The Switch

To Poppy

Enjoy!!

Love Mike,

(aka Tom Wyatt)

Tom Wyatt

Acknowledgements

Thanks to all the members of my family
who supported and even encouraged
me to write this book.
And to Tony, without whose advice
I would probably never have published.

This book is for Penny,
the partner of my childhood friend,
Danny Redmayne

Chapter 1

Danny Redmayne sucked on the remnants of his cigarette, the end glowing brightly between his finger and thumb as he stared at the one remaining illuminated shop across the rainy street.

Through the grimy window, he could just make out the old man moving back and forth, transferring the display stock to the safe at the back of the shop. The cigarette burnt his thumb and he flicked it into the gutter where it was immediately extinguished and carried away by the torrent of rainwater rushing down to the road gully grating.

This was his fourth delivery to London, he reflected, and on each trip it had been raining stair-rods. He adjusted the collar of his trench coat in an effort to reduce the volume of chilly water dribbling down his neck to his shiny, light grey suit beneath.

The old man had moved to the window and was now lowering the steel grille. Time to move, Danny thought. He had to get to the shop before the old man finally locked up, and once inside, with the door bolted and the display lights extinguished, it would look as if the jeweller had already closed.

The old man, stroking his beard, peered over his depressed clerics out into the dusk, as if expecting a visitor. Seeing nothing, he turned and took his coat from the hook by the door. Danny's dripping face appeared at the door window and the old man jumped at the sudden apparition in front of him. He reached for the handle and tentatively opened the door a crack, his foot wedged firmly against the bottom rail.

'Can I help you?' he asked.

'Danny's the name…I have a package from Wilson.'

'Oh yes! Come in, come in.'

The old man removed his foot, pushed the door fully open and waved the rain-soaked courier into the shop.

'Come through to the back room,' he whispered, as if he was not alone. Danny sauntered through to the dimly lit room, took off his trench-coat and threw it over the back of a chair then pulled out a small parcel from his jacket pocket.

The old man, now seated at his desk, slid the parcel into the bright circle of light under the table lamp and opened it to reveal a small suede leather pouch. Danny lit a cigarette and drew heavily on it, leaning over the table for a closer look.

'Genuine stuff that,' he wheezed as he expelled a cloud of smoke which rose up through the metal lampshade and out like jet-streams through the vent holes at the top.

Danny stood around 1m70, stick thin and looked under-nourished. One could only describe him as average looking in his facial features, a little pale with close-set eyes, a narrow nose, faintly pock-marked complexion and a shock of dark hair, which he slicked back with a touch too much gel. Having failed at everything in school, he left at the earliest opportunity to seek his fortune but legitimate employment did not come easily and he was quickly drawn to the darker yet more profitable sector of the economy. He was young and inexperienced. He was certainly unable to tell the difference between a real diamond and zirconium. He was always acting big, but in reality he was a cocky, over-confident, wily little rat of a man. Though likeable in some ways with his quick humour, he was certainly not to be trusted.

The old man opened the leather pouch then stuffed an eyeglass beneath his bushy, grey eyebrow. He examined each diamond carefully, twelve in all. Satisfied, he swivelled in his chair, opened the safe and took out a fat manilla A5 envelope. He passed it across to Danny, who first weighed it in his hand and then flipped it open to roughly check the contents before tucking it into the waistband of his trousers. He reached for his coat and pulled it over his shoulders before leaving the back room and peering out into the street. The old man followed close behind.

There was no one about. Danny turned to face the old man, took a last puff on his cigarette, ground the stub out on the carpet with his heel, then pulled out his Jericho 9mm pistol and shot the old man once through the forehead.

The back of the old man's head exploded, casting fragments of his skull and its contents some distance across the room to the display case behind him. He keeled over backwards, crashed to the floor then lay still, a look of surprise fixed on his sallow face, the blood pumping slowly from the entry wound and running in a thin rivulet down his temple to the shabby, blood soaked carpet beneath.

Danny took out a handkerchief and carefully wiped the pistol clean then walked out to the lavatory at the rear of the shop. Standing on the toilet seat, he reached up and lifted the wrought iron cistern lid and dropped the gun into the murky water. He reeled off a few sheets of toilet tissue, wiped the seat, dropped it in the bowl and flushed it down then retraced his steps to the back room. He picked up the leather pouch, emptied the safe of its contents, wiped his prints and walked quickly to the door.

Checking there was no one about he let himself out of the shop, remembering to drop the latch on the *Yale* lock as he did so and slipped out into the night.

Today was Saturday; nobody will miss the old man 'till Monday, he thought, so he would have plenty of time to get out of London and over to Amsterdam.

Had Danny looked more carefully as he left, he might have seen the man in black tucked into a doorway across the street.

Chapter 2

It was rainy and cold. In the dim twilight of that early winter afternoon, the headlamps of the on-coming cars were mirrored in the wet tarmac, sporadically blinding the driver as the hearse and its entourage made slow passage through the rush-hour traffic toward the crematorium.

In the follow-up car Jeff Blythe sat hunched up, as he peered out, trying to determine exactly how far the procession had got and whether they would make the appointed time. The windscreen wipers squealed as they scraped away the rain for an instant, before it flooded back, once more obliterating his vision.

Jeff Blythe was suddenly a widower. Eight weeks ago he'd had a very good job, a wonderful wife whom he adored, a superb flat in Chelsea, plenty of money, and a fast car. Life had been as good as he imagined it could get. Now, at a stroke, it was all meaningless. He couldn't stop thinking about Sheila and the fate that had befallen her. He would gladly give away all his chattels if only she could be with him again. Tears welled up in his eyes and rolled down his cheeks as he sat there, thinking about her, in the dark interior of the funeral car.

He reached for the freshly laundered handkerchief in his breast pocket and wiped away the damp from his eyes. He carefully re-folded it and tucked it back in place then tried to compose himself. Would he be able to handle the short service? He wondered - particularly his own speech - and he hoped he would not break down during the heart-rending tribute that was expected of Sheila's brother.

He had been married to her for a little under three years, when something quite extraordinary and totally unexpected changed his life forever. He had received a phone-call from a man who would not identify himself. He stated that he had found Jeff's number from a mobile phone in Sheila's handbag, and felt that he'd better phone, as he thought he had accidentally killed her. He stated that as he came round a corner, the end of a scaffold pole he was carrying on his shoulder had hit her full in the face. The caller gave directions as to where the tragedy had taken place, then rang off.

Jeff had phoned the police and then immediately driven round to the address given by the stranger. All the way there he had hoped that it was some kind of hoax, but he knew, deep down, that there was no reason for it to be so. The police were already at the scene when he arrived and had arranged for an ambulance, cordoned off the area and effectively taken full control of things.

Some weeks later, following an exhaustive investigation, no trace of the man had been found and after a long and drawn out post mortem the police had released the body for burial. The coroner had postponed a verdict pending further police enquiries.

And now, here he was in the funeral car, wretched and totally numb. He couldn't actually grasp what was happening to him. He had often read of such bizarre events in the media but he neither considered that such a horror might befall *him* nor had he ever imagined the pain and anguish that he would suffer. Each morning he would wake from a fitful sleep, expecting to see her lying beside him, only to be jolted back to reality with the simultaneous gnawing emptiness in his stomach.

Jeff, to his friends, was a likeable, tousle-haired young man with a sharp sense of humour. Nothing really seemed to phase him. Tall, with a good physique honed from his regular Saturday afternoons on the rugby field, he was reasonably good looking, with a light natural tan, all of which gave him the air of a confident young man.

After his 3 years at Durham University, armed with his 2.1 in geology and a post grad. he had landed a job with the exploration division of one of the major oil companies, investigating findings from prospective drilling sites. It involved regular travel to rigs around the globe and it was at one of these locations that he had met Sheila.

His employer had a major exploration involvement in South Africa, in the Karoo Basin and Jeff had been sent out to assist the team in Johannesburg with his knowledge of shale oil and gas extraction. It was on a visit to one of the sites that he had bumped into Sheila. She too had been based in Johannesburg, but spent much of her time at the drilling sites around the basin.

He had not really noticed her at fist; in fact he had totally ignored her - she had a name that reminded him of his aunt whom he had little liking for - until, one day, she had a confrontation with him over the interpretation of the results of a core sample. It was the closest he'd got to her so far, and it had dawned on him that perhaps there was, after all, quite a lot to get interested in. Her face - tanned and devoid of make-up save for a smidgen of eye shadow - was fine featured and she had full lips and pearl white teeth. He'd felt her warmth, as she stood beside him, her perfume, light and subtle, her breasts, large but firm, straining occasionally against the thin cotton of her pale blue blouse as she vehemently argued her point of view. His eyes had wandered over the enticing cleavage and he had seen the faint bumps where her nipples pressed against the flimsy material. He remembered being highly aroused, and though he had tried to avert his eyes, he'd been incapable of doing so. So intent had he been upon his appraisal that he had heard neither her argument, nor the questions she raised.

She had looked up at him, enquiringly and realised that he was staring at her. It was of little concern to her however, she had just continued her persuasive argument, as if his behaviour was just one of the hazards that good-looking women have to live with. He was not the first man that had drilled his eyes into her curves. She had an answer to voyeurs… stare back!

Jeff's remembered his face being hot with embarrassment. But she had smiled and he'd let her win the argument that day.

He had been due back in London the next afternoon, which meant an early start if he was to catch his BA fight to Heathrow. So when Sheila suggested that if he had nothing much to do that evening, they go out for something to eat, he regretfully declined, offering instead to buy her a night-cap at his hotel on her way home.

An hour later and after swapping phone numbers and e-mail addresses, he had been back in his room packing his things, but his short time with Sheila in the hotel bar was uppermost in his mind.

He had mulled over the happenings of his last day in Johannesburg as he sat on his flight, waiting for the drinks trolley which meandered slowly toward him, pushed, he noticed, by a rather plump, over-made-up, middle-aged hostess and a rather pretty young man pulling on the other end. He had really fallen for Sheila – there had definitely been a lot of chemistry between them. She'd been attentive when he talked of his past, smiled at him frequently and he'd seen the expressions of admiration and affection in her eyes. She had clearly fancied him, he'd thought.

As he walked across the terminal at Heathrow he had made the decision to contact her as soon as he got back to his flat. If he were keen on her he knew he would have to develop the relationship quickly, before someone else beat him to it.

In his urgency he'd rushed to the head of the taxi queue, opened the door and thrown in his luggage before stooping to climb in himself, much to the consternation of the other waiting passengers.

Back in Chelsea, he'd grabbed a couple of groceries and gone back to his flat, made himself an omelette and over a glass of wine, opened up his laptop and composed a quick e-mail to Sheila:

Hi Sheila,
Back home safely. Missing you already!
When will I see you again?
Jeff

He remembered reading the message over, wondering whether he was being a bit forward at such an early stage, but then choosing not to change it. The exclamation mark would soften it. Say it as it is, he'd thought, clicking the 'send' button.

And that was how things started between them. Sheila took a week's leave to stay with him in London – she had never really explored the city - and their relationship grew from that moment.

As he sat now in the funeral car, he reflected on his three wonderful years with Sheila, He felt his whole world had collapsed. He had little appetite for his job or his future.

Chapter 3

George Wilson was furious. He picked up the phone and dialled a local number. The voice at the other end was subservient.

'Listen, Pete!' spat Wilson, 'Danny's not back, he was s'posed to be here last night. His mobile's off. Something's amiss. You'd better get over to Blighty an' talk to the old man…Yes I mean now!' The line went dead and Wilson replaced the receiver.

He stood up from his desk and anxiously paced the room a couple of times before pouring himself a whisky from the cabinet. He took a big swig and grimaced as the amber liquid cascaded down his throat, the alcohol burning his gullet.

It was the first time Danny had been late in the four years since Wilson had taken him on. He had come with good credentials. His father, Alan Redmayne, had been a good friend and 'business associate', as hoods like to call themselves. Danny had shown an interest in the business and Wilson had been looking for a new man. He was a fighter, good with a knife and a broad selection of alternative weapons. He could never be a threat to Wilson though, for although he was wily, he was of low intelligence. Take away the tools of his trade and he was a pussycat.

Wilson had needed a soldier, so it had made sense to take him on, even though he was, at times, in competition with Danny's father. He felt their relationship good enough and besides, he needed acquaintances. 'You never know when you need a favour,' he had thought at the time.

Since the move to Amsterdam, Wilson had never felt totally safe. He had a reputation in London – nobody would have crossed him, but here in Amsterdam he was a new boy and he felt more vulnerable. He didn't know who his real friends were or indeed his enemies, so Danny filled the additional role as protection.

However, now he was late and there had been no word, which was unusual for Danny. What was more perturbing was that he had more than a hundred grand's worth of sparklers on him, unless he'd managed to get to the old man. If so, he'd have the cash. At least that wouldn't be as bad, as it wouldn't necessarily incriminate anyone else. The sparklers weren't registered, so they would naturally be considered illegally obtained. Wilson thought he'd wait another couple of hours then if he wasn't back he'd call in at Alan Redmayne's place and read the riot act.

At four thirty the phone rang – It was Danny.

'Where the hell are you?' Wilson shouted down the phone. 'I said be back here Sunday – that's today you pillock, an' you're not here. I came to the office 'specially for it.'

'Sorry boss,' whimpered Danny, 'I've let you down. I got to the old man but I got jumped. When I came round, the old man was stiff with a hole in his head and the goods is gone.'

'For fuck's sake Danny, how d'ya let that happen? You were s'posed to check the coast was clear before you did the switch.'

'Yeah, I know, an' it was all goin' so smoothly 'till I opened the door to leave. There was a bloke outside. That's all I remember.'

'So you've got the cash?' Wilson knew the question was futile.

'I had it in me pants', said Danny, 'he must've guessed 'cos it's gone'.

'What about the sparklers – you sure they're gone? Did you check the safe?'

'Safe was open, and it was empty,' Danny said wistfully, 'think he must've got them too.'

'Did you get a good look at him?' Wilson asked anxiously.

'Not really, but I remember him pushing his hand in my face an' he ain't got no thumb.'

'No thumb? What bloody use is that?'

'No use if you ain't got one,' Danny quipped, trying to make light of the conversation, 'but at least it's a lead.'

'For fuck's sake Danny, this is serious. Don't you realise the shit you've dropped me in? How can we traipse all over bloody Blighty looking for a guy with no thumb?'

Wilson sighed noisily but his anger subsided a fraction. He knew most of the guys in the business in London – he would ask around, but he didn't hold out that much hope of finding this guy.

'Well get your arse back here, and quick, we've gotta find out who this geezer is an' get our stuff back.' He slammed the phone down in frustration.

It was five o'clock. Wilson quickly jotted a few figures on the blotter in font of him, then swore loudly. The realisation that Danny might have lost him the best part of 3 months profits sent a chill down his spine. While musing over his next move he suddenly remembered that he had a dinner date with his wife's best friend and her old man. He glanced at his watch and realised he would be late if he didn't leave soon.

'Shit!' he exclaimed as he stacked up the papers on his desk, 'that's the last thing I need.'

He locked the side drawer of the desk and re-directed the phone through to his mobile. There was not much else he could do now until he got the call from his man Pete, now on his way to the old man's shop, so he thought he'd go home.

There was just this nagging suspicion that Danny was pulling the wool over his eyes. He didn't want it to be true but for some reason unknown to him he couldn't see it any other way. Danny wouldn't be back at the office 'till the late morning, if he ever came back at all.

He donned his leather coat, switched off the light and slammed the door. Travelling down in the elevator to the basement, he pulled a cigar from his coat pocket and played the flame of his gold *Colibri* lighter over the end, taking small puffs until it was evenly lit. He expelled the smoke with a sigh, feeling somewhat nervous at the day's events. He had been in this business for 17 years, and never had a problem. Now it looked as if Danny had let the cat out of the bag. It all depended on who got to the old man first.

He walked across the underground car park to his Mercedes, blipping the key fob. The direction indicators illuminated the dingy basement. For a split second he thought he saw a figure standing in the shadows at the rear of his car, but as the lights extinguished he was temporarily blinded.

'No,' he whispered, 'I'm just seeing things.' Nevertheless he hastened to get into the car and immediately locked the doors.

'That's the trouble with this game,' he muttered under his breath as he started the car, 'you never know what's coming next – mebbe it's time to call it a day.'

Wilson was home in bed when the call came through. It was 4.30 in the morning.

'What the fuck you doin' phoning me at this goddam time,' he barked down the phone. He was thick-headed having drunk a little too much at the dinner just a few hours before.

'Sorry boss, said Pete, but I got to the old man's like you said, but the place was all locked up, so I went round the back an' broke in through a window. There was no sign of the old man….

'Fuck! Fuck! FUCK!' Wilson's progressively louder expletives woke his wife.

'An' there was stuff all over the place – looked like a fight or somethin', mebbe looking for summat. The safe was open – didn't have nothin' in it though.' Pete continued.

'For Christ's sake Pete, the old man's dead,' Wilson screamed down the phone, 'didn't you see his body? Danny said he was on the floor with a hole in his head!'

'No boss, I'da noticed that if he was there.'

Wilson was flummoxed for an instant.

'What about blood – on the floor or anywhere?'

'No Boss, none.'

'Did anyone see you?' he asked anxiously.

'Don't think so, I was pretty careful.'

'Did the old man have a camera in the shop?'

'Couldn't see no security or nothing,' came Pete's reply.

'Okay mate, then here's what I want you to do. Go back into the shop, Look over the joint for a camera, I don't want nobody comin' back to me with a movie of the job. Check everywhere for the body. If you don't find nothin' then shut the safe, then tidy the place up a bit.' Wilson was desperately trying to think on his feet. His head was reeling and his tongue felt thick in his dry mouth.

'Make it look like it's normal. I don't want nobody thinking he's a fence, OK?'

'Yeah, OK. I'm in the shop now'

'For fuck's sake Pete, not on his phone, are you?'

'Nah! I'm not that daft, I'm on me mobile'

'OK…right…as I was saying, when you leave make sure there's no traces, go to a public phone box an' phone the old Bill. Don't give your name or nothing. Tell 'em you want to report a missing person. Say you've been tryin' to contact him since yesterday, an' you've seen that someone's broken in at the back an' you suspect foul play. Give 'em the address. If they sound like they know about it already, ring off an' scarper. If not, wait around till the police arrive, but don't get seen. Then scarper. Don't go until they arrive, you hear? And don't talk to no one. Chances are they'll just forget about it when they see nothin' much wrong. An' don't forget, wipe all your prints, and in the phone box too.'

It was the best plan Wilson could think of, given the state he was in. He put the phone down, lay back and tried to sleep. He couldn't. He got up and went to the bathroom. He had a shower and got dressed. Even though it was only 5.00 a.m. he knew he wouldn't have been able to sleep with all the turmoil of the previous day. Danny would be back before midday and he was anxious to hear his side of the story. Danny was a poor liar and Wilson knew that once he saw his face he would be able to judge whether he was being conned.

If Danny's story *was* true, who would have nicked the body and roughed up the old man's place, he wondered, as he drove to the coffee shop. Maybe the police? But his little charade with Pete would determine that. On the other hand, Danny might still have the diamonds, having gone to the shop and not found the old man. He then roughed up the shop while he was looking for the cash. He could have made a nice little earner with a hundred grand of diamonds and the cash as well.

Wilson's doubts about Danny's integrity grew stronger by the minute. He stopped the car outside the Café Engel, nipped in and bought a double espresso and a pastry to take out, then drove on to his office.

At 8.30am Danny rang again.

'Boss, I'm late getting' to the ferry, the bloody train's broke down. I'll catch the next one but I won't be in 'till about 2.00 pm – OK?'

'No, it's not fuckin' OK,' Wilson shouted down the phone. You better get here sooner than that. Get a bloody taxi.'

'I ain't got no cash left, Boss,' Danny bleated, 'the bugger nicked my wallet and cards as well.'

Which is it? Wilson wondered. He's either a bloody good storyteller or he really is up shit creek. He decided that he'd have to wait. One sure thing...if he was lying he'd have to go. Pete would get another commission.

'OK! Just get here as soon as you can,' he sighed, dropping the receiver into it's cradle.

At 10.15 am Pete rang back. 'Boss, the police are here an' I'm leaving. I'll see ya tonight.' He rang off without waiting for Wilson's reply.

Wilson smiled with satisfaction. His plan had worked. The police hadn't cleared the body, so now he knew he was safe and that there was some other hood in on the act.

'Just have to find out who an' cut them off' he thought. But he still had that strong feeling that Danny was setting him up.

Chapter 4

The funeral passed with few unusual incidents. Jeff Blythe managed to keep himself reasonably composed, although there was a point when his brother-in-law broke down during his speech, which infected virtually the whole of the congregation, particularly Jeff himself. It seemed like an eternity of silent grieving before the speech continued.

Outside, the air was heavy with mist and the rain steadily persisted, dripping from their umbrellas as the entourage walked in procession through the Garden of Remembrance. One or two people stopped occasionally to read the tributes on the flowers neatly laid out on the turf, but most were just keen to get away.

Jeff felt uncomfortable with his mother's arm through his. They stood at the head of the line of mourners, she, embracing each and mouthing a few words as they passed. Jeff heard none of it. He was somewhere else, where it was warm, Sheila by his side.

He had never been close to his mother. He'd had no real contact with her since her divorce from his father William some 16 years earlier. William frequently worked abroad for long periods and at some point during one of his trips, his mother had had a somewhat torrid affair.

It was not surprising that she got attention. She had been a good-looking, effervescent woman, the kind that can attract men like a magnet. She could draw a room full of them around her at any function to which she was invited and she enjoyed doing so. However, her dallying with her admirers seldom had any intent and she probably would never have ventured further had it not been for the demon drink.

Jeff remembered the difficult periods when he was a lad. Never being fed, often left to his own devices, evening after evening. He would stay awake at night listening for her car in the drive. Then the sound of her stumbling around trying to negotiate the staircase. She would wander straight to her room where she would collapse on the bed and immediately pass out. Jeff would wake her out of her drunken stupor each morning, before making his way to school.

When she became pregnant, it had not been difficult for William to work out that it was not his child and on confronting her, she admitted having had relationships with several of her men friends, some of whom had been friends of his too.

It had all been too much for William. He found that he could no longer trust his wife, his friends and further, he refused to have anything to do with the child, so at three months pregnant she left him, whereupon he had eventually sued for divorce and succeeded, quite unusually, in winning custody of his son. Jeff had been 9 years old at the time. His mother was granted the house and Jeff moved to York with his father.

William tried hard to ensure that Jeff would have the best of everything to compensate for the loss of his mother, but the financial pressure of starting his life again, coupled with his putting every spare hour into his work hastened the ageing process and eventually, his demise. A year before Jeff graduated from university, William died while at work, as a result of a massive heart attack

As sole beneficiary in his father's will, Jeff had become moderately wealthy early on in life, and after completing his degree in Durham he had sold his father's house in York, paid off his debts and bought himself a two bedroom flat in London.

He had always blamed his mother for the way things worked out. At such a tender age he had not understood why she had left. He thought she didn't love him or even want him any more. She had never contacted him after the divorce. But despite all his misgivings, he had felt that she should know about Sheila and be invited to his marriage and now, to her funeral.

He was wakened out of his trance as his mother dragged him toward the funeral car. She seemed steeled during the whole episode.

When she had arrived for the funeral Jeff had hardly recognised her. He had remembered her as elegant, well attired, and certainly attractive. Yet now, here she was, dressed in an old tweed suit and shabby rain soaked suede boots, with her unkempt hair cascading over her eyes like an old sheepdog and a pair of horn-rimmed glasses, all giving her an air akin to a demonstrator at an anti-hunt demonstration.

'Are you sure you'll be alright on your own?' she asked, 'I don't know why you don't come back with me for a few days…Just to get over things.'

The last thing Jeff wanted was to be anywhere near his mother, though he knew she meant well. He needed to be alone.

No, I'll be fine; I want some time to think. I've got to work out where I go from here and do it by myself.'

The Funeral procession drew up outside Sheila's brother's house on Wimbledon Common. Jeff couldn't face attending the wake. All those people he would have to listen to, sympathising with his predicament, then, unable to think of anything else to say, always finishing with a pat on the shoulder and a statement like 'She was a lovely girl, your Sheila, she'll be sorely missed'.

No. He would not attend. He got out of the funeral car with a short farewell to his mother.

'Sorry Mum, but you'll have to take it from here. I can't.' And he ran through the rain to his Jaguar parked under the red maple trees by the drive entrance.

Once back at his flat in Chelsea, Jeff felt as if a huge weight had been lifted from his shoulders. Of course he was still grieving, but the act of running from the wake felt as if he had taken hold of himself in some way, imposed his own will on things and he felt more positive about how he would deal with circumstances from here on. The people at the funeral didn't care about Sheila or him for that matter. They came because of protocol. He hardly knew any of them.

He went over to the fridge and took out a started bottle of Sauvignon Blanc, unscrewed the lid and poured himself a large glass. He walked over to the sofa and turned on the TV before slouching back against the cushions. He flicked through the channels but found nothing to his liking, so he blipped the off button and shut his eyes.

What was he going to do now? He really had no idea. He felt he needed to change everything about his life, as if this might in some way erase the heartache he would suffer if things continued as they were.

He thought about selling everything and moving abroad. A new job, a different country, new house, new friends, etc. No one pretending to feel sorry for him either.

Yes! That's it...That's what he would do. He knew South Africa pretty well, he had worked there and had contacts, and maybe that would be a good place to start over.

He leaned over the coffee table and reached for his laptop. He decided he would start with one of his acquaintances in the Johannesburg branch of the Oil Company, Karl Jongen. Karl had intimated that he would always be welcome if he ever returned to South Africa. Perhaps he would put him up for a few days till he got to know the ropes? He knew from the bulletin board at the UK office that there were positions available in Johannesburg so there was always a possibility of a transfer.

He fleshed out a short e-mail, read it over and corrected it in a couple of places before sending it out into the ether. He would wait for Karl's reply before giving notice of his intentions and applying for his visa.

Pleased that he had made a start, he then went on-line to check his bank accounts. No going back now, he thought, the ball is rolling.

Chapter 5

Danny Redmayne disembarked the ferry at Hook and walked over to the passenger terminal. Looking around the hall he soon spotted the left luggage lockers and walked slowly over towards them trying not to attract attention. Never appear furtive, don't look round, he thought, it always looks suspicious. He picked a half size locker, level with his chest, and covertly transferred the diamonds, the manilla envelope and the contents of the old man's safe. Then, after first removing his cash, he threw his wallet into the locker, inserted a €2 coin in the lock, closed the door, locked it and removed the key. He hadn't even dared to evaluate the stuff he found in the safe yet. He would wait until he picked it up later. As he walked across the apron toward the car park, he removed the tag from the locker key making a mental note of the number upon it, and threw it in a waste bin, then attached the key to his car fob. He collected his car and drove the short distance to Amsterdam.

He felt pretty pleased with himself. Everything had gone according to plan and he was now both relieved and elated. He turned on the radio and at full volume, sang along with the very apt Abba number playing on the station. Yes, he was good – very good. He'd been planning this little heist for some months. Although he was paid well, it paled into insignificance when compared with the huge profits Wilson made on the deals. Yet all that fat bastard did was sit in a chair barking orders. Danny thought Wilson ought to share out the 'winnings' just a little more evenly.

He knew that he had to tow the line for a while to gain the trust of his boss, and it had been difficult having to resist carrying out the plan on earlier trips, especially the previous one which had been much nearer half a mil's worth. He had sussed that if he left that one alone and took a smaller one later he would be seen as above suspicion and besides, he could always do another before scarpering. He just hoped that the old man's body wouldn't be found too soon. The shooter might easily be found when the police combed the joint, but that didn't matter. It wasn't his anyway.

All he had to do now was to convince George Wilson of his story. So far, it seemed that he believed it, but the hard bit would be the face to face row that was still to come. Danny knew that from here-on out Wilson would be watching his every move. He wondered what Wilson's reaction had been like after that first phone call – had he done anything about it? If so, what? No matter - he would find out when he got to the office. Things had gone so well, he had attained a new level of confidence, and nothing was going to bother him from now on – not even Wilson.

The traffic was light and he found himself parking up on the overflow car park - a patch of waste ground outside the office in Wolvenstraat - a bit sooner than he'd hoped. He got out of the car and braced himself for the impending interrogation.

He walked into Wilson's office without knocking, putting on a look of utter dejection.

'Sorry about all this boss, but….'

'I should fuckin' say so,' Wilson cut him off. 'How the fuck did you let this happen? What the fuck did you do with the old man's body?'

Danny stared at him, his face reddening.

'What do you mean boss?'

'The fuckin' body – where is it? It's not there. Where d'ya put it?'

'I never touched it boss, I just left and ran.'

'Pete says there's no body there an' the place is as clean as a whistle, so someone's telling porkies!'

'Well it ain't me,' Danny blurted. He was angry now. So Wilson had sent Pete! Did that mean he already didn't trust him? Eventually, after a long pause, he plucked up the courage to quiz Wilson further:

'Why d'ya do that boss - send Pete?'

'To clean up the place, you twat! Trouble is, when he got there, half of it had all been done for him.'

'Perhaps the old man had a cleaner!' Danny knew it was a poor joke before he said it and it got an apt response from Wilson.

'Listen mate, this ain't no laughing matter. You've cost me two hundred grand up to now. An' now we've lost a link in the chain. We'll have to shut the business down till we find another fence. What ya goin' to do about that?'

'I dunno boss, there ain't a lot I can do or say really, except that if we could find this thumbless guy…'

'Never mind him,' snapped Wilson, 'I'll deal with that.

'So who cleared up the old man's body?' Danny asked.

'How the fuck should I know,' Wilson spat, 'Pete never said but it ain't the Old Bill. They went round when Pete phoned 'em, so they didn't know about it till then. Must've been some other bugger, which means we might get some more bother 'cos someone was watchin' our every move.'

'But boss…I don't understand…Why would Pete call the police?

''Cos I fuckin' told him to, you prat. How else could we find out whether they did the clean up or not?'

'But that means the cops is crawlin' all over the place now, lookin' for me prints an' everythin'.'

'Yeah! But they'd be doin' that whichever way things happened. Anyway, what it means, for us, is that I have to shut down for a while and that means I ain't got much for you to do.'

Wilson shoved a pre-prepared envelope across the table. 'You're outta here Danny, you're finished. Here's your wages up to the end of last week. I ain't payin' you for the run, 'cos you messed up. You can keep the car for the rest of the week…give you time to sort yourself out, but then you bring it back, you hear? OK? If there's work for you when this is all cleared up, I'll let you know. You'd better give me back your shooter.'

'But Boss….'

'Gimme the fuckin' gun!'

'I ain't got it boss, the bastard took that as well.'

Wilson went apoplectic with rage 'You stupid fuck! So now we've got a stiff with a hole in his head, maybe shot with a shooter belonging to me?'

'I guess that's possible,' Danny said sheepishly, 'but they'll never connect it to you 'cos they won't find it – it's probably at the bottom of the Thames by now.'

'How d'you know that? Shit Danny, you'll be the fuckin' death of me, now fuck off, before I do summat crazy.'

Danny got up from the chair and walked aimlessly towards the door. He turned and tried one last apology.

'Go on, fuck off! I don't wanna hear it,' Wilson spat.

He listened for Danny descending in the lift, and when he heard the reverberation of the outer door slamming shut he picked up the phone.

'Pete? Where are you?'

'Just got back boss, I'm grabbin' a bite in Remo's.'

'OK wait there, I need to talk. Order me a club sandwich or summat'…an' a beer, I'll be there in five.'

Wilson had made a decision. He didn't believe Danny's story. Even if he had done, he felt that he was a liability, especially now that he had a murder on his hands. All it would take would be for Danny to spill the beans to the cops or brag to his mates and they'd all go down. In the whole of his shady career, he had never gone as far as murder. Maybe he'd roughed up a couple of guys, yes, but he had no connection to any killings. Now he felt vulnerable. He was not sure how well Danny would cope under pressure. Either way he had to be disposed of. He reached for his jacket and went out into the street.

When he got to Remo's it was heaving. It was only the first working day of the week yet the place was full of the usual business crowd having an early evening quick one before catching their trams back home. He looked around the restaurant, trying to find Pete. He was sitting in the bar at the far end, talking to a young, blond woman Wilson didn't recognise. Perched on the bar in front of Pete were Wilson's sandwich and a 50-centilitre glass of lager. Wilson pushed his way through the hoards of drinkers and stood by an empty stool next to the girl.

'Hi boss,' Pete began 'this is Cheryl....'

'Yeah, yeah, never mind all that,' Wilson interjected, 'We gotta find somewhere quiet, sorry luv, you'll have to bugger off... leave us alone for a bit.'

The girl stared at Wilson in disgust as he took his sandwich and beer and walked towards the restaurant. He nodded for Pete to follow him over to one of the booth tables being vacated against the wall by the phone cubicles

'See ya later,' Pete called to the girl as he made his way over. She gave the pair her middle finger and slipped off her stool into the throng of drinkers, looking for her second catch of the evening.

'We got problems Pete, I need you to do a hatchet job.'

'Oh Christ! Not Danny is it?' Pete asked anxiously.

'Yeah, 'fraid so. He's a bloody liability and I don't believe his story.' He bit a large chunk out of the club sandwich and chewed noisily.

'We're gonna shut down for a while until the heat's off an we've found another dealer.'

'His old man'll kill you.'

'Yeah, but that's why he mustn't find out what happened.'

'How the fuck do I do that?' Pete looked worried.

'We'll have to plan it. We can send Danny over to London or some place and get the job done there. As long as we've got alibis it'll be OK. We can make it look like a reprisal.'

'I dunno boss, I ain't so sure this is a good idea.'

'Look, we've got two scenarios, and only one is the truth. Either Danny's story is true and he didn't kill the old man, got beaten up and someone else has the stuff, or it's a pack of lies, and he did kill him, took the money and the sparklers and hid them somewhere. If he did kill him, where did he stash the stuff and where's the shooter? Come to that, where's the old man's body? Did Danny really cut and run or did he move the body? Is the old man *actually* dead? The whole thing is a bloody nightmare'

'One thing's for sure,' said Pete, 'If it was Danny who had shot the old man, and he had then been mugged, as he says, then he'd still have the shooter. No decent self-respecting hood would take a gun used to kill someone without ensuring the bullet couldn't be found.

Wilson's face suddenly brightened, and a half-smile appeared on his blotchy face. 'That's it! Pete, you're bloody right. Why would he take the gun? Even if either of them killed the old man, the gun would have been wiped clean and left there.'

'But then, maybe it *was* ditched somewhere' Pete added.

'Shit! That's a possibility. Danny did say that he thought the shooter might be at the bottom of the Thames by now. Why would he say the Thames? – Its miles away from the old man's place – he wouldn't go anywhere near the river.'

'Just a figure of speech, I guess,' said Pete philosophically.

'No, it's my bet that the gun is still there in the shop somewhere, but only if it's true the old man *was* actually shot. We don't even know that yet. Not without finding his body.' Wilson drained his glass and slumped back in his chair. He seemed no nearer sorting out this mess.

'Get another beer in,' he ordered.

Pete went off to the bar and Wilson tried to put himself in Danny's position. He remembered that Danny had done a run worth much more the previous month. If he was keen on executing a con, that would have been the one to hit. That's the one that Wilson thought he himself would have done. So did that mean that Danny was telling the truth? Maybe, maybe not.

Wilson wondered whether he should give Danny the benefit of the doubt. No, he thought, if Danny did get nobbled then there's no telling if he'll be any good next time. So whether he did it or not he's let me down an' he'll have to go. I can't just give him the heave-ho either 'cos he knows too much, he thought.

He wondered whether anyone had found the old man's body. It would not make the international news headlines, so no one in Amsterdam would know unless it appeared in an English national newspaper and it would be a day later. It would probably only make the local London papers anyway. What would someone do with a body in the middle of London? Stick it in the boot and drive out to a wood somewhere? Drop it in a River? Down a manhole? Throw it off a motorway bridge? What? Why move the body anyway, especially if you weren't the killer? What would be the point of hiding the body if you intended to hide the gun? None of this made sense to Wilson.

Pete came back with the beers and Wilson quizzed him. 'Imagine you're Danny mate, which heist would you pull off? This month's or last?'

'I'd go for last months – it was five times the size, then you wouldn't see me for dust. But Danny's a bit thick, he probably thought he would get away with a smaller heist and still keep his job.'

'Good point! That's what I thought too,' Wilson lied. 'And if you had shot the old man, what would you have done with the gun and the body?'

'I would've clocked him one, then strangled him or knifed him and not used the gun – I don't like guns, they are too noisy, difficult to get rid of and they leave slugs behind that can be identified.'

‘Yes but Danny’s naïve, he wouldn’t think like that.’

‘OK, then I would have shot him, wiped the gun clean and put it back in the old man's hand to get some prints then left it on the floor.’

‘Exactly.’

‘So do you think Danny did it – the shooting I mean?’

‘Yeah, I guess so,’ Pete replied resignedly, an’ he probably wet himself after, so he hid the body too.’

‘Then he’s got to go. Take him out somewhere quiet, a long way from here and do it. Go in his car then bring it back to the office and leave it in the car park. Whatever you do don’t do it in the car or put the body anywhere near it – I want that car to be as clean as a whistle, an’ remember to wipe your prints. You’ll have to figure something out. Do it right and there’s a nice little earner for you – you can have Danny’s bonus for the switch he should’ve made. I told ‘im that he’d get no more ‘cos he ballsed things up.’

Chapter 6

Jeff took the shuttle to Heathrow. His flight to Johannesburg was at 11.30 am. He had checked in on line to save time as he only had hand luggage.

Following his chat with Karl Jongen, he had managed to get a transfer with his existing company. The interview had been arranged in London at their Strand offices. It had lasted just 12 minutes, largely due to the report sent by Karl from the manager of the Jo'burg office which confirmed his excellent credentials. He would be working in the same site office as Sheila before they were married, which unsettled him slightly, but he was sure any concern would be short-lived.

He had decided not to sell his flat, but to put it in the hands of a letting agent. The rental would easily cover the cost of rent or mortgage for his accommodation in South Africa and if he ever came back he would be assured of an affordable property in UK.

His personal possessions, and the bits and pieces of furniture he wanted to keep had been boxed up and sent ahead. However, he had sold his pride and joy, the Jag XK8 through the London Evening News at a slightly lower than market price in order to get a quick sale. The shipping costs would have been prohibitive, even outweighing the extra cost of buying over there.

As he sat at the gate, waiting to board his flight he felt the excitement of a new beginning mixed with trepidation of the unknown. It was a weird sensation that elated him yet simultaneously made him sweat with apprehension.

The sensation subsided somewhat once he had boarded the flight. The passenger doors were closed and the plane was taxiing out onto the runway. There was no way out now. He had to run with it. The aircraft left the runway and climbed steadily into the clouds.

Jeff closed his eyes and tried to sleep. The last few days had been quite hectic and he now needed to recharge his batteries in preparation for his arrival in South Africa.

Placing her hand on his shoulder, the stewardess woke him from his deep slumber. She enquired whether he would like dinner. He stretched sleepily and looked at his watch. He had slept for six hours. He lowered his table and she leaned across and slid a white plastic tray in front of him. Her perfume had turned and the sour smell, mixed with her noticeable body odour put him off his food. Besides, nothing looked appetising, so he left all but the small bag of biscuits and rubbery cheese, which he washed down with coffee supplied by the follow-up steward.

He turned to the window and stared out into the darkness. He could see nothing and had no idea where he was. He looked for the screen overhead above the aisle, which showed a small plane hovering over the horn of Africa. Not long now, he thought.

A rush of warm air greeted him as he descended the steps from the plane. He had forgotten that it would be early summer here in Johannesburg. It was cooler in the terminal as he joined the queue of travellers waiting for customs clearance.

He made his way out onto the 'Arrivals' concourse and looked around for Karl. At first he couldn't see him, then his ruddy face appeared between two taller men holding up placards.

Karl was of stocky build, about mid fifties with greying curly hair receding from a sunburnt forehead and large jug-handle ears, illuminated by the blinding sun at his back, as it shone through the pink fleshy lobes. He waved over the heads of the two men and shot down to the end of the line of waiting relatives, drivers and reps. He looked genuinely pleased to see him.

'Jeffrey!' He exclaimed. 'So good to see you. Where's your baggage?' His drawl was heavily impregnated with the guttural intonations of the Boer accent.

'Should be here any day now,' said Jeff, 'I asked them to forward it to your address.'

'No problem. OK let's get out of here.' They walked out of the hall and over to the car park. Karl loaded Jeff's trolley bag in the back of his King Cab and pulled the shutter over. 'Gotta keep things safe round here' he advised.

As they drove to Bryanston, Karl gave Jeff a few tips on survival in South Africa.

'You gotta realise that it's pretty lawless here', he started, 'Life is cheap, and even petty crime is often violent.' When you're out an' about, don't wear fancy watches – buy yerself the cheapest mobile you can find and don't carry too much cash on you. If you're out in yer car, keep it locked as you drive, an' watch out at junctions and red lights. If some guy, even a screen washer approaches you, just drive on.'

Jeff listened carefully, but was somewhat taken aback by the emphasis being put on the subject.

They arrived in Bryanston and after driving through some reasonably affluent suburbs, Karl pulled up at a tall pair of wrought iron gates set in a high wall surmounted with razor wire. He blipped the control on his cab roof and the gates slowly opened. He drove through and blipped the control again, checking in his rear view mirror that they had shut properly before driving on. He parked up at the third house on the left-hand side of the estate road. It looked immense in the darkness behind the security lights, which blasted bright white heat toward the pair as they descended the truck.

A young black lad of about 16 came out from the dim alley between the garages and the house and walked excitedly towards the truck.

'This is Jesse, he's our boy – does stuff around the house, garden and so on. He's a Somali. He lives over the garage; he's a good lad. If you need him to do anything just call him.' Jesse gave Jeff a broad smile showing a mouthful of strong white teeth.

'Jesse, this is Jeff, he'll be staying a while, take his stuff up to the guest room.'

Jesse gave a slight bow and a nod of his woolly head.

No please or thank you from Karl, Jeff noted. Jesse grabbed the trolley bag enthusiastically and carried it off in the direction of the side door of the house and the two men went in through the front.

'I guess you could do with a drink after your trip?' Karl enquired.

'A beer would be great,' Jeff replied, he felt very dry after his flight.

'What plans have you got for tomorrow?' Karl asked.

'Well, I don't start the job until next Monday, so I've got a few days to get myself sorted with accommodation. But I've got to get a car first to recce the area....'

'Nope,' Karl contradicted, 'first you gotta get some protection. We'll get you sorted with a hand-gun, *then* you get your car!'

Jeff was apprehensive. He'd never had a gun, let alone used one, in his life.

'I'm not in the office till the afternoon tomorrow so I'll get you stitched up first thing, then I'll show you the delights of Jo'burg,' Karl laughed.

The lounge door opened and a vivacious woman of about 35'ish glided into the room, attired in a long, flesh coloured night-gown with a silk dressing gown over, untied, and slightly parted at the front. Her long, straight, golden hair ran over her shoulders and down to her breast, concealing the gap in her gown. She looked across at the newcomer, holding her gaze, 'You must be Jeff,' she purred, 'welcome to our home, did you have a good trip?'

Karl intervened. 'This is my wife Jenny, Jenny, this is Jeff Blythe.'

Jenny appeared slightly annoyed. 'I know who he is darling,' she said patronisingly, 'nice to meet you, it'll be good to have a man about the house for a couple of days.' Karl's ruddy face reddened further.

Jeff, slightly embarrassed by the put-down, drained the last of the beer from the bottle and looked at his watch – it was 12.30 in the morning. Suddenly he felt tired again. ' Well, if you guy's don't mind, I'll go up to bed – I'm not much good at this time of night.'

'I'll show you to your room,' she said.

Karl gave him a wave but said nothing as Jenny glided out of the room, her hand on Jeff's arm. She took him up to the first floor and stopped at the door of his room.

'I'm sure you'll be comfortable,' she whispered, 'but if there's anything I can get you, just knock. My bedroom's this one opposite.' She tapped the panel on her door, then, squeezing his arm she bade him goodnight.

'Strange!' Jeff thought, 'She said *my* bedroom not *our* bedroom.' He wondered whether her relationship with Karl had broken down.

Chapter 7

The phone rang, waking Danny Redmayne from a doze in front of the television. He reached for the mute button then got up to answer the call. It was Pete.

'Listen Danny, we've got a job. Wilson wants us to pick up some dough in Manchester. He wants us both to go 'cos we may get some bother. How ya fixed?'

Danny thought for a moment before answering. Wilson had just sacked him saying that he was no longer needed. Why the change of plan? He smelt a rat.

'I'm OK for it Pete, but what's it all about? I ain't got no shooter neither.'

Pete had his story ready, 'We won't need that, just a bit of roughin' up, the guy ain't paid his dues, so Wilson wants us to put the squeeze on 'im.'

'When we going?'

'Tomorrow – ferry's at 10.30am from Hook, Can you pick me up? Say 8.00am. Put yer alarm on. Bring some cash – we might get to do a deal.'

The phone went dead. Danny switched off the TV and went to get a beer from the fridge. He was suspicious of the whole thing. Wilson had never mentioned anything about money owed in Manchester and as Danny was his right hand man, he was sure he would have known about it, certainly before Pete. What was all that about bringing some cash? Were they likely to do a deal? It all seemed a bit dubious. He decided to phone Wilson. He dialled Wilson's mobile, and waited, listening to the ringtone. Eventually it stopped and transferred to his landline. Wilson picked up the phone.

'Boss! I gotta call from Pete – what's it all about?'

Wilson was taken by surprise – Pete had acted sooner than he expected – he hadn't even had time to agree a story with Pete. 'How much do you know already? Wilson asked.'

Danny fell into the trap. 'Only that we gotta go to Blighty to rough up a guy who owes you readies.'

'That's right', Wilson was relieved. 'You've gotta get the cash off him – if he don't play ball duff him up good, and get something as a payback.'

'Like what?'

'Like anything that'll sell for 25g's!'

'Shit! That much?' Danny was astounded. He felt sure that he would have known about a debt that big.

'An' what's this about taking some cash with us? Pete said we might do a deal.'

'Yeah, if he pays up, you can do a bit of trading for yourself as a reward for getting the dough – seems fair enough to me.'

Wilson felt pleased with himself. He had corroborated Pete's plan without knowing anything about it.

Danny was easing up. He felt that maybe this was for real and that his disquiet was a little premature. 'OK Boss! It's the least I can do after the balls-up I made earlier. I'll get yer cash, no fear. '

'OK Danny boy, you do that. Talk to you when you get back. Oh, and one more thing…whatever you do, don't kill the bastard, he'll be useful another time. The roughin' up is just to keep him on track.' Wilson rang off.

Danny went into the bedroom and pulled out a small leather case from under his bed. He lifted the lid and admired the contents, fondling a number of items before taking out a switchblade. He was proud of his stash of weapons. They gave him a sense of great safety, knowing that he could tackle virtually any bother that came his way. He pushed the case back under the bed, but then thought better of it and prised up the two loose floorboards under the bed. He placed the case in the hole beneath and replaced the boards. He used the hide-hole during the periods when he would be away for a while. He weighed the 'switch' in his hand and flicked the razor sharp blade in and out with some aplomb. He had used it many times before. It had a smooth, silky action and was his favourite weapon.

He went down to his car in the basement. Opening the hood, he slid the blade in behind the car battery, making sure that it was jammed in and would not vibrate free. Customs won't look there. Never know when it might be needed, he mused, a stitch-up still firmly on his mind. He drove round to the local garage and filled up with petrol, ready for the morning.

Back at his apartment he took the envelope Wilson had given him and stuffed it in his jacket pocket, together with his passport and wallet. He was ready for the trip and could now sleep soundly.

At 7.00 am Danny stopped his alarm and went for a shower. He had slight butterflies in his stomach – he always did before a job. He knew that once they were off it would pass, but no matter how many jobs he did, nothing changed.

He got to Pete's flat at just before eight. Pete was at the window on the first floor, cup of coffee in hand, looking out for him. He descended to the lobby and out into the street, slamming the door then trotted down the path to the car.

'Alright mate?' he asked as he clambered aboard.

Danny thought Pete looked a bit ragged and certainly not his usual self.

'A lot better than you, by the look of it,' he guffawed.

'Yeah! I had a rough night last night – couldn't sleep much. Cheryl wanted a shag at about 2.00 am an' who am I to disappoint her! We ended up in the bath drinking bubbly till about 5.00 so I'm knackered. Now she's flat out, lazy cow, an' I'm on a job. I'll have to give her the push, she's just too much. '

'Who's Cheryl, you lucky bastard?' Danny asked, trying to sound nonchalant, 'Wish I could get laid that easy.'

Pete would not be drawn and stared straight ahead as Danny turned onto the A4.

'OK! Hook here we come.' Danny sighed.

The ferry to Harwich seemed to take an eternity. Pete and Danny sat at the bar drinking lager and reading the morning's English newspapers. There was nothing about any body being found, so Danny suggested that they went to the restaurant for a 'Full English'.

Pete then grabbed 40 winks while Danny sat developing his Plan B. He still couldn't get out of his mind the thought that this might be a stitch-up. Quite an expensive way of doing it though, if that was what it was. Although Pete was quite friendly, Danny detected a slight change in his manner. Initially he had put it down to his bad night, but there were some strange moments when he felt that Pete was trying to stay distant. It was almost as if he didn't want to be *too* friendly.

If Danny were to be liquidated, how would it happen? Had Pete got his shooter or would he have a knife? It was always tricky trying to get through Customs with a shooter and besides, Pete was not keen on guns, so it would probably be the knife – and when he least suspected it. He would have to be on his guard. He hoped he was worrying over nothing.

The sea was rough and after a lot of banging around against the quay, the ferry docked and the pair disembarked. They had some way to go to get to Manchester so they got on the A14 at the first opportunity, to make the best time.

'You got the address of this guy? Danny asked. He knew he would have it but he hoped his question would lead to Pete giving him a clue to exactly where they were going.

'Yeah! It's an old office in one of the sheds in a dis-used railway coal yard just on the outskirts. Bit of a creepy place. Most of the buildings are now used for long term storage. Apparently this guy bought the whole place for bugger all and now he's got his headquarters there…he gets eight quid a cubic metre per week storage charges, an' then the punters have to pay to get it out again.. He makes shed-loads – excuse the pun! There's a lot of dodgy stuff in there too. Once we've done him over we'll take a look. Might find some souvenirs to take back with us.' Pete laughed.

'How did you find out about the guy?' Danny continued his delving.

Pete conjured up a plausible explanation: 'Wilson knew him from years ago – they were involved in a job together at Schiphol airport, they still do things occasionally and I got dragged in on one job but this is the first time I heard that he owes Wilson money.'

That statement made Danny relax a little. So even Pete didn't know. Suddenly he felt much better. Maybe this roughing up was kosher after all, to settle a power struggle between the two bosses.

They stopped off at McDonalds at the junction with the A1. Danny parked the car some distance from the building, it was cold and as they walked across to the restaurant their breath condensed into fog in front of their faces. Danny turned up his collar against the wind. They bought two burgers and coffees to take out and went back to the car. Danny gave Pete the once over as they sauntered back, looking for the bulge of his shooter under his jacket. There was none.

They ate and drank in silence, as if they were strangers in a waiting room with no interest in making conversation.

Eventually Pete lowered his window and threw the empty coffee cup out onto the tarmac, followed by the wrapper of his burger. 'OK, lets go,' he demanded.

'I'll just check I don't need no oil,' Danny bleated, 'burns a lot this old Merc.' He pulled the bonnet lever and the hood clunked. He lit a cigarette then walked round to the front of the car, lifted the hood and pulled out the dipstick. He found an old rag down the side of the air cleaner and wiped off the dipstick, checked the oil level. Then with his other hand, he reached down behind the battery for his switchblade and put it in his pocket. He paced around the front of the car for a few minutes, sucking and blowing on his cigarette, before dropping the hood. He flicked away the butt then got back behind the wheel. 'Nope, we're alright,' he said.

''Bout time Wilson got you a decent motor Danny boy,' Pete joked. Danny just smirked and drove away.

At 7.30 pm they arrived at the coal-yard. It was dark. 'Drive slowly around the site, an' watch out for the canal, it's got no barrier' Pete advised, 'we need to be sure there's no-one else about'.

Danny cut his speed and they cruised in and out of the maze of dilapidated buildings. At the perimeter, every one was empty, glass missing in the windows, doors hanging off hinges, piles of machinery rusting away on the forecourts, the whole area covered with layers of dusty coal slack. It was a macabre sight.

Danny could now understand why Pete thought the place was creepy. Occasionally they came across buildings where the windows had been covered with corrugated iron and the roller shutter doors renewed.

'Storage units,' declared Pete, 'we're nearly there now'.

Danny was looking for a car. If this guy was here he must have driven. There was nothing else around for some distance. No one in his right mind would *walk* into this god-forsaken place.

Suddenly Pete whacked the dashboard with his hand, 'There it is,' he cried pointing at a two-storey building dead ahead. The building had a row of six windows at the first floor, sitting over what looked like a huge hanger with 4 large, rusting roller shutter doors equally spaced down the length of the façade. Danny could see nothing unusual. There was no car, no lights were on and there was no sound of activity. It didn't look as if this building was even *partially* occupied. He suddenly realised that if anything were to happen to him it would be here...Now. He thought the best plan would be to play along, so that Pete would be off his guard.

Danny felt so sure now that this was a set-up. There was no debt to chase...no duffing up...no deal. The whole thing was staged for his execution.

'I'll go in first,' said Pete, 'I'll try an' talk to him. If things get sticky, I'll get you up there. Look out for me signalling at the windows and listen out for my shout'.

Danny felt sick. He now knew how Pete intended to do it. He would call for him and then Danny would have to run the gauntlet within the labyrinth of dark corridors until Pete jumped him. He stood no chance. Desperately he tried to formulate a strategy for his survival. Why not drive away and leave Pete there? No, It would only prolong the situation. He'd always be looking over his shoulder. Pete or Wilson would find him eventually. He had to go in, otherwise, Pete would realise that he knew he was to be liquidated. The best way to stay alive was to play along. He would go in, but he would turn the tables. He would find a hide, pretend to be confused, and wait for Pete to come looking for him. Then he would get him first.

Pete got out of the car, checked his pockets then walked slowly over to the building. He disappeared into a small doorway adjacent to the first roller shutter.

'Funny!' said Danny under his breath, 'Wasn't even locked, no bell or nothing'.

He lit a cigarette to calm his nerves and let down his window. The smoke billowed out into the cold air in great swirling clouds.

Ten minutes went by. There was no sign of activity, no signal from Pete. Danny threw the cigarette butt out of the window and watched it spark brightly as the wind fanned the glowing end while it rolled away toward the building.

Then, through the grimy glass of the third window, he saw Pete's face. He was gesticulating wildly.

'This is it,' he thought. He reached into the glove box for his *mini-maglite* torch, got out of the car and ran across to the entrance, checking that his switchblade was at hand. He swung open the small metal door and it screeched on its hinges. Pete would know he was there. At first he could see nothing. The building was in total darkness, so he paused, hoping it would allow his eyes to become accustomed to the lower light level. Anxiously he looked around for a suitable place to hide. He decided to stay on the ground floor and pretend that he couldn't find the stairs. He went as far as he could down the thin corridor, silently, feeling his way, then found a small room at the end with a window, which gave onto the corridor. The room was almost totally dark. From here he might be able to see Pete coming. He cupped the torch in his hands and switched it on. In the dim pink light shining through his fingers he could make out a steel locker against the back wall. Danny switched off his torch and walked over to it and tried the door. It opened smoothly with no sound. He left it open and fumbled his way back to the window.

He could hear Pete descending the staircase, the sound of leather on metal ringing down the long corridor. He heard Pete's whisper:

'Danny – where you got to?'

Danny made no sound but watched the corridor intently. Pete was pacing down the corridor now, looking in each room as he went. Danny caught the faint glint of his stiletto blade as it swayed back and forth in his hand.

'No doubt now,' he thought, 'I'm the target. Well it's not going to be that easy for him.'

He turned and went over to the locker, climbed in quietly and slowly pulled the door until it was only slightly ajar. Through the vent slits at the top he watched the doorway of the room.

'Where the fuck are you Danny?' Pete called in a subdued voice, 'the guy won't play ball, so we've gotta job to do.'

Danny didn't reply, he just waited, trying to breathe as quietly and steadily as he could.

Eventually, Pete's frame appeared, filling the doorway of the room. He stood there for a moment, then walked in a couple of paces and stopped again, looking around. Then he stared at the steel locker.

Danny made no sound, his switchblade in his hand ready to strike.

Pete was reluctant to go over to the locker and check the contents, he had seen plenty of others in the offices he had already passed, but somehow he felt this one was different. He could almost smell Danny in this room and the only hiding place was the locker.

'No,' he thought 'Danny won't be in there, he's not that stupid, he would know that I might have a gun and could shoot him dead through that flimsy door. He wouldn't hide in there.'

Pete had almost convinced himself that the locker was empty and he dropped his guard a little. He walked cautiously over to the locker and with the tip of his stiletto he flicked the edge of the door.

As it swung open, Danny's arm shot out and with a single horizontal movement slashed Pete across the face with his blade. It tore through his right cheek, across the bridge of his nose and through the lower lid just beneath his left eyeball. For an instant Pete just stood there, immobile, a look of shock on his face, then the edges of the wound turned crimson and the blood shot forth from the open slit like wine from an upset glass.

Pete groaned and put his hands to his face. Danny seized the opportunity and thrust his switch with both hands into Pete's chest, screwing the blade in a circular motion to ensure maximum internal damage.

The force of the blow sent Pete backwards.and off balance. He fell to the floor, screaming.

The scream turned to a gurgle as his mouth filled with blood and he choked and spluttered, his body convulsing as he sobbed for air.

Danny stood there watching him die, panting hard. The sudden burst of energy had tired him. His teeth ached from clenching them for so long. He knew Pete's life was now slowly ebbing away. He'd done it! He'd managed to turn it around. He couldn't believe how easy it had been. He pulled the switchblade out from Pete's chest and wiped it on the dying man's shirt. He searched his victim's pockets and found a handkerchief, which he forced into the slack mouth, stuffing it in, tight, both to stop the terrible noise of his gurgling and to stem the flow of blood from his lips. Pete lay motionless but his eyes were darting this way and that, watching Danny's every move.

'Got you, you bastard!' Danny spat, looking straight into those flickering eyes. It was several minutes before they dulled and the eerie gurgling ceased. Pete was dead.

With some difficulty, Danny pulled off Pete's blood stained jacket and removed his phone, money clip and all signs of identity, slipped the lot into his pocket, then he laid the locker on its back and lifted Pete's inert body into it. With the jacket he mopped up most of the blood and threw it into the locker. He closed the locker door, locked it and took the key, before lifting it back to a vertical position against the wall. It was now quite heavy with the dead weight of a body and the exertion brought beads of sweat to his forehead. He found some old papers in the corner of the room and scattered them over the bloodstains, tramping them into the concrete with his feet. Satisfied with his work, he wiped away any trace of his being there and quickly ran out of the building, 'Pete should have brought a shooter,' he thought, with a wry smile.

Danny looked around the yard. He needed to wash his hands and clean off some of the blood spatters on his shirt and windcheater before it fully dried. In the dim moonlight he saw an old rusty digger bucket at the foot of a pile of scrap. It was half full of filthy rainwater.

'Better than nothing,' he muttered under his breath as he went about his ablutions. He found an old paint tin and tipped in Pete's passport, papers and cards, lit the papers with his cigarette lighter and patiently waited until he was sure the passport was burning furiously, helped by the burning liquid plastic of the credit cards. When he was sure they were all burnt beyond recognition he stirred up the ashes a bit with a stick and threw the paint tin into the pile of scrap, together with the key from the locker. He was still shaking, so he sat on the edge of the digger bucket and lit a cigarette to calm his nerves. He sat there for a full five minutes steadily drawing on his cigarette, until he felt calmer.

At his car, he hid the switchblade again before driving out of the coal-yard.

'Obviously no-one ever comes down here,' he thought, 'so the body will be well decomposed before it's found, and once I get that bastard Wilson, no-one can connect me to it.'

Back on the road, he drove quickly back to the sea terminal. It was 1.30 a.m. and he had missed the last boat. He went to the waiting area, parked the car then got out for another cigarette. There were two or three other cars there and a large camper-van. The smell of onions frying reminded him that he had not eaten since lunchtime. No matter – better to lie low for a bit rather than show his face around the terminal.

He finished his cigarette and went back to the car. He opened the window a fraction, locked the doors, reclined the seat, and settled down for the night. He lay there for some time trying to decide how he would deal with Wilson. There was that Cheryl bird too. She might have buggered off by now, but she must have known where Pete was going. What would she do when she found out that her stallion had disappeared?

The more he thought about it, the less he liked the idea of going back to Amsterdam. The best thing seemed to be to disappear for a while, maybe after he got Wilson. But how could he get Wilson without being seen by anyone? He opened the window and lit another cigarette. He found they helped him think.

Then there was the car. Maybe someone would have seen it in Blighty. Maybe even the security cameras at the terminal – it would also be recorded on the tickets. And of course, the two passengers, him and Pete, they'd be on the tickets as well. Shit!

Danny found himself panicking a bit. He was finding it difficult to resolve things in an orderly way. He'd go down one avenue and all was hunky dory, but then something would crop up which cocked up his theory and he'd have to start again.

He lit a fourth cigarette and inhaled deeply.

Then a light came on in his head. Burn the car, buy a separate ticket, preferably from another port and go back to Amsterdam. Burn Wilson and the girl, pick up a fake passport and go to Spain or some place.

He couldn't fault the plan – mainly because he was totally confused now, tired and hungry – so he decided to act upon it.

He started the car and drove out of the terminal, toward Parkeston, then took the A120 towards Colchester. He knew the area fairly well, having lived there for a couple of years before moving to Amsterdam.

After driving about 10 miles he found the sprawling great scrapyard where, in the days before he moved up in the world, he used to get the spares for his old *Mondeo*. He parked up outside and tried to sleep while waiting for the gates to open in the morning.

At 7.30 a.m. he was awakened by the sound of a diesel truck idling alongside his car. Dave Beatty, the scrapyard boss was fiddling with the lock on the gate. Danny got out of the car and walked over to him.

'Danny boy! Long time no see! Where ya been?' Dave seemed genuinely pleased to see him.

'Hi mate, yeah, I've been working away. Look, I need a favour,' Danny said sheepishly, 'I gotta get shot of this car.'

'Is it a goer? Dave asked, 'I won't get a lot for it – it's left-hand drive.'

'No, I want it scrapped, unidentifiable - comprendo?'

'Yeah, I guess so, I'll get the mechanicals out pronto and crush it.'

'OK, but I want to take off the plates, and the VIN, then I'll leave the rest to you.'

Danny slipped his hand in his inside breast pocket and pulled out a small wad of notes. 'No questions asked, OK?' he insisted as he held out the cash.

'Fine by me,' Dave replied, taking the cash and folding it into the top pocket of his overalls, 'I'll get you a chisel.'

Danny drove the car into the yard and parked up by the dismantling bay. Dave came over with the chisel and a 4lb lump hammer.

'I'll have to bust the screen,' said Danny, 'but your gonna crush the car anyway,'

'No problem,' Dave replied, and with a wave, walked over to the site hut.

Danny set about removing all identification from the vehicle. He whacked off the registration plates with the lump hammer, then smashed the windscreen to get at the VIN number at its base. He chiselled it out, and put the alloy tag in his pocket.

He pulled the hood lever and lifted the bonnet to reveal the VIN stamped into the metal of the wing channel. With the chisel he defaced it until it became unreadable. He chipped off the embossed engine number, removed his switchblade and dropped the hood. Then he moved to the front doors, taking off all identification plates and labels from the base of the B pillars.

He checked all the windows for etching, checked the boot, flipped open the glove box and removed the service record and other documents and checked over the car for anything else he might have left in it that could identify either himself or the car. Finally, he carefully wiped the whole interior and external door handles to remove his prints. He took out the keys, removed the left luggage locker key from the fob and tucked it in his jacket pocket. He polished the ignition key with his handkerchief, carefully replaced it in the ignition and picking up the plates he walked over to the smouldering bonfire at the back of the yard. He dug a hole in the embers with a piece of rusty metal and one by one, he threw the plates, labels and service records into the red-hot glowing coals he had uncovered. He watched the registration plates contort and liquefy in the intense heat, blue flames and black acrid smoke spiralling upwards, then, satisfied with a job well done, he went over to the site hut.

'Thanks Dave, I'll see you around,' Danny shouted over the noise of the kettle whistling on the stove.

'Not stopping for a cuppa'' Dave enquired.

'Nah! I'm knackered, 'an' I've got a long way to go. Thanks for everything.' He gave a wave, turned on his heel and walked out of the scrapyard, looking for a bus stop.

Chapter 8

Jeff Blythe woke early. At first he was confused by his new surroundings, then he remembered where he was. He drew open the curtain to reveal a French door leading out onto a small veranda, which overlooked the rear garden of the house. The sun had just broken over the sprawl of elegant houses within the high wall, TV aerials and satellite dishes sparkled as they reflected the intense rays slanting towards him. He went into the en-suite, showered and shaved, then donned a pair of slacks and a black T-shirt. It was 7.30.

He went down to the kitchen, following the smell of baking bread. Karl was at the table with a coffee and his laptop.

'Sleep well?' he enquired, 'Hope you didn't find Jenny too full on last night, but she gets a bit flirty sometimes. I think she does it to make me jealous.'

Jeff didn't know quite what to say. He had thought her manner was a bit forward, almost contemptuous of Karl, but he had enjoyed it to some extent. He had assumed she found him attractive and that made him feel good.

'Got some rolls in the oven,' Karl said, changing the subject, 'help yourself to some coffee.'

Jeff poured a large mug of the dense black liquid from the Kona Coffee jar on the stove and added two spoons of sugar, stirring it furiously.

'When you're ready we'll go into town,' Karl suggested. He opened the oven and took out the four steaming rolls. With a carving knife he slit them and inserted a large slice of cheese and an even larger slice of ham. He put two on a plate and offered them to Jeff. They talked as they ate the huge rolls, washing each mouthful down with the coffee. Jeff could only manage one.

'I'll leave your other one for Jenny,' he said, covering it with a tea towel. 'She'll not be up for a while.'

The pair left the house, climbed into the King Cab and Karl reversed out onto the estate road.

'Munitions first stop,' he said.

They drove out through the prison-like gateway and turned Southwest. Leaving behind the relatively wealthy area of Bryanston, they drove on through what to Jeff's eyes looked like the outskirts of any other major city.

'Carry on down here and you get to Soweto' Karl volunteered. 'I guess you'll have heard of it on your English news programmes. Used to be quite a lot of violence down there. Mainly blacks.'

They crossed the Western Bypass and headed down Hans Schoeman Street then turned right onto Beyers Naude Drive, pulling in at the Honeycrest Centre and parking up. They walked over to a tall-fronted shop emblazoned with its name, 'Kalahari Arms', in metre high letters above it's doors.

Karl knew exactly what he was looking for. There was no discussion with Jeff. He just asked for a Magnum Research 9mm – the same handgun as he himself used. He handed the pistol to Jeff, suggesting that the balance was good and the weight just right. Jeff weighed it in his hand. It felt heavier than he imagined. He had no idea as to whether it was a good choice or not, he had never handled a gun and doubted whether he could even fire one in anger.

'Very smooth trigger,' Karl added, 'you'll like it a lot.'

'With a holster and a box of slugs that'll be 13,500 Rand, d'you wanna try it on the range?' the gunsmith asked casually.

Jeff declined and reluctantly pulled out his wallet and handed his credit card to the gunsmith. He did a quick conversion in his head and was staggered that he had just spent the thick end of £650 without blinking. Quite unusual for a Libran, he thought.

The gunsmith bagged up the goods and they left the shop and returned to the King Cab.

'Next stop, we get you fixed up with some transport,' Karl dictated. 'D'you wanna buy or rent?'

Jeff hadn't really thought about it yet. If he was to stay in South Africa for some time, it made sense to buy, he ventured.

'No, what you wanna do is to get a contract hire job,' Karl barked. 'Cheaper in the long run, 'specially if you get cover for insurance thrown in. Cars in SA cost a bomb, 30% more than UK, so you take out a year's rental and renew it each year. What car d'you want anyway?'

'Well, I'd quite like a Jeep, the big one. Diesel auto. perhaps.'

'OK, so they cost about R850 to 900.000 - about £37 - 40,000 English. But you can rent one for a year for about R16,000 a month. You'd have to rent for about 7 or 8 years before you covered the purchase price if you take into account insurance and servicing. By then it would be worth bugger all anyway.'

Although it made sense, once again Jeff felt pressured into complying with Karl's advice. He thought about Jenny and her offhand manner towards Karl – perhaps she was pressured in the same way as he was now experiencing. She had probably been suffering it for several years. Little wonder she acted the way she did.

They drove to the Jeep showroom downtown and selected a standard *Jeep Cherokee Limited* for R11,500 a month. Once again it was Karl who was doing the deal. Jeff signed all the documentation as it was put in front of him, and Karl did all the talking.

The car would be ready for pick-up the following Monday morning, which coincidentally was Jeff's first day at his new job. He didn't want to be late in on his first appearance.

'Don't worry, I'll fetch it for you,' Karl volunteered, 'it'll be all ready for you on the drive when you get back from work.'

Jeff winced at the thought of Karl being the first to drive his new transport. But again he found it difficult to do anything other than accept.

'Next, the Rental Agents?' Karl suggested.

'Well, I'd better get some brochures and prices, but I haven't a clue which are the best areas to live....'

'I can help you there!' Karl interjected.

'God! Is there no end to this guy's controlling instinct,' Jeff muttered to himself. He was by now becoming heartily sick of it and really wanted to go back to the house and up to his room for a bit of peace and quiet. He wondered how long he would have to live under the same roof and the thought galvanised him into searching out a property with renewed vigour.

'Right, lead me to an estate agent,' he sighed.

'We ain't got long,' said Karl, 'I've gotta be at work this afternoon, We'll get a bite to eat and then I'll drop you home an' nip off to the office. But I'll be back around 7.00 pm to give you a hand.'

Chapter 9

Back at his office, Wilson picked up the phone. It was 4.00 pm nearly 48 hours had passed since Danny had phoned him, so Pete should have done the job by now. He rang his mobile. It rang about six times, then went dead. 'Funny!' Wilson mused, 'he's switched it off.' He tried again and it went straight to message service.

He wondered whether Pete had a problem, but there was no other way of contacting him… 'Unless…I phone Danny's mobile,' he thought. He tried it. It rang, but not for long. Then it too went dead.

'Shit! Something's gone wrong,' he mumbled. They were not supposed to switch off their phones – they had to be available full time – they both knew that.

Wilson knew Pete was cleverer than Danny, but Danny was the better fighter – had Danny managed to turn the tables? He hoped not, because that would mean *he* was also now in danger. Danny would know that the order would have come from him.

'Fuck!' Wilson shouted, 'this is getting outta hand.' He was furious with himself for allowing the situation to develop. He should have taken more care over the selection of his boys. Pete was OK, but he needed a helping hand in most things. Danny was cocky and reckoned he could do it all, but in fact he was a bit thick and only saw things in outline, not a guy for detail.

He needed a stiffener so he walked over to the cabinet and poured a large scotch. He drank heavily from the thick-bottomed tumbler, it made him feel better. He decided to wait 'till morning and if he heard nothing then he'd tackle things in earnest. In the meantime, he decided to call Al Redmayne, Danny's father.

'Danny's gone missing Al, he was on a job over in Blighty for me, helping Pete with a guy who owes me. Did ya hear from him in the last few days?'

Al was not surprised.

'He's got a mind of his own, that lad,' he chirped, 'wouldn't surprise me if he's gone on a spending spree with your cash' he quipped.

'He better bloody not have,' Wilson growled, 'but if you do hear from him, get him to ring me. I can't reach Pete either, I reckon they've fucked up on this one!'

Al sounded uneasy, 'What was the drill?' he asked anxiously.

'Oh nothin' much, just a bit of rough and tumble, the guy owed me 25 g's.'

'I'll keep an eye out,' Al replied.

'Oh! And by the way, d'ya know a guy in our line of work who ain't got no thumb?'

'What the hell's that got to do with anything?'

'He duffed Danny up good last time he ran a package for me,' Wilson explained.

'The only guy I know without his thumb is an old mate of Danny's from school days. Cut it off with a chain saw, helping his dad. That was sort of like years ago an' I'm sure he ain't seen him since.'

'OK, Al, just thought I'd ask,' Wilson replied. 'Don't forget to ring me if Danny shows up. Cheers.' Wilson waited for a response but the phone went dead.

Can't be him, thought Wilson, if Danny hadn't seen his thumbless mate since school, it must be someone else.

Then the penny dropped. 'Silly bugger', he blurted to himself, 'Danny's used this school pal in his scam, but only because he knew him as a kid. There was no guy with no thumb. Danny was setting me up.' Wilson was now sure that Danny was bent. He hoped he had got what was coming to him.

He shut his office and went down to his car. He had begun to hate walking across the basement, ever since he thought he saw that man standing in the shadows behind his car. Now, with his fears over Pete and Danny, his disquiet was accentuated to the extent that he could barely bring himself to exit the escalator. If Danny had managed to deal with Pete, even he could be waiting for him down there.

As the escalator came to a stop he pushed the 3rd floor button again and returned to his office. He went over to the safe and took out his little Colt handgun and slipped it into his coat pocket. He closed the safe, twirled the knob and shut the office again. Walking back to the lift, the presence of the gun in his pocket gave him the confidence to tackle the car park.

Once back in the relative safety of his penthouse he relaxed a little. He poured himself another drink and slumped into his favourite armchair in front of the television. His wife came out from the kitchen, glass of wine in one hand and in the other, a small bowl of peanuts. She sat in his lap, placed the peanuts on the rise of his stomach and with one arm around his neck, lay against him, forcing one thigh down between his legs. Suddenly he felt better. Marion always knew how to get him away from his demons. She felt him stiffen against her thigh and she slowly rubbed her leg against him. They sat like that for a while, eating the peanuts and quietly drinking. Wilson reached over to the side-table for the TV remote and switched to the BBC News Channel. There was nothing about a body being found in London – not that it necessarily meant that there wasn't one, but it helped reassure Wilson. He switched off and put his hand up Marion's skirt...

She was a tall, slim woman of 48, the daughter of a train driver on the London underground. She had a somewhat sophisticated air, acquired not through her background but more from the friends she had made following Wilson's rise into the richest 5%. She dressed impeccably, was amusing as a hostess, cooked beautifully, made love expertly and was fiercely loyal to her husband. Wilson had no desire of other women. No need to seek sexual gratification elsewhere. He had it all in one place. 'How many men can say that?' he thought to himself.

By contrast Wilson was short'ish, plump, thin haired with a ruddy face, a broad Cockney accent and a fiery temperament. By 35 he had made enough money to buy outright his dream cottage in Eaton Mews, London SW1, and from a financial viewpoint, he'd never looked back. Here he was at 51, with an extremely lucrative, if shady, business in Amsterdam, which now, unfortunately, if current events were anything to go by, might go tits up! How would Marion feel about that, he wondered? Would she still remain loyal as he rotted in some jail somewhere, with no money to maintain her current levels of expenditure?

He put it out of his mind.

Danny Redmayne stood on the side of the road thumbing for a lift. He had walked about 3 miles and not yet come to a bus stop. He was now cold and extremely tired. He'd had nothing to eat and hadn't slept well. Although he'd managed to sort things out so far, he knew that the worst was yet to come. He was nervous about where he went from here. He hadn't really thought out the rest of the plan, nor could he do so when his mind was numb and in need of sustenance. He didn't want to be noticed by too many people in the area so he only put his thumb out when the occasional lorry approached. Eventually a large truck and trailer pulled up and Danny gratefully climbed aboard.

'Harwich mate, how's that?' the chubby, black-bearded driver offered.

'Fine by me,' Danny replied. 'I'm going to see my old Granny down there, me Granddad died last week an' she's all by herself.'

'Oh! That's tough,' said the driver, 'where's she live?'

Danny was caught out. He had no idea of street names in Harwich. He'd have to pick a name that most towns had and hope for the best.

'Main Road,' he said lamely, hoping he'd picked a suitable one.

'Oh yeah! I know it,' said the driver, It runs parallel to our route, straight down to the terminal,'

Danny breathed a sigh of relief.

'Where abouts?' the driver asked, 'It's a long road that one.'

'Shit!' Danny thought, wishing the driver would mind his own business. 'It's an old council flat about a mile from the docks I think,' said Danny tentatively. 'I ain't bin there since I was a kid'.

'Yeah! I think I know the one,' the driver replied. The council are pulling down them flats, does she know where she's going?'

'For Christ's sake, shut up!' Danny thought. If this guy carried on, he was likely to trip him up. He scrabbled around in his stupor desperately trying to think of a reply that would terminate this farce.

'Actually, she's too decrepit to live on her own now. She's 87 an' her legs is gone. So they're moving her to a home.

'Oh yeah! Which one?'

'Fuckin' Hell mate, how should I know? Why all the bloody questions?' Danny had lost his rag. He hadn't intended to, it just blurted out like that.

The driver looked surprised. 'Sorry mate, I was just making conversation.'

'Yeah, I know… sorry,' Danny cooed, 'I'm just a bit upset at the moment, you know…with my Granddad an' all.'

'Yeah! I guess so.' The driver studied Danny's face for a couple of seconds but didn't appear to think there was anything unusual in Danny's response,

'Well I hope all goes well for the old lady,' he said with a kindly smile.

'Me too.' Danny replied.

The remaining 5 minutes to his drop-off was conducted in silence. Danny was thankful for the interlude. He closed his eyes and leaned back against the cab door. He had been lucky so far. He hoped it would continue.

Danny had to walk the last bit. The driver had guessed the rough position to drop him, at a point with the shortest distance to Danny's imaginary council flats. The wind was still strong and bitterly cold as he made his way down Main Road toward the terminal.

Suddenly he was aware of a phone ringing. It was not his ringtone and he had forgotten that he had Pete's in his pocket. He pulled it out. Wilson's name was flashing on the screen. Danny panicked and pressed the cancel button. Then, a few seconds later, his own phone rang. Again it was Wilson. He pressed the cancel button again.

'Shit!' he muttered. He knew that Wilson would think something was up, but on reflection he didn't really care. The next time he saw Wilson face to face he would be a corpse. He didn't matter any more. The phone calls were worrying him though. He realised, suddenly, that his movements could be traced if he kept the mobiles. As he walked he removed the sim-cards from both phones and with his switchblade he poked a hole straight through the chip on each. He threw both phones on the ground and stamped on them, grinding his heel onto the shattered casings, then threw them in a waste bin. Once at the terminal he jettisoned the damaged sim-cards in another bin and headed for the passenger hall, where he found a seat and waited until the call for his crossing was announced.

His return ticket was for a car and two passengers, but he thought he could dream up a suitable excuse to get him back to Holland without having to purchase another ticket. However, it eventually dawned on him that he might be safer by buying a single ticket, as when the hunt for him started, they would probably be checking the ferries for a car and passengers. It might even be better to take a boat from somewhere else, he thought.

After deciding on this new plan of action, he walked out of the hall onto the apron and climbed into the first taxi in the line.

'Where to mate?' the driver asked.

'Dover,' Danny replied.

The taxi driver looked surprised but said nothing. This was going to be his best fare of the day.

Chapter 10

Jeff and Karl arrived back at the house at 1 o'clock. Karl never bothered to get out of the truck, he just waved as Jeff walked up the drive, and drove off.

'No goodbye to Jenny or anything?' thought Jeff, 'no wonder there's no magic between them.'

He thought he'd better knock, rather than just walk in.

Jesse came to the door, a big, white, toothy grin appearing on his face as he recognised the caller.

The hall felt cool after the heat of the city. Jeff stood for a moment under the revolving ceiling fan, relishing the cold torrent of air it thrust down at him. At first he didn't notice her standing at the top of the staircase, leaning on the balustrade. Jenny called out to him softly, 'I expect you'll want some lunch?' she asked.

He looked up to see her still in her nightclothes, her hair neatly brushed and her face made up. 'I'll be down in a minute, once I'm dressed.'

'No, honestly, it's OK, Karl and I had a sandwich and a beer in town. I'm a bit hot, so I thought I'd take a shower.'

'That's fine,' she said 'you know where it is'.

Jeff climbed the stairs and went into his room. He threw the brochures on the bed and walked over to the wardrobe and placed his newly acquired pistol in the sock drawer.

He slipped off his T-shirt and sat on the edge of the bed, idly sifting through some of the house details.

He heard her knock on the door, but didn't have time to make himself presentable before she opened it quietly and slipped into the room. She no longer had her nightdress on, but had replaced it with a black silk shortie petticoat with a lacy bra top. As she walked over to the bed it was clear that she had nothing on beneath it.

She sat on the bed beside him, crossed her legs and studied the reading matter in his hands, her bare arm brushing the skin on his chest as she leaned toward the pamphlets.

'So you've been down to the agents already!' she exclaimed. 'That's a nice looking place,' she said, pointing with her forefinger to the picture in his lap. He felt the pressure on his leg and watched in astonishment as she dragged her finger along the brochure until it passed over the edge and onto his leg near his groin. She was very close to him now, almost nuzzling against him. He stood up 'I'd better have my shower now,' he blurted, picking up his towel from the back of the chair.

She lay back on the bed, resting on her elbows, her slip riding up her thighs, exposing more than a suspicion of golden curls. 'I'll get you a cool drink,' she said.

Jeff averted his eyes and went into the en-suite shower room. He felt flattered that she fancied him, but apprehensive about taking it anywhere, as he could see it would cause problems with Karl. 'Never shit on your own doorstep,' he heard himself whisper, with a certain lack of conviction.

He got into the shower and turned the temperature down to cool. He stood there, his forehead resting against the white tiles, savouring the icy jets on his skin and wondering how he could dampen Jenny's ardour.

Before he could come to any conclusion, she was there behind him, wrapping her arms around his chest and thrusting her hips into his behind.

'Come on,' she whispered, 'you know you want me.' He felt her hands moving down his torso, reaching for his groin. He put his hand on hers, in an effort to stop her caressing him, but it was half hearted. 'I can't do this Jenny,' he began, 'it wouldn't be fair on Karl.'

'Fuck Karl, he's an old man, I haven't had sex with Karl for years, he can't get it up any more, but clearly you can, big boy!'

She had both hands on his semi-erect manhood now and was trying to turn him round in the confines of the tiny shower cubicle. He caved in and so she succeeded, dropping to her knees.

'Oh God! No, not here, not now, Jenny,' he heard himself say, but he was actually powerless to stop it. He took her head in his hands, his animal instinct had kicked in and he was now fully aroused and enjoying it.

They dried themselves in silence, neither really knowing what to say. Jeff wondered where things would go from this point. He was the first to break the silence.

'Jenny, look...that must be a one-off. We can't continue like this. Karl doesn't deserve it and I don't want to be dragged into the feud between you.'

'I'm not leaving Karl or anything like that,' she replied, 'I have a good life here, but I need to occasionally satisfy my sexual desires. That's where you come in. It won't happen often, we can chose our moments and Karl need never know. What the eye doesn't see, the heart won't grieve over. Surely you enjoyed it too?'

'Yes, but I don't want the lies and deceit that will inevitably be part of it. Furthermore, I will be finding a place of my own soon and I don't want it to continue there.'

'But surely that will make it easier for us. We will be alone, and Karl will be none the wiser.'

Jeff could see that the subject was moving into nightmare territory. He had visions of Jenny as a sex starved stalker, following him around wherever he went, unable to shake her off. He should have been more severe with her in the shower. He had to stamp on it now.

'It's not going to happen Jenny, We're through. It was a mistake and one I'm not prepared to perpetuate.'

'Well, I could speak to Karl and make it legal...'

'For fuck's sake Jenny, what are you trying to do? Are you trying to make us enemies? Firstly I'll deny it and secondly he probably knows what you're like, you've been married to him for long enough.'

'Forget Karl, Jeff, think about us. We're good together. You certainly fit my idea of a sexual partner. I can show you a good time too – you seemed to be enjoying yourself just as I was. What's wrong with us getting it together once in a while? Don't you find me attractive? For God's sake, there's a need for some comforts now and again in this unfair world. How do you think I feel being married to an impotent? I'm a full-blooded sexy piece of arse, as all you men like to put it, just crying out for some attention. Surely you can see that?'

Jeff sighed. He could see that no amount of cogent argument was going to alter her point of view. He was forced to capitulate, in part because he sympathised with her over her predicament but mainly because it was now getting late and he didn't want Karl to come home and see or hear them arguing the point.

'OK,' he said, 'we'll play it by ear, but the moment it gets too hot, or one of us decides enough is enough, then we pack it in, OK?'

'OK,' she confirmed, but Jeff knew that saying it was going to be easier for her than actually carrying out their tentative agreement.

Karl arrived at the house promptly at 7.00 pm Jenny hadn't made anything for supper and instead suggested that it would be good for Jeff to sample one or two of the local restaurants. '…As you probably won't be cooking your own meals when you move into your own place,' she added, winking at him.

They all climbed into the King Cab and went the mile and a half down to the LBV Bistro & Wine bar in Main Street, it was Karl's favourite. 'Best food in Jo'burg here,' he added. 'You'll love it.'

Jeff was getting that feeling that he was about to be 'controlled' again.

The restaurant was modern in style, somewhat cool in feel, with lots of *Formica* in greys and blacks and globe lights on long flexes hanging from the ceiling.

Karl and his companions were immediately shown to a table by an enthusiastic young waitress who asked if they would like a drink before the meal.

'No, we're gonna have the Salsa Prawns with Curried Carrot Purée and Horseradish – as a main, not a starter, so make plenty of 'em - followed by Salted Caramel Affogatto, Karl insisted. The waitress turned to put in the order.

Oh! And bring over a bottle of Sauvignon Blanc, chilled really cold, Boschendal would be fine.'

Jeff stared at Jenny in amazement. She grinned sheepishly.

'Karl always knows what we would like,' she said sarcastically.

Jeff was beginning to warm to Jenny in a big way, despite his initial misgivings. There was no doubt that he found her extremely attractive, but he also felt so sorry for her. He wanted to put his arms round her, console her. She was living in a totally controlled environment, which did not permit her to express her own needs or desires. Even if she insisted, she would be beaten down until she was weary of it. She had reached the stage after many years, where it was easier just to resignedly accept it, rather than suffer the heartache created and the argument that always followed. Jeff was beginning to understand why she felt that he was a breath of fresh air in her life.

Of course, any relationship with her should really be taboo, because of Karl, but he knew that if one developed it would be difficult to terminate. Love was like that. It conquered all. However, Jenny was possibly some 8 - 10 years Jeff's senior, despite her youthful looks. It wouldn't matter much now, he thought, but would he feel the same way when he was 20 years older? He put it out of his mind. Any fling with her would have to take its course and be played out in accordance with the circumstances arising.

After the meal they drove back to the house. Karl insisted that they had a nightcap before retiring, and brought out a bottle of Dutch Kümmel liqueur.

He poured three generous glasses and handed one each to Jeff and Jenny. 'Here's to a successful day!' he said. We fixed you up real good, didn't we Jeff? You are now officially an Apprentice South African.' Jeff raised his glass in acknowledgement then sampled the nondescript smelling, sweet liqueur and winced. The taste reminded him of the *Gripe Water* he used to be fed as a windy toddler.

Jenny raised her glass too and gave Jeff a knowing smile. 'You've really settled in well now haven't you? You know you'll always have a nice snug little nest here when you need it.' Her glaring innuendo was missed totally by Karl. Jeff's face reddened. He hid his embarrassment by bottoming his glass of Kümmel, grimacing at the power of the liquor.

Chapter 11

George Wilson woke with a start. He checked the alarm clock – it was 5.30 am The problems with Danny flooded back into his mind. He would have to sort things out today, somehow, though so far, he couldn't find a solution. Neither had he any *concrete* evidence that Danny *had* hoodwinked him. He went hot and cold thinking about Danny being rubbed out, leaving no lead to the money or diamonds. He might have to accept that this would be a totally irrecoverable loss and he'd have to press on regardless. First though, he'd have to set up the chain again, find a new fence and with Danny gone, recruit a new soldier. He was assuming that Pete would eventually return, although he was still doubtful as to whether he had managed to pull off the hit.

He turned toward his wife sleeping soundly beside him. He wondered how much longer he could continue in this shady business. By now he should have made enough to pack it in. He dreamed of spending his remaining years in Spain, lapping up the sun, with a nice little villa and a boat on the Med. Danny's antics had caused him a bit of a set-back, so the other thing he would have to do today was to evaluate his assets. Marion deserved better than to end up visiting him in a jail somewhere.

He rose from the bed, careful not to wake her. He gently turned down the duvet, exposing her naked breasts. Stooping forward he lightly brushed his lips across them. She smelt warm and sweet. She stirred a little, murmured something he couldn't decipher and promptly fell back into her dreams. Even after all this time he loved her dearly, she was his all, his desire for her had never diminished. He covered her again and walked across to the bathroom.

He studied his face in the mirror as he shaved. He was beginning to look old, he thought. All this stress was not good for him. It spurred him on to get to the office and sort out his financial affairs.

'Where d'ya want droppin' off?' the taxi driver asked.

'Take me down to the entrance to the ferry terminals.' Danny replied. 'I've gotta get a ticket'.

Danny reached into his windcheater pocket and took out Pete's money clip. 'Can I pay you in Euro's, mate?' he asked.

'No problem, it'll be 160,' he said, as he put his 'for hire' sign back on. Danny passed him four €50 notes.

'Keep the change,' he said.

For the second time that day the taxi driver looked surprised.

Danny stood on the pavement and watched as the taxi swung round the traffic island and raced back up the hill towards Dover town centre. He walked over to the petrol station and with the remains of his sterling he bought himself a sandwich and a bottle of cola. He was starving hungry. He swanned around the station eating his sandwich, then lit a cigarette and walked over to the line of taxis. He felt that he needed to add one more detour in order to ensure his return would be untraceable.

He took a ride back into town and asked to be dropped at the railway station.

'Where do I go?' he murmured to himself. At the ticket office he decided to buy a standard single to Portsmouth. There were ferries there, to the continent. He wasn't sure which ports they sailed to, but he knew it would work out with his plan. His return to Amsterdam would be so convoluted as to be virtually untraceable.

'That'll be £65.00,' said the desk clerk.

Danny's eyes popped at the price. 'Christ!' How much is that in Euro's mate?

The clerk looked up a figure on a chart hanging on the window and did a small calculation on his calculator. 'That'll be €90 mate' he said 'you have to go via London, St. Pancras, change for Waterloo, then on to Portsmouth,' the clerk volunteered, noticing Danny's shocked expression.

Danny wished he'd picked another port, but it was too late. Change his mind now and it would arouse suspicion. He stuck with it and passed over the cash.

'Train leaves in 4 minutes,' said the clerk, 'you'll catch it if you're quick. Platform Two.'

Danny walked quickly over to the platforms, found the train and jumped into the first carriage just as the guard was whistling and waving his 'table tennis bat'. He walked slowly down the aisle from one carriage to the next until he found an isolated seat with few other passengers around him. The train lurched forward before he had time to sit down and he fell onto the armrest between them, bruising his arm.

'Shit!' he swore, loudly. The one passenger in earshot some 3 rows away looked up.

'God!' thought Danny, she's clocked me now. He imagined wanted posters pasted up all over UK with his mug shot on it and that one passenger rushing down to the station 'I saw him! I saw him, he was on my train....'

He put it out of his mind. He decided that he would read his magazine en-route to London, then sleep all the way to Portsmouth. He needed the rest to clear his head. He hoped that his diversions so far would be sufficient to avoid detection.

Portsmouth was the end of the line and Danny was still asleep as the train slowly came to a halt at the platform. A guard passing through the carriages woke him up from his slumber.

'This is Portsmouth and Southsea station, mate' he chirped.

Danny shot up, at first not really taking in what he had said. He looked around anxiously but there were no other passengers about. He got up and thanked the guard, trying desperately to sound gentlemanly then got off the train.

At the end of the platform, he walked over to the information desk and asked if there was an exchange bureau in the station. He had no English money left and was starving again.

'We can do that for you sir' chirped a chubby little woman of about fifty.

He changed another €150 from Pete's money clip and went into the snack bar to buy a hot pie and a cup of coffee. He chose a small circular table in the corner and quickly consumed his purchase.

On his way out of the station he asked the guy on the news-stand if he had a copy of the previous night's London Evening News.

'Not a fresh one mate, but you can have mine,' he said, 'I've done with it.'

Danny offered him some change, but the man refused it.

Outside the station Danny took a taxi to the Port. He scanned the paper as the taxi made its way down Park Road to the Sea Terminals. Nothing! No mention of any bodies being found, so it seemed the coast was clear so far. But he did wonder who had taken the old man's body, why and where it had been hidden.

Danny was thrown across the back seat of the taxi as the driver did a quick U-turn at the end of his fare, and came to a sharp stop at the entrance to the passenger-booking kiosk.

'Will this do mate?' he asked.

Danny got out and passed the driver some cash through the front near-side window, turned and walked up to the kiosk. The attendant studied him for some time, then asked him for his ticket. 'I ain't got it yet,' Danny replied 'can I get a single ticket to Cherbourg?'

The clerk prepared the ticket. As he did so, he leaned over the counter and looked down at Danny's feet. Danny did the same, wondering what the guy was looking at.

'Just wondered if you had any luggage?' he said.

'Christ! Danny thought. Might look a bit suspicious going over on a single with no luggage. Still, it's too late now.

'Don't need it', Danny replied, 'I'm staying with me brother. Left some stuff there last time.'

His second invention of the day seemed to satisfy the clerk's curiosity. 'Leaves tomorrow at 0830 arrives 1345. You'll hear the call for foot passengers at about ten past eight. 'That'll be £30, please.' He pushed the ticket out towards a relieved Danny who swept it up, sliding the fare in the opposite direction and quickly left the kiosk. He was surprised by the fact that a ticket to a foreign country cost him less than one from Dover to Portsmouth

Danny glanced at his watch. It was 3.45 in the afternoon. What was he going to do between now and boarding time tomorrow? He knew he had to lie low and not cause suspicion but it was cold, and he had to spend the night somewhere.

He left the terminal and started back towards the town. About half a mile from the Port, he found a small Bed & Breakfast, '*Sleepholme*'. The vacancy sign was up in the front window so he enquired whether there was a room available. An old lady showed him up to a shabby room overlooking the street. It was freezing. The noise from the road funnelled through the half open window. 'Aint'ya got some pyjamas?' the little old lady asked, noticing that he had no baggage, 'I can lend you some, if you like. Used to be my old man's, but he passed away last year.'

The very thought of a dead man's pyjamas put Danny right off. 'Nah, I was s'posed to be back in London tonight, but summat's come up. Caught me unawares love, but don't worry, I can sleep in me boxers.'

Danny decided he would stay in his room and get an early night.

'What time's breakfast?' he added.

The old lady opened the door to leave, 'Any time you like after 7.00 she replied, bathroom's across the landing,' as she closed the door behind her.

Danny shut the window and lay back on the bed. He was dog-tired. He set the alarm on the clock radio next to the bed and crashed out.

The next morning, at breakfast Danny ate quickly. He was a little later than he had wished. He had worked out that he could get to the terminal in about 10 minutes, in time for the call for foot passengers, but he hadn't reckoned on the old lady taking so long to cook his eggs and bacon. He had to rush. He took a last swig of his coffee and taking £40 out of his money clip, he placed it under the saucer. As he opened the front door, he called down the hall,

'Gotta go missus, he shouted, money's on the table.'

He rushed down the street towards the Port, then through the terminal, arriving just as the foot passengers were filing onto the ship. He was hot and sweaty as he walked up the gangway but he suddenly felt safe, as if leaving England was somehow the end of his problems. It was, he thought, the start of a new life. It would be even better when he had completed his mission and moved elsewhere.

Chapter 12

It was Monday, Jeff's first day at his new job. Karl offered to drive him in and take him to meet the team, after which he would get one of the lads to run him to the garage to pick up the new Jeep.

Jeff sensed that the colleagues he had met before, during his previous involvement, were rather subdued. It took him some moments to realise why. They had all known Sheila of course; she had worked there since graduating from University. Jeff had only been widowed for a short time, and perhaps they were unsure of quite how he would react. He knew he would never forget Sheila but the sombreness of the re-acquaintance with his colleagues made him feel as if he had taken a step backward in the healing process.

Following the introductions, Jeff was taken to meet his Group Leader, an amiable, heavily built, strawberry-nosed, Scotsman whose beard matched his copious ginger hair.

'Gordon McKlintock,' he bellowed in a deep Glaswegian accent, offering a huge hairy-backed hand.

He filled Jeff in on the rôle he would perform and where. It turned out to be essentially the same rôle that Sheila had vacated when she moved to England and married Jeff. McKlintock had decided not to seek a replacement preferring instead to spread her duties amongst other staff. Unfortunately that had not worked well, as there had been a degree of duplication, many misunderstandings and much dissatisfaction from staff. Jeff hoped that he would fulfil this position at least as competently as Sheila had and that comparisons would not be made.

At Lunchtime, Karl came into his office with the keys to his new vehicle.

'Took it for a spin,' he said enthusiastically. 'It's real good off-road.'

Jeff felt his anger rising. Karl had taken yet another liberty, another example of his controlling character and his lack of respect for other people. He said nothing, but Karl's attitude galvanised him into ensuring an early move to a place of his own.

They walked over to the canteen together in silence. As they sat eating, Karl seemed a little pre-occupied. He looked as if he wanted to say something, but then he'd hesitate and instead fill his mouth with another fork-full of the *bobotie*.

Jeff looked at him enquiringly.

'I can tell that you want to tell me something…what's the problem?

Karl looked up from his plate, his face reddening.

'Am I that transparent? It's just that I guess I need to straighten out a couple of things with you Jeff, it might make it easier for us to get along.'

'Like what things, Karl?' Jeff was hoping the subject of Jenny would not come up.

'I think you've seen how Jenny is with me. Truth is, that although we stay together, we lead separate lives. You might have noticed that she gets a little bit touchy-feely with you? Well, it happens with all my friends too. I think she does it for two reasons. Firstly, to get me going, but secondly, because she is starved of a good sexual relationship.'

Jeff winced. This was not the sort of conversation that manly chaps had. Little did Karl know just how far things had gone.

'How do you mean?' Jeff enquired, trying to sound intrigued.

'Well…. I've got a bit of a problem.….Which I don't really wanna go into…but basically it means I can't satisfy her…if you know what I mean?

'Oh come on,' Jeff tried to play it down, 'surely it's only temporary – have you been to the Doc.?'

'Too late for that – it's been going on for years.' Karl replied. 'The point is, you now know why she is the way she is. What I'm really askin' is for you not to take advantage of the situation, which I'm sure you won't, but I feel I've gotta tell you.'

'No worries on that score Karl,' Jeff lied, 'You've done me too many favours for me to disrespect you in that way.'

'I knew it,' Karl replied, 'I knew we were buddies, and I feel a lot better about it, now I've told you. But remember, I can be a real bastard if I find out anything different.'

'I'm sure you could,' Jeff said, knowing that there was every likelihood that Karl would probably kill him if he found out the truth.

'Now we've got that out of the way, are we going property hunting after work?' Jeff asked, trying to avoid continuing the subject.

'Yeah! I s'pose we better get you fixed up, but I can't help you tonight, I've gotta see a guy about a shipment I'm making shortly.'

'A shipment? For the Company? Jeff was puzzled.

'Yeah…No not the Company, I've got a little sideline business, import/export type of thing, makes me enough to build my pension for when I retire to Belgium.'

'Belgium? What do you deal in?' Jeff was interested.

'Oh, anything that comes my way, no questions asked. Mostly game trading, like skins, the odd bit of ivory an' stuff, maybe some gold or stones.'

'Isn't that illegal?'

'Yeah, but everybody's at it, an' the overheads are low. Blacks will work for almost nothing and the profits are real good. I've got a few good suppliers, one's a game hunter, he takes tourists out on a shoot, they take the animal head and stuff it for their lounge wall, I take the skin after the boys have tanned it and sell it on.'

Karl noticed Jeff's look of astonishment. 'You clearly don't approve?'

'Well, I think there are issues with supporting the killing of animals, especially endangered species.'

'Don't you believe it mate, there's enough game out there, especially 'Boks an' Zebra, like…millions of 'em. Their skins sell fast and furious. You can make a shed-load of money in just a few years.'

'You mentioned stones…'

'Yeah, look, this is confidential OK? Diamonds mostly, smallish ones that can get smuggled out of the mines. I send them to a contact in Amsterdam and he passes them to a guy in London. By the time they get there they are untraceable, cut and mounted in rings and things and sold on, some as second hand. Everybody takes a cut, but it's hard to get a regular supply. All depends on the amount the boys in the mines can get out. Sometimes we get lucky and get a few from Namibia or Angola, even from miles away like the CAR, smuggled over the borders. By the time they get to us they've passed through so many hands nobody knows where they originated.'

Jeff couldn't believe what he was hearing. He had suddenly seen a side to Karl that he found totally abhorrent.

'How do they get the stones out of the mines?' he asked, 'Surely they would be searched – I mean really searched – full body stuff etc.'

'Yeah! But it depends on what sort of mining and how much labour is involved. There's a lot of smuggling goin' on by the black diggers. They find all sorts of methods. We don't generally ask. Better that way. One guy I did hear about was catapulting them out of the compound, over the fences, then coming back after dark to find them. He didn't get many back, but as they earn bugger all in the mines, even his cut on one stone would be worth a few month's wages. He's dead now. Found with his throat cut. They reckon it was the mine staff that saw to it.'

Karl changed the subject of their discussion, cutting off Jeff's next question mid sentence. 'Tell you what! As I can't make it today, why don't you ask Jenny to show you round and help you with your searching? She needs something to occupy her and she'd be happy to do it.'

Jeff looked at his watch. It was time to get back to his office. 'I'll have a word with her when I get back this afternoon,' he said feigning reluctance. He knew it would not be that simple, but he was drawn toward the idea, not just by Karl, but by his own insatiable desire to spend more time with her. He was surprised, however, by Karl's willingness to suggest that he enlist Jenny's help, after all that he had said previously. He obviously trusted Jeff and that, he found somewhat embarrassing.

Jeff arrived back at the house around 4.30pm and buzzed Jenny to open the gates. He was parking up his new Jeep on the drive when she came out to have a look at the car.

'Nice motor!' she said, 'Are you going to take me out for a spin.'

'Better than that,' Jeff replied, 'We're going house hunting.'

'But Karl will be back in a minute.'

'No…he's got a meeting and won't be back till later. He suggested you help me, he said you'd enjoy the challenge.'

Jenny looked quizzical, 'That's not the Karl I know,' she said with disbelief.

'I know, but we had a heart-to-heart at lunchtime and he told me about the trouble you two have been having with your love life and everything. He was quite candid. Then he made me swear I wouldn't touch you, but of course it's too late for that now. I guess we'll just have to be careful.'

Jenny did a little skip and turned toward the house, 'I'll just go and change,' she said.

Jeff had not been happy with the properties in the brochures he had so far collected. Most were too big for a single person and would probably involve far more maintenance than he was prepared to give time for. He decided to go for something much smaller, yet more salubrious. It would involve a further visit to the agents but this time Jenny would be with him and he would find the experience far more enjoyable.

They set off for the town, both with a sense of adventure, excitement and the smell of new leather in their nostrils. They had not gone far before Jenny placed her hand on his thigh. ‘There’s a nice park up ahead, we could park up for a while, maybe go for a walk?’

‘I think it would be better to get the brochures first,’ Jeff retorted, ‘I don’t want to arrive back at the house with nothing, because the agents had closed before we got there. It would be too embarrassing to explain that to Karl.’

‘OK then. We’ll get the brochures, then maybe make out in the back of your new car? Sort of christen it!’

‘OK, sounds good to me,’ he replied, sheepishly, knowing that if he had said anything to the contrary he would have been arguing all night.

Chapter 13

Danny woke to find that the ferry had already docked and the call for foot passengers had been issued. Impatient, inconsiderate vehicle passengers were already thronging around the stairwells, preventing the foot passengers from descending, so he remained in his seat, waiting for the queue to die down. He tried to organise in his mind how he would get back to Amsterdam and finish the job, once and for all. He had to be careful, one slip-up and he would be a dead man. It would be stupid to hire a car; it would give away his presence in Cherbourg and identify where he dropped it off. He thought that maybe he should buy a cheap motor bike.

He didn't fancy confronting Wilson, he was a heavy guy and quite strong. Furthermore he had an armoury of weapons, so it would be useless trying to take him out at his house. He would have to take him by surprise, do it at the office – say at closing time – perhaps wait for him in the basement car park. He decided he would go for the girl, Cheryl first, then Wilson, and jettison the bike somewhere near Cherbourg again. If he travelled at night there would be less chance of anyone spotting him.

His thoughts were interrupted by the call over the Tannoy. Danny made his way to the gangway with the handful of remaining passengers, making sure that he was the last to disembark.

He walked through customs without being challenged, the officer just waved him through without even looking at him, while deep in conversation with a colleague.

'So far so good!' Danny whispered to himself.

He decided to walk into Cherbourg town and look for a bike shop. By the time he got sorted it would be dark and he could start out on the trip to Amsterdam. He would need a map too, so he could plan the route. He had absolutely no idea how far it was, nor how long it might take him. As he walked briskly down the Quai de Normandie, it became apparent to him that he would have quite a walk to reach the town centre so he passed the time by firming up his plans.

He thought about the girl, Cheryl. Did he really need to deal with her? He doubted that Pete would have told her he was going to kill someone in Manchester. It would be too risky. Was Cheryl Pete's girlfriend or just someone he'd picked up for the night? Danny had never heard of her before so chances were that she would have moved on. He decided that he would go to Pete's place and if she didn't turn up then he would assume that there was no need to deal with her. He certainly wasn't going to prolong his stay in Amsterdam by hunting around for her.

He decided he would deal with Wilson in the basement garage. He would let down one of his tyres, then, while Wilson was occupying himself with the wheel change he would jump him. It would all be so easy. Then he would get back on the bike and scoot across to Hook, pick up his goods and go back towards Cherbourg, dump the bike somewhere, buy a car and drive south.

It took Danny a good three quarters of an hour before he arrived at the town centre, having lost his way a couple of times. He looked around for a Tabac sign, they often had a *papeterie* attached - maybe maps as well, he thought. He found the sign over a café on the next corner. Looking through the window he could see a wire rack of French newspapers and above them on the wall a shelf with magazines and maps.

He went in and decided to buy a pack of cigarettes and order a coffee. The noisy bar fell silent as every face in the place turned to eavesdrop while he explained, in his pidgin French, his requirements to the barman. After what seemed an eternity and a good deal of sign language, an embarrassed Danny got his point over. The barman suddenly guffawed and raised his arms as if he was addressing the crowded bar.

'Ahhh! Oui, oui, une carte routiere d'Europe, oui, oui, une carte Michelin, oui, on a – la…la, en haut!'

He gesticulated wildly at a selection of red coloured, folded maps on the wall at the end of the bar. Danny walked over and looked for one marked 'Europe'. There were none. He chose instead to buy one each of France, Belgium and the Netherlands, and waved them at the barman.

'Eh, voila Monsieur!' the barman beamed 'Avec le café et les Gitanes, c'est trente-quatre Euros.'

Danny had no idea how much that was so he just peeled off a 100 Euro note from his wad and passed it across the high bar-top, hoping it wasn't more than that.

The barman stared at the note then turned to the light, studying it carefully, before opening the till and counting out Danny's change. 'Voila Monsieur, et merci bien!' The noisy conversations resumed and Danny carried his wares over to one of the small round, aluminium tables in the window, to drink his coffee and study his route.

As he poured over the maps, he became aware of just how far it was to Amsterdam - he reckoned about 800 kilometres, possibly in the cold and rain, but he knew he couldn't do much else. To buy a car would involve so much red tape that it would be some time before he would be able to continue his journey. He drained his coffee, folded the maps and went in search of a bike shop.

As he needed to travel south-south east to get round the peninsular upon which Cherbourg was perched, he headed in roughly that direction. He zipped up his windcheater to the neck and walked into the cold headwind, along Rue du Val de Saire. At the entrance to the Louis Pasteur Hospital he stopped a young woman with a small child in a pushchair and asked in English if there was a motorbike shop in the area. He was relieved to find that she spoke enough English to understand his request. 'Moto

Magnifique,' she said. 'Continue along Rue du General Leclerc and take a right, down Rue du Bois to the D901. It's a little way along I think. You can ask again. I go a little that way too.'

'Moto Magnifique' had a veritable forest of wonderful motorcycles, but many were way beyond Danny's self-imposed, limited budget. He checked how much of his pay packet he had left and came to the conclusion that it would be wise to spend as little as possible, especially if he was to ditch the bike later. He trialled a Peugeot XPS 125 for €950, which looked the fastest he could find for the minimum outlay and a helmet for an additional €60. He didn't know what regulations were in force for French bikers, so he attempted to convince the salesman that his driving licence covered him, that his car insurance entitled him to ride a bike and that no further bureaucracy was required.

It seemed to work, although the salesman didn't really seem to be bothered. He'd made a sale and was not going to argue with him.

Danny wheeled the machine out of the shop and down to the nearby petrol station for a fill-up. He also considered buying a mobile phone, one with a French sim-card, but he had second thoughts and decided to wait until he had completed his mission in Amsterdam and returned to France. It would be safer, he determined.

It was 5.30pm and practically dark. The cold wind persisted but the sky was clear with a crescent moon as Danny made his way out of Cherbourg on the N13. He planned to reach Lille around 2.00 am on the first leg of his journey, then hopefully tackle the remaining 300 km the following day. He decided he would eat and drink at the filling stations while re-fuelling to save time, and buy a pair of gloves at the first opportunity as his hands were already numb with cold.

Chapter 14

Jeff was somewhat preoccupied as he drove into town with Jenny. He still couldn't understand how Karl could have got himself mixed up in the shady business of contraband when he had a perfectly stable and reasonably lucrative job with the Oil Company. He was itching to question Jenny about the revelations, but he was unsure about how much she knew. The last thing he wanted was to create a rift between himself and Karl, because he now knew that Karl was, without doubt, a ruthless individual who would stop at nothing to protect his interests.

If Jenny didn't know about his extra curricular activities, then telling her was sure to cause a scene, which would then implicate Jeff himself. He decided to keep quiet about it.

Their first stop at Kingston's Estate Agency on 7th Avenue proved to be their only visit. Jeff had straight away spotted a suitable property in the window, which to his mind seemed ideal, both in terms of accommodation and location. The agent sauntered over and introduced himself:

'Hi, I'm Jim Barber, how can I help you?'

Jeff relayed the spec he was looking for in the order of rental cost, accommodation and location, as Jenny had directed him. Jim winced a little and suggested that renting for the sum Jeff had tentatively suggested was unlikely (in his opinion) unless he went a little too far down-market.

'As a matter of fact, at the moment there's a bit of a lull in the selling market, not yet reflected in rentals, so you may get a better deal if you buy, depending on how long you'll be in Jo'burg,' he offered, 'what's your planned length of stay?'

Jeff gave a vague figure of around 3 years, and the agent called over one of the assistants. 'Karen, where's the details of that 3 bed in Parkhurst, R4.5 mil?

Karen duly came over with the papers. Jeff was a little concerned over the location – Parkhurst was a prison in the UK – until he saw the photos. The property had three bedrooms; a beautiful covered terrace with columns looking out over a tree bordered garden mainly grass, with a central pool. The house appeared empty in the photos but there was generous space across the reception areas and at only R 4,500,000 or approximately £215,000 sterling, it seemed extremely good value.

Jeff decided to buy and asked if a cash offer at 10% less might be accepted, subject to viewing. Jim advised that he would get in touch with the client and get back to him.

'Give me your phone number and I'll phone you later tonight. I'm sure Mr Lewis will agree a deal in that area,' he said. 'Have you time to view the property now?'

Jeff and Jenny agreed to follow the agent to the property and give it the once-over. It was getting late, and would be dark in an hour or two, so they left immediately.

At the house, Jim walked the couple through the rooms, then out onto the terrace and into the garden. It was a balmy evening and the sun was just setting over the front of the house, the sun's rays shining through the windows and reaching the terrace at the rear. Although the house was empty, it was clear that the place was being maintained as the pool was clear and the water bright and Jeff could hear the faint hum of the pool pump in the small pool shack at the bottom of the garden. He immediately felt that this was just the place he wanted. He imagined the rooms filled with his minimalist furnishing, the verandah with barbecue, bar, table and easy chairs, friends sitting around drinking and lazing by the pool. Yes. It was just his style.

'OK Jim, If you can get me that deal, I'll take it,' he said.

'I'll get back to the office now, and make the call.' Jim confirmed.

'Tell you what, why don't you stay and give the place a real going over, you can just drop the latch and lock the gate when you go, and I'll see you again once the deal is struck. How does that sound?'

Jeff looked at Jenny, as if for approval. She nodded excitedly. 'OK, sounds fine with me.' Jeff replied.

Jim Barber left the house and drove off, back to his office.

Jenny immediately walked out to the verandah and started to undress.

'What the hell are you doing?' Jeff asked anxiously looking around in case they could be seen.

'I'm in that pool as soon as I've got my undies off,' she replied, and she ran naked across the grass and dived into the crystal clear water with a neat splash.

'Come on,' she cajoled him, 'it's absolutely gorgeous.'

Jeff took off his clothes save for his briefs and dived in after her. It was true the water was good. From his vantage-point in the pool he looked back at the house, hoping that the news Jim would give him that evening would be positive.

Suddenly he found his briefs being pulled down over his knees. Jenny was underwater, desperately yanking at his last item of attire, and fondling the goods they had previously concealed. She surfaced alongside him, shaking the hair from her face and leaning towards him, her breasts rising to the water surface appearing bigger than they actually were, her nipples occasionally breaking cover then dropping back below the surface. 'Come on, big boy, have you ever fucked under water? She asked, drawing him toward her.

'So, what do you think?' he eventually asked her.

'Oh I think it will do. The area is OK, it's not like our place, but it'll do for a randy bachelor,' she joked. 'And I won't mind coming over occasionally, I'm not proud.'

Jeff was exasperated. No, I'm being serious, do you really think it's OK?'

'To be honest, I think it's a bargain,' she said, 'you'll always be able to sell it again, 'cos it's probably worth more. And it's secluded, rooms are nice, so take it.'

'I definitely will!' he replied.

Jim Barber's call came through at around 9.30pm while they were eating a late dinner that evening. Karl answered the phone and was surprised when the voice asked for Jeff. He passed the phone over.

'Good news Mr Blythe,' Jim announced cheerily, 'the client has made a counter-offer, but it's only a rounding up really. He wants R4,100,000. How do you feel about that?'

Jeff calculated that the price increase was only a couple of thousand pounds more. To quibble would be cheese-paring. He accepted.

'Then the place is yours!' Jim confirmed, and after congratulating Jeff and making a further arrangement to tie up the deal, he rang off.

'This calls for a celebration,' Jeff crowed. 'I'm now a resident of Johannesburg!'

Karl looked up, both surprised and pleased for him – and possibly for himself. He broke out a bottle of bubbly from his stock and the three of them celebrated the news. Karl did not understand why Jenny was so enthusiastic about it all; he just put it down to the quantity of alcohol she had consumed that night.

Chapter 15

Danny reached Amsterdam at midday on the second day of his gruelling journey. His bike had been capable of a good turn of speed but he found it most comfortable to ride, with more acceptable noise levels, at about 85km/hour. He was not properly dressed for biking and his thin windcheater had not lived up to its name, furthermore the gap between his socks and slacks had allowed the cold wind to funnel through to his lower torso, freezing his nether regions. He was stiff, cold and extremely tired. He had not slept the previous night, choosing instead to make as much headway as he could.

He knew he was in no condition now to carry out his plan but to go back to his flat for a sleep would be too dangerous. He parked the bike, found a coffee shop and dosed himself up with caffeine. The warmth of the place soon defrosted his weary frame and sharpened his mind.

He thought again about the girl, Cheryl. He wondered what she looked like. What would happen if he left her alone? He conjured up a scenario in his mind: Pete's body being found, she, finding out about it through the media and going to the police, the police going to his employer, Wilson. Wilson giving the game away, and finally the police arresting him.

'No,' Danny said out loud, 'she's got to go.'

He decided he would go first to Pete's flat and check whether she would still be there. He would have his helmet on, so nobody would recognise him.

Danny parked up outside the low-rise block and walked up the path and into the lobby. He looked over the mailboxes, to find that Pete's was stuffed with circulars and odd letters. It had obviously not been emptied for days. He rang the bell push below Pete's name. He was not really expecting to find anyone in, so when the Tannoy responded with a shrill female voice he jumped.

'Yes?' the voice demanded.

'I'm looking for Pete, he's a mate of mine, is he there?' Danny replied.

'Not back yet,' came the reply.

'Who are you?' Danny asked

'More to the point, who are you?' the voice responded.

Danny wondered whether she was alone. Could he chance giving her his name? It would probably be the only way he'd get into the flat.

'I'm Danny,' he said.

'Oh yeah! He's mentioned you,' the voice said, 'I'm Cheryl,' and he heard the lobby door lock release.

Danny ran up the stairs to the first floor and pushed open the door, kicking it shut with his foot. He removed his helmet and was immediately stunned by the image in front of his eyes. She was virtually naked apart from a pink lacy thong, which left nothing to the imagination and a large towel over her head, draped over her upper body, thus retaining a little modesty.

'I was just washing my hair,' she murmured, 'I won't be long.' She turned towards the bathroom, her beautifully rounded bottom, cleft by the thin strip of lace, jiggled as she padded across the floor. .

Danny walked over to the lounge and paced up and down the room trying to formulate how he would carry out the hit. He had to do it now - she knew who he was.

He was still pondering when she returned, now dressed in a low cut, navy cashmere jumper, no bra, a pair of tight stretch jeans, and sequinned silver ballerinas. Her long hair flowing like spun gold over her shoulders and down her back. Her cockney accent did nothing to enhance her sensuous appearance.

'How come you're back an' he ain't?' she enquired. 'You were both s'posed to be on a job weren't you? Stuffing some guy over in the UK or somethin'!'

Danny felt himself reddening. He was temporarily stuck for a reply. His mind raced, trying to find something convincing to say. A few seconds later, it came to him.

'You're not s'posed to know about that. Pete's back with the boss for a de-briefing and to give him his money back. I need a place to stay so Pete told me to come straight here.'

Cheryl eyed him up and down and a sly smile crept across her face. 'Well that's just great,' she said, 'are we gonna get to have a threesome?'

'I'll start with a drink,' Danny replied, knowing that the third person would never show.

She walked over to a cupboard and took out a bottle of cheap whisky and two glasses. She waved the bottle at him, asking if it was all right.

'It'll do the job,' Danny responded.

As she poured the drinks, her back to him, he studied her intently. She was slim, with a neat little bottom, which filled the stretch jeans perfectly. He wondered if he could have some fun with her before he carried out his hit. Then he remembered something about DNA testing, whatever that was, and thought better of it.

She offered him a glass of the whisky and he took it, making sure that he did not touch her hand as he did so. He didn't know whether touching could transfer his DNA to her skin, but he would not risk it anyway. They drank in silence, Danny consuming his in one mouth swilling gulp and proffering his glass for more.

'When do you think Pete'll be back?' she asked

'A couple of hours I should think,' Danny replied, guessing what she might say next and smiling lewdly.

'So shall we warm up the bed while we wait?' she asked bluntly.

'If you like,' came his rather lame reply.

Cheryl walked over to the bedroom doorway, peeling off the sweater as she went, her breasts swaying gently as she shook off her silver ballerinas. As she approached the bed she undid the top button and zip of her jeans and pushed them down over her thighs. Bending to free them from her lower legs and feet she offered a tantalising glimpse of everything she had between her thighs. Danny was now in a highly aroused state, but he knew he could not afford to go through with her invitation.

She slipped between the sheets of the double bed and beckoned him over. 'Come on, get your kit off, let's see what you've got' she cackled.

Danny steeled himself, walked over to the bed and straddled her. He leaned over her, as if to kiss her, but instead he pulled out the pillow from under her head and pressed it over her face. She let out a muffled scream and writhed beneath him, but he had her pinned between his thighs, his knees on her upper arms. He pushed down on the pillow with the flat of both hands and all his strength, trying to maintain his position as her body writhed and her legs flailed wildly under the restraining sheet. Gradually her screams grew weaker as her lungs deflated and he heard her sucking desperately through the pillow for air, but to no avail. Her thrashing around eventually ceased but her hoarse sobbing for air was, for a while, still discernible. Danny kept the pressure on for some minutes, until she was silent to ensure that she really had expired.

He eventually lifted the pillow, to reveal the horror of her contorted face, her mouth a huge circle surrounded by lips already bruised purple from the force of the pillow, her blue eyes wide open in terror and blood trickling from her broken nose. He could barely look at her. He lifted himself from the bed and taking hold of the corners of the pillowcase, he shook out the pillow, and folded the flimsy cover carefully before stuffing it into his pocket. He then fetched his gloves from his upturned helmet in the lounge and pulled them on. Retracing his steps, he summoned the courage to pull back the sheet from Cheryl's cadaver and cast his eyes over her body. She was beautiful to look at and he felt a twinge of resentment that he had been unable to even touch her let alone have sex with her. He stood there, studying her torso for several minutes, making sure he did not look into the vacant, staring eyes, before covering her body once again with the sheet and pulling it up over her head. Then he left the room, closing the door behind him. Picking up his whisky glass, he took it to the kitchen. He removed his gloves, washed the glass then re-donned them, dried the glass and returned it to the cupboard. He wiped his prints from the areas he believed he had touched, slid his helmet over his head and quietly let himself out of the flat.

Down in the lobby, he removed as much of the mail and circulars as he could extract through the top slit in the mailbox. Hopefully, no one would consider that there was anything amiss, he thought as he stuffed it all into his windcheater.

After a quick look out through the glazed entrance door, he dropped his visor and walked out to his motorbike.

About a mile away, he came upon a large waste bin at the back of some flats and tipped in the mail, and the pillow case, covering them with a couple of the black plastic bags already occupying the stinking receptacle.

'Nice one Danny boy ' he said to himself as he sped over to Wilson's office. It was 4 o'clock in the afternoon.

Chapter 16

At breakfast Jeff tackled Karl again about his extra curricular activities. Jenny was still in bed, as usual. Although Jeff felt that Karl was involved in something he considered morally wrong, he showed a great deal of interest and derived much excitement from it. He was keen to find out more.

'How did you get on at your meeting last night, Karl – I didn't get a chance to ask you yesterday, with all my own developments?'

Karl took a swig of his coffee and looked at him suspiciously.

'You're getting' mighty interested in my dealings,' he said. 'You keen to get involved or something? And by the way, I don't like talking about it except in private. Jenny doesn't know that most of the money I give her comes from my sideline and I don't want her finding it out from you either.'

Jeff found his tone rather aggressive and he wondered whether they would remain friends after he moved out. But he couldn't let the subject rest. He was fascinated by the way Karl had infiltrated this world of criminal activity, yet he remained, externally at least, the very model of South African society.

'I am interested – it's rather exciting, but I'm not sure I would want to be involved.' He said at last.

'In that case, we'll talk no more about it.' Karl replied sternly.

'But you haven't told me how you got on. You raised the subject in the first place, remember?'

'It was OK. I got the package away. It's on its way to the Netherlands as we speak.'

'What was it – the package I mean?'

Karl looked at Jeff and studied his expression for a few seconds before answering. 'You really can't leave it alone, can you? You're either keen to get involved or you're under cover or somethin'.'

'No, I'm just interested, we're mates remember.' Jeff tried to sound hurt.

Karl opened up a little.

'OK, so the package gets to a guy in Amsterdam who has a contact in London. One of his guys couriers it over on the ferry. Amsterdam is the diamond capital of Europe, so a lot of the unregistered stuff goes un-noticed. The UK has a huge community of dealers in London, many in the diamond and gems trade. It all gets lost in there. Simple as that. I'm actually doing guys a favour, helping to make diamonds cheaper for everyone in the trade!'

'How does it get to Amsterdam?' Jeff enquired.

'We find a different way each trip.' Karl said. 'I can't tell you any more as you are not involved an' I'll get shot if anythin' slips out, so keep this shut.' He motioned with his hand as if zipping up his lips.

'Don't worry, I won't say a thing. It's nothing to do with me, but I think you are foolish continuing with it, particularly as you don't have long to go to retirement. Imagine what would happen if you got caught. You'd be in jail, probably for years, you'd lose everything including Jenny.'

'Fuck Jenny, I wasn't planning on her being part of my retirement plans anyway. She probably wouldn't come with me to Belgium, she'd stay here – especially if I gave her the house. She's got plenty of guys interested in taking her on, so she'd want for nothing.'

Suddenly Jeff had a clear - if somewhat appalling - vision of his future. Karl leaving Jenny. Jenny moving in with him. Getting a divorce from Karl…

He hoped he was wrong. In fact he would ensure, if he could, that it didn't happen. Yet somewhere in the depths of his conscience he was persuaded that the idea was irresistible even enticing.

'So why Belgium?' Jeff asked.

'I dunno, really…maybe because a long time ago some of my family came from there, maybe because Jenny and I had a great holiday there, I dunno…the food's the best in Europe – better than France. I just like the place I guess.'

'And when do you plan to make the move?' Jeff pushed his luck.

'I haven't made up my mind yet, but even if I had, I wouldn't tell you until it was sorted with the Company, Jenny and just about everyone else,' he spat scathingly, 'What the fuck is it to do with you anyway?'

'It's not, I'm just interested. It's a big moment in your life and I feel your decision is not so very different from the one I took in coming out here – giving up everything I knew to start again – that's all.'

'Yeah! I guess you're right. I didn't mean to chew your head off, I'm just a bit wary of things at the moment – you know, seeing stuff which isn't actually there, worrying about whether I'll actually get the chance to do it. More than anything else, it means I'm gonna have to pack in my little out-of-hours business, and I'm not sure how the others will take it. Their income depends on me.'

Jeff then said something he never intended to say. It just spewed out of his mouth, no pre-consideration, no hesitation, it just came out as if it was the voice of someone else in his head.

'I could take over where you leave off,' he heard himself say, to his horror.

'There you are! I knew it. You *were* interested in coming in with us after all. You sly old bugger.' Karl took a pace towards Jeff and slapped him hard on the back. 'You were just pumpin' me for more information weren't you?'

It was too late to change his statement. Jeff had unconsciously sewn the seeds of how Karl could extricate himself from South Africa without breaking the chain.

'If you're serious, we'd better sort you out a role, to get you into the team, so that when the time comes you can slide over to my role, like a seamless take-over....'

'Well, hang on a moment,' Jeff interjected, alarmed at the prospect. 'I've only just arrived here. I need to settle in and get to know the routine etc. before I start taking an involvement in something like that.'

Karl rejected his misgivings. 'Nonsense, we'll find you a small role to start with, one that you can easily do without much knowledge or expertise, maybe acting as a courier or summat.'

Jeff began to sweat. He realised that Karl wasn't really bothered about a decent role for him, he was just using this pact with him as a means to recruit another courier, the worst job in the team, the most dangerous.

'It'd be easy. You'll be flying back to the Company in both Holland and UK from time to time. You could take stuff. No one would ever dream that you were bent. You could even use Jenny as a decoy – pretend to be on a little holiday. They'd be even less likely to suspect you. Separate beds though!'

Jeff stared at Karl, trying to understand how his mind worked. One minute he was warning him off getting anywhere near Jenny. The next, he was advocating that they should go on holiday together. Did he really think that nothing would happen if they took him up on his suggestion? Jenny, the sex starved temptress sleeping in her own bed? It didn't seem even remotely likely. Had Karl decided that in order to set the wheels in motion, he must now give up ownership of his wife? Did Jenny know anything at all of these plans? Presumably not.

Jeff was anxious that Jenny understood the position, but the more he thought about it the more he realised that remaining silent, in the short term at least, would give more time to decide how he could extricate himself from this mess.

At that moment, Jenny glided barefoot into the room, still in her flimsy nightdress, all but naked as her shapely figure was silhouetted by the shafts of sunlight slanting through the window as she passed by. 'Hi boys, I thought you'd have left for work by now,' she purred, reaching for the coffee pot. Jeff melted.

'We're just going,' Karl said, flatly. Jeff glanced across the room at Jenny, smiled and gave her a wave as he left the room. 'Don't forget we're going back to meet Jim again tonight,' she called to Jeff as the door slammed behind them.

Karl frowned at Jeff. 'What's all that about?' He asked.

'Oh it's just signing up some papers and stuff to do with the purchase.'

'So why does Jenny need to go with you?'

Jeff hesitated. He knew she didn't have to, but he found himself desperately wanting her to. 'She's going to witness the paperwork, that's all,' he heard himself say.

Karl seemed satisfied with the response, but reminded Jeff not to be too late, as they would be going to another restaurant that evening. Jeff's heart sank. At best, he hoped he would get the chance to order something he liked.

Chapter 17

Danny arrived at Wilson's office at about 4.20 pm. It was not yet dark, so he would have to wait for an hour before Wilson would be finished for the day. He knew that there may be more activity in the basement at leaving time than in the middle of the afternoon, and it would make sense to nobble his car first and return to the basement later to deal with Wilson. It would also give him the opportunity to check he was actually at work too. 'No car, no Wilson, so plan B' Danny said under his breath. Trouble was he didn't have a Plan B. He went down to the basement to see if he needed one.

Wilson's car was there, in its allocated parking place. Danny walked over and peered in through the passenger window. On the seat was a small parcel with gold ribbon around it. Another present for Marion, he thought.

Danny crouched down beside the car and gingerly undid the valve cap of the rear wheel. He took his switchblade and pushed the point into the valve until he felt the air rushing from the tyre with it's accompanying shrill squeal. He held the blade there while the tyre deflated, looking around furtively to ensure he had not been seen or heard. He then repeated the performance on the other side of the car. It now assumed a slightly squatting position at the back. Wilson will definitely notice, Danny thought.

Pleased with his handiwork, he checked his watch. Twenty to five. He just had time to leave the basement, get something to eat to pass the time. He planned to return to the car park at about 5 o'clock. He knew that Wilson seldom left his office before then.

George Wilson sat back in his chair staring at the ceiling of his office, as if looking for divine inspiration. He had weighed up the possibility of retiring and had completed his exercise to see if he could do so whilst maintaining the standard of living that he presently enjoyed. He had been pleasantly surprised by the advice given by his financial advisor and so he had begun the winding up of his business.

However, he felt that he could not fit all the pieces together until he received news from Pete. It was now some four or five days since he'd first rung him and he had done so again and again since, but with no reply. It concerned him greatly and he couldn't help feeling that Danny may have escaped his execution and might even have managed to get the upper hand and dealt with Pete. Or maybe they had a car crash he pondered. Maybe they were in hospital in England somewhere. He really had no idea. He wondered if he could track the mobiles of the pair. They were not supposed to have the location tracker switched on – George didn't like the idea of the police following them around. But their phones were under a business contract with his own phone, so maybe he could get information from the service provider as to where they last phoned from. He decided he would dig out the contract and give them a ring in the morning.

He walked over to the safe and pulled out the contents, tossing them onto the desktop. There were several bundles of banknotes, some papers, a small leather bag containing a variety of precious stones and his two handguns: His small, Colt short barrelled revolver - his *Mafia* gun as he called it - together with a much heavier weapon, a Glock 17, 9mm semi-automatic pistol. At the bottom of the safe were a couple of cartons of ammunition.

Wilson fanned out the cash on the desktop and idly counted the notes. €30,000 in €50 notes in one large bundle and €10,000 in each of the other two. He poured out the contents of the leather bag onto the desk blotter.

Six uncut diamonds and a handful of blue sapphires. He turned toward the safe and replaced each wad of money one at a time in a neat pile. Then transferred the papers, guns and their ammunition. Lastly he scooped up the gemstones and put them back in the leather bag before picking up the phone and dialling Al Redmayne.

'Still no news I guess?' he asked.

Al confirmed that neither Danny nor Pete had shown up at his place.

'Bloody nuisance this. Fucked if I know what's happened.'

'Don't worry George, you'll find out soon enough,' replied Al. He didn't seem the least bit worried. Danny had always been a pain that way. 'As a young lad he would often be out for days with his mates somewhere,' he continued.

'Look Al,' said Wilson, 'I've got a few sparklers that I need to offload cheap – you interested?'

'You know me George, always got an eye for a bargain. What's the deal?'

'Six uncut diamonds, they'll make two one-carat and four two-carat diamonds, I'd say VVS1's, and eight blue sapphires, about 2 carats each, medium/dark, minor inclusions. You can have the lot for €40k, but I'm open to negotiation once we agree the quality.'

'I'll come an' have a look, but I don't wanna pay silly money for 'em.'

'OK, fair enough, come round first thing tomorrow, I've got 'em out ready, but I need the cash so bring it with you.'

'OK George, I'll be at your place around 7.30'ish. It'll be quiet then an' there won't be no-one else about.'

Al Redmayne put down the phone and went down to the cellar to obtain some ready cash for the deal. He had converted his cellar into his office. He didn't trust banks and instead had dug out a huge hole in the cellar front wall, under the skylight, into which he had formed an open fronted hollow concrete chamber. In the opening of this chamber he had installed a *Chubb Trident Grade 6* Safe with a 60-minute fire rating, weighing almost 900 kg, bolted into the concrete on the base. The whole ensemble probably weighed some 3 tons but it could not now be removed from either inside or out because the concrete box also served as underpinning for the bay window above, which had been the original reason for the work. Redmayne had just adapted the design to incorporate his safe foundation.

He had managed to carry out all the work without recourse to outside tradesmen. He had even taken delivery of the safe at the works and with a great deal of difficulty, a JCB and a heavy duty trolley, installed it himself in order to maintain it's secret location. The two keys required to open the safe were always kept in different locations and Al was the only person who knew where. Danny was not privilege to even know of the safe, let alone where the keys were kept. Redmayne now swung away the heavily framed map of the world that served to conceal it and inserting the two keys one by one, he unlocked the door and yanked the three-spoked wheel around, simultaneously pulling the heavy door outward.

The top shelf of the safe was his money shelf. Notes were bundled in two-inch wads, piled up on top of each other, stacked end on, three deep, six wide and six high, almost totally filling the allocated space. On the shelf below was a collection of stacking trays. These contained Redmayne's personal items: some of his and his wife's jewellery, watches, gold and silver items, a small revolver and of course, his own trading goods, for he, like Wilson was a dealer in gemstones. The base of the safe contained three document boxes, full of papers, contracts, accounts, deeds etc.

Al Redmayne removed three of the bundles of notes and pushed the safe door closed, swinging the three-spoked handle over with a satisfying clank. He locked it and removed the keys.

'Thirty grand should get me this deal,' he said quietly.

Three miles away, Wilson put his gems back in the safe and was about to shut it when he remembered the little Colt revolver. He took it from the safe, reached for his camel hair coat and slipped it into the right hand pocket.

He checked the time – it was five fifteen. Time he was away. He draped the coat over his shoulders and searched out a cigar from his jacket pocket, lighting it as he walked to the door. He switched off the light, slammed the door and made his way over to the elevator.

Danny heard the elevator coming down the shaft and looked at his watch. This would be Wilson. There was no one in the basement and only two other cars left, so his job would be easy he thought. He hid behind one of the remaining cars about 5 metres away from Wilson's Mercedes and squatted down below the window line of the intervening vehicle. He heard Wilson's footsteps approaching.

Suddenly they stopped.

'Good,' thought Danny, he's seen the tyres'

Wilson kicked himself. 'The bloody safe!' He said out loud. He had forgotten to shut it. He turned, and walked back to the elevator.

Danny had heard his exclamation and realised that he might have to adjust his plan, particularly as the added benefit of an open safe and it's contents appealed to him.

As soon as Wilson was in the elevator, Danny ran over to the stairwell and shot up the stairs two at a time. At Wilson's floor he stopped and quietly waited behind the small glass pane of the door onto the landing until he heard the elevator motor stop and saw Wilson exit the lift and cross the landing to his office. Again he waited until Wilson had opened the door, then, switchblade in hand, he walked silently over and followed him in.

Wilson had gone behind his desk and almost reached the safe when he heard the intruder behind him. He turned, saw Danny and immediately knew what he was going to do. The bastard had got Pete, he thought, and now me, well, he won't last long. He pulled out his little Colt revolver and aimed it at the slit in Danny's unzipped windcheater.

Danny saw it coming and dived toward the opening in the front of the knee-hole desk. He slid along the carpet and crashed through the space as the shot rang out, the bullet splintering the far edge of the desk, sending shards of wood slivers into the air.

He could see Wilson's foot by the revolving chair on the other side of the desk. Raising his arm he smashed his switchblade down into the toe of Wilson's moccasin, the blade sliding easily through the leather to the flesh and bone beneath.

Wilson screamed in pain and tried to shoot through the desktop at Danny below, peppering the green leather top with neat round holes until the magazine was exhausted. But nothing penetrated the desk, the files and books in the drawer below absorbing the slugs. Danny left the switch in place and grabbed Wilson's other leg and pulled it, with all his might, into the recess under the desk. Wilson's leg twisted then cracked as the knee joint broke and the ligaments were torn out of place. Wilson collapsed sideways, heavily, his screams were now more desperate. His gun was empty, the pain was excruciating, but he knew he had to shut the safe. He tried desperately to reach it but Danny was holding him back by his damaged leg, inflicting further pain. He knew that he would be a dead man…unless he could reach the safe. He had remembered the Glock automatic. He couldn't decide whether to nudge the safe shut or to get the gun and kill Danny. He knew that latter would be more difficult – he had to get further towards the safe.

Danny, now kneeling on Wilson's leg, was pulling the switchblade from his other foot. It was difficult for he had used such force that the blade was embedded in the shoe's leather sole. Wilson realised that if he managed to extract it he would use it again. He grabbed the end of the desk and with all the strength he could muster, tried to pull himself further toward the safe, simultaneously gauging the distance with his other arm. About two feet away, he thought, but he just couldn't summon the strength he needed to get there.

'What the fuck, Danny! What the fuck are you doin'?' Wilson pleaded.

'Danny laughed.

'You really are a fuckin' prize shit boss. D'you think I'm stupid or what? You sent Pete to top me, but I done him in good. D'you wanna know what I done to 'im? You should see his face. He's split from ear to ear. He looks like a fuckin' Muppet. Dead meat. And now it's gonna be you, an' you ain't getting to that safe neither.'

'No - please Danny, I never meant for you to be topped. You were only to be learnt a lesson. I knew you'd stashed the stuff from the old man. But I couldn't have you makin' the rules, so I was going to give you a lesson in manners, that's all.'

Danny had managed to withdraw the switchblade from Wilson's other foot.

'Well, you ain't wrong! I did stash the stuff, an' I topped the old man. And another thing…you don't learn me a lesson with a stiletto,' said Danny 'I took Pete out, an' now you're gonna see what my switch feels like jammed into your bollocks, you've gotta go, you bastard.' And he thrust the switchblade hard into Wilson's lower stomach. It was as far as he could reach without allowing Wilson to improve his progress towards the safe.

Wilson's scream turned to a deep moan as the pain intensified. He was now gasping for air.

'No, Danny…No more…Please, listen to me, we can sort this out…please…' Wilson screamed again as Danny wiggled the switchblade out of the wound and moved up Wilson's body, pushing the thin blade under Wilson's ribs and through his diaphragm, to his heart beneath. Wilson writhed in his death throes, a deep blood-curdling moan signalling that it was almost over.

He lifted his head, beaded in sweat and stared at Danny, mouthing silent words, his bulging eyes wild with the terror of what was to come, then, slowly, they dulled and his head slumped back to the floor with a thud, his body limp, his ragged breathing fading fast.

Danny stood up and waited until he could hear no further sound from Wilson, then he prodded the body sharply with his foot. There was no movement. Panting and in pain from the impact of crashing his shoulder and thigh into the desk, he hobbled straight over to the safe. He was afraid that the door might somehow shut itself. He took out the contents and placed them on the table. He limped to the door, wincing with the pain and checked the corridor, listening for any sign of the other office tenants. All was quiet, so he went back in and dropped the latch. He didn't want any inquisitive visitors until he was well away from Wilson's office.

He removed his switchblade from Wilson's now lifeless body and wrapped it in a couple of sheets of paper then stuck it in his pocket. He was careful not to touch anything that might leave traces. Grabbing Wilson's feet, he dragged his body fully behind the desk and placed the chair in the knee-hole, so that from the door, the body would not be immediately seen. He picked up the money, the gemstones and one box of ammo, checked the magazine of the Glock pistol then tucked it into the back of his pants. He took Wilson's little 'Mafia' gun from the floor by the safe and stuffed it in his windcheater pocket. He was just about to leave when the phone rang.

He wondered how long it would ring if he didn't answer it and whether it had an answering service. After what seemed an eternity, he picked up the receiver and waited for a voice. 'Hi Darling, How long you gonna be? I've done my shopping, I'm down at the car. Looks like you've got a puncture. I'm coming up.'

It was Marion.

'Shit!' Danny mouthed, his heart leapt. He slammed the phone down and ran for the door. He looked out into the corridor. No one about. He heard the whirring sound of the elevator motor, the delta-shaped red light over the door indicating that the car was travelling up the shaft. He dropped the latch and closed the door, hoping that she didn't have a key. He needed time to get away.

Danny went for the stairs. He knew he had to escape quickly. Once the police had been informed, there would be roadblocks and all sorts to contend with.

In the heat of the moment he forgot about his limp and he flew down the stairs as fast as he'd come up them, wincing with pain, he waited to check that the lobby was clear before making his way out into the street. Walking as naturally as he could, he skirted round the side of the building, to where he'd hidden his motorbike behind the bushes adjacent the car park extract ventilators, jerked on his helmet and, trying to control his shaking body, he set off for Hook. He needed to deal with his stash in the left luggage lockers. This would be his only opportunity. As the police intensified their search for Wilson's killer, the ports would be watched carefully.

His trip to the port was uneventful and there were no signs of any unusual police activity, but Danny knew that by now the situation in Amsterdam might be quite different. If she had carried a key to Wilson's office,

Marion would have found his body and raised the alarm by now. The police would be crawling all over the office and the surrounding areas would be road-blocked. He was also sure that they would very soon be watching the ports and he was glad that he would not be making a crossing and would not have to show his papers.

At the terminal he went over to a shop selling travel aids and bought a small holdall then he walked across to the lockers. Taking the key from his pocket he recalled the locker number and sidled towards it. He opened the door and one by one took out the contents and placed them in the holdall. He then took the Colt pistol from his pocket, wiped it clean and placed it in the locker After closing the door and re-locking it, he arranged the items within the bag and walked over to the toilets. Selecting the disabled cubicle he went in and locked the door.

He set the small pouch of diamonds and the A5 manila envelope to one side on the basin worktop and put his wallet back in his breast pocket. He began to examine the stuff he had removed from the old man's safe. A black velvet folded pouch contained thirty-two small diamonds, none more than about a carat or two each. A couple of trays of assorted diamond rings, pendants and earrings and a cigar box secured with a band of insulation tape containing a flat purple velvet cushion in which were set eight rings with various large gemstones. Danny didn't really know what they were. In addition, there was a bundle of cash. He counted it out, all in €100 notes, €35,000. He gave a low whistle. He was rich! He had no idea what the diamonds were worth, but he guessed at about €5,000 a carat. If that was true, he thought, he'd got about €200k in sparklers! Never mind the rings, there was enough here to set him up for life. With the contents of Wilson's safe and the stuff from the heist, he reckoned he had well over half a million in total. Furthermore, he had the remains of his wages. He was truly loaded.

He suddenly felt very vulnerable. Someone somewhere must know that all this stuff had gone missing and they would be looking for him. Tucking one of the old man's manilla envelopes into his jacket inner pocket, he transferred the rest of his haul to the holdall and zipped it up. He shouldered the bag, passing the strap over his head for safety, left the cubicle and walked, as casually as he could, across the concourse to the exit and back to his motorbike.

He felt elated. He could never have envisaged the ease with which he had arrived at his goal. All he had to do now was to be careful not to arouse suspicion. Uppermost in his mind was the dilemma of how to dispose of his newfound wealth.

He desperately needed more sleep, but he felt that he would be safer getting out of Holland first. He wondered how he could guarantee that, given that he had to cross the border into Belgium. He studied his map, looking for little used border crossings that might be un-manned. He decided that they couldn't possibly all have customs posts. He would do a quick *recce* when he got down there.

Marion stepped out of the elevator and walked across to Wilson's office. The door was locked but a thin strip of light beneath it told her that he was probably still at his desk. She knocked twice but with no response.

Funny, she thought. Who had answered the phone? Perhaps it had been the answering machine – there had been no voice. Yes, that would be it. She wondered whether he had forgotten to switch off the light, gone down to his car and seen the puncture, then decided to get a taxi home. She tried the door again then decided to do the same.

Back at their penthouse, there was no sign of Wilson. Marion set about making supper. She was used to him working peculiar hours, particularly when he had meetings with his cronies. He would occasionally arrive back, having consumed more than his usual quota of alcohol, following the settlement and celebration of some lucrative deal or other.

She had no reason to think that there was anything untoward. But the punctured tyres on his car perturbed her somewhat.

'Why didn't he get it sorted?' she wondered.

By 10.30 Wilson had still not turned up. Marion left his food in the oven and turned it off. He could reheat it in the microwave as he often did.

She went to bed.

Al Redmayne arrived at Wilson's office at bang on 7.30 am. He too found the door locked and no sign of Wilson. He noticed the light at the foot of the door and knocked again, only much louder. There was still no reply. He wondered whether he had got the location of his meeting wrong – Did George say 'office' or his 'home'? He couldn't exactly remember.

He heard the elevator arrive and turned towards it hoping that it was Wilson. The door opened and the cleaner, a small rotund lady in her 60's, leaned on her trolley laden with cleaning materials, mops and brushes and pushed it gingerly out of the elevator.

'You waiting for Mr Wilson?' she enquired.

Al Redmayne acknowledged and decided to wait a few more minutes.

'I can let you in if you like?' the cleaner persisted.

'Yeah! OK.' He replied, as she unlocked and opened the door with her master key.

'I always do Mr Wilson's room first because he's the early bird,' she said, pushing her trolley through. Al Redmayne followed her in.

There was a peculiar smell in the room, detected immediately by both parties. The light was on, the splintered desk and rucked carpet showing that there had been some kind of incident and the safe door was open.

'Oh Christ!' Redmayne groaned, 'I bet he's been robbed!'

He walked towards the safe, and as he rounded the desk he almost tripped over Wilson's body on the floor. At first he stood there, immobile, he couldn't believe what he saw. He stooped over his body looking for signs of life, but the pallor of his skin and the extent of blood soaked into the carpet told him otherwise.

'Christ! He's dead.' Redmayne whispered, failing to find a pulse at his neck.

The cleaner screamed and started crying. Redmayne eyed the safe. It was empty, yet Wilson had said he had the stones ready for examination this morning. That meant they were probably in the safe. Whoever killed Wilson must have made off with them. Who else would have known about it? He wondered.

He reached across the desk for the phone and called the police. He told the cleaner to go and clean another office, but to be ready to speak to the police when they arrived. He doubted it would do any good, as she was probably too distressed to even think about her work.

Turning his attention to Wilson's desktop, he had to make sure there was nothing that might incriminate him. He didn't want the police to be knocking on his door when everything was cleared away and the investigation began. He particularly didn't want them to get hold of Wilson's diary, address books and mobile phone. He noticed the peppering of shots through the desktop and he suddenly realised that he would not be able to remove anything from that drawer. If the slug was not found in the carpet beneath and there was nothing in the drawer to stop the bullet, the police would know something had been taken. He opened the drawer gingerly, taking care not to disturb anything, but the items he sought were clearly elsewhere. Frantically routing through every other drawer and cupboard in the room, he eventually found the diary and address book in the midst of a pile of correspondence in Wilson's out-tray. He then checked Wilson's pockets and found the phone. He switched it off, stuffed the three items into his trench-coat pocket and then sat waiting for the police to arrive.

Al Redmayne had a bad feeling about Wilson's demise. The possibility that it was somehow linked to his son, Danny, was gnawing away in his mind. Something had gone down. Pete and Danny were missing and now Wilson was dead. He remembered Wilson's disquiet over Danny during his previous phone call. Clearly Wilson knew there was something up.

Who was this bloke in Manchester that owed Wilson money? Al Redmayne knew nothing about any of it but he realised that getting hold of Danny might be the key. He would have to wait until Danny contacted him.

Al Redmayne heard the police sirens as they raced up Wolvenstraat. He went down to meet them at the entrance. The three police officers, two tall, wiry looking, uniformed young men and a shorter slightly tubby, older man with a pencil moustache, wearing a grey mackintosh, checked over Wilson's corpse and briefly looked around the office. The older man, who was the senior and clearly a detective, took charge, issued a warning not to touch anything then suggested that Redmayne should leave the room so that it could be secured, but wait to be questioned.

He then pulled out a radio from his jacket and mumbled into it in Dutch for several seconds.

'We wait for forensics,' he said in English, 'is there a room where we can conduct our enquiries?'

Redmayne shouted down the corridor for the cleaner and asked. She ambled across the landing and disappeared around the back of the lift-shaft, beckoning the officer to follow. She showed the officer to a small kitchenette, containing a sink and worktop on which stood a kettle and microwave oven. In the corner, next to a small cupboard, were a table and two chairs.

'Thank you, that will be excellent,' said the officer. He beckoned to Redmayne to follow him into the tiny room.

Both men sat at either side of the narrow table, the officer taking out a small black notebook and pen and laying them down on its Formica surface.

'Full name and address?' the officer asked.

Redmayne gave his details.

'Do you know the name and address of the dead man?' he asked.

Redmayne gave his friend's name, but hesitated over the address, deliberately making it sound as if he was not that familiar with Wilson.

'I think he lives on the Amstelkanaal Block 5 or 6 I think, I can't really remember.

'Was the deceased married?'

'Yes, her name is Marion'

'Have you contacted her?'

'No'

The officer scribbled some notes in his little black notebook.

'Were you the person who discovered the body?' He asked.

Al Redmayne explained how the body had been discovered, but was not prepared for the next question:

'What was the nature of your business with the deceased?'

Redmayne paused, frantically concocting a coherent response.

'We were mates, going back a few years, and I hadn't seen him for a while, so I invited him over to my place for a drink and a chat. But he was busy, so we made an arrangement to meet here this morning instead.' Redmayne replied, somewhat hesitantly.

The policeman scribbled again in his notebook.

'How long has it been since you last saw him alive?'

'Oh! I dunno, maybe six months.'

'So you have no business connections of any kind with the deceased?'

'No, none at all,' Redmayne lied.

Their 'interview' was interrupted by one of the young policemen entering the room. He leaned over the detective and whispered something in his ear.

'We need to find out who visited Mr Wilson yesterday. Would he have had a desk diary or something to record his meetings? My guys can't find anything in the office.'

Redmayne rubbed his chin, pretending to think for a moment before answering: 'These days I think most people use their mobile phones – I know I do' he replied. If that isn't in his pocket, then I expect it might be at home.'

He hoped that the policemen would not ask him to turn out his pockets, for that would certainly incriminate him in the murder.

'Well, that will be all for the moment Mr Redmayne,' sighed the officer, 'but we shall be speaking again soon, I have no doubt. Please ensure that you remain available at the address you have given me.'

'Who will speak to his wife?' Redmayne asked anxiously.

'We will send round one of our female officers,' came the reply.

Redmayne's relief was reflected in his expression. He hadn't fancied calling on Marion to give her the news. She must already be wondering what had happened to Wilson when he didn't return the previous evening. She was probably frantic by now, he thought.

Redmayne walked back to Wilson's office and took one last look through the door. One of the policemen was taking measurements of the position of the bullet holes in the desk. 'Excuse me sir,' he called, just as Redmayne was turning away, 'do you carry a firearm?'

Redmayne froze. He knew he would now be implicated. The policeman would insist on searching him if he said 'No'.

'I do occasionally,' he replied nervously, 'but not today', opening his coat and jacket beneath to demonstrate that he was clean.

'Is your firearm licensed?' Continued the policeman.

'Of course', Redmayne was becoming more anxious by the minute.

'Then if you don't mind, would you please bring your firearm, two rounds of ammunition and your licence to the police station, later today – just so that we can eliminate you from our enquiries, you understand.'

'Of course, no problem' Redmayne replied, doing his best to hide his apprehension. He waved to the Officer then went down the elevator to the main entrance and walked out into the cool late-morning sunshine. He was desperately in need of a drink and decided to drive to his local café for a quick one before going back home.

He was sitting at the bar with a measure of whiskey and an espresso, mulling over the events of the morning when his mobile rang.

It was Danny.

'Danny boy!' Redmayne was relieved. Where the hell are you? He whispered.

'Oh!' said Danny, 'I forgot to tell you. I'm havin' a few days off in France.'

'I thought you was s'posed to be in Manchester?'

'Who told you that?'

'Wilson rang me. He was worried 'cos he hadn't heard from either of you.'

Danny was quick with his reply. 'No, I never went. Wilson had laid me off for a while 'cos I fucked up a transfer in London. Then, 'cos there wasn't much going down, an' there was only a bit of ruffin' up of a guy in Manchester to take care of, Wilson paid me off an' Pete reckoned he could do the job by himself. So I left 'im to it.

I've just met this French bird an' we got chattin', as you do. She'd been backpacking' in Blighty and was goin' back home via Amsterdam. I asked her where 'home' was an' she said…' Danny paused, trying to remember the name he had seen on the sign for the little port on his way back from Blighty. '…Diélette or summmat, in Normandy. Her Dad's got a big place down there near the beach, so I said I'd go with her…give her a lift on me bike. And here I am.'

'What bike? You ain't got a bike, you lyin' little toe-rag.'

'Hey! Steady on Dad, I have now…Wilson took me car back. Pete took it to Blighty an' I bought a cheapo bike to get around on with me redundancy money. Great little machine.'

'So you got the sack and never went to Blighty with Pete?'

'No, I said that already. I was tryin' to get in on the job, so I could get me proper job back. But Pete was bein' a bit of a pain about it, sayin' Wilson didn't need me and he could do the job on his own an' that I would just get in the way. So I left him to it. I ain't too bothered about missing out on givin' someone a good kickin'. Besides, this French bird's really hot an' I didn't wanna miss out on a chance with her.'

'So you haven't heard the news yet?'

'What news?' Danny tried to sound alarmed.

'Wilson's been robbed'

'You're jokin'…Poor bugger, what'd they take?'

'Cleared his safe…' Redmayne stalled, '…then killed him.'

Danny whistled under his breath and held back his reply until he felt he had left enough of a pause to appear genuinely surprised.

'What? You're kidding,' he said, trying to sound incredulous.

'No, it's true,' Redmayne insisted 'I found him this morning with the cleanin' woman, he'd been cleaned out and looked like he'd been knifed two or three times.'

'Well fuck me! Who'd've done that?'

'I dunno Danny boy, but you gotta be careful in this business. Could've been anyone.'

'So how come you was goin' round there anyway?' Danny knew they never met often. It was too dangerous.

'He phoned me the night before, asking if I wanted a deal on some sparklers, an' I said see you in the morning, an' there he was dead'. Redmayne realised as he was speaking, that he had been the last to talk with Wilson. He hoped that his call couldn't be traced, as the sparkler deal would be a great motive for the police to latch onto.

'So what's your plan now Danny? You comin' back soon or what?'

'No, I'll stay a while with this bird, Marie-Christine summat. The family's got pots of money, so don't worry 'bout me. I'll see you when I'm broke!' He laughed.

'Well you take care, I don't want to find out that you've gone the same way as Wilson. Don't get mixed up in nothin' you can't handle.'

'OK Dad, don't worry about me, I can handle myself, you'll see one day,' and he rang off.

Al Redmayne drained his glass, slid off the barstool and made his way home. He was relieved that Danny was OK, but the fact that Pete was not back clearly meant that something had gone wrong. Had this guy in Manchester managed to rub out Pete then set up a revenge attack on Wilson? It seemed the most likely course of events, and one theory he would maybe offer the police if he were to be questioned again.

Danny was really pleased with his invented story. He was so used to lying now, that he could do it without hesitation or contradiction. His father had obviously believed every word, and would no doubt be passing on the tale to the authorities if they ever discovered that

Danny had been working for Wilson. All he then had to do was to corroborate his own story, if it ever got to that. If they ever found Pete's body, they would be looking for some imaginary guy in Manchester dreamt up by Pete himself. So that would come to a dead end.

Danny had successfully reached France, and he felt that now he could relax a little. He had crossed the French border near the Belgian village of Doorntje about 10 km from the coast. There was a sign indicating the border with France, but no manned crossing. He marvelled at how easily he had made his journey.

'If there is a God, he must be on my side,' he whispered.

In Saint Omer he decided to buy a new mobile then look for somewhere to spend the night. He rode into the centre of the town and searched out a supermarket. He thought that would be the simplest way to buy one – no language problems, he would just choose the one he wanted and pay for it. On the Rue d'Arras he found a Carrefour Hypermarket with a technology department. The phones were all in transparent plastic boxes, so choosing was easy. He picked one with a *Bougitel* sim-card, only because most of them used that brand.

Mounting his motorbike once more he rode out to the suburbs to look for a cheap hotel. He found a *Formule 1*, just outside the centre, parked up, paid the €26 and dog tired, crashed out on the thin mattress.

Chapter 18

Jeff had no sooner got to his office than he received a call from Gordon McKlintock, his group leader.

'We've got a little problem,' he understated. 'You know the current situation with the oil price at the moment and that we are struggling to keep our shale oil and gas production viable?'

Jeff acknowledged.

'Head office wants a meeting to discuss strategy. Meanwhile, we've gotta' look at ways we can trim back, until things get back to normal, but do it in such a way that we can re-start without major re-development upheaval when the situation changes.'

'So what can I do?' Jeff asked, although he knew he was a target for some involvement due to his shale background.

'We want you to go to the meeting in London and cover our side of operations, our costs and resource levels etc….'

'When? I'm just in the middle of negotiations to buy a house.'

'Right away – well at least in the next day or two, the first meeting's scheduled for Monday.'

'Where are they being held?'

'The Strand Offices.'

'Oh Christ! I'll need some time to sort things out here first,' Jeff stated.

'You've got 24 hours, then you need to be on that plane.' McKlintock insisted, emphasising his statement by pushing the flat of both his hairy hands down on the table with a dull thud. 'It's all booked already.' Sandra will give you your tickets. Unfortunately due to the short notice you're flying KLM via Schiphol. You've got one night at a hotel near the airport, then you're on the early shuttle to London City airport the next day. Your meeting is in the afternoon. You'll probably want to book a hotel in London yourself?'

It was not that Jeff didn't want to go, it was just bad timing. Furthermore, he dreaded breaking the news to Karl and Jenny. Karl would undoubtedly see this as an opportunity to use him as a courier and Jenny would be pestering him to take her with him. Neither prospect really appealed to him. But he felt flattered that after such a short time in the company, they would consider putting their trust in him over such an important issue.

'OK, I'll go pack my bags.' Jeff proposed, trying to sound enthusiastic.

'Great stuff laddie!' McKlintock appeared genuinely grateful and proceeded to brief Jeff on the strategy he had devised for the meeting.

After some two hours of discussions, Jeff, weary from assimilating so much information, phoned Karl to tell him the news and advise that he was leaving the office early, then picked up the necessary documents, collected his air tickets and got in his car to drive back to the house. He needed first, to sort out his own house purchase, then pack a suitcase.

Jenny met him at the door as she was leaving for her coffee morning with some friends downtown.

'You're back early,' she said, 'If I'd known, I'd have changed my plans.'

'No need,' Jeff replied, 'I've got a few things to sort out then I fly out for meetings in London - day after tomorrow.'

She looked at him aghast. 'Don't tell me you're leaving me already?'

'No, it's just some meetings. I'll be back in a week or so, but I need to sort out my house and get the papers signed up etc.'

Jenny seemed relieved. 'Look, I'll be back in about 2 hours,' she said, 'We'll go and do that together. Besides, if you are away for a week, I need a top-up if I'm gonna survive that length of time without you. Wait for me.' And with that she climbed into her Golf and drove out of the gates.

Jeff groaned and went into the house and up to his room to make some phone-calls. He kicked off his shoes, lay back on the bed and phoned Jim Barber first to set up his meeting to sign up papers for the house. Then he sorted out a hotel in London.

He was about to leave his room when he heard faint footsteps on the landing and the familiar squeaking sound of Jenny's bedroom door being slowly opened. He knew that both Jenny and Karl were away, so it was with some reluctance that he tiptoed to his door and gingerly opened it a crack. Jenny's door was ajar and through the narrow slot he could see the shadow of the intruder on the wall. He opened his door enough to slip through it and crept over to her bedroom. The intruder was going through the drawers of her dressing table, examining the contents of each, then re-arranging things just as he had found them. It was Jesse. He was obviously totally unaware that Jeff had returned to the house. 'What's he looking for?' Jeff murmured. He wondered whether he should confront him now or wait until he had taken whatever it was he was looking for. He decided on the latter, and waited behind the door.

About 2 minutes later Jenny's door was swung open and Jesse slipped out, straight into Jeff's restraining arms.

'What are you doing in there Jesse?' He demanded sternly.

'Oh! Sahib Jeff, please, don't hit me, I was jus' doin' something for Sahib Karl.'

'Like what?'

'He jus' called me on the telephone and told me to do something for him. I can't say what it is. He tol' me to keep quiet 'bout it.' You'll get me into trouble if I tell you.'

'You'll be in a lot more trouble if you don't show me what you've done, Jesse,' Jeff's voice was getting sterner by the minute.

Jesse's head hung low on his shoulders. He looked as if he was going to burst into tears. 'He asked me to hide something for him.' He say that Memsahib is going away and he has a package to send, and I must hide it in her airline toilet bag.'

'What sort of package?'

'Very small, she will not find it, I put it in a small bottle, and filled it up with cooking oil, just like he asked me.' Jesse said with a pleading look on his shiny brown face.

'Show me, quickly.' Jeff gave Jesse a mild shove on the back, pushing him towards the bedroom.

Reluctantly Jesse went over to the dressing table and opened the bottom drawer. He took out the toilet bag, full of small tubes and bottles and held up a small bottle of what appeared to be translucent nail gloss. At first, Jeff couldn't see anything untoward about the contents, but when the bottle was inverted he could just make out a lozenge shaped capsule at the neck of the bottle. He knew what it was immediately. This was Karl, doing another diamond run. He wondered whether he had ever used Jenny before, and how the goods got collected at their destination.

'Why cooking oil, Jesse?'

'I don't know but he say it fool x-ray machine at airport.'

Jeff doubted that that could be true, the density of the two contents were totally different. It was more likely that Karl was relying on luck to get them through. The emphasis now, at airport security, was on terrorist activity, guns and explosives, not on contraband. So he probably felt that he had a better chance of getting away with it. The diamonds would probably be lost in the clutter of items in the bag.

But Jeff was appalled that Karl could actually implicate his wife in this way.

'OK Jesse, put it back. I won't say anything. You are not in trouble. Off you go now.'

Jesse's face brightened immediately. 'Thank you Sahib, I no say that you know 'bout it either.' And he trotted off to his quarters.

Jeff went back into his own room, in a quandary. How was he to deal with this now? Karl was obviously going to recommend that Jenny went to London with him. He must have had advanced warning of the trip. Where did he get that information? He was setting up his wife for the transfer en route at Schiphol, and possibly implicating Jeff himself as well. He knew he would suffer the wroth of Karl if he brought up the issue or, even worse, if he stopped it altogether. On the other hand, If Jenny was caught, he had no visible relationship with her and could deny any involvement, but that would mean leaving her to defend herself alone, and he couldn't bring himself to allow that, even though it would resolve the problem of her infatuation with him.

He lay back on his bed and closed his eyes, trying to conjure up a solution. The most obvious thing to do was to get Jesse to go to the authorities and spill the beans, but the repercussions from both Karl and the organisation behind him would undoubtedly put his little black life in serious danger. The same might also apply to Jeff himself.

He could see no way out of it other than to run with Karl's plan. He would wait initially to see if Karl made any reference to Jesse's act, before doing anything else, because there was just a possibility that Karl was not actually involved, and Jesse was lying to get himself off the hook, the instruction being given by someone else, albeit unlikely.

The sound of Jenny's Golf on the drive broke his chain of thought. He jumped off his bed, put on his shoes and went down to meet her.

'I'm ready to go,' she said eagerly. 'I think we should have one more look at the house.'

Jeff knew exactly what she was thinking. There was no way that he was going to comply with her request.

'No, we don't need that now, we're going to get the papers signed, then if all is OK you can help me decide what decorating & furnishing it needs.'

She seemed happy with that. They would have to go back to the house in that case, so in a way she was still on course to fulfil her aim.

Chapter 19

The sound of footsteps, voices and doors slamming in the hotel corridor woke Danny from a deep sleep. He sat up, his head reeling and his back sore from lying on his pistol. Realising with horror that he had been asleep fully clothed, he stood up and tried to straighten his crumpled trousers. He checked the position of the Glock in his belt, at his back and put on his windcheater jacket. He combed through his hair with his fingers until eventually he felt tidy enough to leave his hotel room. He grabbed his holdall, thought about breakfast but dismissed it and instead went out into the car park, jumped on his motorbike and rode out into the countryside.

He had decided to head for the west coast of France, have a little holiday, but first he had to get rid of his bike and buy himself a decent car. He had already had his fill of 60mph wind tearing through his windcheater, driving rain soaking him to the skin and the intense cold that came with it all. He thought Rouen would be a good place to start looking. It looked a big place on the map. It was also far enough into France to be unconnected with Amsterdam. If his bike had been seen when he was there, no one would be looking that far away. Besides, there were lots of bikes like his in France.

As he rode along the tree-lined D928 heading for Abbeville, he found himself addressing his predicament over the contents of his holdall. He had absolutely no idea how to get rid of hot diamonds, let alone the rest of the jewels he was also carrying. The rings and jewellery were probably the easiest things to deal with, he thought. If all else failed, he might be able to pawn them one at a time in different brokers, He might not get reasonable value, but at least they would be gone. He also needed to deposit his pile of cash into a new bank account. He had realised that to use his existing account would be folly as the authorities in Amsterdam might already be watching for his transactions. He didn't have much cash left in there anyway, he was not the saving type, so he could just disown it.

But how would he open an account in France and deposit at least a quarter of a million without creating some suspicion? He wished he could talk it over with someone, but he knew that was totally out of the question. He also felt exceedingly vulnerable to robbery. He couldn't envisage going everywhere with his fat little holdall, having to worry about losing it somewhere or having it stolen.

Somehow he had to find a way to stash it all safely, to save carrying it everywhere, yet maintain easy access to it as needed. Furthermore, he would never be happy until he had rid himself of the diamonds and other gems.

He tried to imagine what his Father or Wilson would have done in his situation. He knew his Father didn't like banks, and Wilson wasn't much better. He always kept his business money well away from his banked 'domestic' funds.

Danny was rapidly coming to the conclusion that he needed to be established somewhere if he was to attain any sort of safety. Somewhere where he could hide his cash, from where he could operate a legitimate business and live a reasonably normal life. He didn't need any further shady deals, violence or murder. Once he'd sorted out the stuff he was carrying he'd live a normal life, stay clean and get himself a nice girl and enjoy himself. No more doing other peoples bidding, he'd do his own thing from now on. But he needed a town big enough to guarantee anonymity and he felt that Rouen was that place. So he headed down there with renewed vigour.

Rouen was also close enough to Paris to enable Danny to access the black market there. He would initially need to find such connections if he were to rid himself of his stash.

On reaching Abbeville, Danny looked about for a café. He was now starving hungry and his throat was dry from riding into the wind all the way from Saint Omer.

In the Place du Grand Marché he found a small café-bar, 'Le Bistrot des Halles'. He parked his bike directly outside, and sat at one of the small aluminium tables on the pavement. Why did the French like so much aluminium? He wondered._Every café looked the same, no individuality, but practical nonetheless. He found himself much more relaxed now that he had managed to put some distance between himself and Amsterdam. He felt he had escaped. It was almost as if he had cut a slit in the backdrop of his life and climbed through into another, safer dimension.

He leaned back in his chair, enjoying the late morning sunshine and lit a cigarette, drawing strongly on his first of the day and exhaling the smoke through his nostrils, like a rampant bull.

A weary looking man wearing a small grey cotton apron appeared at the door of the bistro and curtly enquired what he would like.

Relying solely on his poor French vocabulary Danny asked for some coffee then hand-signalled some bread by bunching his fingers and moving them back and forth in the direction of his mouth. The waiter asked something which Danny could not comprehend, so he asked for a menu. 'Il n'y a pas Monsieur' he said pointing to a board in the bar.

A youngish woman at the adjacent table leaned across and asked Danny what he wanted. She spoke almost perfect English with just a hint of a French accent. Danny explained and she fired a string of words at the waiter who shrugged his shoulders and went back into the bar.

'Unfortunately, my name is Liliane Duval,' she said, 'I hate it but it was not of my choosing. I would have liked to be a Sylvie or perhaps a more exotic name like Crystale or Sophia, but there we are. Are you English?'

Danny looked at the woman, studying her face for a few seconds before answering. She looks about thirty something, he thought, tidy looking, cheap but nice clothes, figure's not too bad either.

'I'm Danny,' he said jauntily, 'Yeah, I'm English, just on my way to Rouen for a cheap holiday for a few days. How about you?'

'I have the misfortune to live and work here in Abbeville,' she replied resignedly, 'I used to live in Paris, until my divorce, but then had to get a job and move into something smaller. I got a job with the 'Bureau des Impôts' in Paris but then they posted me out to Abbeville. Not quite the same, wouldn't you agree?'

'Dunno,' Danny replied, 'I ain't never been.'

'That's a double negative,' she replied, laughing.

Danny didn't respond, as he didn't understand what she meant. He took another cigarette out of his pack and lit it with the stub of his first.

'Do you have another for me?' she enquired.

Danny looked into the pack and, satisfied that there were several left, he offered her one and leaned over with his lighter. She sheltered the flame with one hand and guided his hand toward her cigarette with the other, looking into his eyes as the flame danced upon the loose French tobacco.

Danny didn't read anything into it. 'How come you ain't workin' today?' He asked.

The waiter arrived at the table, and placed on it a basket with two croissants, a large, thick, white bowl containing a huge quantity of frothy black coffee and a small *Bakelite* saucer under which he placed the bill.

'Tu as ramassé un autre client?' he asked, winking at the woman.

Liliane ignored him and turned to Danny. 'I only work four days a week, Tuesday to Friday. We are closed Monday, which is good, because I get a long weekend.'

She looked at Danny expectantly, waiting for his next question, but it never came. He was busy with his croissant, brushing the flakes off the front of his windcheater.

'Would you like a tour around Abbeville?' she asked eventually.

'Well, I ain't in any rush,' he replied, 'but I ain't really stayin' here for long, so I don't see the point.'

'It would make me happy to have something to do,' she replied, 'then perhaps we could have lunch together before you leave for Rouen?'

Danny concentrated on her face again, trying to read what she was up to. She just looked at him her expression bland, but her eyes were smiling. He thought it unusual that she seemed to be making all the running. Normally he had a job getting girls to even talk to him, but this one clearly found him interesting. He didn't really want to get distracted from his mission to get to Rouen, but he sensed that he might regret not fully pursuing things. He decided to go for broke.

'We could go back to your place.' He offered, testing her, hoping her response would be decisive, one way or the other.

'We could…' she replied, '…but I have only known you for fifteen minutes. How do I know you won't take advantage of the situation and have your wicked way with me?'

'I probably would too, but if I did, I might like it, I might change my plans and I might decide to stay in Abbeville.'

'Oh my God! Don't do that. Compared to Rouen it's not such a great a place, it would be far better if - were those circumstances to occur, you understand - that you take me there for the weekend.'

'But my bike has only one seat.'

'True, but I have a car.'

Danny was enjoying the banter, but he wondered how serious she was. He decided to push her to the limit.

'So you're really saying you quite fancy us getting together, but you want more time to suss me out?'

'I guess so. Don't you want to get to know me a little better too?'

Danny wasn't that bothered, although the idea of getting her into bed quite appealed to him. But he wondered what would happen after their weekend. Would she go back to her job? Would that be the end of it all? He wasn't that happy about being alone in France and she just might turn out to be a suitable partner in the short term. He could get shot of the bike here in Abbeville, as alternative, more comfortable transport was temporarily available. Besides, if anyone were looking for him, he would be less conspicuous with a girl on his arm.

The more he thought about it, the better the proposition seemed.

'OK! Tell you what…we'll get rid of my bike an' we'll go to Rouen in your car. How's that?'

'I'll have to get some things from my flat first, and my car is at my home too.'

'OK then, let's go!' Danny stood up, and searched in his pockets for some money. He threw a ten Euro note on the table and placed the *Bakelite* saucer on top then picked up his holdall.

Danny wheeled his motorbike along the pavement, Liliane walking beside him, as they covered the short distance to her flat. She made no attempt at physical contact. They arrived at a small, double fronted electrical hardware shop with a side door leading up a flight of stairs to a first floor landing.

Danny parked the bike and they went up. Liliane inserted her key into the lock of the door opposite the stairs and beckoned Danny inside. She shut the door, taking care to deadlock it before removing her coat and hanging it on one of a row of hooks in the narrow hall.

She led him into a small kitchen-diner with a tiny window, which overlooked a courtyard full of old, rusting washing machines, fridges etc. at the back of the shop. In the room there was a dining table, a few chairs, one velour upholstered easy chair with wooden arms and a sideboard upon which stood an old tube-type television. All the furniture was old fashioned, what in England would be termed 'brown furniture'.

'Have a seat for a minute,' said Liliane, disappearing into an attached bedroom.

Danny cast his eyes around the flat. It was a bit of a dump, he thought. Clean enough, but he could understand why she was fed up with her life here. His thoughts turned to Liliane herself. He had noticed her trim figure earlier and pert little bust, nicely accentuated as she stretched her arms backward to remove her coat. She wasn't a bad looking bird compared to some he had befriended in Essex. She also was a lot more presentable. Maybe he was being a little too reserved? He wondered.

He walked over to the bedroom and pushed the door open. She was sitting on the bed, cross-legged, shoes off, whispering into the handset of the telephone on the bedside table. She looked up and blushed, then said something in French which, to Danny, sounded like a parting shot and she replaced the receiver.

'A friend of mine…' she said looking rather guilty, '… he's the local butcher, had his eye on me for some time and won't leave me alone.'

'Funny,' thought Danny, 'I didn't hear the phone ring.'

She leaned back on the bed and looked up at him. 'I think I might be starting my life again, so I told him we were finished,' she said. 'I hope I'm right, Danny?'

Danny swallowed hard. He suddenly realised that he was in a little deeper than he had intended. She was now looking to him for a new beginning. He wondered how many 'new beginnings' she had had.

He sat down on the edge of the bed and turned toward her. She took it as a signal of his intent and sat up, putting her arms round his neck and pulling his head towards her.

'We can make love if you want,' she whispered in his ear, then we'll eat something and go.'

For the first time in his life Danny was in a quandary over a woman. He could not see how to deal with this amorous interlude yet maintain his plans for self-preservation.

It was too much for him to immediately evaluate, so he felt the best thing to do was to let nature take its course.

He suddenly remembered that he hadn't had a wash for several days, and he had been wearing the same clothes for even longer.

'Where's the bathroom?' He asked, 'I've got to take a shower.'

She pointed to a pair of full height cupboard doors. 'There's no toilet,' she said, 'that's on the landing.'

He opened the cupboard doors to reveal a small shower cubicle with a basin. To use either, the doors had to remain open, as there was no light.

She lay back on the bed, smiling broadly. 'I am going to watch you now,' she smirked, 'I'm going to give you marks out of ten for your body, your bum and your little *zi-zi*.' She was now rolling around on the bed laughing. 'If you get more than twenty points you can have me when you're done.'

Danny ignored her, took off his clothes as quickly as he could then jumped in the shower, pulling the translucent curtain across, hoping it would give him at least a degree of privacy. It did while it was dry, but once wet the curtain became totally transparent and he could see her clearly on the bed. The water was hot and he savoured the warmth on his skin.

He heard her gasping with delight as he soaped himself all over, but she made no move from the bed. He rinsed off, then realised that he had nothing with which to dry himself.

'Have you got a towel?' he called through the steamy curtain.

'Yes I've got it here, but you'll have to come and get it,' she said, still laughing.

He pulled back the curtain and stood there facing her, totally naked save for the thin gold chain at his neck. She stifled a scream, her hand over her mouth, disbelief written all over her face.

Danny had always been ribbed at school over the size if his kit. The jealous stares in the shower after football were largely from boys endowed with lesser stuff.

Now here he was facing this French girl, with his slack testicles looking like two apricots swinging in the bottom of a plastic bag. His thick, pendulous penis curving gently downward and swaying slowly from side to side.

Liliane was still in shock, on the bed, not moving while Danny dripped all over the floor. Then suddenly she jerked upright and leapt from the bed, grabbed the towel from behind the door and rushed over towards him.

'My god! You are built like a donkey! I'm giving you ten out of ten for this!' She said, wrapping his member in the towel, 'five out of ten for your body - you're a bit skinny, but I haven't really examined your bum yet. Turn round.'

Danny duly turned around to get his score. She patted his wet backside and gave him a seven.

'Twenty two,' she shouted excitedly, simultaneously peeling off her jumper.

Danny recoiled in horror as the sweater came away from her slim shoulders and he swore under his breath.

'Now you can understand why I divorced', she said mournfully.

Tattooed across her chest, just above her pert little breasts, in Roman script letters about five centimetres high was the name 'Jean-Claude'.

'Was that his name – your old man?' Danny enquired.

'Wait, there's more,' she replied, as she removed her bra. On each breast around the aureole of her nipples, was a tattoo of a gargoyle, the nipple itself forming the nose of each beast.

'What the hell is that all about?' Danny was stunned. He stood before her, naked, looking at the disfiguration before him. She began to cry.

'This is why I am now single and penniless,' she stammered through her tears, 'one day I will tell you the story. But not now, I want you to hold me.

Danny felt a twinge of sorrow for her and took her in his arms, walking her slowly to the bed. He lay there with her, wrapped around her for a while, waiting until she calmed down. Then he opened up the bed and laid her between the sheets, gently lying beside her. He kissed her and stroked her hair.

'You never know,' he said, 'it might have been the best move you ever made.'

Danny pulled back the sheet and looked again at the faces on her breasts. He bowed his head and kissed each one.

'Well, my name's not Jean-Claude, but it doesn't matter. I still fancy you.'

It was no lie. He was actually becoming aroused. Although he had said it to make her feel better, he *did* actually want to make love to her.

She felt him stirring against her thigh and reached down, attempting to encircle it in her hand. 'I've never seen anything quite like this before she said, squeezing it gently, I hope I can manage it.'

Danny pulled the sheet back a little further and kissed her flat, taut stomach, then continued, working his lips down her body to the rise of her downy pubis. He moved down the bed and between her legs, exploring her damp earthiness.

She was moaning in ecstasy now and grinding her pelvis up and down on the mattress. He had both hands under her bottom squeezing her buttocks, pushing his face into her, thrusting into her hidden depths. Her breathing was spasmodic and her calls for him to enter her were intensifying. Once he was sure that she was ready, He knelt before her, fully erect and massive. She grabbed him with both hands, and pulled him toward her, urgently, gasping as he plunged his way into her. They were both thrusting now, working in unison, their movements increasing in tempo, until, shuddering in ecstasy, they climaxed together.

They lay there, still entwined, in silence for a while, the sweat from their exertion drying cool on their bodies.

'You know…' she whispered, '…I think, in my whole life, that was probably the best sex I have ever had with a man.'

Danny, not realising the full significance of her statement, smiled inwardly but said nothing, he felt much the same too.

They didn't go to Rouen that day.

'I said I'd tell you how I got my tattoos,' she whispered hoarsely, 'I'm going to tell you now.'

Danny lit two cigarettes, lay back on the pillow and put one between her lips. 'Here, let's have a fag first, we've got all day for that.' He said.

Chapter 20

That evening, following their meal, Jeff, Karl and Jenny repaired to the lounge with a brandy, to catch up on the world news on the television.

Following the international news events there were a couple of items of London news. One was a report on police breaking into a shop in a back street off Hatton Garden and finding a partially decomposed body in the attic with half its head blown off. The police spokesman said that the body had been identified and that according to records found in the shop, the motive for the killing was probably linked to a diamond smuggling ring operating out of Amsterdam. So far, neither the murder weapon nor the murderer had been identified. Enquiries were ongoing.

Karl had seemed quite agitated during the broadcast, telling Jenny and Jeff to shut up as he tried to listen to the piece. Neither noticed his particular interest in the article, they just thought he couldn't hear what was being said.

Karl flicked the remote and the TV fell silent. He was extremely restless following the news broadcast, draining and refilling his glass several times before having the courage to speak

'So Jeff…you're off to London soon?' he asked, suddenly fully composed.

Jeff played along with his rather obvious charade. 'Yes, I don't know why, but it seems that The Oil Company have greater faith in me than I have myself. They seem to think that I can be the mouthpiece for the Karoo Shale Fracking Division, despite only having been involved for a few days. I'm really rather chuffed.'

'More like they've set you up as the fall guy,' Karl responded, with a degree of venom in his voice, 'a lot of 'em will do anything to save their necks. But look at it another way: you get to see England again, and London at that. You can do a bit of shopping, go to some good restaurants…'

Jeff cut him off. 'I've been there and done all that stuff with Sheila,' he said. It's not that much fun on your own.' He suddenly regretted his statement, as Jenny leapt into the conversation. 'Well I could always go with you. I haven't been there for years. I could look up my old Auntie Sybil in Putney, and we could do a show or something.'

'But I'll probably be much too busy with work to pay you the attention you deserve,' Jeff answered sarcastically.

'You know…that's not actually such a bad idea,' Karl chipped in, 'It'll give you a bit of a break love, and god knows, you could do with one...'

Then he spoilt things by adding: '…freshen you up a bit.'

So that was it. Jeff's trip to London had been sorted. He just hoped that she wouldn't be able to get a flight at such short notice. But of course, he didn't know that Karl had already arranged it through his pal in the Travel office, even down to seating her next to Jeff in Business Class, both ways, open return.

It seemed that Karl was not going to say anything to Jeff about the small capsule that he had instructed Jesse to hide in Jenny's belongings.

Jeff thought that he, perhaps, was hoping that the less said, the more likely it would get through. Maybe he thought that once Jenny or Jeff knew about it, their demeanour might change during transit through customs, thus giving the game away.

Jeff wondered whether he should let Karl know that he was aware of what Jesse had done, but decided against it as it might have been difficult for Jesse. Besides, he had promised Jesse he would say nothing. Better to deal with the situation once he had left and was safely on his way to the airport. However, he was in two minds whether to just ignore it, as he was actually fascinated to know whether the transfer could be achieved.

It was now 10.30 pm and Jeff had still not packed for his trip. He was going to be tied up early next day, sorting out the remaining problems with his new house, so he wished his host goodnight and made for the stairs. Jenny followed suit. Karl had drunk far too much and was slouched in an easy chair, his glass in hand, but he looked ready to fall asleep at any moment.

'Leave him there,' Jenny said to Jeff, 'he'll probably stay there all night. But as always he'll sober up by morning and still be able to make your breakfast.'

They climbed the stairs together, and went into their separate bedrooms.

Jeff gathered his clothes for the trip. His flight was at 11.15 pm the next evening, arriving in Amsterdam in the morning of the following day. He wondered which plane Jenny would be on. In many ways he hoped they would meet up and spend his free time together. She was, after all, the closest he had to a companion at the moment.

Having sorted out sufficient clothing for 5 days, he stacked it all in his open trolley bag and transferred the bulging mass to a chair in the corner of the room.

He undressed and fell into his cool bed, pulling the sheet over his torso. He lay there thinking about his trip, the diamonds and how the meetings with the Oil Company might go. He hoped he could give a good account of himself. But his thoughts kept returning to Jenny. Despite his reticence to continue with it, he felt he really had to stay involved. He wondered whether this was love. It was certainly different from his feelings for Sheila, yet in a peculiar way, he felt just as smitten this time around. There was no way he was going to sleep tonight. Everything was racing around in his head, and he felt he had to seek a solution to it all before he submitted to oblivion.

The faint knock on his door jarred him from his thoughts as Jenny crept silently into the room, slipped off her night gown and climbed in beside him. 'I told you I needed a top-up, before you went.' She said.

'Yes, but you're coming with me aren't you?'

'I have no idea,' she replied, 'Karl mentioned that it might be a good idea but he hasn't told me anything, but it would be great if I was. We could have a ball together.'

She straddled him, pressing her hips against his groin and lying against his chest. 'Come on big boy, get some life into it, let's go to town!' She whispered.

For one reason or another Jeff could do nothing for her. Making love was the last thing on his mind and the pressure of his trip and of finding a way to resolve the issue of the diamonds was totally occupying his thoughts.

'Jenny, Karl is downstairs and might come up any minute. Do you want him to change his mind about your trip to London? Besides, I'm not really in the mood at the moment, I have too many things to think about right now.' And he pushed her gently off him.

She rolled onto the mattress and sat up, throwing her night gown over her head and pulling it down over her torso. 'I can wait another night, but I won't wait for ever Mr 'Booby' Blythe,' she said sharply and stormed out of his bedroom, slamming the door behind her.

The next morning Jeff showered and dressed and went down to the kitchen for some coffee. There was no sign of Karl, neither in the kitchen nor the lounge. He put on the kettle and threw a couple of slices of bread into the toaster.

He was halfway through his breakfast when Karl and Jenny came into the room, both very chirpy. Jeff wondered if they had spent the night together, but it turned out that her sunny disposition was down to the fact that he had told her about her flight arrangements and that she was to be chaperoned by Jeff himself.

'Guess what Jeff! I'm on your flight tonight, but better than that, I'll be sitting next to you all the way there and all the way back. Isn't that great?'

Jeff feigned a groan and a look of sheer disappointment. 'Oh God forbid!' he blasphemed, 'that's all I need.'

Karl shot over to Jeff and grabbed the front of his shirt, roughly pulling him into the utility room. He shut the door.

'Yeah? Well, let me tell you this, punk, she's gonna get me at least a hundred and eighty grand outta this trip. I ain't telling you how, but if it gets through, you might get a cut too, if you help her any way you can.' He let go of Jeff's shirtfront and smoothed down the material with the flat of his hand. Jeff tried to maintain his cool. He knew Karl could turn really nasty, and he didn't want to inflame the situation.

'OK. So what've you done this time?' Jeff tried to feign ignorance.

'Best you don't know, but it's a test to show you how easy it's gonna be. You'll be doin' one of these runs next time they ask you to go to London.

'Not the stupid nail-varnish bottle trick, is it?' Jeff asked nonchalantly, 'I fell out of my pram using that old trick.' He hoped that his response might lighten up Karl's demeanour and at the same time give him inkling that he was aware of his plan.

'What the fuck are you on about?' Karl bellowed, 'you been snoopin' around in the house have you?'

'Sorry Karl, it's just a joke. I actually caught Jesse in Jenny's room yesterday. But it's a good plan. We'll see if it works.'

'It better bloody had, or I'm out to the tune of ten grand of your British pounds mate,' Karl spat.

They walked back into the kitchen to see Jenny slumped at the table with her head in her hands, waiting for the outcome of their little fracas. Karl tried to make light of it.

'OK Jeff! This is what we'll do:' He was controlling things once more. 'You go off and do your stuff this morning, I've got an important call to make first, then I'll go to work as usual, but I'll be back for an early dinner tonight – we can have it together, maybe out somewhere. I'll sort that then I'll take you both to the airport, straight from the restaurant, around 8pm, so you get plenty of time for your flight. OK?'

'That's fine, thanks.' Jeff tried to sound genuinely pleased.

'And what do I do today, Karl?' Jenny asked, tongue in cheek.

'Why not go with Jeff? I'm sure you can while away some time shopping or something while he's sorting his paperwork. That would be OK Jeff, wouldn't it?'

Again Jeff nodded but tried to look unenthusiastic.

Secretly he wanted to be with Jenny, and he still found himself wanting to take part in the 'smuggling' venture, even though he knew it was against his better judgement. Whether it was the money beckoning, or just the thrill and excitement of carrying out the act, he didn't know. However, he felt that if he was to become involved, he would eventually want to do it his way, based on a coherent plan with a proper risk analysis carried out. But of course, this was not the time to lecture Karl on the niceties of smuggling.

Karl waited until the pair had left the house and then went to his safe and took out a mobile phone. He dialled an Amsterdam number.

'Al…Karl! I just heard the story last night. Am I right in thinking it's our man?' He didn't want to give away too much over the phone, but he knew it would be enough for Al Redmayne to understand.

'Yeah! It seems so. But worse than that, Wilson went too.'

'You sure they went with the same guys?'

'Couldn't be anyone else. It'd be too much of a coincidence. We think one of Wilson's soldiers went with them too, 'cos he ain't shown up yet.'

'Shit!' Karl swore. 'That really messes things up. I gotta party coming over tonight. What do I do with him?'

'Keep him comin' – I'll see to him, but you might have to wait for the weather, it's a bit dicey out there. I'm gonna wait till the fog's cleared.'

'Good idea. No problem. We'll see how things are later in the week. Cheers.'

And he rang off, 'Shit!' he shouted. He switched off the phone, put it back in the safe, spun the tumbler, checked the door and walked out to his car.

Jeff managed to stall any further paperwork on his new house until his return from London. Jim Barber had seemed a little disappointed because it was the end of the month and he had hoped that the deal could have been completed, thereby improving his earnings related income, but no matter, he assured, it would enhance the following months figures, which were usually a little slacker.

Jenny finished her shopping and met Jeff for lunch, during which they drank a little too much and spent the afternoon back at the house, getting to know one another a little better.

He was longing to tell her that she would be smuggling diamonds into the Netherlands but he was equally desperate to see if the plan would work, and he knew she would be much less assured going through customs if she knew the truth.

Chapter 21

Alan Redmayne went down to his basement office and sat at the huge mahogany desk, his elbows on the leather clad blotter, the fingers of both hands pressed together, as he contemplated the current situation.

The old man - the fence in London – had been found with the back of his head blown off, Pete had not come back from Manchester, and George Wilson was now in a coffin in some funeral parlour, waiting for his cremation next Thursday. A police manhunt was under way concentrating in England, mainly because their chief suspect was Pete himself, largely because he remained elusive, but also because they believed that the car he had travelled in to England had not left the country. They had also determined that he may have had an accomplice, but would not release his name at this time.

Redmayne knew Danny had been doing the runs for Wilson, and that he had carried out the last mission, but he couldn't imagine that Danny would have had an involvement in any of this. He was a good lad, always did as he was told. A bit slow on the uptake perhaps and not too clever, but he always did his job well. Why wouldn't he? He was making good money and he stood to take on a big chunk of Wilson's business at some point.

Al was furious with himself for not getting Danny's telephone number off him the last time he called. He desperately needed to talk to him, if only to allay his fears that he had been involved. Now he would have to wait until Danny phoned again, which might not be for some time.

On top of all this he had Wilson's wife, Marion, phoning him every day, asking for help in sorting out bits and bobs, consoling her in her grief and taking her out frequently for meals to encourage her to keep eating.

She appeared ready to give up at first, but gradually over the last few days, she seemed to have come to the conclusion that a tub of aspirin and a litre of gin are not the best means by which to end a life alone. She had made the hasty decision to go back to the cottage in Eaton Mews, London. Although she liked Amsterdam, now, without George, she felt lonely and vulnerable. She had family and friends in London, so continuing her life there would be more familiar - more normal.

It was 6 o'clock. Redmayne picked up the remote from the desk and turned on the television. He tuned to the BBC News channel. Maybe there were some further developments, he wondered.

Nothing there. He switched to the Dutch News.

A rather over made up young lady with an impeccable accent announced that police had been called to a block of flats in the Rozengraght area of Amsterdam, following reports of a bad smell emanating from one of the premises. Residents had been worried because they had not seen the occupier for some weeks. Police had broken into the flat and discovered the naked and decomposing body, yet to be identified, not of the tenant, but of a young Caucasian woman, believed to have died from suffocation. The police had also discovered that the tenant of the flat was none other than the person they were looking for in connection with another killing. It was therefore being treated as a double murder investigation.

As is often the case, the media, having extracted snippets of information from various sources, conjectured that the tenant had murdered the girl and fled to England, although this had not been formally confirmed.

Redmayne studied the backdrop as a reporter at the location gave his spiel. He was sure he recognised the building. It was the same type of block as that containing Pete's flat.

Strange coincidence, he fleetingly thought.

He flicked the off button and replaced the remote on the blotter. He picked up the telephone and tried Karl Jongen's number.

'What have you arranged for my client?' he asked, without any salutary greeting.

'0710 tomorrow. KL0592 into Schiphol. Jongen and Blythe. Ibis Hotel.'

The phone went dead. Redmayne quickly jotted the information on the notepad by the phone, then called one of his boys to do the collection.

Chapter 22

Liliane rolled off the bed and walked naked into the kitchen. She opened a cupboard over the sink and reached up for a bottle of Martini Rosso, and two glasses. Danny followed her every move from his prone position on the bed, marvelling at her smooth, tight skin. Although she was very slim, her body was totally in proportion with a perfect little bum, shapely breasts - marred only by those dreadful tattoos - and long slim legs. Nothing wobbled or shook, her flesh everywhere was firm and she walked with the 'toe out' gait of a ballet dancer, barely did her heels touch the worn carpet.

She poured two generous measures and walked back to him. Danny sat up and took the proffered drink, sticking his nose in the glass and sniffing it before taking a sip. He had never had Martini before. Liliane looked at him fondly, she had such a lot to teach him, she thought.

'So come on then, what's the story behind those colourful tits of yours?' Danny asked impatiently.

'You see me now,' she started, squatting on the bed beside him. 'I am just an ordinary woman, living in an ordinary, cheap flat, with very little money, no future... nothing.

But when I was twenty-four, I met a man whom I thought was wonderful, with an enviable job and lots of money. After a very short romance we married and moved into a large 19th century house in Le Vesinet, a really smart suburb on the outskirts of Paris. He had a Ferrari and I had a Mercedes sports car, jewellery and we had two beautiful Belgian Shepherd dogs, which I adored. I didn't have to work, we had a cook, a maid and a gardener and life was beautiful. We had friends, mostly his originally, a lot of friends, and we seemed to be dining out somewhere nearly every night.'

Danny listened intently. ‘So what changed it all?’ he asked.

‘I wanted children.’ Liliane paused; recalling these events was obviously upsetting her.

‘Go on…’ Danny was getting impatient again.

‘We tried and tried, but nothing happened. I would wait, hoping my period would not come, but it always did. He blamed me saying that I was barren and that he knew he was OK because he’d got someone in trouble before, when he was at the Sorbonne. To be sure, I made an appointment with our doctor for a test. It proved that I was fine, so I asked him to do the same. He refused. That was the beginning of our breakdown.

After that, we never really talked, never touched each other, let alone make love; we slept in separate bedrooms, all because he didn’t want me. He became abusive and at times violent toward me and would go out of the house for days, then turn up with another girl on his arm, bringing her into the house and treating her as if *she* was his wife… sleeping with *her* and not with me.’

‘So, how did you get the tattoo’s, for God’s sake?’ Danny asked, wishing she would get to the point.

‘I was lonely, with no one to turn to. I didn’t want the embarrassment of talking to our friends about it, so I started taking my solace from a bottle.’

‘You mean drinking?’ Danny enquired, not quite understanding.

‘Yes, I would get through perhaps a bottle of Martini or Dubonnet a night. Sometimes, I often ended up totally incapacitated - comatose.

‘Bloody hell! How long did that go on?’ Danny asked.

‘Not that long actually, because Jean-Claude, my husband, had a friend who had a tattoo parlour…’

‘What’s that got to do with anything?’

‘Well, one evening, Jean-Claude had a party and asked his tattoo friend to bring his kit so that he could give his friends a small tattoo as a present. I think he had in mind something like a small butterfly on the derrière for the girls and an armlet for the men, perhaps.

At the party, during the meal and in front of our friends, he started criticising me for various things…the cooking was badly supervised or the wrong glasses had been put out, or whatever. I'd had quite a lot to drink already, but I did what I always do. I went to the kitchen and got even more drunk. Unfortunately I passed out, but I can vaguely remember people carrying me into the lounge, ripping off my clothes and there was a lot of laughter. But I was so drunk I was totally incapable of doing anything about it.

The next day I woke up with all this.' Liliane waved her hand over her chest. I was so ashamed and at the same time, angry that our friends could have allowed him to do something like that. I mean, it's so permanent, I have to live with this for the rest of my life.

I went to a lawyer to get advice about a divorce, and that's when the real problems started. When he found out that I had started divorce proceedings he went mad and took his shotgun into the garden and shot my two dogs as revenge. I was totally heart-broken.

After all this, during the divorce settlement meetings, it turned out that Jean-Claude was in debt up to his neck. The house was rented, the cars were on lease-hire, and he had no money in the bank and thousands on his loans and credit cards. His salary from his job was going towards paying off an element of all these debts, and we had no savings. All I got out of it was a share of his pension, but I won't get that until much later.

'So, what's he doing now?' Danny asked.

'I have no idea, he might be in jail for all I know. I haven't seen him since the divorce went through, and the legal bill is still not paid. I keep getting letters from the lawyer, but I can't pay him, in fact I won't pay him, I think it is Jean-Claude's problem.'

'So what are we going to do now?' Danny asked.

'How do you mean, 'we'?'

'Well, we were going to go to Rouen together, remember? We've just been to bed together, we seem to get on ok, so where and how far do you want to take it?' Danny was attempting to be rational.

'Are you saying we stay together?'

'Well, I think we could try.'

Liliane threw her arms around him and hugged him.

'You really are cute, but I can't come with you. What about my job, and this flat? I already owe the rent for this month, so I must work to get the money.'

Danny wondered whether he should tell her about his newfound wealth. He dearly wanted to help her by paying off her rent. He wondered whether she would become greedy if she knew the truth about his worth. No, he thought, she had been through a lot and deserved a little compassion and help.

They were both still naked, lying on the bed, her head on his chest. 'You see that little holdall hanging on the hook in the hall,' he began, 'It's got a present for you in it.'

She looked up and across to the hall. 'For me? Are you joking. How can that be, as you have only just met me?' Liliane was wide-eyed with excitement.

He got off the bed and walked over to the hooks. Liliane watched, smiling and shaking her head as she stared again in wonder at his magnificent, but now flaccid appendage. She could still not believe how easily she had accommodated him.

He returned to the bed unzipping the holdall as he approached her. Fumbling about inside the bag, he reached for the cigar box with the rings, pulled it out, peeled off the tape and opened the lid.

'I'm not saying we are engaged or nothin',' he stammered, but I'd like you to have one of these.' He passed the cigar box to her and waited for her response.

Liliane studied the contents of the box for a few seconds, then looked up at him in amazement.

'Danny, do you mean it? These must be worth a fortune. And you're giving me one?'

'Yeah! Why not? I think you deserve it, and besides, I think we'll get on, so I want you to have one.'

Liliane was beside herself with a mixture of joy and admiration for Danny's generosity. 'You know you've got a fortune in that cigar box,' she said, selecting the big blue sapphire ring and sliding it onto her finger. 'Oh, Danny…it fits perfectly,' she purred.

'That's not all I got either.' He replied, as he upturned the holdall and tipped the contents onto the bed. 'I reckon I've got about a million Euros in here,' he said quietly.

Liliane stared at the pile of money, ring trays and velvet pouches on the sheet in front of her, eyes wide in amazement.

He reached over and pulled her to him, shaking the contents of one of the envelopes over her head. €100 Euro notes fell all around them and he suddenly felt in need of sex again.

They made love on top of the contents of the holdall, laughing and making innuendoes. 'Here's a good one Danny bleated, 'looks like we've come into some money.'

They both laughed, but eventually reality got the better of them and they realised that they had a problem to resolve. The mood changed.

'Now I've shown you all this, you will know that I'm serious about us,' Danny ventured.

'Yes, and I can't believe it,' she retorted, 'I only met you today, and already I've made love to you, told you my life story, and received a very expensive present from you. Now I feel as if we are going to have a life together. It's unreal.'

'It's not quite that simple,' said Danny, 'You haven't heard my story, and I'm afraid that once I have told it you will not feel the same and probably hate me for ever.'

'How could I do that? You seem such a nice guy, I could never believe anything else.'

'Then I'll tell you my story,' said Danny.

He recounted his involvement with Wilson and how he had escaped his planned execution by Pete. How he dealt with both Pete and Wilson and how he had, so far, evaded being found out. He told her of his crooked lifestyle but he didn't tell her about shooting the old man in London, or about smothering Cheryl in Pete's flat, as he felt some remorse for what might have been the needless killing of those two. As far as he was concerned, his treatment of Pete and Wilson was morally acceptable, but he wasn't going to create greater doubt about his integrity by bringing up the less savoury aspects of his personality or recent past.

Liliane listened intently to his story, making no comment until he'd finished. 'I can't believe you've killed someone…twice in fact,' she said in a subdued voice. 'How did you feel, when you'd done it?

'They were different,' Danny shrugged, 'In the case of Pete, it was really self-defence. It was him or me. I thought he was a friend, so I felt betrayed I suppose. It made me even more adamant that it would be me who survived.'

'As for Wilson, I thought I was his right hand man, yet he had issued orders to have me killed. He had to pay for that. I don't feel guilt for any of that. Although, as I was doing him in, he was rabbitin' on about how he hadn't given Pete the order to kill me, he only wanted to learn me a lesson. But I knew he was lying, so that made me think even less of him.' He said.

'*Teach* me a lesson.' She corrected. 'So where did all the money and stuff come from?'

'From Wilson, he was a crook anyway, so I thought it would be my compensation. Now I've got to get rid of it, somehow.'

'Was Wilson married?'

'Yeah, to a cracking woman whom he didn't deserve.'

'So shouldn't you give back the stuff to her, maybe anonymously? After all, she had nothing to do with any of this, she was probably totally oblivious of what he was doing or what his business was all about.'

'No way! As I said, this is my compensation for four years of his lack of respect and doing all his dirty work for him. Besides, he had loads and loads of money…and property…She won't want for nothin''

'OK, so what you are saying is that you aren't really a murderer, but that you were forced into it to avoid being murdered yourself, initially by Pete, but then when he failed, subsequently by Wilson?'

'Yeah! I guess that just about sums it up. I'd never have done it if I hadn't been pushed.' Danny knew that this was not strictly true, but to fully explain might jeopardise his new plans with Liliane.

Liliane thought for a while then tentatively offered Danny an option.

'OK I believe you. Now, I know we haven't known each other for long, but do you think *you* could trust *m*e?' she began.

'Do *you* trust *me*? Are you sure I won't slit your throat when you're asleep?' he retorted.

Liliane laughed. 'I don't believe you would do anything like that… not without me giving you good reason.' She replied. 'I think I trust you. Time will tell, but you can't blame me if I'm a little nervous, given what you have told me so far.'

Cheryl's tortured face came into Danny's mind and he visibly shuddered. She was such a gorgeous looker and had not deserved to die. It was just the result of a set of circumstances. A means by which he could save himself. He wished those circumstances had been different. That Pete had not met her before the trip. He'd never have needed to kill her then. He turned to Liliane: 'I would never hurt you, Lil,' he said tenderly.

'No, I don't believe you would,' she replied, kissing him full on the lips.

'So here is my plan,' she continued, 'I have a bank account, which, if necessary, I can transfer to Rouen, we can deposit money into it, bit by bit. I can get a safety deposit box too, and we can put all the gemstones in it until we get someone to buy them. We can keep most of the money in the safety deposit box, transferring just enough into the bank account, regularly, to cover our expenses. I also have a savings account, which has a small amount in it – about 70 Euro's, I think - so we can periodically deposit even more money. It would all look quite normal.'

'There's just one snag to your idea.' Danny countered, 'how would I draw money on your account?' He was slightly suspicious of the plan.

'Well, initially you could use my bank card if I gave you the PIN, but later, when we are married, it could become a joint account….'

'Whoah! Steady on girl. Goin' a bit fast ain't you?' Danny exclaimed.

'Well, there's no harm in being ambitious, is there?'

'I s'pose not. An' I can't think of a better plan at the moment,' Danny replied.

Liliane put her arms around his neck and kissed him again.

'So you'll marry me then?' She asked.

Danny didn't respond immediately, it looked as if he was considering the request. 'If we are still together in 6 months time, we'll marry,' he assured her. She jumped off the bed, arms akimbo and danced round the little room.

'Why don't we have a shower, get dressed and first we'll sell your bike, then go out and get something to celebrate our agreement?' She suggested.

Danny agreed, but with the proviso that he bought some fresh clothes first.

Liliane walked over to the old television and switched it on. After some minutes the silver screen slowly gave way to a faded colour image of a newsreader animatedly discussing a multiple murder with a foreign correspondent. Danny couldn't make head or tail of it but he thought he recognised the location where the correspondent was standing.

'What's that about Lil?' he asked anxiously.

'Oh just someone who has been murdered in London. They found a body in the attic of a shop and they think it is linked with another murder in Amsterdam…' as she said it, she realised that they were probably talking about one of the two murders that Danny had committed.

'Apparently,' she continued, 'a third person is missing who has connections with the two dead people. They think that he may be the murderer and is hiding somewhere in England. He has been traced going to England on the Ferry but never coming back. At first they thought the same man did the two murders, but now they think there may be another person involved. They now have estimated the time of death of both victims and they believe the two murders could not have been done by one man, unless he came back to Amsterdam by another route.'

Danny swallowed hard. That sounded like the beginning of his manhunt. 'Dunno about the London one, but the Amsterdam one is probably Wilson. That was mine,' Danny blurted.

'But you said you did Pete in Manchester, so who was this London guy?'

'Search me!' Danny replied, 'I ain't the only guy killin' people in England, you know.'

'So what about this third guy they are talking about?'

'For fuck's sake! I don't know.' Danny was getting irate.

'How did you get back to Amsterdam after you'd done Pete?'

'I took a long way round,' But look, it don't matter now. They'll think I didn't have anything to do with it, 'cos I've got a guy in Amsterdam givin' me an Ali Baba'

She laughed, 'You mean Alibi?'

'Yeah! Same thing.'

'So what do we do now? Do we just carry on as if nothing happened?'

'Yeah! I guess so. If Al says the right thing, they won't be looking for me anyhow. I don't suppose they'll find us down there in Rouen anyway, if we go.'

'So we'd better go soon then. I just hope they don't stick your mugshot on the telly.' Liliane was now quite concerned for Danny.

'There is one problem that might trip you up.' She continued, thinking on her feet, 'you are a tourist over here, and you might be asked for your passport if you get caught doing even the most simple thing, like crossing the road where there is no crossing, or being involved in an accident, no matter how small. Your passport has a picture which might match one they circulate. There's not much we can do about that, but we'd better change the way you look so people in the street don't make the connection with any published photo of you. Maybe give you a different hairstyle. Can you grow a moustache fairly quickly?'

'Dunno, never tried,' Danny replied. He didn't really see the need for such subterfuge.

'Well you'd better stop shaving now. On second thoughts maybe we'll lie low here for a couple of days while your new look takes shape, then go on to Rouen.'

'That's fine by me,' Danny said with a twinkle in his eye.

'We need some food. And we need to move your motor bike round to the back of the shop. If the police are looking for one, we don't want it to be yours.'

'OK, Lil, You go out and get some supplies, here's some money.' He handed Lil a note.

'I can't use that Danny – I've never seen a €100 note before, nor have any of the shops I would think, it'll cause a massive talking point and might attract the attention of the authorities. Haven't you got anything smaller?'

Danny, still not dressed, walked over to his trousers and searched the pockets. 'No, that's it.' He said.

'OK then I'll use my own money, though I might not have enough.'

'So change some of mine at the bank,' he suggested.

'Same thing Danny, they'll wonder why we've got such big notes. No-one uses €100 notes anywhere, unless they are paying a huge sum. Even banks don't issue them as standard.'

Danny gave in. 'OK, you go shopping – use your card - and I'll wait till it's dark and move the bike round the back, for now at least '

'Whatever you do don't bring it into the yard. If it gets found, it's nothing to do with me…us I mean.'

Once she had left the flat, Danny dressed and went over to the kitchenette to get another drink. He half filled the tumbler from the Martini bottle and then went back into the bedroom, sipping his drink as he went. He pulled open a couple of drawers of Liliane's shabby, dust laden dressing table and examined the contents, most of which were lingerie, make-up and sundry tubes of creams of various types. He moved down to one of the larger drawers below. A few items of clothing – jumpers, a skirt and a couple of blouses – but not the extent of quality clothing that one would have expected for a girl who had once had everything. He found that slightly disconcerting. Surely she would have kept some of the expensive clothes she would have bought with Jean-Claude?

He began to wonder whether she had made up this whole story. Was any of it actually true?

He moved down to the third row drawer, the last, and tried to open it. It was stiff and something inside was caught which prevented it from opening more that about 5 centimetres. He peered through the gap at an object wrapped in newspaper. He pushed his fingers into the drawer and felt the object. It was of hard material, rectangular, almost the shape of a cash-box. Above it he could feel books and files, which were probably the reason why the drawer wouldn't open. He tried again to dislodge the obstruction but to no avail. Then he had the bright idea of taking out the drawer above, thinking it may reveal the contents of the one below. He was just about to do so when he heard the key being inserted in the door. He hastily pushed the drawers shut and stood up with the remains of his drink, pretending to look out of the narrow window.

Liliane called out for him and he responded with a jaunty 'In here! Hope you don't mind but I had another drink.'

'Oh! You are dressed,' she replied as she came through the door, sounding disappointed. 'I was looking forward to another session in that lovely bed of mine.'

Danny winked. 'Yeah! But you've gotta cook dinner an' I've gotta move that bike now it's nearly dark, then I'll sort you out after.' He walked over to her pressed his hand on her rump and squeezed it playfully.

Chapter 23

Karl dropped Jeff and Jenny at the airport terminal apron. He didn't bother to park up and come into the building, making some excuse about the cost of the car park. He gave his wife a peck on the cheek, but there was no sincerity in it, then shook Jeff's hand firmly.

'Take it easy,' he said, and don't get worked up.' He said.

'What did Karl mean by that remark?' Jenny asked as the two of them walked over to the baggage X-ray machines.

'Oh I guess he was just a bit worried that we might get a bit pissed off with the new customs procedure.' Jeff lied.

They queued up for the X-ray machines and put their pull-along cases on the belt. Jeff removed his trouser belt and deposited it in the tray with his wallet, mobile phone, watch and loose change.

His belongings disappeared into the machine and re-appeared the other side without incident. He then walked through the scanner. No alarm, so all clear.

Jenny followed suit. There was a build up of cases on the X-ray machine, so she passed through the body scanner and waited for her case to pass through. She watched as the attendant studied the screen. Suddenly the belt stopped and her case was retrieved and put through again. Again it was stopped. An official enquired as to whose case it was. Jenny indicated that it was hers

Jeff's heart was in his mouth. He heard it pounding so loudly he felt others might hear it too. .

'You've got some nail scissors in there,' the official said gruffly, 'open up the case please.'

Jenny unzipped the case and took out her toiletry bag. And handed it to the attendant

He studied the contents of the bag for a short while, foraging through the bag with his fingers. Eventually he found the scissors and confiscated them. ‘No sharp instruments allowed madam,’ he said placing them on a shelf under the baggage belt.

Nick heaved a sigh of relief. If this had been an initial test of the system, it would bode well for their arrival in Schiphol.

The pair walked into the business Class lounge, and selected a sofa near the bar. Jeff needed a ‘pick-me-up’ and ordered a couple of drinks. He couldn’t tell Jenny how relieved he felt, but he guessed it must have shown on his face because she was looking at him in a rather bemused manner.

‘You look like you’ve seen a ghost!’ She said.

‘No, it’s just a bit hot in here,’ he replied, ‘besides, I hate airport lounges.’

The drinks arrived, and they toasted their start to their ‘mini-holiday’. Jeff could tell that Jenny was excited. She was clearly looking forward to spending her days shopping and site-seeing and whiling her nights away in a series of passionate embraces with this irresistible Englishman who was successfully fulfilling the role of her dream lover, an immeasurable improvement on her current husband.

‘There’s one thing I’ve never done, but I would love to try…’ she began. She leaned across the sofa and whispered in his ear: ‘…Join the Mile High Club.’ She waited for a reaction from Jeff, but all she got was a ‘What’s that?’

‘Have you never heard of it before?’

‘No – can’t say I have,’ he replied.

Again she put her lips to his ear and whispered softly.

‘No way – I’m not going to do something as sordid as that. Where would we do it? In the toilet? Here in our seats? It’s horrendous just thinking about it.’

‘Yes, but wouldn’t you enjoy the challenge? Think of the buzz you’d get, when everyone guessed what we had done.’

'For God's sake Jenny, you're sex mad. I think we can wait until we're in the hotel, thank you very much.'

Jenny put on her disappointed look, picked up a magazine from the coffee table and pretended to read it.

Ten minutes later their flight was called and they walked over to the gate.

Once on the 'plane, Jenny settled down and fell asleep very soon after take-off. Jeff sat sipping his whisky, dreading the passage through customs at Schiphol. He thought about Karl and his total lack of respect for his wife. He wondered whether Karl would even care if she got caught. It would probably be just a small blip in the greater scheme of things. No one would be able to reliably tie it to him, so he'd just find another carrier and another route.

Jeff tried to sleep. He looked at Jenny, she was still sleeping soundly, without a care in the world. She seemed even more attractive when she was asleep. Her face was relaxed, her features almost child-like, her hair cascading over her face and wafting gently as she breathed. How could anyone behave the way Karl had toward her? Jeff wondered.

He found himself falling deeper and deeper into his relationship with this beautiful creature with every passing hour.

He wondered whether he could concoct a story just in case she got stopped at the customs. After all she truly did not know what she was carrying and Jeff himself was not involved. He could spin a story involving Karl. But how would he do it without the authorities realising that he knew the transfer was taking place? He sat back in his seat and tried to think.

He came to the conclusion that the best defence was to feign ignorance and if that didn't work, to then implicate Karl by substituting him for Jesse as the planter of the contraband. He thought he would recount hearing someone in Jenny's room, going to investigate then coming face to face with Karl, but that he had not been aware of what Karl had been doing in her room. He couldn't quite put it all together in a totally coherent statement now, but he felt that he could make it so, if and when the time came.

Satisfied that he had the semblance of a plan, he tried to put it out of his mind and turn his attention to the main reason for his visit to London, the meeting at the Oil Company. He wondered how many people would be involved and how much weight his contribution might carry. He reached up into the overhead locker and took out his document case to go over his papers once more.

The drinks trolley meandered down the aisle again and Jeff ordered another whisky from the hostess. He tore open the complimentary bag of peanuts and after pouring the meagre contents into the palm of his hand, he threw them into his mouth, chewed them to a pulp and washed them down with his drink. Suddenly he felt hungry. He looked at his watch. There were still a couple of hours to go before any food would be served, so he settled down, leaning gently against Jenny, to sleep for a while.

Chapter 24

Three days later, Danny's new hairstyle, parted in the middle and combed back, each side over his ears, together with the slightly droopy, downy beginnings of a moustache, began to look less like a disguise and more like a narcissistic pop star trying to be different. But the slightly retro appearance made him look a little out of his era. Liliane quite liked it, but Danny thought he looked gay.

However, they decided that it was now a good time to make their move. Danny had very little to pack and spent most of his time helping Liliane sort out what she would keep and what was to find it's way into the bins behind the shop. Danny was keen to find out what it was that he had discovered in the bottom drawer of the dressing table in her bedroom, but each time he volunteered to clear it, she kept giving him plastic bags of rubbish to take to 'les poubelles.' He eventually completed his tasks only to find that the bottom drawer was now empty and its contents packed into a battered over-stuffed suitcase, which she again asked him to carry down to the car. He decided to investigate further when they found somewhere to stay in Rouen.

It was now midday. After a last check around the flat, Liliane closed up and went down to her car. Danny collected his bike, climbed on and followed Liliane down to the garage.

Pierre, the garage owner obviously knew Liliane quite well as he greeted her like a long lost friend. She tried to avoid his oil stained *salopette* as he leaned over to kiss her on both cheeks. She introduced Danny as her 'Ami Anglais' and he eyed Danny up and down with a somewhat suspicious look on his face, but following some amicable, if long-winded haggling entirely between Liliane and Pierre, Danny was handed €400 for his bike and helmet. It was a lot less than he had paid, but he didn't want to make an issue of it as it might lead to further interest from the wily garage man, so he thought he would just do the deal and run. Pierre seemed well pleased at getting the bike for such a reasonable price and Danny felt that he had at least managed to offload it with the minimum of fuss.

Following another round of handshaking and cheek kissing they bade their farewells and walked over to Liliane's battered, powder blue 2CV, climbed in and set off for the B*ureau de Poste.*

There, she wrote a letter to her employer, resigning her position and apologising for such short notice, saying that she had had news of a dying relative and now had to spend her time looking after her.

She also wrote a letter to her landlord, enclosing the keys and some money that Danny had given her for the outstanding rent, saying that she would forgo the deposit, as she had to leave at short notice. She passed both letters to the counter clerk and asked them to be sent express and recorded, paid the woman on the *Caisse* then grabbed Danny's arm and pulled him out into the street.

They chugged off towards Rouen in the 2CV, well pleased that they could now forget the past and look forward to their future together, without a care in the world.

Liliane placed her hand on Danny's thigh as the tiny car bounced its way down the A28, 'You know, I am really looking forward to our future together, I just hope that nothing happens which might cut it short in any way,' She said.

'Such as what way?'

'Well, you know…with the police looking for you…I would hate it if you were taken away from me now.'

'Don't worry,' he replied cheerily, 'we don't even know that they are looking for me yet.'

He was sure that she was sincere though. There was no way that this was all about his money. He looked at her and smiled. Her face was radiant in the early spring sunshine, her eyes sparkling like the jewels in his holdall. Apart from the fact that he really liked her, he also felt so much more secure with her on board. It would give him better cover, which would mean that he would be less conspicuous to those who might eventually be tailing him, and she was going to be his passport to solving the problem of the contents of his holdall too. Things couldn't be better, could they?

Just to reassure himself that all was ok, he thought he might give Al Redmayne a call once they arrived in Rouen. He reckoned they would be there in about an hour and a half, then they would have to find a hotel for the night. He determined that it might be best to phone after he had watched the latest news on the T.V. That way the information would be up to date.

However, the more he weighed up the pros and cons of phoning, the more apprehensive he became. On thinking it through, he arrived at the conclusion that maybe making contact with his father would bring the whole enquiry a step nearer to him, especially as during the last few days he had been able to put it all to the back of his mind. Lil had helped very much in that regard. There was also the possibility that Al's phone would be tapped. He wondered whether he should forget about getting in touch and just enjoy himself – wait for things to develop. There was just a chance they might not.

He decided to send a text instead, a sort of 'wish you were here' greeting. He didn't know whether that would give his phone number, but he was sure it would not give his location. Nor would it get picked up, he assumed, by any cop tapping his phone. Then he'd just wait for a reply. That way, Al could contact him if there was any news and for the time being, the current period of respite would hopefully continue.

He turned to Liliane. 'We ain't decided what we're gonna do for digs yet Lil. I reckon we should get a hotel room for a couple of nights, that'll give us time to look around for a flat or somethin''

Liliane agreed. 'If anyone asks – like when we book in – you are my boyfriend from England, you've come over to see me again, and we're having a few days away from your future mother-in-law. OK?'

'Yeah! But why all the camouflage?'

'You mean subterfuges don't you?' she corrected, 'Well, because we might have to hand over our ID cards or in your case, your passport. So the moment they hear any news about looking for an Englishman in France, they might wonder about you if you haven't explained why you are there. It may be that nothing will happen, but it's better to have a story ready to give them.'

Danny wondered what they would think if the receptionist was to compare his passport with his new 'look'. That might make him seem even more suspect. Unconsciously he ran his fingers through his hair, trying to arrange it more like his usual style. The facial hair was one thing, but the hair-do was never something he felt happy about. If his mugshot appeared on the telly, it would be his passport photo, which would not match his current look. That was the only advantage.

The sun was hot and the glare through the windscreen made it feel even more so. Danny needed a cigarette. 'Pull over at the next junction,' he demanded, 'I'll roll down the roof a bit.'

They stood leaning on the car, smoking and staring over the gently waving winter wheat at the spire and the very tips of the towers of Rouen Cathedral in the distance. The city was in a valley in the landscape, the bulk of its buildings concealed.

'Not long to go now.' Danny said, stubbing his cigarette out on the sole of his shoe. He sidled up to Liliane and put an arm around her shoulders. 'I still can't believe I got myself a babe!' he crooned, 'an' a cracker at that.' And with his free hand he grabbed her left breast and squeezed it gently. She turned towards him and hugged him. 'Come on, lets find a hotel, quickly,' she whispered, a degree of urgency in her voice.

They set off on the short leg to Rouen and within fifteen minutes or so, were cruising the tree-lined streets, looking for a small hotel-bar within the centre of the city.

After several attempts they found a hotel with rooms available. Hotel Kyriad also had parking at a reasonable price and was pretty much in the centre of Rouen, a stone's throw from the Seine on Quai Gaston Boulet.

They registered under Liliane's surname, using her ID card. No mention of Danny's passport was made much to his relief. In fact the receptionist asked, in French, whether they needed help with their baggage, 'or can your husband manage?' she asked.

Liliane felt herself blush a little, but declined the offer of help.

Once in the room, immediately, without any discussion and as if of one mind they stripped off their clothes and fell onto the small, overstuffed double bed. Liliane grabbed him and with gentle hands and soft lips she coaxed him into life.

They explored each other's bodies, kissing, caressing and clambering around on the soft, spongy bed they noisily made love until they were both exhausted.

They lay there, quietly, for a long period, resting, she with her head on his chest, Danny sharing his cigarette, not talking, just savouring the moment.

It was a new chapter in both their lives, and one that neither had expected just a few short days before they met.

Eventually Danny spoke. 'Let's go eat,' he said.

Chapter 25

Jeff woke with a start. The whirring sound of the plane's lowering undercarriage signalled that they had missed breakfast and he grimaced at the thought that in a few short minutes they would be running the gauntlet through Schiphol immigration and customs. He felt cheated, as if a few more hours of enjoyment should have been their entitlement before having to confront the ordeal that was awaiting them.

How would the diamonds be collected and who by? Did they know where they were stashed? Was there someone at the airport in Karl's pay? He wondered. Of course Jenny was blissfully unaware, so he would have to be careful not to give any indication of his anxiety.

They left the aircraft and fought their way along the Air Bridge and into the terminal amongst the bustling crowd of passengers. At the Passports section they had to part, Jeff passing through the EU side and Jenny through the Foreign Nationals. Jeff was through quickly and waited as Jenny made her way down the long queue. Eventually she presented her passport and passed through without incident.

'So far so good,' he thought. There was only the 'Goods to Declare' section to deal with now. He looked down the baggage hall to the illuminated sign over the walkway. Again there was the division of EU citizens and Foreign Nationals. He couldn't see how Jenny was doing, as her route had a dogleg in it, behind which she quickly disappeared.

Jeff walked fearfully through his own section to see two customs officials leaning back against the counter, studying the passing passengers. He certainly felt apprehensive and it must have shown on his face, as he was initially waved through but a split second later, called back to the counter.

'Please place your bag on the table and open it, sir.' The burly officer demanded politely in English.

Jeff obeyed, feeling himself sweating profusely. He had nothing to hide, but his guilt had got the better of him. The Customs official studied his face for a few moments before rummaging through his case.

'Are you travelling alone?'

'No, I'm with my girlfriend.' He blurted, suddenly aware he had said the wrong thing.

'Where is she? He asked.

'She's not an EU citizen.' He replied.

'Are you coming to Holland for long?' he asked, looking in Jeff's shaving bag.

'Just passing through,' Jeff responded, 'A night in a hotel then off to London the day after, for a meeting.' It was probably more than he needed to say, but he felt it might just make things seem more natural.

The officer dropped the bag back into the case, pressed all the contents flat and pushed the case back towards Jeff.

'You look hot!' he said looking at Jeff somewhat suspiciously and waiting for his reaction.

Jeff removed a handkerchief from his pocket and wiped his forehead.

'Yes, I think I've picked up some sort of flu bug or something.' He replied meekly.

He zipped up the case, pulled it off the counter and walked as naturally as he could out of the customs hall.

Jenny was waiting on the other side.

'What took you so long?' she quizzed. 'You look awful – did they give you a rough time?'

Jeff was so relieved to see that she had got through without problems that he almost broke down. Gathering his composure as quickly as he could, he took her arm and guided her out to the concourse without replying.

They took a Taxi to their hotel and checked in. The room was typical of a low cost airport hotel – a rectangle with an en-suite bathroom set in the corner, a bed, TV, small desk and chair, a coffee tray, built in wardrobe, a noisy air conditioning unit and no room to move. Jeff made a note to give the Company travel department a piece of his mind.

'Look at these terrible blankets, why do they never use duvets?' Jenny complained, stripping them from the bed.

It was late and they hadn't eaten, so they quickly showered, one by one, standing in the tiny bath, then dressed and went in search of some brunch.

Breakfast had finished and the hotel did not serve lunch, so they decided to get a taxi and spend the day in Amsterdam.

The taxi driver took them to the main train station in Central Amsterdam, suggesting that they could catch a tram to any part of the city from there. There were cafés and restaurants in the vicinity he assured them.

Jeff and Jenny crossed the busy street taking care not to be run down by the trams plying back and forth in front of the station. They found a small restaurant on the opposite side, and sat in the small glass atrium on the front of the building. They ordered coffee, juice and pastries, which arrived accompanied by warm bread, Gouda cheese and thinly sliced ham.

They ate in virtual silence, just looking at each other as they ate. Eventually Jeff drained his coffee cup and lounged against the back of the banquette replete and totally relaxed. 'You know…this is the first time we've been together and not had to look over our shoulder, yet somehow it doesn't seem quite as exciting.'

'You are probably a bit drained after the trip,' she replied, 'you'll feel better after a good night's sleep – if I let you!'

Jeff realised that she was right. Not just the trip but the whole episode of the diamond smuggling had worn him down and now that it had all gone according to plan, the weight of anxiety had been lifted from his shoulders, leaving only fatigue and a sense of relief. Jenny by contrast, was raring to go. This mini-trip was the highlight of her year and she wanted to make the most of it.

'What do you want to do today?' Jeff asked, 'There's the Van Gogh museum, the Rijksmuseum, Anne Frank's house, Rembrandt's house….'

'No, I don't want to do any of that,' Jenny said firmly, 'I just want to casually walk about with you, along the canals maybe. Then have a nice lazy lunch somewhere, maybe buy a couple of things…then get a taxi back to the hotel and we'll have a rest.'

Jeff knew what she really meant by 'a rest' and he agreed immediately, largely because he wanted to get back to find out how the pick-up would be carried out. He was acutely aware that their visit to the city might provide the ideal opportunity for the diamonds to be collected from their room. He needed to surreptitiously check her toilet bag as soon as they got back.

OK! Let's get on with it then,' he said, trying to sound enthusiastic. He took a couple of bills from his wallet and placed them on the table and they left the restaurant and hand in hand, walked over to the tram stops outside the station to look at a map of the city.

'Looks like we'll have to cut across the Red Light district to get anywhere,' Jeff said, winking at Jenny.

'Oh good! She replied, maybe we'll get some good ideas.'

Chapter 26

It was Tuesday morning. Danny and Liliane breakfasted in the bar in the hotel and then went swiftly in search of a branch of her bank. She made an appointment to see the manager to organise the transfer of her accounts and to enquire about safety deposit boxes.

Monsieur Paul Chave looked the typical old school type of bank manager. Short, in a smart navy blue suit, striped shirt, spotted tie and black lace-up shoes. The thick lenses on his horn-rimmed glasses made his eyes much bigger than they could possibly have been, making it appear as if he was staring intently at his clients, which gave Danny the creeps.

'With modern technology, there is no need to transfer your accounts,' he explained. 'You will be able to access them anywhere,' he assured, waving a hand in the air. 'However, a deposit box is not included with your account at the moment and that would mean a small additional monthly charge.'

Liliane agreed charges with Monsieur Chave, signed the relevant paperwork and they followed the manager down to the vault and through to the small room lined with deposit boxes. He inserted two keys into the door of one of the mid-sized ones, opened the door then handed one of the keys to Liliane and put the other in his pocket. He slid out the box and placed it gently on the central table. 'When you have completed your transfer, shut the door firmly to ensure it is locked,' he said as he left the room.

Danny looked at Liliane incredulously. 'How simple was that!' He exclaimed. 'I thought we might get a bit more of a grilling.'

He took his holdall from his shoulder and placed it on the table next to the steel box. He unzipped the bag and took out one of the bundles of cash. He counted out ten thousand Euros and gave them to Liliane. 'For our first bank deposit,' he said.

'Why so much?' Liliane queried.

'Well, we need to pay the rent when we find a flat,' Danny reminded her. 'And we don't know how much they'll want for a deposit yet.'

'Good thinking, Danny,' she replied.

Danny started to transfer his booty. The box had a low partition dividing the base in two so he put the gems in the rear portion then stacked the money in the front section. Finally he placed the cigar box of rings and the box of ammunition on top of the lot. He slung the empty bag over his shoulder, took the box and carefully slid it back into position. He was about to shut the door when he remembered the pistol. He pulled out the box again and removed the Glok 9 mm automatic from his belt, slid out the magazine and dropped both in the front section. 'Don't suppose I'll need this for a while,' he whispered to Liliane, 'if I get any bother I've always got me switch.'

'That goes in there too,' Lil said emphatically, 'We're decent, honest, straightforward people from now on.'

Reluctantly Danny reached into his pocket and dropped the switchblade into the box, although he knew he would feel naked without it.

Once again he closed the flap and slid the box into its recess. He checked that Liliane still had her key, before pushing the door firmly shut and listening for the latches to drop.

She put her arms round him and gave him a hug. 'Now we really are on our way,' she said.

They walked upstairs to the teller and Liliane made her first deposit, asking that one thousand Euro's be put into each of her two accounts.

They walked out of the bank into the bright sunshine, Danny ecstatic at having at last relieved himself of the holdall's contents and the associated stress that had been building within him over the last few days.

Let's have a fag, then we'll look at some flats,' he offered.

Liliane grabbed his arm and they meandered up the street.

It was 11.30 a.m. 'Time for our casse-croûte,' Liliane suggested.

'What the hell's that?' Danny enquired.

'Oh, it's something the older generation used to do all the time, but is now falling out of fashion. I rather like it so I try to keep up the tradition. Trouble is, old Frenchmen in their salopettes surround me when I go into the café and they all stare as if I'm an alien. Most young people now tend to sit outside and maybe have an espresso or something.'

'So what is a casse-croûte?' Danny was still none the wiser.

'It means 'break a crust', usually with a glass of white wine – 'Un petit Alsace'.

'Ok! I'm game for that,' he said, 'You'd better order, I'd take all day.'

They sat outside in the sunshine, sipping their wine. 'God! That's sharp,' Danny whispered, his face contorted with the sourness of it.

'That's because you're having it in the morning and without any food. It'll get better,' she assured him, laughing.

He looked across the table at Liliane. She looked so happy, he thought. He felt proud of himself, not just for engineering his own good fortune, but for being able to help her too. For taking her out of her miserable past, and giving her something to look forward to. He was grateful too, for her interest in him, and the strange feeling he had inside now he was with her. He couldn't imagine what he would do if she weren't there. Was he falling in love? He didn't know, but he had never felt this way before.

Their eyes met and she smiled at him. He was sure she felt the same way. Yet there was something nagging away at the back of his mind. His encounter with Liliane seemed to him to be too good to be true. When he looked back to their initial meeting in Abbeville, the speed with which they moved from introductions to sharing a bed was unnatural. She seemed too trusting, too ready to move on to the next stage. He'd had a few birds in his time, but he'd always had a hard job getting them into the sack, and certainly never on a first date. Was there some ulterior motive behind her latching on to him. Could it be something to do with her ex? Was she looking for someone to do something for her? A revenge attack, say? Or was it just his money? Although he was grateful to have the weight of the holdall lifted from his shoulder, he was somewhat concerned that it was Liliane who now had control. He wanted to put these suspicions out of his mind, but they remained, niggling away in the background. He recalled her comment as they shut the deposit box…'now we really are on our way'. Did she mean perhaps that *she* was on her way? He hoped he was wrong.

'So…We get a flat. Then what?' he demanded,

'I don't know,' she replied, 'I suppose we look for a job, although with the amount of money we have we don't need to worry too much just yet.'

He noticed that she said 'we' rather than 'you'. She clearly felt she had a share in all his wealth, maybe more than a share? He wondered. The niggling started again.

'Come on, let's get the flat sorted,' she said, draining her wine and sliding her chair back to get up.

Danny looked at the bill and left the required amount on the table with a small tip, then stood too. She leaned over the table and kissed him and in an instant all his disquiet was forgotten.

'*Apart-mart Immobilière* was the first agents that they found. They stood at the window watching the screen of a large video display firing out images of the properties on its books and the associated prices. Some were for rent, some for sale and a good deal of them were identified as already sold but had been left in the display in an attempt to demonstrate the speed with which the agent did business.

The display rolled over to a rather nice two-bedroom apartment with a terrace, situated at roof level in a large old block. It appealed to them both and although the rent was higher than they expected, they went into the shop to enquire further.

The assistant brought out a two-page brochure of the property. There was a small kitchen, bathroom, two bedrooms and a 'S*alle de sejour*' or living/dining room. It was on the fourth floor of the building and the terrace of apparently 10 square metres looked out over the rear of the property just above tree level. It was €1,200/month with a €5,000 returnable deposit subject to condition survey and repairs. It was fully furnished to a high specification but unfortunately, it was under consideration by another couple who would give their decision by the following Friday morning.

Danny and Liliane were recommended to call again at lunchtime on that day to check whether it was still available, in which case the agent would be delighted to do business with them.

Danny imagined sitting out on the terrace in the sunshine with a cold beer and Liliane in his lap. It really appealed to him. The terrace seemed to be quite secluded and, being high up, it was not overlooked by any other window.

'We should go for this,' he whispered to Liliane under his breath. She agreed and they confirmed that they were interested, left a mobile number and said they would call on the Friday. If not taken, they would view the property then.

They did not have long to wait. Following a long lunch of *charcuterie* and *steak frites* under the awning of a pavement restaurant, the agency phoned to say that the interested party had made a counter-offer for the rent which did not satisfy his client, so the couple had abandoned any further negotiations. Danny and Liliane were now free to view the property at the first available opportunity and would have first refusal.

'Let's go now,' Danny suggested, 'we could be in by tomorrow.'

They walked back the short distance to the agents, discussing whether to make a reduced offer themselves. 'I think we should get as near to their figure as we can, in case we lose it too,' Liliane advised. 'Maybe we offer €1,100 because there is no garage?'

'OK, we'll go with that.' Danny agreed.

The agent introduced himself formally, now that he realised the couple were serious about the flat. 'Monsieur, Madame…Pierre Mansard...Enchanté,' he offered, shaking hands with each of them in turn. He reached into a drawer and took out a small bunch of keys then with a curt 'Suivez moi, s'il vous plait' he motioned the couple to follow him out to his car. Danny thought he was swearing, but was swiftly enlightened by Liliane.

They walked back out into the sunshine and clambered into the roasting heat of the interior of Pierre's Citroën.

He lowered the windows to alleviate the unbearable conditions and apologised. 'It will not be long, it is just a short distance, but it will be quicker by car, and I am needed at the office more today as my assistant is sick.'

Liliane retorted, in French, that it was no problem, and they travelled in silence to their destination, in all about 5 minutes from the agency.

The stone façade of the building had a number of smallish windows at street level, all barred. The upper windows were full height with delicate wrought iron balcony rails; the stonework terminating in a frieze at the fourth floor with a fine, slate covered Mansard roof. There was a large central archway with a pair of heavy doors of what looked like mahogany with massive wrought iron hinges and studs all over it. The door-knocker was in the style of a lion's head the size of a football. Pierre leaned hard against one half of the doors and pushed it open to reveal a small courtyard with a raised circular flowerbed around which were scattered a bicycle and two Velocette-type mopeds. Just within the doorway, to the left, was the entrance to the upper floors.

'I am sorry but there is no lift,' Pierre apologised as they ascended the corkscrew staircase with its massive turned wooden handrail, up to the fourth floor of the building. There were two large, panelled doors on each level, and at the fourth, a large glazed dome over the staircase, flooding it with light. Pierre inserted one of three separate keys into each of the three locks on the left-hand door, unlocking each in turn. 'Very secure flat,' he said assuredly, 'this door is the only way anyone can get in, so no…how you say…*Voleurs*?'

'Thieves.' Liliane translated.

He pushed the door open and courteously waved them into the entrance hall.

The flat was a lot bigger than either Danny or Liliane had imagined and it was beautifully furnished in the old French style. The entrance hall, in itself a large space, hadn't featured in the brochure yet it gave the whole place a more classy, airy feel with its high ceiling and moulded plaster cornices. Off the hall were four panelled doors, leading to the *Salle de sejour*, the two bedrooms and the bathroom. The kitchen was accessed from the *Salle*.

Danny walked over to the windows. Two sets of full height French doors, opening inwards, each giving access to the terrace. He looked over the railing to the trees and gardens below. It was three o'clock and the terrace was in full sun, facing Southwest. With the doors fully open the outside seemed to enter the room as the sun reflected off the parquet floor, lighting up the walls of the interior.

Pierre was ushering them round the flat a little too quickly for Liliane's liking and she nudged Danny and held him back briefly to signal a message. Danny knew what she was thinking: 'Don't let on about how excited we are.' He could see it in her eyes.

After the full tour, drawing attention to the various key benefits of such a property, Pierre gave them a few moments to themselves to revisit the rooms, and talk amongst themselves.

They were in no doubt. They were going to have this flat even if they couldn't get a reduced deal.

'Let's discuss it back at your office,' Liliane suggested to the agent, ' you need to get back, and we have plenty of time.'

Pierre gratefully showed them out and locked up.

'Do you like it?' He asked.

'Yes, it's OK,' was Liliane's non-committal reply, 'but we need to discuss maintenance charges and things like that before we make a final decision.'

Danny nodded.

Back in the air-conditioned comfort of Pierre's office, Liliane queried the standing charges that pertained and asked if there were any imminent maintenance due which would not be covered by the normal maintenance charge.

Pierre ran through the financial aspects and then paused and looked intently at Liliane and Danny in turn. 'So… have you decided to take it?' He asked.

'We are prepared to make an offer,' Liliane began, 'as we think the rental is a little higher than market rates.'

'But Madame, you have seen the flat, its quality and the standard of furnishings, surely you can see that the price is reasonable in the circumstances?'

'We're willing to offer €1,100 and a reduced deposit of €1,000 but we *are* prepared to pay 6 months rent in advance. That would be our best offer.'

Danny winced – Lil hadn't discussed this particular option with him at all. The nagging feeling in his stomach started again.

'I can put that to my client, Madame,' Pierre replied, picking up the telephone, 'but I think there is little chance, as the offer is not so different from that given by the previous couple.'

'In which case we must be making a competitive offer, reflecting market conditions,' Liliane retorted.

Pierre's call connected to his client and he conveyed the basis of Liliane's bid. Danny could faintly hear the agitated voice at the other end of the line, and his heart sank. However, Pierre had saved the best bit until last. 'But they are prepared to pay the rental in 6 monthly intervals, in advance, Monsieur,' he proffered, 'and they are a nice couple, very interested in the property and you will have no trouble from them I am sure.'

There was more faint discourse from the earpiece, before Pierre, with much bowing and scraping, was heard to thank his client profusely and adding 'You will not be disappointed Monsieur, merci beaucoup!'

'You have got it!' He said, turning to each of them in turn and shaking their hand. 'However there is just one small thing required to seal the deal. The Client wants you to go to his house tonight for aperitifs, to meet you and to discuss a few things about the flat. Are you able to do this?'

Danny looked at Liliane nervously. 'I can't speak French, so you'll have to do all the talking Lil'.

'It's no problem,' interjected Pierre, 'he speaks perfect English, in fact he was teaching English at the Lycée Pierre Corneille, here in Rouen.'

'Nevertheless, I'll probably be doing most of the talking anyway,' Liliane said firmly.

Danny wondered why.

Chapter 27

After a lazy day in Amsterdam, Jeff and Jenny took a taxi back to their hotel. Jeff was keen to check out whether the diamonds had been collected.

They picked up their key from the reception and went up to the room. Jenny had a twinkle in her eye, which Jeff interpreted as an expectation of some activity on the thin and somewhat shabby mattress. Instead, he went into the bathroom and locked the door. Jenny's cosmetics bag was on the vanity unit, next to the basin. He quickly scanned the contents, looking for the nail-varnish bottle. It was still there. He held it up to the light over the mirror. He could clearly see the contents and in the misty liquid, the lozenge containing the diamonds resting at the bottom of the bottle.

So whoever was involved hadn't collected them yet. He wondered when the pick-up would take place.

After placing everything back in the bag and positioning it as he had found it he flushed the toilet and washed his hands before leaving the bathroom. Jenny would suspect nothing.

She was already in bed when he walked into the room. She smiled and threw back the sheet to reveal her glorious, naked body and beckoning him to join her. He slipped off his clothes and climbed in beside her.

They were woken suddenly by the strident tones of the fire alarm. Jeff checked the bedside clock. It was 3.45 a.m. Jenny rushed over to the door of the room to check their assembly point. They made themselves decent and went down the corridor to the fire escape.

They joined the queue of guests making their way out of the building but there seemed no urgency for there was no evidence of a fire in the immediate vicinity. Jeff, still in a slight stupor from being dead to the world less than 3 minutes previously, didn't immediately realise what was happening. Then it hit him – this was the sideshow. The main event was the pick-up. It was probably going on at this very moment. There was no fire. It was a diversion. No doubt the incident would shortly be declared a false alarm and everyone would be told to go back to bed. He hoped it was so, for he feared that otherwise he might not be able to offload the diamonds and he'd be forced to take them on to London. That would mean the further anxiety of getting them through the British Customs, which had a reputation for being far more fastidious.

After a roll call of guests and a short consultation with the fire service, the fire officer did indeed declare a false alarm but nonetheless congratulated everyone on their speedy execution of the fire drill.

The crowd of guests pushed and jostled as they squeezed through the fire doors, and down the narrow corridor to the staircase.

Back at their room, Jeff went into the bathroom and locked the door.

He checked the toilet bag again and was relieved to see that the varnish bottle had disappeared. The transfer had been completed and he could fully relax again.

'You're looking pretty pleased with yourself,' Jenny cooed from the bed, 'are you expecting to get laid again?'

'I rather think I am,' he replied, climbing in beside her.

Chapter 28

'What am I s'posed to wear to this dinner tonight, Lil?' Danny asked. He had no clothes, other than those in which he had travelled from Amsterdam. 'I'll have to get a few things before the shops shut, and as it's now 4.30 we'll have to get a move on.'

Lil was stooped over the hotel bed, sorting out her own clothes for the evening. 'I'll come with you. I think I might have a better idea of what you should wear. You'd probably just buy a pair of jeans and a T-shirt, but I think we need to make a better impression than that.'

She straightened up, hands in the small of her back, trying to relieve the tension.

They went down to the hotel reception and asked the young woman at the desk where the best place to find men's clothes might be. She unfolded a map from the counter display and gave directions, marking where the hotel was and the proximity of the shops.

Danny took the map and they walked out into the street. The air was somewhat cooler now that the sun was lower in the sky and already the café terraces were filling with people taking their evening aperitif.

They found a department store and Lil selected a pair of beige coloured chinos, a navy checked shirt and a light blue sweater for Danny, while he foraged for some new underwear

In the shoe department he found some Italian slip-on moccasins with a discreet gold buckle.

'With some red socks, you're going to look really cool in that lot,' she whispered, as the shop assistant rang up the goods on the till. 'I'm going to have to get a dress or something too, just to keep up with your image.'

On the floor above, Liliane sorted through the dresses on the stands but without success. Eventually she made do with a new top and some black leggings, which accentuated her neat round bottom and shapely legs.

'Bet our new landlord won't be able to take his eyes off you tonight,' Danny joked, 'you'll be getting' him all hot and bothered, he won't want to say no to us havin' the flat.'

'Lets hope so,' Lil replied.

The address, which Pierre had given them, was a short distance outside the city, so they took a taxi.

After a short climb out of the city and up onto the surrounding plain, they eventually pulled up outside a large set of wrought iron gates set in a low wall topped with railings. The taxi driver leaned out of the window and pressed the button on the intercom. After a brief sentence, the gates slowly opened and he drove through and up the long tree-lined drive to the Manoir at the end.

'Blimey,' Danny exclaimed, 'some pad this…look, he's even got deer in the park.'

They began to wonder what they were letting themselves in for.

'What are you going to say you do for a living, if he asks?' Lil enquired.

'God knows! I work for myself, so I s'pose I'm an *entrepreneur*, whatever that means,' he replied.

Lil thought for a while, then came up with a suggestion. 'Why not say that you've just sold your business in England, and you are hoping to start a new one here in France, as you are shortly to marry me, the girl of your dreams. He's bound to ask what your business was, and you could quite genuinely say that you had a small security company offering personal bodyguards to the wealthy.' You'd know about that sort of thing if he quizzed you, wouldn't you?'

'I could probably flannel my way round the subject,' Danny agreed.

'If you get a question you don't know how best to answer, just look across to me and I'll cover you.' Liliane felt that the less Danny invented, the smaller would be the hole he would dig for himself.

The car reached the Manoir and drove round the circle of grass with it's central fountain, to pull up on the gravel at the front door, identified by the position of the stone steps at the middle of the building. The front door itself was exactly the same as the four other French doors that stretched along the terrace.

Most were open, as although it was nearly dark, the evening was still warm, with only a faint breeze. All the ground floor rooms were dimly illuminated.

The Taxi driver, hoping for a big tip, offered his card and telephone number, suggesting that they phone when they were ready to be picked up at the end of the evening. Danny offered him some money, but he refused it, saying he would collect it upon his return. Danny thought that most unusual. Taxi drivers were not usually that trusting.

An old man in a black suit appeared at the door but neither Danny nor Liliane could determine his face, backlit by the candelabra in the Hall behind him.

After a solemn greeting in French he showed the pair into the adjacent sitting room and then promptly left.

Danny walked around the room looking at the antiques and paintings, which adorned the furniture and walls of the room.

'Cor! There's a few bob here,' he whispered to Lil as the door opened and a young man, of about twenty-five or so, entered the room.

'Yes there is indeed,' he said with a smile, 'in fact most has been in the family for generations.'

He introduced himself in perfect English. 'Monsieur et Madame Duval, please let me introduce myself, I am Antoine Durand, and it is with great pleasure that I invite you to dine with me and my wife Yvette tonight. She is organising the kitchen staff and will be with us shortly, but meanwhile, can I offer you something to drink?'

Liliane responded immediately, 'A glass of whisky - for us both - would be wonderful, thanks, but Monsieur Durand, unfortunately you are under the impression that we are married. In fact this event will not occur for some months. I am Liliane Duval, and please meet my fiancé, Daniel Redmayne, but I must insist that you call us Liliane and Danny. We are so pleased to have this opportunity to meet you. We are so excited about the flat.'

Durand walked over to the fireplace and pulled the red and gold bell rope. 'Then you must call me Antoine, and yes, it is a very nice flat. In fact, until recently I was living there myself. In fact I own the whole building. You see, my parents died a short time ago, whereupon, as sole heir, I inherited the Manoir and with it all the splendid artwork and trinkets that you were admiring earlier, together with various other properties in Rouen. I have unexpectedly had to completely change my life in what seemed like a split second, from being a graduate student who had just started teaching in Rouen, to the master of this monstrous house, its staff, its 70 hectares of parkland and its associated cottages. The responsibility I now have to assume is formidable for me, even after having been born into it. You see, most of my liquidity was used to pay the crippling inheritance tax, so I will now be hard pressed to carry out the necessary maintenance. How I envy you, replacing me as the tenants of my lovely little flat.

'How awful for you,' Liliane responded, 'and please accept our condolences over the deaths of your parents.'

'Yes, it was a most unfortunate accident, and in fact very inconvenient for me at the time. They were involved in a car accident whilst on holiday on the Riviera. A bus pushed the car off the road on a narrow stretch and they skidded over the edge and down the cliff. My parents and the chauffeur were killed outright. It was a nasty business and took quite a while to sort out, as you might imagine.'

The door opened and the old man who had greeted them earlier appeared.

'We'll have some whisky André, find a good one, perhaps the Tomatin, that's always a favourite - and bring plenty of ice.'

'Certainment, Monsieur' he replied with a slight nod of his bald pate and he disappeared again.

Liliane glanced across at Durand as he took up the silver cigarette box from the table and offered it to Danny. For one so young he had certainly assumed his new role admirably. He was mature, polite but firm and clearly quite capable of running a house such as this, and the servants in it.

The door opened again and Yvette appeared, closely followed by André carrying a silver tray upon which were the whisky, some elegant cut glasses brimming with ice and a bowl of mixed nuts.

Durand introduced his wife. She looked about the same age, was tall, slim and tanned with auburn hair, drawn back from her forehead and held in a bun with a silver pin. She wore a simple emerald coloured tunic with leggings and matching flat ballet pumps. She smiled broadly at Liliane and the two of them moved to a chaise longue and sat chatting.

André opened the bottle of whisky and poured a good measure into each glass and passed the tray round the party, then set it down on an occasional table and slowly walked out of the room.

'A toast I think,' Durand began holding up his glass, 'to a successful business relationship between us, and may you enjoy my little flat for many years to come!'

Liliane and Danny raised their glasses in response and took a sip of the whisky.

'Now let's get down to the business of our agreement before we relax over dinner,' Durand continued. 'The agent will deal with most matters but I just have a few points which I must make, so that you are fully aware of the responsibilities which I expect you to undertake during your tenancy of the flat.

You will appreciate that there are some long-standing tenants in the building, a number of whom are a generation or two older than you are. They have certain standards, with which we too had to comply during our tenancy, so wild parties, excessive noise and loud music will be very much disapproved of.

You will understand that in our new position we neither wish to fall foul of the other tenants nor allow the degeneration of standards which so often affect the rental market generally. As far as the latter is concerned, I would warn you that I shall expect a fastidious attitude towards the care and maintenance of the flat, and in particular the furnishings and *objet d'art* within it.

Of course I do not doubt that you will comply with my wishes, but you will understand that I have to draw attention to these points as a matter of course.

Danny and Liliane nodded simultaneously, 'Of course,' replied Liliane, 'we are actually very quiet, careful people'.

Yvette Durand smiled. 'Of course, I'm sure you are!'

Durand continued: 'Now we have got that over, I think we should relax and get to know each other a bit better. Do you work Danny or are you a gentleman of leisure…?'

Chapter 29

The relief of having finally offloaded the diamonds transformed Jeff's manner from that of nervous wreck to his more usual happy-go-lucky, laid-back self. Even Jenny noticed the marked difference in his behaviour. She had initially put it down to his brooding over the meeting in London, but he clearly had no issues in that regard, as he neither discussed it nor undertook any further preparation for it. Instead, he devoted all his time to ensuring that he and Jenny enjoyed their short break together.

How shall we play it today? Jeff asked, as they rode the shuttle into London from Heathrow. 'I have to be at the Strand for my meeting at 2.00 pm but I have absolutely no idea when it will finish. You might be waiting for me for ages. It will be too early to check in at the hotel now, so I have a suggestion….'

Jenny was unperturbed. 'We have the rest of the morning to ourselves, and don't forget, I have to go to Putney to see my old Auntie Sybil and it would be ideal if I could call on her during your meeting. Then in order to leave promptly, I can use the excuse of meeting you for supper.'

Jeff smiled at her. 'You've got it all planned already, haven't you,' he said. 'But we need to agree when and where to meet.'

'Well, you could get a taxi and pick me up when you're done. Just ring me when you think you'll be arriving. I'd like Sybil to meet you anyway.'

They agreed to do a spot of shopping before his meeting, heading all the time towards the Strand. They lunched at the 'Four To Eight' Italian Restaurant in Catherine Street, not far from the location of Jeff's meeting.

Jenny left her suitcase with Jeff and headed for Temple underground station and took the district Line to East Putney for her afternoon with Aunt Sybil.

Jeff grabbed a taxi for the short ride to his meeting at The Oil Company's headquarters. He didn't fancy walking – one pull along case was bad enough, but two would have been impossible.

On arrival, he identified himself at the entrance desk and asked if there was somewhere he could leave his luggage. The security officer seated at the desk had already spotted the cases and was about to stop Jeff entering the main foyer. He took both the cases and summoned one of his colleagues with his walkie-talkie, to deal with them. Jeff was told to take a seat – someone would fetch him. It was 1.45 pm.

At 1.55 pm a tall slender woman of about 45 dressed in a white blouse, navy blue two piece suit and black high heels walked up to him.

'Mr Blythe? I am Daphne Lawrence, David Robinson's PA,' she started, offering her hand. Jeff shook it lightly. 'Please follow me.' And she walked over to one of the four lifts in the lobby and summoned the car. On the way up to the 12th floor she explained that her boss David Robinson would be chairing the meeting, and that all 32 delegates would be expected to report on their specific region, with particular emphasis on productivity, volumes and production costs. Jeff remained unfazed, having garnered a full account from his colleagues in Johannesburg.

'How long will the meeting last?' Jeff asked.

'Oh, quite some time I would think, David is not one for skipping lightly over anything – he likes to get to the kernel of every issue. I would guess it would be around 5.30.'

Jeff said nothing, but he hoped it would end earlier than that. He had his rendezvous with Jenny to think about. It was only now that he realised how much he missed her not being with him. He was slowly falling into the abyss that was love.

At the 12th floor Daphne steered him out of the lift in the direction of the conference room. The pair walked noiselessly across the thick piled carpet and into the huge room, now filled with the delegates to the meeting, sitting around the heavy table, drinking coffee and chatting amiably.

The room quietened as Jeff walked in, looking for a vacant seat. Daphne announced him as 'Jeff Blythe from the Johannesburg Office' and there were murmurs of 'Oh Yes!' and 'Welcome to sunny UK' etc…

He was offered a cup of coffee, given a name badge and with these in one hand and his briefcase in the other, he continued walking around the massive table until he spotted an empty chair.

He sat down between a large, ruddy faced man on his left, and an even larger but younger man on his right. The latter introduced himself as Walt Deanburger, who from his accent was from the Southern end of USA. On interrogation, it turned out to be Corpus Christi in Texas.

'How 'bout you' the Texan drawled, 'where's your base?'

'As Daphne said, Johannesburg,' Jeff replied, shifting his chair away from the encroaching belly of the Texan, 'although I've only been working there for a week.'

'How come you're here at this meeting then?' the Texan queried, loudly enough to attract the attention of the other delegates around him. The room quietened again.

'I guess it's because of my knowledge of Fracking and Shale Gas Extraction, otherwise I have no idea,' Jeff replied, 'I don't know how much I'll be able to contribute.'

The not so fat man on his left then chipped in with his pennyworth: 'You got your figures, and that's about all you can do. The board'll take any decision, not us. I reckon we may be getting our cards today, if they think there's no future in Fracking for some time.'

The three men were considering this when the door opened again and Daphne Lawrence and David Robinson came into the room. He took the chair at the head of the table but did not sit. Daphne squeezed in on his left, sat down and took out a note-pad.

'Good afternoon gentlemen,' Robinson began, 'Thank you all for coming here today, especially those of you from the far-flung corners of the globe. I hope you all had a good journey. I'm sorry it's a bit of a crush, but it was important that you were all here, so that we all come away from this meeting singing from the same hymn-sheet, with one objective. After all, the clock won't work if there's a cog or two missing.'

There was a muted outpouring of forced laughter, then Robinson continued:

'We must all realise the seriousness of the situation in which we now find ourselves, largely none of our own doing, but which will affect our industry, and more importantly, our turnover, profits and the money in all our pockets.

As you all are aware, the price of oil has fallen dramatically, currently $35 a barrel, due of course to the lack of agreement by OPEC to regulate the flow of oil to the markets. They consider that we, together with other western countries, are responsible for the drop in price, due to the remarkable production levels we have been achieving using the technique of Fracking. This has been so successful in America that there have been suggestions that they may eventually become self-sufficient in the near future.

However, the Saudis believe that by increasing their own production levels, thereby creating a glut in the market, it will reduce the price of oil further and drive the Frackers out of business, as the production costs are much higher. This they say, may have a short-term economic effect on their GDP, but they insist that they can maintain this policy long enough to force Frackers out of the market. Not all OPEC members are happy with this proposal, but due to the Saudi's huge resources and their influence in the market, they are likely to tag along.

If we add to this problem the fact that oil sanctions against Iran have been lifted, and they are now pumping furiously, you will all have, no doubt, realised that it could be some time before there is any let up.

On the table in front of each of, you will find a single sheet, upon which I have indicated the main points for discussion forming our agenda for today, but first, does anyone wish to add anything to what I have just said'

One of the delegates stood up. 'John Gilchrist, Mr Chairman, I'm based in Oman, where I think the situation is quite dire. The Omanis as you will know are looking to safeguard their future GDP by investing in areas other than oil. Their oil revenues have reduced to such a degree that many of their investments and projects abroad are now suffering financially and in fact some are being put on hold or cancelled altogether. I don't think they will be able to support the Saudi proposals for much longer. Other smaller producers are in the same boat. In fact I would go as far as to say that there is a likelihood that the OPEC group may disintegrate if the situation continues beyond this year.'

'Yes, thank you John, the knock on effects of this crisis will eventually affect world growth, no doubt. Any one else got a view on this?

Several delegates wished to make their points, and it was some time before the Chairman got round to broaching the topics on his Agenda. David Robinson was not one to rush things, he was quite happy to allow the attendees to air their views. At one point it seemed the chairman had lost control of the meeting as delegates started arguing the points made by others.

Jeff sat quietly occupying himself with his proposals, not wishing to be seen to be a participant in the mêlée.

Eventually Robinson wrested back control and continued going through his agenda points, one by one.

It was already 3.45 and item 3 of 12 was under discussion. Jeff sensed that with so many bodies round the table, there would be no firm policy developed today. The Chairman and his board would gather the cost and value statements from each delegate's location, listen to their theories on the viability of each site, and consider their solutions for maintaining operations, but any overall strategy would be developed elsewhere by a much smaller, elite group.

Unfortunately for Jeff, his quiet and somewhat reclusive approach to the meeting had got him noticed. Robinson, having got through his agenda, was casting his eyes around the ring of delegates, probably pigeon-holing them into type and capability, when they fell on Jeff and stayed there for some seconds, before diverting to the name card on the lapel of his jacket.

'What about you…er…Mr Blythe is it?' He couldn't quite read it without straining forward.

'Yes Mr Chairman, Jeff Blythe from Johannesburg. Well, as you are aware, we have the beginnings of a very large operation in the Karoo basin, and our research has confirmed some relatively large reserves, mainly in shale gas, overall figures indicate a possible 300 t.c.f. in the southern Karoo basin. However, this is only an estimate and unfortunately the figure is being revised downward rapidly, as more investigation is carried out. One of our problems is obtaining licences. It is taking years. However, where we have succeeded, our extraction cost per volume of recovery is lower than average, and we reckon the price could drop to an oil equivalent price of around $30 a barrel before we become neutral, at which point we'd have to consider our options. The situation is doubly difficult for us because if the estimates of overall resources fall significantly, and the trend suggests they might, we may have to reconsider our further involvement here.

As far as the oil price is concerned, personally, I can't see oil dropping to $30 for long, if at all. I would suggest two reasons for this: One, The implosion in the Gulf States would have too severe an impact. The likes of Kuwait and others are already seeking major banks to manage the sale of their international debt in order to shore up their finances. And two, I think the Russians themselves might step in to prevent any further reduction in price.'

'And how do you see that happening?'

'Well, Russia is having a hard time of it at the moment. They are, as you know, a major producer, under sanctions from the West, and they are suffering these low oil revenues too. They are not members of OPEC, so at the moment they have little influence, but it is my belief that they will not stand idly by for much longer and will force the issue with OPEC and Iran in particular. I think prices will be back at about $55 - 60 a barrel by the end of the year.'

'You seem very sure of yourself Blythe…'

'No sir, but you asked for my view, and that's what I think.' No-one can second guess this situation, all we can do is make the best assessment we can and act upon it.'

'Good point, well made. I tell you what, Blythe; I'll lay a rather large bet with you. If the oil price is above $55 by Christmas, and you are still producing in Karoo, I'll bring you up to the twelfth floor of Head Office. If not, the operation will probably be gone anyway, and you with it. How does that sound?'

There was a stunned silence in the room. What everyone around the table inferred from Robinson's statement was that if Jeff was right he would make Director by Christmas, otherwise he'd be out.

'I'll take that bet sir,' Jeff replied, showing absolutely no emotion.

'Good man! And with that, Gentlemen, I think we'll call the meeting to an end. Thank you all and keep up the good work. It was 5.30 precisely.

Jeff thought he was off, but Robinson was making a beeline straight for him.

'Ah, Blythe, come through to my office, I'd like a quick word with you before you go.'

The London Hilton on Bayswater Road, Hyde Park – was a good deal grander than their Schiphol Hotel. Far more in keeping with her position in life, thought Jenny, as they registered in the foyer. Jeff had booked a deluxe room with full height windows overlooking the park.

They asked for their bags to be taken up to their room and made straight for the bar for a drink.

'God, Jeff, this is the place I'd rather be, you know, here in London, its so much more sophisticated than SA. You and I, we could make a great life here. I'd love it.'

'Well, you never know. After the way the meeting went today, that may become one option.'

'Really? How's that?'

'Well, I made a bit of an impression with the Chairman. But what about Karl? You said earlier that you didn't want to leave him.'

'Yes but that was before…'

'Before what?'

'Before I fell in love again.' She leaned over on the sofa and laid a hand on his thigh, before kissing him gently on the cheek.'

'Hey! Watch it, not here, save it for later, ' Jeff replied, looking around the room in embarrassment., 'you'll get us slung out.'

She smiled sweetly and took another sip of her Champagne.

'Anyway, what was that you were saying about making a good impression?'

Jeff recounted the events of his afternoon at The Oil Company. 'It was all pretty dull really, until the Chairman asked for my views. I gave them, then he made me an offer I couldn't refuse.'

'Really? But he doesn't even know you.'

I know, and that was what made all the other delegates sit up. He virtually said that I would make Director if my views actually came to fruition. And then, after the meeting he called me into his office and reaffirmed what he had said, saying that I had handled myself well in the meeting, not getting involved in the various arguments, but just keeping my own council so to speak. He seemed to like that. He said I had shown an assertive manner when questioned and he wants to be kept informed personally through me on the day to day business in Johannesburg. He said he doesn't have a good rapport with the current regime over there. It all seems a bit strange to me.'

'How old is he?' Jenny asked.

'Oh, I'd say about 55 or so. Why?'

'Well, you don't think he's on his way out do you? He might just be looking for an ally, someone to provide him with ammunition to safeguard his position.'

Jeff thought about her question for some time before answering. 'No, I got the feeling that there was more to the meeting than was conveyed to the attendees. At one point Robinson was looking intensely at each individual and at times making notes. I wondered whether there was a hidden agenda, I mean he was possibly looking for successor material.'

'Wow! So you think you've made the right impression?'

'Let's hope so. Only time will tell. But now, for the moment, I've got the unenviable task of reporting back to him – privately – on the business in Jo'burg.'

'You know I think you should send him a letter or memo, confirming what has been agreed, just in case he reneges on his agreement, or if he isn't still on the board at Christmas.'

'No,' Jeff replied, 'suppose oil doesn't reach $55 by Christmas – it would be like signing my own death warrant.'

Jenny sidled closer to him and gave him a hug. 'Anyway, I knew I'd made the right decision in seducing you,' she whispered, nibbling his ear.

They sat quietly for a while, each thinking about their futures. Then Jenny broke the silence:

'Shall we have dinner here or do you know a good restaurant in the area?'

'Or maybe we could have something sent up to the room, then we could make the most of our first evening together, in the dim light of our comfy little boudoir?'

'You sexy beast!' She retorted, 'Yes, let's do that.'

They finished their drinks and went up to the room. The curtains had been drawn and the covers turned back on the bed. Their cases had been set out on the stand by the bathroom door, and the hotel information folder was laid out on the desk at the page giving details of room service. It was almost as if the hotel staff had anticipated their every desire. Jeff picked up the telephone and booked a simple meal for 8.00 p.m. from the Hotel's 'Aubaine' French Restaurant menu, then without further ado, started to undress.

Jenny was already naked, but for a little black g-string, and was peeling back the bedclothes in anticipation when Jeff's mobile rang.

'Shit!' Jeff spat, 'Who the Hell can that be?' He looked down at the screen. It was Karl.

'See mate,' he began, 'wasn't that tricky after all was it? A little bird tells me that the delivery has been made and all's well. How's that wife of mine? You looking after her for me?'

'Yes, Karl, all's well here. We're just about to have dinner. Do you want a word?'

'No, you're alright mate, I'll see you both when you get back. Enjoy London. By the way, I've been thrashing your Cherokee around the Vaal a bit today, goes real well in four wheel drive. See yah' he laughed like a drain then without waiting for a reply, rang off.

'Bastard!' Jeff swore.

Chapter 30

Danny felt the vibration of the mobile in his pocket. It was a short message from Al Redmayne. 'Danny, phone me on 07981 264911 from a public box quick.'

Danny felt a lump in his throat. 'Shit,' he murmured to Liliane, 'summat's up back home. I've got to phone me Dad.'

'Well phone him then.'

'No I've gotta do it from a box.'

Liliane then realised that something was seriously wrong. Al Redmayne wanted to avoid any possibility of the call being traced. Presumably, she thought, something to do with the police and their investigations into the killings.

Danny donned his windcheater and went out into the darkness of the night to look for a phone-box. He started to shiver involuntarily, even though it was not cold and he zipped up the neck of his jacket in a futile attempt to warm up. It was eerily quiet. The streets were empty, with just the odd light showing dimly here and there through slatted shutters. He walked faster, full of apprehension, as if he was being followed. As he looked around, his mind was racing. He was trying desperately to guess what had happened back in Amsterdam to spook his Father. So much had happened since he last spoke to him that he could no longer remember exactly what he had already told him. He realised that he would need to be careful not to contradict himself.

At the junction at end of the road, he came upon a small tree-lined square on the edge of which was a *Bureau de Poste* with a telephone box outside it. The figure inside, dimly lit, was that of a young girl of perhaps fourteen or fifteen. Danny waited outside, making sure that she had seen him, hoping it would speed up her call. He could vaguely hear the conversation but only guess at what was being said, though her tone and facial expressions led him to believe she must have been speaking to a boyfriend. His presence seemed to do nothing to accelerate her phone call and Danny was swiftly becoming impatient.

Eventually he could wait no longer and he pulled open the door and bellowed at her to hurry up, in English. She stared at him for a few seconds, dropped the handset and pushed her way past him then ran down the street shouting obscenities.

'Good!' muttered Danny, 'that had the right effect'.

He searched his pockets for the right change and dialled the number Al Redmayne had given him. It rang for what seemed an eternity, before Al answered.

'Dad, its me, Danny,' he started…

'Danny! You in a phone box?' Came the reply.

'Yeah, there was one down the street.'

'Listen, you got your mobile?'

'Yeah, but it's a new one.'

'Give us the number.'

Danny obliged.

'You ain't registered it yet have you?'

'No, I ain't used it much yet either.'

'An' you ain't got the location thingy turned on?'

'No'.

'Right, well don't, or they'll trace you. Use the number I gave you when you need to get in touch, it's my safe phone, but only do it by text message – never call me, ok? I'll text you on your mobile.'

'Who's they?'

'The police. Things have moved on a bit since we last spoke. They found a dead girl in Pete's flat. They seem to think that Pete must've got back to Amsterdam, murdered the girl and maybe Wilson, and then disappeared somewhere. They know from the Ferry Company that he went to Blighty and 'cos you're on the ferry ticket too, they think that he may have done you over somewhere there, because they found a note scribbled by the phone in his flat.'

'What did it say?'

'I dunno *exactly*, they came to talk to me and explained that they thought you might be a gonner cos the note was a list of things he had to do, one of which apparently said something like 'Top Danny'. The stupid bastard wrote it down. They found out who 'Danny' was by chance 'cos they was investigating the George Wilson murder and your name came up in his books, that tied up neatly with the Ferry booking details, so they put two and two together and came to see me. It seems that they've taken that note to mean that you must be dead meat, somewhere in Blighty.'

'But I told you I never went,' Danny whispered, 'I'm in France. Ditched the bird from Lyons cos she was a P.T. an' now I'm with another bird, livin' in Rouen.'

'OK, so answer me this then…if your name was on the ferry ticket and Pete's note said 'Top Danny', that indicates to me that he was goin' to top you in Blighty, when you went to rough up the other guy. If that was what he had to do, how come he didn't insist you went with him?'

Danny was cornered. 'I dunno Dad, maybe the note was for a different date?'

'OK, maybe, but there's still a problem. I haven't told the police that you never went, or that you was in France, cos they didn't think you were alive, so there was no point. If they ever find out that you *are* alive, they're goin' to assume you were the killer and not Pete. And as Pete's disappeared, they'll think you did him in too. Do you get it?'

'Yeah – course I fuckin' get it,' Danny cursed, 'an' cos Pete, the girl and me and Wilson were all connected they'll probably think I did the fuckin' lot! Shit! I gotta lie low for a while. Are they comin' to see you again any time?'

'I expect they will at some point but I ain't got no more to say to them. They ain't sussed out yet that me an Wilson were workin' together.'

'What about Marion? She might drop you in it.'

'Nah! She won't do that. She knows we was friends, but she don't know nothing about the business.'

'So we're all good then?

'Yeah, for the moment. Just keep quiet an' don't do nothing that might arouse suspicion. Especially, don't do nothing against the law, cos the coppers in Blighty will be working with the French, looking for Pete, an' you might just get mixed up in it. An' don't forget...never phone me...text OK?'

'OK, Dad, I'll get to you later. Don't expect me to make contact often, an' only text me if I need to know summat.'

'OK Danny boy. By the way, who's this new bird you got?'

'Liliane – she's a cracker. We're getting' married in a few months.'

'Look forward to meeting her, Danny, don't forget my invite to the wedding.'

The line went dead.

Danny foraged around in his windcheater pocket for his pack of cigarettes. His hands were shaking so violently that he had difficulty lighting up. He inhaled several times before releasing a stream of smoke, which hung in the air like a fog in the confined space of the phone box.

The last few days had been so relaxing he had been able to put all this aggravation to the back of his mind. Now it was very much to the fore. The pressure upon him to keep an extremely low profile would now be unrelenting.

'Strange how the police had got the wrong end of the stick,' Danny thought, 'Pete killing me then Cheryl then Wilson.'

It all hung together quite well, but there was one aspect that Danny couldn't get his head round:

If he was discovered by the police to be alive, and he maintained his stance that he didn't go to Blighty with Pete, wouldn't the Ferry Company catch him out? Did they not check that all booked passengers actually passed through the terminal? Wouldn't the Customs guys have a record of him passing through? He had done that crossing so many times but he couldn't remember whether on this particular occasion he had actually presented his passport or just been waved through.

As he approached the hotel he came to the conclusion that the police must have investigated these aspects and concluded that he did actually go. That was fine as long as they kept thinking that Pete did the killings. The one remaining problem was that he had lied to his father. What would Al's reaction be when he found out that Danny was the real villain, if it ever came to light? Meanwhile, there was always the chance that Al, on further questioning, would insist to the police that he had stayed behind and that might set the police off on a completely different tack. The whole scenario was more than he could mentally cope with.

He went straight to the bar in the hotel, lit another cigarette and ordered a much-needed whisky. Downing it in one, he chucked a €5 note on the bar and went up to his room.

'That took a long time,' Liliane remarked as he entered the room, 'how did it go? What's happened?

'It's a bit of a fuck-up actually, Danny began, 'but I think we might be off the hook, if we manage to keep a low profile. The police found a dead girl in Pete's flat and think that Pete must've killed her after he got back from Blighty, and they think he maybe killed Wilson too. They also think he killed me 'cos they found a note at Pete's saying 'Top Danny'. They think I've been disposed of somewhere in Blighty and they're looking for me but they ain't found my body yet.'

Liliane stared at Danny, amazed but confused. 'I don't get it, let me just think this through.'

'It don't need no thinkin' through Lil, so long as we lie low we're gonna be in the clear.'

'But Danny, listen to me, we've got to understand the situation to make sure we don't slip up, and more importantly, if we get caught, we both need to tell the same story.'

'You don't need to say nothing, it don't involve you.'

'Of course it does, I'm an accessory to the facts, I should be turning you in, not helping you avoid custody. Let's just go over what the police think, from the beginning.'

Danny slumped down on the bed and leaned back against the pillows. Liliane tried to piece together the police theory:

' So far, the police think that you and Pete went to England – do they know what for?'

'No idea. Al didn't say.' Danny replied.

'OK, but because they discovered the note, they assume that Pete killed you in Blighty?'

'Yeah!'

'There must have been other things on the note, like a list of things Pete had to do for the trip, which would have made them think that you were killed over there, otherwise it could have been anywhere, any time.'

'OK, that's true,' Danny agreed.

'So, do they know where the pair of you went in England?'

'Depends what Pete wrote on the note, but no one else alive knows that we were going to Manchester – except you. Our phones were off an' we made no calls. We never used cash machines or anything either, so there's nothing to trace.'

'Good, so, Pete supposedly kills you in Manchester, then what?'

'I dunno, but the police might think that he came back in the car and went back to his place.'

'Talking hypothetically, could he have got rid of the car before he left England?'

'Yeah, and come back by a different route.'

'OK, but why would he have murdered the girl?'

'Cos she knew he was s'posed to be killin' me, an' she might talk?'

'Good point. So far so good. But what about Wilson?'

'I was a mate of Pete's, maybe he was upset at having to kill me and then Cheryl. Maybe he felt that Wilson had gone too far in asking him to do his dirty work. Maybe he even asked for more money and the bugger wouldn't pay him? Maybe he fancied a share of the loot in his safe? I dunno.'

'OK, there are enough options there, but what do you think the police will do now?'

'Look for Pete I expect.' Danny concluded.

'Yes but where?'

'In Amsterdam I s'pose.' Danny replied.

'Or England, Belgium or France!' Liliane said, 'that would bring the investigation much closer to you.'

'Yeah, but it ain't me they're looking for.'

'No, but they are looking for an Englishman who's not been in any place for long. You fit that category, and people might talk. They'll have pictures of you and Pete. We've therefore got to be very careful.'

'Yeah,' Danny added, 'there's another thing too. We can't afford to touch none of our 'stock' at the bank vault neither. Maybe the money, but not the stones. We'd be bound to get clobbered.'

'Ok good point.' Liliane agreed. 'You know I think we're going to have to be extra nice to the neighbours when we move in to the flat tomorrow. There's nothing worse than suspicious folk pushing the word round. I think

I'll go round to the bank tomorrow too, and get out a few thousand from the deposit box so we don't need to show our faces there too often.'

'I'll come with you,' Danny offered.

'Best not,' she replied, 'the less you are seen about, the better.'

Danny felt the gnawing in his stomach return yet again.

Chapter 31

'Now listen Jeffrey Blythe,' Jenny began, 'I think we need to decide what we are going to do from here on. We need to plan our future. I can't go back to SA and put up with Karl without having something to look forward to, a target to aim for, if you like.'

She pushed back the sheet on the bed and sat up, lifted her pillow against the headboard and leaned back against it, her arms folded across her naked breasts.

'Something to stop me going round the bend. To be honest I would prefer to give up this masquerade entirely and get everything out into the open.'

Jeff lifted himself up one elbow and placed his other hand on her smooth belly, idly stroking the smooth downy skin. 'Hang on a bit, Jenny, we can't do anything yet. I've only just started the job, not yet sorted my house, and I'm still living at your address. To spill the beans now would be lunacy,' he countered.

'We must wait at least until I am in my own home, secure in my job at the Company and in a position to defend any flack that might come our way once Karl finds out what's going on. He could make my life at the Company quite difficult and I certainly don't want to lose the opportunity of a promotion.'

'OK, I can understand that, but how do we deal with it? What's our plan going to be? We must at least agree when and how we are going to sort this mess out. Once you have moved in I will be alone with him and I don't know whether I will be able to cope with that. He's a bastard to live with and the only reason I stay, aside from the fact that I haven't, until now, found a suitable replacement, is because of the money. He doesn't know, but I have managed to salt away quite a tidy nest egg out of his frequent gifts.'

'How do you mean?' Jeff was intrigued.

'Well, we always rowed a lot, over all sorts of things, like… to do with his not being home much…our sex life, or should I say the lack of it, then, gradually over more trivial issues. The rows usually developed to such an extent that he would get quite violent and started hitting me, sometimes hard enough to cause serious bruises. I would then start to cry, then he would become ashamed and try to apologise, and alleviating his guilt by giving me money and saying things like 'I'm so sorry darling, here, take this and go buy yourself something nice.' It was his answer to everything.'

The amount of money I have saved up is testament to the frequency of these episodes. I should have left him years ago but I had nowhere to go and no one I could confide in, so I just carried on.'

Jeff was boiling now. His hatred of Karl was growing by the second. Was it time to tell Jenny about his dirty secret? He really wanted to. But he knew that if he did, then it might exacerbate the problem and they would be unprepared for it.

He leaned forward and kissed her. 'Tell you what, let's say that we'll persevere until Christmas by which time we'll know whether I've been made a Director. And if so we'll be moving back to UK or if not, I'll be sacked anyway and still have to leave. I've still got my flat in Chelsea and we can always live there.'

Jenny beamed with delight. 'Now you're talking Mr Blythe, I can definitely live with that.'

She leaned towards him and slid her hand under the sheet, reaching for his groin. 'How about I come on top this time?' She suggested, lightly fondling him.

Karl met them at the airport on their return to Johannesburg. Jeff was annoyed to see that he had brought the Jeep, rather than use his own vehicle. He noticed that it was filthy and covered in the red dust of the Transvaal.

'Had a good trip?' he asked jovially as he loaded the cases in the back of the car. 'You ain't missed much over here.'

He tossed the keys at Jeff, 'You'd better drive, I've had enough for this week,' he said provocatively.

'I don't remember giving you permission to use my car Karl, so I'll tell you now. You don't drive it unless I have specifically given my approval.' Jeff blurted it out. He was so annoyed that he just couldn't just ignore it. It had to be said. He was furious with himself for leaving the keys available.

Was he being petty? He wondered. He didn't want to fall out with Karl on his immediate return; after all he had four months to wait until Christmas. He would just have to grin and bear it.

Karl didn't respond, but looked a little sheepish and changed the subject.

'I've booked a table for lunch at the LBV Bistro, our favourite,' he said, 'I thought it would be a good place to celebrate …er… your successful trip.' He nearly let the cat out of the bag. He was nearly a hundred grand richer and actually meant his own good fortune, but of course, it had to be kept from Jenny.

The following morning Jeff called in on Jim Barber to finalise the transaction on his new house. Barber had been progressing things while he had been away, and advised that the solicitor had agreed a completion date by the end of the month – just 3 weeks away. With no mortgage to organise, the move would be reasonably swift, he assured, provided there was no hitch with the money transfer. Jeff advised that the transfer from his account in the UK had been successfully organised.

Jenny was thrilled at the news, seeing it as a further step in her quest for freedom.

The next day at work, Gordon McKlintock called Jeff into his office for a de-briefing.

'Well, laddie,' he began, his hairy hands spread on the desk top, 'How did it go?'

'To be honest, I have no idea,' Jeff replied, 'the meeting was not at all what I expected. Yes, they asked for performance figures from everyone, but there was little discussion over the way forward. David Robinson was more concerned about what our individual views were. He had a short agenda, a copy of which I have for you,' Jeff passed it across the desk. 'Robinson rattled through it and I've made notes against the various items, but no edicts were issued, and we all came away none the wiser.'

McKlintock glanced down the list of items, studying Jeff's notes. 'So we carry on as we are then,' he confirmed, 'I didn't expect much else actually, there will never be a decision made by one Director. The full board would have to ratify any plan and a gaggle of senior employees round a table certainly wouldn't be made aware of any proposals until the board had chewed them over. I guess we won't get any directive for at least a couple of months. I wonder how much that meeting cost, getting everyone together like that? Bloody typical!'

'Yes, I can see your point, but it is interesting that when I gave our figures, he seemed very impressed that we could operate right down to $30. Most of the others are already squirming.'

Jeff stopped at that point. He was not going to divulge any detail of his personal discussions with Robinson. As it was, he would find it quite difficult to perform his role as 'informer', without having the people around him wondering what he was up to.

He was already finding it difficult mentally, reconciling his new company role with his involvement in Karl's illegal sideline, albeit in it's infancy. He was going to have to make a choice sooner or later.

He thought it was time to tackle Karl about the venture as soon as possible, preferably before he prepared the next run.

That evening, Jeff returned to the house to find Karl alone. Jenny had gone shopping for something to eat for supper. He was in a jovial mood again, and poured them both a large whisky before sitting at the kitchen table and motioning Jeff to do the same. He reached into the table draw, took out a wad of notes and passed them across to Jeff. 'That's your share, for the run,' he said, 'your first pay packet, as you might say. And there will be plenty more.'

'I can't accept that, Karl, it would mean that I am condoning what you are doing.'

'But you are already in mate. You've gotta accept it. I can't have people on board not taking a cut. It would look like they're not committed. They might even think you were a stoolie.'

Jeff fanned through the wad of notes. Possibly as much as 10,000 Rand he guessed.

It was obviously based on the value of the transfer. 10% perhaps and not an amount to be sneered at. But was it worth the risk?

He weighed up the odds. There was another aspect to consider now: The fact that he *was* in the know. If he chickened out, could they trust him to keep quiet? What would they do to him if he either did or didn't? He didn't like to think about it. Let's wait until the next run, he thought, I can decide then.

With some reluctance he took the money and he stuffed it into his trouser pocket just as the door opened and Jenny waltzed in with her bag of shopping. 'Ah! You two are getting along fine I see.' She cooed, unpacking her purchases onto the kitchen worktop.

Karl nodded at Jeff, concluding that Jeff's pocketing of the wad deemed acceptance. With a broad smile on his face he turned to Jenny, 'We're gonna have another drink, what about you, love,' he asked.

It was some years since he had called her 'love' and it took Jenny by surprise. 'I'll have what you're having,' she replied, laughing, 'but what's the celebration for so early in the evening?'

'Oh, I've just had a good day, that's all.' Karl replied.

Chapter 32

Moving in day! Danny and Liliane gathered together their meagre belongings and packed them into the 2CV's tiny boot.

Liliane went into the bar to pay the hotel bill while Danny checked over the room to ensure nothing had been left behind. He went down to the car to wait for her, lit a cigarette and leaned back against its flimsy boot lid.

He felt a little calmer now. The pair had chewed over the various scenarios they had conjured up the night before and concluded that as long as Pete's body was never found, and they quietly went about their business without arousing suspicion, there was probably nothing to worry about.

However, the one remaining issue niggling away in Danny's mind was how he could convert his booty into cash. It was neither an asset nor an investment locked away in the bank vault. He needed to find a dealer, someone under the radar, but he knew that would be difficult in a foreign country where he had neither the contacts nor the necessary know-how. If only he could discuss the problem with someone, say like his father.

Liliane came out from the hotel and walked over to the car. 'OK Danny, we're off!' She jumped in and started up the engine. Danny took one last puff of his cigarette, stubbed it out with his foot and climbed in beside her. 'Our new life begins here,' she said with a grin.

They drove over to the Estate Agent to collect the keys.

'I gather your evening with Monsieur Durand was a great success,' Pierre Mansard cooed jovially, 'he seemed very happy to have you as his tenants when he confirmed this morning'.

Liliane smiled, 'Then there is just the matter of making the first payments and picking up the keys?'

She didn't really like Pierre much. He had an inflated view of his role in the whole transaction. Almost as if he had a special relationship with his client.

'Of course, but first, a couple of points regarding your tenancy.'

'Just give us the keys, Pierre,' Liliane spat, reverting to French, which to Danny made her sound much more irate, 'We've been through all that with Durand.'

Pierre retreated a little, suggesting that he only had his client's interest at heart, but yes of course, the keys, and a receipt.

Liliane reached into her bag and pulled out the remains of the wad of notes that Danny had given her. She counted out the required €7,600.00 to cover the six months rent and the deposit and handed the money to Pierre. She then grabbed the receipt off him and with a weak acknowledgement, beckoned Danny to follow her out.

'Lil, remember what we said,' Danny scolded as they walked up the street to the car. 'We need to be on our best behaviour – be nice to people.'

'Fuck him,' she replied, 'I don't like him, he's a creepy fat-headed pillock.'

Danny was amazed at her command of the less savoury elements of the English language.

They drove round to the block and took their bags up to their new flat.

Danny unlocked the door and pushed it open then picked up Liliane and carried her over the threshold, laughing, 'I know we ain't married yet, but we're as good as.' He quipped.

She gave him a hug. 'Well, you know what we'll be doing tonight…just as soon as I get some bed linen! I think you call it consummation?'

'You mean shagging?' Danny asked, not having heard the word before.

'But I must go to the bank again too. Can you go to a shop for some groceries? We need coffee, milk bread and stuff. I'll get some sheets for the bed, towels and things like that, then go to the bank. We can eat out this evening.'

'Good idea,' Danny replied, feeling less wary of her intentions.

They left the flat together, separating at the entrance, Danny walking down to the row of shops at the bottom of the street, Liliane jumping into her car to drive to the bank.

However, she didn't start the car, she waited until Danny had walked far enough away, then quietly got out and ran back up to the flat to collect the square tin box wrapped in newspaper that had so intrigued Danny at her previous address. She then set off again. On the way to the bank, she stopped off at a small shop selling smart leather goods. She bought a large brown, leather brief case and placed the tin box inside it.

Arriving at the bank, she purposely ignored the tellers and walked over to Paul Chave at his desk by the window.

'Bonjour Monsieur Chave…' she began with a beaming smile. He recognised her instantly and jumped up out of his seat to greet her.

'I have a couple of things to drop off in my deposit box…'

'Of course, Mademoiselle,' Chave interjected, 'this way please.' He took her arm and led her off toward the stairs and the vault in the basement.

Once her deposit box was opened and she was sure Chave had got back to his station, Liliane laid her newly purchased briefcase on the table and opened it, then set the combination codes. She removed the tin box from the briefcase and placed it on the table. After pulling out the deposit box, she took a sheaf of bank-notes and put them in her handbag then began to unload everything else into the briefcase, including finally, the gun, the switchblade and the ammunition. By arranging things carefully she was able to get everything into it, although closing the case deformed the lid a little. But with some gentle pressure she managed to close the clasps and spin the combination locks. She then took the tin box, still wrapped in its covering of newspaper, placed it in the deposit box, closed the lid and replaced it in its station. Once she was sure she had properly locked it she picked up the briefcase and left the vault. The case was much heavier now and she was aware that she had to make it appear to others to be empty, so she swung it about as she strode out, giving a curt smile and wave to Chave as she passed.

Her plan was not yet fully developed and she had absolutely no idea how she would pull off the stunt that she was about to carry out. Her hair-brained scheme had not been worked out beyond the left-luggage office of the railway station, but she knew that she would have to be quick, if she was to get there and back *and* get the bed-linen before Danny got too impatient waiting for her return.

Liliane pulled up directly outside the railway station and ran up the steps into the hall. She found the left luggage office and placed the briefcase on the counter in front of the attendant. He squinted through his thick pebble glasses at the ledger on the counter and wrote out a ticket, tore off her portion and passed it across to her. The remaining portion he ripped from the ledger and stuck it around the briefcase handle. Walking over to the slatted racks at the back of the baggage area, he neatly placed it in a narrow gap between two overstuffed soft bags on the top shelf.

Satisfied that the briefcase was safely stored, Liliane placed her half of the ticket in an inner pocket of her handbag and carefully zipped it up then trotted back to the car, pleased that all had gone so smoothly.

Danny was waiting by the entrance to the flats, leaning against the wall, smoking a cigarette as Liliane drew up and parked the car. She thought he looked quite agitated.

He walked over to her. ‘Where the fuck have you been?’ he cursed, ‘I’ve been waitin’ here for ages. You’ve got the keys remember. I thought you must've had an accident or summat.'

'Oh Danny, I'm sorry,' she purred 'Didn't you take yours? I went to the bank and got into a long conversation with our friend Paul Chave. I think he fancies me, you know.'

'Fuck Chave,' came Danny's heated reply, 'he can piss right off – creepy little bastard'.

'Then when I got to the shop I couldn't find the right size pillowcases and the assistant had to go into the storeroom to get them. It all seemed to take ages. Anyway, I'm here now and we can get settled in.'

How much cash did you take out?' Danny asked.

'I've no idea,' she replied, 'I just took a handful of notes. It's in my handbag.'

Danny opened the bag and fanned through the notes. 'There must be a couple of grand in here Lil, should last us a while.'

'Yes, you'd better keep it, Danny, I don't want to be walking round with that much in my bag, it might get taken.'

Liliane opened the boot and took out her purchases and passed them to Danny.

'Hang about Lil, I've got the bloody shopping to carry up first.'

He was still angry but had begun to calm down a little, soothed to some extent by Liliane's innocent responses and her readiness to allow him to rifle through her handbag. She had been clever enough for him to think that she was not holding anything from him and the misgivings he had earlier, as he had waited outside the flats, were subsiding gradually.

Back in the flat, Liliane occupied herself with the bed making and arranging her new purchases. Danny dropped his groceries on the kitchen worktop and went out onto the balcony for another cigarette. He leaned on the balustrade, looking out over the gardens, listening to the birds and the faraway sound of children playing in the park. He felt a sense of calmness and serenity, which he had never experienced before in his murky life. To him it appeared that his troubles were behind him, he had money, a nice girl and, sitting in the bank, his nest egg. Now all he had to do was to work out how to convert it. But there was no rush, after all, there was plenty of cash to use up first.

Liliane called to him softly and he turned and wandered over to the bedroom, pausing to watch her for a few seconds. She was lying on the newly made bed, totally naked, her legs apart, and her hands clawing at her crotch.

'Come on Danny,' she panted softly, 'I need you now, please hurry.'

Danny hadn't waited for her words. The scene as he entered the bedroom had already given him a massive arousal, such that he was having difficulty getting out of his boxers. He fell upon her and she took him in both hands, guiding him into her. She climaxed almost immediately, moaning loudly, her back arched, her hands grasping his buttocks, her nails piercing the taut thrusting flesh.

She knew this would be the last time they made love so she wanted to make it a moment he would remember forever. She pushed Danny over onto his back and straddled him, taking him up again and working herself against him, thrusting her tongue into his mouth and tasting the bitter remains of his last cigarette.

At last Danny came, and she felt the warmth of it as he bucked beneath her. She lay against him and panting, put her lips to his ear.

'How was that Danny…was it good?'

'Yeah! It was OK,' Danny replied nonchalantly, 'It'll do for now,' reaching for his cigarettes.

Liliane smiled, 'Let's get dressed and go find somewhere to eat,' she suggested.

Chapter 33

Almost three weeks to the day, Jeff received a call from his solicitors to say that the financial transfer on his new house had gone through and he was clear to take possession.

The news put such a spring in Jenny's step that he had to take her aside and admonish her for fear of giving their little game away.

Gordon McKlintock approved Jeff's application for a week's leave so that he could organise the purchase of furniture and decant from the Jongen residence. Jenny couldn't wait to accompany him on his buying spree, making the most of any opportunity for them to be together.

Karl didn't seem bothered by the idea, largely because he was heavily involved in his secondary business – a deal involving a bush shoot and the shipping of some animal skins for an American client who was upgrading one of his properties in Tuscany.

Jeff had started making lists of his requirements, by category. Kitchen equipment, Dining furniture, Lounge, Bedroom, Outdoors, etc. That way, he hoped he could just locate everything in each category in just one store, getting it delivered in one drop, enabling him to furnish one room at a time.

'We need a trip out to the house again before we start,' Jenny began as they ate supper that evening. 'We need to look at the overall colour scheme, then we'll have to look at the size and positioning of each room so that we can decide on the best type and arrangement of furniture.'

'Hang on, Jenny, what's all this 'we' business?' The total lack of subtlety on her part was embarrassing Jeff, especially when discussing things directly in front of Karl.

'Well, I'm just assuming that you will want my advice. You've often said that you like the way I've furnished this place, so I might just have a few ideas to help you do it right.'

Karl looked up from his plate and slowly wiped his mouth on his napkin. Replacing it in his lap he spoke for the first time since sitting down to the meal. 'She's got a point you know Jeff, a woman's eye can make all the difference. I'd just let her get on with it.'

That was the signal they both needed. There would be no need to be wary about it. They could just get on with it without fear of inquiry. Jenny glanced at Jeff with a twinkle in her eye.

The process of furnishing the house took much longer than Jeff expected. Jenny's involvement meant that decisions were slower as searches for exactly the right piece of furniture or accessory covered more and more shops, studios or galleries and as a consequence costs spiralled beyond Jeff's planned budget. Nonetheless, she had excellent taste and despite being a woman, she was quite well able to interpret his male tastes. Gradually as the empty spaces filled, the house took on an elegant, sophisticated air interspersed with reminders of its location and heritage in the South African bush. Animal skins were bought to adorn the hall walls; woodcarvings and local art were sparsely sprinkled around the rooms. Out on the patio, dried elephant grass was used to make a roof covering for the mandatory new bar area, where large earthenware pots with a variety of mature plants were arranged, semi-enclosing the dining area and barbecue.

Jeff was well pleased with their work and wasted no time in getting settled in.

Jenny, on the other hand, was not so happy, now that her involvement had ceased. The realisation that she would have little excuse to be there with Jeff was now all consuming.

'I guess this is the end of things for a while,' she said solemnly as they sat drinking on the patio, soaking up the last of the warmth in the evening twilight.

'Yes, but I'll be here if you need me,' Jeff replied, 'If you can get away. But don't forget you can always invite me over for meals, and you can always do your 'shopping' here. It'd only be until Christmas after all. Just two months or so, then things might be totally different.'

She understood but his assurances didn't alleviate her misery. The thought of being alone with Karl again was more than she could bear.

Chapter 34

Liliane woke to an empty bed. She could hear Danny in the kitchen making coffee and from the smell of baking reaching the bedroom, she deduced that he had put croissants in the oven to warm.

She felt a degree of remorse for what she was about to do to him, but consoled herself with the fact that, in view of his past actions, he didn't deserve better.

During a fitful sleep that night she had slowly developed her strategy and now she felt that all the loose strands that might trip her up had been tied together. She couldn't fault it. It was bound to work out. She would be free and rich.

Danny came into the bedroom carrying a plate of croissants in one hand and two mugs of coffee in the other. He was still naked and she took what was to be one last look at his physical attributes. She knew she would never again see such a majestic sight and it tugged at her heart a little.

'Here we go Lil,' Danny whispered, 'tuck into this little lot.'

She sat up in bed, cross-legged, and placed the plate of croissants in her lap. 'Thanks Danny, I'm feeling ravenous.' And she dunked a croissant in her coffee and took a large, soggy bite.

'What we gonna do today?' Danny asked, his mouth full, the crumbs cascading down his chest.

'Well, I've got to go down to the chemist, then depending on the results, we may be registering with a doctor fairly soon.'

'What do you mean?' Danny didn't comprehend.

'I think I might be pregnant,' she lied.

'Oh Christ! I hope not,' Danny moaned, 'that's the last thing we need at the moment.'

That was the second stage of her plan.

Stage one: Get the money, stage two: Find a way to get some time alone, away from the flat so that she could progress her little scam. The rest would happen by itself.

Danny grabbed his boxers and went into the bathroom. Liliane had been surprised by his reaction. She had been afraid that he might want to settle down, lead a normal life and do all the things a family does. But clearly he wasn't ready for all that.

She was glad in a way, because it indicated that he was not actually the right person for her. She never intended him to be in any case, at least not after she had seen the money and the diamonds. She had, however, developed a soft spot for him, and she knew that she would never find another so willing to accept her. Nonetheless her newfound wealth was to prevail at all costs.

Danny came out of the shower and began dressing.

'So you're going down the Chemist, I've got to get some clothes – jeans and stuff – I ain't got much to wear at the moment if I put me others in the wash.'

They agreed that they would go their separate ways and meet back at the flat for lunch. Liliane would get something from the *Charcuterie*.

'Listen Lil, whatever the result is, I love you and I can try to live with it,' Danny conceded as he walked out of the door, 'but if it's true you *are* pregnant, we've got some difficult decisions ahead… An' as I'm not sure how to cope with a kid, we've got some serious talking to do.'

'Not as much as you think.' Liliane muttered under her breath.

Once Danny had gone, Liliane quickly dressed and went out to find an Internet café. She didn't quite know the best way to shop Danny, but she thought that if she got in touch with the Dutch police, they would then organise his arrest. That might be better than calling in the French police as they would no doubt wish to get involved in the investigation and possibly make a mess of things, as in her experience, they often did.

Liliane found a computer in the Bureau de Poste, and Googled 'Amsterdam Police'.

She was spoilt for choice – there were several addresses. She chose the one that seemed to be nearest the centre of Amsterdam at Elandsgracht 117, and made a note of the telephone number.

She walked over to the phone kiosks, inserted one Euro into the pay slot on one of the phones and dialled +31 9008844. She could hear the phone ringing at the other end, but it was a while before she heard a male voice responding to the call, even then she didn't understand what was being said, for it was in Dutch. She asked if he spoke French. He replied 'No, but can you speak English?'

At last she manage to explain that the person who might have murdered the man in the office in Amsterdam was here in Rouen, living at her own address.

'Which man was that Madame?' The policeman asked.

'I don't know, but it's the one that has been on the news this week. Wilson I think his name was.'

The policeman casually asked for her name, age and address, then what her relationship with the murderer was and finally, would she like him to pass on the information to the relevant department? Did she have a number they would be able to contact her on? Liliane gave her mobile, asking that any contact be only in exceptional circumstances, in case it aroused Danny's suspicion

She then rang off, full of a combination of remorse for her act and anxiety at how things might develop.

Danny had not gone far before he found a small boutique selling cheap casual wear. He found a couple of pairs of jeans, a short sleeved shirt and a *Lacoste* tee shirt.

He was on his way back when he saw Liliane leaving the post office some way ahead of him. He ran to catch up with her.

'What's up Lil? Saw you comin' out of the post office.'

Liliane blushed severely. 'Oh nothing much, I just had to make a call to the Office in Abbeville to be sure they had received my letter of resignation.'

'Would it have mattered if they hadn't? Danny quizzed.

'No, I suppose not, but I just felt that I needed to know.'

'So what did they say?'

'Not a lot really. They reproached me for not having given notice, but what else can they do.'

Danny reluctantly accepted her explanation, but he couldn't really understand why she thought it was necessary at such a late stage. Was she actually telling the truth? He remembered the phone call she had made when he first went to her flat in Abbeville. It was to her old boyfriend. Could this one be to the same guy? Was she stringing him along?

Danny reflected on his chance meeting with Liliane at the café in Abbeville. He remembered how forward she had been, how quickly she had accepted his suggestion that they go back to her flat. Was she actually what she seemed? Perhaps it was all a set up. Maybe she had been waiting at the café for someone to come along and by chance it was he. She probably pushed things along further when she found out about the diamonds.

Danny's disquiet was making him sick. He realised that he might be just another victim. Her story about living the life of luxury was probably just bullshit, but how could he find out the truth?

He decided he would watch her like a hawk from now on and try to analyse everything she said or did.

'By the way, did you go to the doctors?

'No but I tested myself at the pharmacy, and I'm definitely pregnant.'

'Fuckin' Hell,' Danny swore. 'What are we gonna do about that?'

'It doesn't change anything, does it?' Liliane asked, trying to look anxious.

'Well I wasn't plannin' on havin' a kid in tow this early in our relationship, Lil.'

'Well, we've got time to decide what to do about it – about 24 weeks I think,' she replied.

Was this part of her plan? Danny wondered. Could she possibly be faking the pregnancy to put him off? He'd have to wait and see.

'We'd better get back so I can change into some new clothes,' Danny suggested, 'Don't forget we're eating out tonight.'

'Yes, and I'm looking forward to a nice romantic dinner with my favourite man,' Liliane replied with a smile. But Danny noticed that the smile was cold and her eyes lacked any expression.

Once back at the flat they quickly washed and dressed. Danny noticed that though they shared the bathroom, there was no physical contact between them. Previously she would have been touching, stroking or embracing him, but not any more. She went about her toilet single mindedly, as if she couldn't get out of the bathroom fast enough.

'What's the matter Lil,' Danny asked as he came back into the bedroom, 'you seem pissed off with summat.'

'No, I'm fine, I'm just a bit disappointed in your views about the baby.'

'Well, what did you want me to say? I just wasn't expecting that quite so early in our relationship. I was hopin' we could have some fun first, then maybe think about a baby in a year or two.'

'But I'm 34 now and I should have had kids long ago,' Liliane exclaimed, 'besides, if you didn't want me to get pregnant you should have done something about it. There are such things as condoms you know.'

'Yeah, but I just assumed you were takin' somethin', it was your invitation, if you remember.'

'Well I wasn't, so you'll have to put up with it.' She replied firmly.

Danny got dressed, determined not to say any more on the subject. Liliane squirted a bit of perfume around her neck and went into the kitchen in a huff.

'I don't know why we're bothering to go out,' she moaned, 'you'll be like a bear with a sore head.'

Eventually Danny too was ready. The pair left the flat and started down the stairs. The sound of many feet on the marble treads below them grew louder until, at the second floor, they sighted the blue uniforms of the gendarmes rounding the curve in the stairwell.

The lead policeman called up to them: 'Madame Duval?'

'Mademoiselle,' she corrected, 'why do you want to know?

'Would you please accompany us back to the station, with your friend.'

Danny froze on the staircase. He knew he wouldn't be able to get past them, there were three of them. He looked over the stair rail. It was about seven metres to the ground floor. He wondered whether he could jump over the rail and land safely.

He glanced back up the stairwell and decided that was his only option. Would he be able to get to the top, unlock and open the flat door and lock it again before the gendarmes got to him? He doubted it, but it was his only safe option. Lazily, Liliane had only locked one of the three locks, so there was just a chance he could make it.

He grabbed Liliane and, as hard as he could, he pushed her down the staircase at the ascending gendarmes and turned and ran back up the stairs two at a time.

The lead policeman fell backwards under the force of Liliane hurtling into him. Her scream, as the air was punched out of her chest, echoed around the stairwell. Valuable seconds were lost as they got back on their feet. Liliane was too injured from the blow to stand and her foot had been wrenched, caught in the wrought iron of the decorative balustrade. By the time the gendarmes had got past her, Danny was at the top floor searching in his pocket for the key. He was shaking so much that even that small activity took precious seconds. He could hear at least one Gendarme coming up the staircase behind him, then a shot from a pistol and the simultaneous thud of the bullet splintering the door near his head. A split second later, the door opened and Danny shot inside and shut it, taking care not to be standing directly behind it in case the policeman fired again. Fumbling, he tried desperately to bolt all three locks, dropping his keys on the floor as he did so. He was now sure that the police really meant business.

He also knew that unless he could find another way out of the flat he would eventually have to give himself up. He ran out onto the balcony and looked up at the mansard roof. The parapet around the building was just a few feet above his head. He thought that he could perhaps reach it if he stood on the balcony railing. He dragged a chair out of the salon and pushed it up against the railing. From the chair he gingerly climbed onto the railing and balancing himself, he reached up to the parapet, hauling himself up onto his elbows, he was then able to swing a leg over the stonework and into the gutter behind and pull himself up. He ran along the parapet to the flat adjacent and swung himself down onto the balcony. The French doors were open and he cautiously entered the flat. Two occupants, a man and a woman both in their latter years were watching the news on television in the corner of the room, the back of their sofa towards him. Judging from the volume of the TV the two of them were hard of hearing. Certainly neither had heard Danny, so he was able to quietly move to the hall and their door onto the landing. He flicked open the observation peephole and put his eye to it. On the landing he could see Liliane, supported by one of the gendarmes, searching in her bag, probably for her set of keys. Another gendarme was on his mobile, presumably calling for back up. The third was nowhere to be seen.

Danny stood by the door, peering out, waiting for their next move. Then Liliane found her keys and started to unlock the door.

All three entered the flat together and Danny realised that if he was to make a move it had to be now. He unlocked the door as silently as he could and crept out onto the landing. The door to their flat was still open, but the neither Liliane nor the gendarmes could be seen. Danny ran down the stairs as quietly as he could and reached the entrance to the courtyard. Rounding the corner of the entrance, he ran headlong into the third policeman who was smoking a cigarette and answering his car radio, the handset cord uncurled and extended out through the passenger window. He saw Danny just in time to avoid collision, but simultaneously encircled the microphone cord around his head as he passed. Danny was brought up short with a jerk, which nearly choked the life out of him. The gendarme neatly put him in an arm lock and pushed him face first into the bonnet of the Renault. Within seconds Danny was cuffed and the chase over.

'So I was right,' Danny thought. 'Liliane has shopped me. She was after the money and the diamonds all along.' He could kick himself for being so naïve. He had no idea how he was going to get out of this predicament now.

The policeman opened the rear door of the car and asked Danny to get in, a helping hand pushing down on his head as he did so.

Danny saw the other two policemen carrying Liliane over to the second car and putting her in the back. One of them then walked over to him and climbed into the driving seat, the third got in the back with Danny.

'What the fuck's goin' on?' Danny asked feigning innocence.'_

The policeman didn't reply as they raced off down the street.

Chapter 35

It had been three weeks since Jeff had moved into his house. The temperatures were beginning to soar as full summer approached and the swimming pool was in constant use. His routine involved an early morning swim before work, then another immediately on his return in the evening, before retiring to the patio for a drink and the occasional *al fresco* meal.

However, today was a little different. It was Saturday and Jeff was still in bed when Jenny's call came through.

'Hi Darling!' She said cheerfully, 'Karl thought it a good idea to invite you over for a few drinks and a lazy lunch today. What do you think?'

Jeff thought for a minute before giving his reply. It seemed unusual that Karl would have suggested something like that.... Unless there was an ulterior motive. Was it time for the next run? He wondered.

'Are you still there?' Jenny asked anxiously, then she whispered 'I really need to see you – it's been too long.'

'OK, I'll be round about 12.00. But listen Jenny, Karl does know about this doesn't he?'

'Yes, sure, it was his idea after all. But we'll be able to have some fun together in the afternoon because he's off to see a client at 3.00 p.m. and won't be back for several hours. Sounds good doesn't it?'

'OK, I'll see you shortly,' Jeff said, before hanging up.

Jeff pulled up at the estate at exactly midday, and phoned Jenny to open the gate. The heat was unbearable so he left all the Jeep's windows open when he parked up on the apron in front of the house.

Jenny had rushed out to the drive and was waiting to greet him as he arrived. She gave him a big hug. Karl met them both as they entered the hallway. 'We're having drinks out on the terrace – it's nice and shady there' he said, without any greeting.

He beckoned Jeff to follow him out, while Jenny went across the hall to the kitchen.

'I expect you know what this is all about Jeff,' he began.

So it was true. Jeff knew it. It was exactly as he expected. There was to be another run.

'I can guess.' He replied.

'Well, Christmas is a good time,' Karl continued, 'There's always a good number of travellers to give you cover. And the reason I'm sending' you over is because the boss at the Amsterdam end wants to meet you. We need new people after all the problems we've seen with one of his associates. He wants to be sure that in future the guys we take on are up to it. He won't just take my word for it, so you're going to have to go to Amsterdam on 23rd December. But I don't want you saying anything to Jenny about this one, OK?'

Jeff was taken aback by the way Karl had issued the edict. How should he react? Why not just refuse to have anything to do with it? That might be a little dangerous, perhaps.

'You've sprung this one on me a bit suddenly, Karl I don't know whether I will be able to do that date, there are a few things happening at work right now and I might have to go back to London around that time.'

'Good, then you can combine the two jobs,' Karl beamed, 'just take a flight to London via Amsterdam as before and I'll organise the rest.'

Just like that! Jeff thought. But he knew he was caught and could do little about it.

'Who is, and where do I meet this guy?'

'You don't meet him, he meets you. Nearer the date he'll contact me and give me the details and you'll be given a time and a location.'

'What's his name?' Jeff asked.

'Alan Redmayne, he's a Brit, based in Amsterdam. He and another guy ran this business and acted as middlemen for our 'exports' but they had some aggro with a couple of the runners which enforced a cooling down period but thing are back to normal now. So we're gonna get our shipments moving fast and frequent at last.' Karl rubbed his hands together with glee, relishing the thought of all the money he would make.

Jeff sat back in the chair, staring across at Karl who was now busying himself at the icebox opening a couple of bottles of Castle lager. He passed one to Jeff across the marble-topped patio table. 'Here,' he said 'nice and cool, help get your temperature down, you look a bit hot.'

Jeff was indeed hot, but mainly under the collar. Karl was gradually drawing him deeper into this murky world of contraband. He was passing him information, little by little, which would make his position more and more difficult for him to safely extricate himself from.

He tried to reconcile this with his job at the Oil Company. If things worked out with David Robinson, how on earth would he throw off this millstone without endangering himself? He had no idea.

But on reflection, if things went sour with the Oil Company, he might be glad of the involvement, at least until he could find more worthy employment.

'OK, Karl, I'll do it, but with one condition.'

'And what's that?'

'That if things go the way I hope at the Company and I get a senior post, you'll allow me to back out gracefully, knowing that I'll keep quiet.'

'I can only say that I'll do my best, but there are others to consider. You'll have to convince them too.'

'Yes, but if you put in a good word it will help.'

'OK, I'll go along with that,' Karl agreed 'but I don't think you've got much chance with the Company – it's too big.'

'We'll see about that,' Jeff replied. Of course Karl was unaware of Jeff's discussions with David Robinson, so he would naturally be sceptical.

'We'll talk about this again nearer the date,' Karl continued. 'No more now, not in front of Jenny.'

As if on cue, Jenny came out onto the terrace with a bowl of olives and a tray of garlic bread. Karl made her a Dubonnet, poured over a tall glass of crushed ice, her customary pre-lunch, patio drink.

'Lunch will be about 20 minutes,' she said.

By the time they had finished their drinks, the sun had turned and the patio was now unbearable. The three of them moved inside and were grateful of the shade and the soft breeze from the ceiling fan over the kitchen table. Jenny had prepared a fillet of cold salmon with salads and baby potatoes, which they washed down with two bottles of Karl's favourite ice cold Boschendal Sauvignon Blanc.

Karl soon rose somewhat unsteadily to his feet, 'I'm gonna have a shower, then I must go.' He said, 'It's nearly 3 o'clock.'

Jenny looked at Jeff and smiled, unconsciously placing both her hands in the crook of her thighs. It would not be long now before she had Jeff all to herself.

Twenty minutes later, Karl was back down, changed into fresh clothes and looking a little less inebriated.

'OK I'm off. See you Monday if you've gone before I get back, Jeff,' he said with a wink, 'I'll be in touch.'

He left the house, climbed into his truck and drove off.

Jenny got up from her chair, sidled over to Jeff and sat on his knee. She leaned back and whispered in his ear. The two rose and arm in arm, made for the stairs and her bedroom.

It had been three weeks since they had last made love and they set about their quest with a mixture of excitement and urgency, each undressing the other.

It was at that moment, locked in their union, that Karl chose to walk into the room. He had quietly returned to the house, padded gently upstairs and caught them both in full flight.

He was once more apoplectic with rage.

'You fuckin' bastards,' he shouted as he rushed over to the bed. He grabbed Jeff around the neck and pulled him to the floor, naked and still erect. Jenny screamed, and reached for the sheet to cover herself, as if it would give her some protection. With a swift, well-aimed kick, Karl's unshod foot made contact with Jeff's testicles with a resounding slap. Jeff creased up in pain, bent double and writhed on the floor. Karl then turned to Jenny. He swung his arm behind him and then released a mighty lunge at her face with his open hand, catching her full on the side of her head, so powerful was it, that it knocked her off the bed and across the polished wood floor. She screamed again as her shin hit the corner of the wardrobe. 'You dirty little bitch – I knew you were up to something - that's why I conjured up that little meeting tonight. I knew you were shagging each other. Well, you can go and do it elsewhere. Get your stuff and get out, you filthy tart.'

He walked over towards her, 'maybe this'll help you on your way,' and with his foot, he kicked her in the stomach, his instep meeting the soft flesh below her diaphragm.

There was no scream now, just a low moan as Jenny lay on the floor clutching her abdomen.

Jeff raised himself from the floor, desperately trying to get up and stop Karl from further injuring Jenny, but it was too late. Karl was walking to the door, 'You've both got 15 minutes to be gone, otherwise I shall not be responsible for my actions,' he said, slamming the door behind him.

Jeff crawled over to Jenny, and kneeling before her, took her head in his lap. She was crying and in severe pain.

'We've got to get you to a doctor,' Jeff whispered, 'that kick in the stomach could have caused some serious damage.' Jenny nodded, but she didn't have the strength to move.

'You can phone for the doctor,' she panted, 'the number's in my mobile in the kitchen.'

Jeff lifted her onto the bed and dressed quickly before rushing down the stairs 2 at a time to the kitchen.

Karl was there, at the kitchen table, head in his hands. His handgun was on the table.

Jeff was enraged to see him sitting there feeling sorry for himself. 'You've really done it this time Karl, you might have severely injured Jenny. This is the last time you touch her. I'll fucking kill you if you go anywhere near her again.'

'Karl looked up, his face contorted with anger. 'I don't think you're in a position to make that statement. I'm the one with the gun, an' I'm on the right side of the law, morally speaking. We had an agreement, you bastard, it's entirely your fault, you caused the problem. I only did what any self-respecting bloke would do. You both deserved what you got. In fact you should be grateful you didn't get worse. You don't have the right to dictate to me what I do and don't do with my wife. This ain't the first time she's screwed around you know. I've been living with her dirty little games for years.'

Jeff didn't reply, concentrating on his search around the kitchen for Jenny's mobile. Eventually he found it in the fruit-bowl and cursored down through the numbers looking for the doctor. He made the call, giving a brief description of Jenny's injury, hoping that it might convey greater urgency.

Karl got up from the table, picked up the pistol and grabbed his car-keys 'You'd both better be out by the time I get back,' he shouted. Then he swore under his breath and left the house.

Jeff wondered why he had taken the gun.

The doctor arrived forty minutes later, a young, white South African, tall and self-assured. He examined Jenny carefully, but appeared suspicious of Jeff's explanation of events leading to her injuries. A fuller more candid explanation of the whole episode had to be given, rather embarrassingly, before the doctor seemed satisfied. 'You should press charges,' he added, it sounds like this was a major assault. Luckily, it seems, he has not done any lasting damage, but to be certain, come and see me in a week' He then gathered together his kit and before leaving, added, 'If in the meantime you get any further pain, or feel sick at all, come straight back to me.'

Jeff saw the doctor out and turned to Jenny. 'You can come back to my place now, but we'll have to get your stuff together – at least enough for the time being. I'll come back for the rest when Karl's cooled down a bit.'

Jenny smiled weakly, she realised that what she had been hoping for had arrived sooner than expected, although not without a good deal of pain and suffering.

Chapter 36

At the police station Danny and Liliane were searched, their belongings taken away in huge, expanding manilla envelopes then they were led to adjacent cells.

The Police Chief explained that a couple of Amsterdam policemen were on their way to Rouen to assist in the interview of each of them, and depending upon the outcome, extradition proceedings would probably begin and Danny would be extradited to Amsterdam. Meanwhile, A doctor would be brought for Liliane, but they both would remain in their cells overnight.

They were brought some coffee and blankets and told to settle down for the evening.

Danny deduced that Liliane was not badly hurt, for although the doctor's visit lasted quite a long time, he left alone and Liliane remained in her cell. Then all was silent.

The cell light went out at 10.00pm and Danny lay back in the dark on the hard mattress, trying to work out how things had gone so wrong.

The one aspect he couldn't come to terms with was why Liliane had turned against him. Things were going so well between them. Or at least *he* thought so. But there again, maybe she had planned to do this right from the start.

One thing was sure. She wouldn't declare that she had the cash and diamonds in her deposit box. She wouldn't want to lose her grasp on them. So as long as he could weasel his way out of custody, he would be able to get back at her *and* recover his booty.

Danny tried to clarify in his mind just how much the police knew about him. As far as he could tell, his whole involvement in the murders hinged on whether they had concrete evidence that he went to England with Pete. They certainly wouldn't know they had been to Manchester, nor would they know why they went. They would have found out that the ferry office had the record of the pair booking a crossing with the car, but would they actually know whether they both went over? They also would have discovered that the car didn't return. And that no one came back to Amsterdam through Harwich.

He had told his father that he didn't go, so there would be some fairly weak corroboration of his story there. All he needed now was to find some simple alibi to prove that he was in France for the period in question.

If he could achieve that, then the scenario the police had developed with Pete as the prime suspect might prevail…

Thinking it through in more depth, his heart sank. 'Oh God!' he groaned aloud, as he remembered that he had told Liliane all about his trip to Manchester, the reasons why and what he had done to Pete. She was the only other person alive who knew, but she was now batting for the other side and would no doubt spill the beans. Danny felt sick. He realised that he wouldn't get out of this mess unless she kept quiet. But why would she? She had already shopped him, so she would be unlikely to hold back.

Then an idea struck him. He walked over to the door of his cell and with his finger tried to slide the external peephole cover open. It eventually moved aside sufficiently for Danny to see that it was dark in the corridor. He deduced that there would be no one there in the dark, so he might be able to call out to Liliane without drawing attention.

He tapped on the dividing wall between their respective cells. After a short pause, Liliane tapped back.

'Can you hear me Lil?' he called.

A muffled voice called back, but Danny couldn't really hear what she was saying.

'Go to the door,' he shouted.

Then he heard her reply more clearly.

'Sorry Danny,' she said, 'I shouldn't have done it but it wouldn't have worked out.'

'But you could have just said so. You didn't need to get the police in. What else are you gonna tell 'em?'

'I won't drop you in it Danny, I just want the money, then I'll leave you alone.'

'Well you ain't gonna get the money, 'cos if you squeal, I'll tell em about it and you won't get your greasy little mitts on it.'

'You're too late Danny, I've already got it, so you're up the creek anyway.'

'You've turned out to be a real little shit, Lil, do you know that. I really thought we was good together….'

Liliane didn't reply, although she did inwardly accept that there had been a spark between them but the money was now a bigger draw.

Somewhere down the corridor a door opened and slammed shut. Danny could hear footsteps approaching. He heard the rattle of the bolt being slid back and the door swung open.

One of the two policemen crowding the doorway entered the cell and demanded that Danny bring his blanket and follow him down the corridor. The last cell door at the end of the corridor was opened up and the second policeman pushed Danny in. 'Now keep quiet,' was all he said.

Danny wondered whether they would have heard the detail of what he and Liliane had said, rather than just indistinguishable words. He doubted they would have been able to, unless there was a bug in the room. He started to look around the cell, just in case.

Satisfied that there was nothing, he came to the conclusion that he should stick with his story and see what course his interrogation would take, but he knew he wouldn't sleep that night.

At six o'clock in the morning the lights came on again and the two policemen returned with coffee and some baguettes spliced with a meagre layer of ham.

Danny asked for an update.

Neither policeman could speak English, but Danny gleaned from the statement that the Amsterdam police would be arriving mid morning, and that he would stay in his cell until then.

Danny wondered whether Liliane was getting the same treatment.

She might be released before him, and that would be the last he would see of her and the money. If the worst happened, he might not be released at all. Whichever way, he was doomed.

What did Lil mean when she said 'You're too late, I've already got it?' Was she reaffirming that the account was hers and only she could access it, or did she mean that she had moved the contents of the deposit box? No, he thought, she wouldn't have had time. She never had it with her when she came back from the bank. Even if she had, where could she possibly have put it? No, it was not true. The stuff will still be there in the vault. He was sure of it.

Despite the desperate situation he found himself in, Danny was still convinced that he could pull off his escape from arrest. But he knew that he had to find some way to fool the police into thinking that he was in France at the time of the crossing to Blighty.

How could he do that when he was here in custody? He thought back to the evening when Pete had phoned him. He wouldn't be able to erase the call - it would be on his phone records and his bill - but the conversation wouldn't have been recorded.

Danny tried to develop an alternative scenario for his interview:

He would convince the police that Pete had phoned him to ask if he could take the car to do a job in Blighty, of which Danny would say he knew very little. Pete would have known that Wilson had given Danny his marching orders, so why would he expect Danny to go with him? The car belonged to Wilson, and Danny had been relieved of the responsibility of looking after it. It would therefore be quite normal that Wilson would suggest that Pete take it.

Meanwhile, Danny had met this bird in a club in Amsterdam. Her name was Marie-Christine. She had then spent a couple of days shacked up with him in his flat before deciding to go back home to a little town called Diélette, near Cherbourg. So Danny, with no job and nothing better to do decided to go with her. He could take her down there on his motor bike…

Danny stopped his scenario for a moment. There was a glitch. He realised that he didn't have a motor bike at that point in time. Furthermore, he had bought the bike in Cherbourg - which was very close to Diélette - some time later than when he was supposed to have met the imaginary Marie-Christine. It would make sense to tell the police he had bought it after dropping her off. He would have to say that they hitched a lift down to Diélette. There was another problem too. If he had actually done all this, the police would surely expect him to be able to direct them to her, identify where she lived, etc. But of course he couldn't do that.

He would have to invent some reason for not actually taking her all the way. Perhaps, say they had an argument and decided to go their different ways. Yes! That would do. But he would have to have dropped her somewhere near Cherbourg, otherwise he would not have bought the bike there.

All this confusion was doing Danny's head in. It was far too complex for his slow brain to manage and he knew he could so easily make a mistake, especially if he couldn't think fast enough during the interview. The police would be firing questions at him one after another, try to trip him up and although he was sensible enough to know his limitations, he knew he could easily mess up.

It was a bit like a row of dominoes, he thought. One down and they all go over, one after the other.

Where could he have dropped Marie-Christine off?

He was in a police cell, with no map, his mobile confiscated, with no knowledge of the towns and villages around Cherbourg.

The time was ticking away. The Amsterdam police would be here shortly and Danny was now sweating with apprehension. He had to get his story together before they arrived, but a coherent solution seemed to elude him.

He sat on the edge of his bunk bed, racking his brains, head in hands, eyes closed, trying desperately to think of something.

It would have to be a bar in Diélette. He hoped it had one. Yes, it must have one, he thought. All French towns do. But they didn't have a motorbike shop, so he went to Cherbourg. Yes! That would do. That would work.

Having now woven this lie into his scenario, he could now continue with the more truthful portions of it:

He would say that he then set off back to Amsterdam, but stopped in Abbeville and met another girl, Liliane in a café and he was so taken with her that he changed his plans entirely.

From that point he knew the rest of his tale would be easy. A piece of cake! If Liliane was true to her word and didn't drop him in it, then all would be hunky dory. Danny thought he would run with this plan, sure that it would work.

He lay back on his bunk and tried to calm himself. He knew that if he was to be believed, then he would need to give his account in an unflustered way, answering the police questions politely, without showing any sign of nervousness, or worse still, aggression. He felt he could do that.

He was running through his scenario for the last time, when he heard the familiar sound of the corridor door being opened and footsteps approaching. His cell door clanked open. It was the same two policemen that had incarcerated him the previous night. 'Venez,' said the first policeman as the second beckoned Danny to leave the cell.

They marched him down the corridor and into one of the tiny interview rooms. It had a barred window and the sun was streaming through it, casting alternate broad, light patches and thin, dark streaks across the leatherette surface of the table.

The table itself was bare except for a recording machine at the end against the sill of the window.

Danny was made to sit down and wait.

After some ten minutes or so, one of the policemen entered the room with two trench-coated men, an older moustached man and a younger, slighter man who carried a blue folder, and a third, affluent looking fellow, in a blue suit.

The policeman introduced them as Inspecteur (Inspector) Lars Daalmans and Hoofdagent (Senior Constable) Daan Cuypers and a French lawyer, chosen to represent Danny named Phillipe Corneille.

'I don't need no lawyer,' Danny said scornfully, 'I ain't done nothin'.'

It cut no ice with the four men, who all drew up chairs at he table.

The French policeman reached over and switched on the recorder, then leaned over the microphone and identified the participants to the interview, the time, date and subject matter, then asked Danny to state his name and address.

The Inspector started questioning Danny in a soft but firm voice, in perfect English.

'So Mr Redmayne, you presumably know what this is about?'

'Yeah!' Danny began, 'but I ain't got nothin' to do with it.'

'To do with what, exactly?'

'I'm not daft, you know, I seen it all in the papers.'

'Yes, of course you will have. But if you had nothing to do with it, why did you try to evade the police when you were arrested?'

'Well, I ain't got the sort of job that the police would be happy about have I?'

'Oh, so you *did* work for a Mr George Wilson then - a British man with a rather shady business in Wolvenstraat in Amsterdam?'

'Yeah, but I got the sack and me cards, and had to find other employment.'

'Why was that?'

''Cos he said that I'd cocked up on one of the jobs, and he couldn't trust me again.'

'When was this job?'

'Back in August I think, can't remember the exact date.'

'What exactly was the job?'

'Oh just delivering summat in England for him.'

'What was that?'

'Search me! I just do the delivery.'

'Who did you deliver it to?'

'To a guy he dealt with.'

'And who was that?'

'I dunno, I just ask him for the code word and if he says it right, I give him the package.'

So how do you meet up with a man you don't know?'

'It's at a place agreed in advance.'

'Agreed by whom?'

'My boss, Wilson.'

'OK, so how did you mess up?'

Danny wasn't expecting this line of questioning, so he was unprepared and had to think on the hoof. It was not his strong suit.

The more the police delved into this particular aspect of the case, the more likely he was to demonstrate his involvement. All they had to do now was to establish the dates of his visit and tie them up with the old man's murder. Danny knew things didn't look good for him.

'I lost the package, cos I got jumped by a guy when I got off the tube.'

'Where did you agree to meet the pickup?'

'At the tube station where I got off, by the ticket machines.'

'And which tube station would that be?'

'Chancery Lane, near Hatton Gardens'

'Was all this happening in broad daylight?'

'Sort of. It was in the tube station and the lights were on.' Danny smirked.

'No, I mean, it must have happened with lots of people around - witnesses, especially if you were by the ticket machines.'

'Well, I wasn't actually standing by them, I was walkin' around an' just got round the corner, by a pillar, when he jumped me.'

'Did you get a good look at him?'

'No, cos he was hidin' round the back of the pillar an' took me by surprise. His fist came out an' hit me an' that's all I saw.'

'So what did you do?'

'I couldn't do nothin' cos he smacked me so hard in the mouth I went down. Then he nicked my wallet, cards and cash and scarpered. So after I stopped the bleedin' I borrowed a phone off a guy standin' there, to tell the boss an' he said come back to Amsterdam.'

'And did you?'

'Yeah, I had to hitch a lift to Harwich 'cos I had no readies.'

The lawyer sat in silence, busily making a series of notes in his black leather notebook, before standing and inviting the Inspector to step outside the room for a moment.

'So far, my client's story ties up with the date of the Hook / Harwich crossing, Monsieur Daalmans, and from the speed of responses and their plausible nature, it would appear that he is perhaps telling the truth, wouldn't you say?'

Lars Daalmans was less convinced. 'We'll see when we get to the main areas of this investigation, but I agree that he doesn't seem to be holding anything back. It is perfectly feasible that his boss, for fear of incrimination would not give him too much information. Let's move gently on to the murder of the two victims.'

They walked back into the room and asked the French policeman if it was possible to have some coffee.

He immediately jumped up, apologised and left the room.

Danny asked if he could have a cigarette and the Inspector reached into his pocket and pulled out a packet of Stuyvesant and flipped it towards Danny. It was Danny's first smoke since his incarceration and it tasted good, helping him think through the next chapter of his invented story during the short interlude.

Inspector Daalmans waited for the French policeman to return before continuing. Meanwhile, he studied Danny intently. He didn't look much like a crook, he thought, even less a murderer. Maybe he was just some small fry caught up in it all. His nervousness showed on his face, but not in his responses, which he thought, might be a sign of inexperience, innocence and youth. He fidgeted like a small child might, and became suddenly much more calm with the offer of the cigarette. He was obviously scared of something, but was it the police presence or was he hiding something. We'll wait and see, he thought.

Lars Daalmans nodded to the French policeman who switched on the recorder again and stated the time, and the interview continued:

'Are you aware, Mr Redmayne that your boss, George Wilson has been robbed of quite a lot of money and then murdered?'

'Yeah! Course I am, me dad told me when I was here, in France.'

'Yes of course, Al Redmayne is your step-father – we have already interviewed him...'

'Father actually,' Danny interjected.

'Can you remember exactly when you found out?'

'Yeah, it was about 2 weeks ago, I can't remember the day, but you can find out from my phone company. I was shocked, cos although I didn't like the way the old bastard sacked me, he didn't deserve to die.'

'That's exactly the point Danny – May I call you Danny?'

'Yeah, can I call you Lars?'

'If you wish, but the point is Danny, you are a suspect largely because you have a motive for robbing him and possibly even for killing him. You lost your job, and your wages. Many would commit such crimes for much less than that.'

'That's as may be, but seeing as I was in France and not Amsterdam, It couldn't have been me.'

'OK, we can check out dates and times, to see if they support your version of events, but first let's move on to your former colleague Pete Radbourne. Do you know of his whereabouts?'

'Not exactly. I know he went over to Blighty cos he nicked my car to make the trip. But I ain't heard from him since.'

'Why would he take your car?'

'Well, it wasn't actually mine. It belonged to Wilson who lent it me. But Wilson wanted it back so he got Pete to get it, an' he used it for the job in Blighty.'

'What job was that?'

'I dunno really, except that he was goin' over there to rough up some guy for not paying his dues.'

'How did you know that?'

'Cos Pete told me.'

'Can you explain why your name was on the Ferry tickets?'

Danny froze. The one thing he knew he couldn't cover up had surfaced. He took a last puff of his cigarette, thinking desperately and taking what seemed an age to stub out the cigarette in the small *Bakelite* ashtray. Once he had completely extinguished every red ember of the stub and rubbed it round the perimeter a couple of times, he replied: 'I was probably s'posed to go with Pete when Wilson booked the tickets, but I got the sack before the job went ahead. So he had to go on his own.'

'So when exactly did you get the sack from Wilson.'

Danny realised that Daalmans was hoping to catch him out. The wily cop was trying to show that the tickets were bought after he got the sack. Danny knew however, that the only people who could confirm the date he was sacked were both dead, so he could alter the time a little.

'It was the same day that Pete left for Blighty. He took the car off me at eight o'clock and I got the sack when I got into work at nine.'

'Can you remember what day that was?

'Yeah, course I can. It was the day after I got back from Blighty when I did the drop, as I told you before. The 27th August I think it was. It was a Tuesday.'

Danny knew that Pete had bought the tickets on the evening of the 26th. He felt a smile creeping over his face. He tried to stifle it, but it did not go un-noticed by Daalmans.

They ain't got nothin' on me, Danny thought, an' I'm walkin' through this, no problem. He felt more confident now.

'Do you know anything at all about Pete's job in England, where it was, who he went to see etc.'

'No, all Pete told me was that the guy owed Wilson twenty-five grand. I'd worked for Wilson for a while, but I never knew he was owed money from someone in Blighty – he never said anythin' about it to me.'

'And you don't know where Pete might be at the moment?'

'I got no idea.'

'Did you know Pete had a girlfriend?'

'Nah! Pete's never had no girlfriend. He picked up a few scrubbers here an' there, but never had nobody steady or nothin'.'

'You've never heard of someone called Cheryl?'

'No, who's she an' what's she got to do with anything?'

'She was found murdered in Pete's flat.'

'Shit! I don't know nothin' about that, but maybe that's why Pete ain't back. Maybe he did it.'

The inspector looked at the Lawyer and nodded imperceptibly.

'OK Mr Redmayne, I think that will do for the moment. We'll continue our interview tomorrow.'

'Oh! One last thing. Why did you come down here to Rouen?'

'Met this bird, didn't I. We got on well to begin with, an' I came down with her but then she buggered off but I thought I'd stay around for a bit. Met another bird, and here I am.'

'And that other bird – would that be Miss Duval?'

'Yeah, that's the one.'

'So when did you actually leave Amsterdam and begin your journey around Europe?'

'After I got the sack, I went to this club, and that's where I met the first bird. She stayed with me a couple of nights, so it must have been about the Thursday, 29th I think, although I'm not 100% on that.'

'OK Danny, we'll continue this conversation in the morning.'

The French policeman picked up the microphone and stated the time then switched off the recorder and the four men left the room.

Danny leaned back in his chair and put his hands behind his head, lifting his feet onto the table. He felt very pleased with himself. The interview had gone like clockwork and the police had gone away no wiser than when they had arrived. He was clean!

His two jailers returned while he was still congratulating himself and shuffled him back to his cell. It was 11.20am.

Chapter 37

It was the 16th December. In one week's time, Jeff reflected, he would be on his way to Amsterdam. The Oil price had recovered quite considerably and the shale extraction process was becoming increasingly economic once more. His target of $55 a barrel had not yet been reached but he still had hopes. There were 9 days to Christmas and anything could happen, although the prospect of his being elevated to the twelfth floor in the Strand seemed to now be pretty remote. In fact, despite his fastidious weekly reporting to David Robinson, there had been no contact with him since the original conference in London. He remembered Jenny's comment back at the Hilton in London. It could be that David Robinson was now *persona non grata,* and no longer held the tiller, hence no call. On the other hand perhaps he had not been that impressed with the slower than anticipated recovery.

It seemed therefore, that his trip on the 23rd might be solely a return ticket to Amsterdam.

Karl had phoned Jeff and given him a further briefing on the trip. It was a strange conversation. It was as if nothing had happened between them. Jenny was with Jeff now and yet Karl behaved as if he had never been involved with her. He didn't refer to the fight nor could Jeff determine any animosity on his part. Karl was solely intent on getting this latest transaction properly planned and accomplished.

Jeff allowed the situation to settle down too, for he realised that if his plan to keep both fronts operating, was to work, he would have to maintain a working relationship with Karl long term, even though he abhorred the guy and his principles.

The drop involved 12 uncut diamonds, weighing 64 carats in all, and these would be placed in a compartment in the heel of one of Jeff's shoes. Jeff was to bring the pair of shoes to Karl's house and he would then organise the modification. Karl emphasised that any method of transporting the gems would be used only once. He believed that this would lessen the chance of being caught. The shoe compartment would not be discovered unless there was a tip-off or if the courier looked suspicious, as it would not be passing through the scanner, nor would it set off the walk-through alarm.

However, it was important that both shoes made exactly the same noise as Jeff walked over the polished concrete and marble floors of the airports. In order to achieve this, the diamonds would be wrapped in plastic, evacuated, then inserted into the hollow heel, and encapsulated in resin, whereupon once set hard, the final layers of leather and rubber would be glued and nailed in place. The outward appearance of the two shoes and the density of each heel would be absolutely identical.

Jeff was to collect the completed shoes on the day before departure.

As the date for the drop got nearer, Jeff was getting more and more anxious. He still had no word from David Robinson, yet the oil price now stood at $56 and fracking was virtually back at production levels seen before the slump. What excuse could he give Jenny for his trip to Amsterdam? She would wonder why he didn't want her with him. He had to find a reason and fast.

But then, as luck would have it, the call came through. It came in the form of a summons from his boss Gordon McKlintock.

'I've just had a call from David Robinson,' he said, leaning back in his chair, a quizzical look on his craggy, bearded face, 'from what I understand, you seem to have made quite an impression on him, laddie,' he said with a wry smile. 'He wants you to meet him in London immediately after New Year – first day back after the holiday – 3rd January.'

McKlintock looked at Jeff, waiting for a reaction but saw none.

'What does he want me for?' Jeff tried to sound apprehensive.

'How the hell would I know,' retorted McKlintock, 'he didn't say, but he sure as hell likes you. He couldn't stop bleating about your report at the meeting last month. Said you were exactly the type for fast tracking through the business. You're a lucky little sod by the sound of it. What do you say to that, laddie?'

'I don't know what to say actually – is it OK with you if I go?'

'Not even I can counter the demands of the Chairman, laddie, of course you go, but I'd give you a word of warning. If he offers you a deal, don't accept it if it's in Finance – they could be looking for a scapegoat.'

That was the second time he had heard that remark. Karl had said much the same earlier. Was there some truth in what the two of them were saying?

'You're not the first to say that.' Jeff eventually said.

'That's because traditionally, when things go wrong and profits drop, the Finance and Marketing teams are the first to feel the sharp edge of the axe.' McKlintock affirmed. 'So just watch it, laddie. They'll be lookin' for somebody to blame.'

Jeff left McKlintock's office feeling ten feet tall. He knew he had made it. He was going to be a big fish. And as a bonus he had an excuse for Jenny. He was now able to take her to London for Christmas.

Even though he still had the drop to consider, there was none of the apprehension that he had endured on his first trip. He was confident that Karl's ruse would work and he certainly would not permit himself any doubts over the successful execution of the task ahead.

When Jeff arrived back at his house that evening, Jenny was still in the pool. He sat down on one of the sun-loungers and watched her lithe body scything through the water as she completed her daily 25 lengths. As she climbed the pool ladder to greet him he marvelled at her glorious, naked, lightly tanned figure. She was a beautiful specimen, he thought and it gave him great satisfaction to know that he had finally prized her from the clutches of her disturbed, bullying husband. She was his now and all his earlier misgivings over their developing a relationship were in the past.

He walked over to her with a towel and draped it over her shoulders before embracing her and kissing her full on the lips. 'I've got some great news,' he said, smiling broadly, 'we're going back to London.'

She looked at him incredulously. 'You mean you've got the promotion - already?'

'No, not yet, but I've been summoned to meet the Chairman.'

Jenny was over the moon.

'There's just one small thing I've got to do on the way – I have a meeting with someone in Amsterdam, but it won't take long, it just means that we will be staying over again.'

'I don't care about that,' replied Jenny, 'just as long as you find a better hotel this time. Who are you meeting?'

'Oh, just one of the Company guys for a meeting and to drop off some reports,' he lied. He did not want Jenny to be aware of what he had agreed with Karl, under any circumstances.

'If it all worked out, and we moved back to UK, what would you do with this place?' Jenny asked.

Jeff paused before answering her, he hadn't actually thought about such things yet. 'We could keep it, and use it as a base for our holidays,' he joked. But the more he thought about it, the more sense that made. If he were still carrying out his 'second job' he would probably need a base in South Africa. He would know more after his meeting with David Robinson.

‘I’m not sure I would ever want to come back,’ Jenny stated, ‘knowing that Karl was nearby, I would hate to see him again after what he did. Besides, I’ve lived here so long, there’s nothing new here for me any more. I would prefer a second home in, say, France or Italy - Rome perhaps.’

Well, by that time Karl might have moved on, and in any case, we can decide what we do with the house when we know a little more,’ Jeff replied, ‘meanwhile, we’ve got to plan our trip.’

Chapter 38

Lars Daalmans and his colleagues called for Liliane Duval to be brought to the interview room. He thought they would get a short interview in before lunch.

After the introductory formalities, Daalmans broached the subject of how she had met Danny.

'We met in a café in Abbeville,' she replied. 'He was struggling with the menu as he didn't speak French.'

'And from that chance meeting, you decided to live together? A bit sudden wasn't it?'

'Yes it was. It even surprised me, but we got on really well.'

'Yet despite getting on really well, you still felt you should turn him in?'

'Well, yes, it was a difficult decision, I admit, but I couldn't bear the idea of living with a murderer.'

'Who said he was a murderer?'

'He was bragging that he'd done it when we saw it on the news.'

'Which murders did he say he'd been involved in?'

'He said two, a bloke called Pete and his boss'

'Can you remember how he put it to you?'

'Well, I told him about my past, because we were going to live together, and he thought I should know that he too had a somewhat murky past. But I didn't expect it to include murder.'

'So you didn't shop him for the money?'

'What money?'

'Well, we know that whoever killed Wilson made off with loads of his cash from the safe in his office.'

'Danny never said anything about money. In fact he seemed to be completely broke when I met him. All he had were the clothes he stood up in and an old motorbike.' I've paid for everything so far, but even I don't have a lot of money.'

'We've inspected the inventories of your belongings held by the station, and it seems that Danny had some two thousand Euro's on him at his arrest, and you had a couple of hundred Euro's and a ring probably worth some €5,000. Can you explain where that came from?'

'Yes, Danny gave it to me.'

'What, just like that?'

'More or less, yes. He said we weren't engaged, but would I like it.'

'But not a moment ago you said that he didn't have any money or anything.'

Well, that's what he told me. He is obviously lying.'

'Why would he have nearly two thousand Euro's on him when you both were arrested?'

'I have absolutely no idea. I assume he was keeping his financial affairs a secret from me.'

'Do you have a bank account here in Rouen?'

'Yes, two, with the same bank, but I've got very little money in them, probably no more than a couple of thousand Euros or so.'

'But you live in a very nice flat, which must be costing you a lot per month. How do you pay for that?'

'I have paid so far, for six months, but we anticipated getting jobs here in Rouen. However all that has changed now.'

'May I ask which bank you are with so we may check out your statements?'

Yes, it's the Credit Agricole, the branch in the Place Saint-Marc.'

'Thank you'

Lars Daalmans glanced at the clock over the interview room door. It was twelve fifteen – time for lunch.

'OK Mademoiselle Duval, we will continue later this afternoon, we should break for lunch now.'

'I don't get it,' Daalmans said, shovelling another forkful of Caesar salad into his mouth, his jaw clicking incessantly as he chewed. They've only just met, shacked up together, and then she's shopped him. Why would she do that now, after taking on the flat and spending all that money? And another thing, why would Redmayne admit to murdering people if he wanted to hang on to his bird? If Redmayne did murder Wilson, where is the money that was taken? His wife said that there was loads of it, apparently.'

Dan Cuypers poured himself another glass of wine before answering, he was just as perplexed, but gave his view:

'I think that before we go any further we need to establish exactly how much money they both have. We should go to Duval's bank first and check it out, then quiz Redmayne about his. He's got no ties in France, so it seems unlikely to me that he would open a bank account here, particularly as he would need to give away too much personal information to do so, which would be stupid if he really was the murderer. He might have a bank account in Holland, but he wouldn't be drawing money from it here if he were the murderer. It would identify his location. No, it's my bet that he's using her bank account to stash his haul. Where else would he have got the two thousand from?'

Daalmans agreed. 'OK, we'll do that first. Then grill Redmayne some more. Got your phone?'

Cuypers took his mobile from his pocket and waved it at Daalmans.

'Call the office and get Anna to check the banks in Amsterdam for an account in Danny Redmayne's name. There won't be another English name like that in Holland. Tell her we want balances of all his accounts and frequency and size of deposits over the last couple of months. Check whether he had a deposit box too.'

Cuypers busied himself on the phone while Daalmans signalled the waiter for coffee and *l'addition* before tackling his crême brulée.

The pair strolled back to the police station, discussing the situation.

'I'll have a further chat with Redmayne,' Daalmans said, 'and you get yourself down to the Credit Agricole and suss out Duval's bank account. They'll probably ask for a warrant and if they do, we'll just have to bring the woman with us next time we call in.'

Cuypers was just about to peel off in the direction of the bank, when his mobile rang. It was Anna from the office in Amsterdam.

He listened intently for some time before turning to Daalmans.

'They've found his bank account and apparently there's only a current account with about €400 in it. He hasn't made a deposit for two months, but a withdrawal by debit card was made...'

'And?..' Daalmans asked impatiently.

Cuypers smiled and continued. '…And guess what! The debit card payment was to a petrol station in Amsterdam the night before the crossing to England!'

Daalmans was confused. 'I thought he said he didn't go to England.'

'Yes he did say that, but this proves that he planned to go. Why would he put petrol in a car before handing it over?'

Daalmans didn't answer.

'And there's something else too.'

'Yes what is it? For Gods sake Cuypers, just get on with it.'

'The guys at the office have discovered that Pete Radbourne had been over to England the day before that. He went over in a different car.'

'So that would be when…the Sunday?'

'Yes, that's right.'

'But that's roughly within the time-span that the lab boys in UK said the old man was murdered.'

'Yes, so now we might have to consider which of two possible killers actually carried out the murders.'

'Yes,' said Cuypers, 'but on the other hand, it might also back up Redmayne's story about being mugged in the tube station. It could have been Radbourne'

'Shit! That rather complicates things. Especially as we don't have Radbourne's whereabouts. It means we must put extra pressure both on our team and the British police to find him.'

'I'll get Redmayne up again and quiz him some more, you get down to the bank. This is getting more complex by the minute.'

Danny entered the interview room sandwiched between his two French gendarmes and was made to sit down opposite Daalmans. His solicitor had not returned, so Daalmans decided to continue without him. 'Do you have any objections Danny?' He asked.

'He wasn't much use anyway, and besides, I ain't got nothin' to hide.' Danny replied disdainfully.

'OK, so, can you explain where you got the two thousand Euros found on your person when you were brought to the police station?'

'Yeah, Liliane got it from the bank that morning. She gave it to me because she didn't like carrying that much money around in her bag.'

'Why did she draw out so much?'

'I dunno exactly, we'd only just moved, an' she had said summat about buyin' some stuff for the flat. I didn't have much in the way of readies, so maybe she was gonna give me some of it, I ain't got a clue.'

'OK, so let's now go to the weekend of your trip to England, when you attempted to make the exchange. Did you know that your colleague Pete Radbourne also went over that weekend?'

'No, He never said nothin' about that.'

'Do you know why he would have gone?'

'No, not unless he was goin' to see his folks or summat.'

'Is it possible that he could have been the person that jumped you?

'Maybe, and maybe he went on to do the exchange himself?'

Danny had seen where Daalmans was coming from and was happy to go along with his thinking. It might just get him off the hook.

'And you got back from your trip on the Monday, right?'

'Yeah, that's right.'

'You went by car?'

'No I went over as a foot passenger.'

'Why was that?'

''Cos I'd damaged my knee playin' football an' couldn't bend it, so I thought it'd be safer not drivin',' Danny lied.

'But you drove to Hook?'

'Yeah, an' it was driving to Hook that made me realise. It hurt so much that I just parked it an' got a foot passenger ticket.'

'Can you explain why you filled up your car at the petrol station on the Monday night?'

''Cos the tank was empty, that's why'

'But you were going to have the car taken off you.'

'Yeah, but I didn't know that at the time, did I?'

Daalmans realised that he was none the wiser, but the recent new information from Cuypers did provide evidence of another possible scenario. He went through it in his mind: It was just possible that Danny was telling the truth and that Radbourne, knowing Danny was to make the exchange, had jumped Danny, taken the money carried out the exchange and shot the London dealer, taken the goods and then returned to Amsterdam. He was presumably hoping that it would be pinned on his colleague. Once back, he'd had a phone call from someone instructing him to 'Top Danny' – there had been a note made on his message pad by the telephone – Maybe the girlfriend knew too much and had to be disposed of too. But who killed Wilson? Was it possible that the 'Top Danny' note was the result of a call from Wilson? Could Radbourne have refused and had a showdown with Wilson, resulting in his murder? In that case, why would Danny brag about having done it? Had he actually said he did it or was Liliane Duval lying to try to implicate him? Daalmans was gradually doubting Duval's version of events, in part because Danny appeared so naïve but natural in his responses and also because he seemed to be virtually destitute. There was no record of him spending large amounts of money, as might be the case had he committed the murder and robbery, nor was there any sign of his having stashed the stolen hoard.

The interview room door opened and Daan Cuypers, breathless, signalled to Daalmans. He rose and the two men left the room.

'I've been to the bank,' Cuypers blurted, his chest heaving. 'Duval has two accounts, a current and a deposit, with not far off €1000 in each.

But get this! She's also got a deposit box, she only asked for it a few days ago. The Assistant Manager, a fat little creep called Paul Chave wouldn't divulge anything. He said that we either had to get a warrant or accompany the customer to the bank, if we wanted any further information.'

'OK then,' replied Daalmans, that's what we'll do.'

He called for the gendarmes to take Danny back to the cell.

'And while you are there, please bring Liliane Duval up here. We need to take her to the bank.'

Liliane arrived at the front desk looking bewildered. She didn't understand what was happening. She was apprehensive, hoping she would not be confronting Danny. But when Daalmans explained that they were taking a little trip to the bank, he noticed that, rather oddly, she became much more relaxed and receptive. 'We need to take your key to the deposit box,' he said offering Liliane the manila envelope of possessions, 'would you find it for me please?'

'Liliane feigned reluctance, but nonetheless obliged and Cuypers took her out to the car while Daalmans signed her out on the police register.

At the bank, Paul Chave was all smiles again as he led the three down to the vault. The keys were inserted and once the box had been opened, Chave left the room.

Liliane flipped open the lid and lifted out its contents. 'What's that?' Daalmans asked, as Liliane removed the newspaper wrapping its contents.

'It's the ashes of my two dogs,' she replied softly, 'I cannot bear to part with them. But I need to keep them safe, so I thought a safety deposit box would be the best thing.'

Daalmans sighed, looked across at Cuypers and lifted his eyes to the heavens. 'What else do you have in there?' he asked tersely.

'Nothing, I don't have anything else worth storing at the bank.'

Daalmans glanced again at Cuypers, a look of desperation on his face. They were getting nowhere. He was beginning to wonder whether there was any point in continuing further with this line of enquiry, as it seemed that neither Redmayne nor Duval were hiding anything. Their stories did not coincide, but neither story could be disproved, yet the one remaining puzzle was, 'Why had Duval made the phone-call to the police in Amsterdam?'

'OK. We'll go back to the station. We need to ask you a few more questions,' Daalmans said resignedly, 'pack that thing away and lock up, quick as you can'.

Back in the interview room, Daalmans questioned Liliane over her phone call to the Amsterdam Police.

'Miss Duval,' Daalmans began, 'what I don't understand is why you suddenly felt the need to inform us about Danny Redmayne, such a short time after what seems to have been such a whirlwind romance. Can you explain this a little bit better please?'

Liliane hesitated for quite some time before responding. She was trying to develop a coherent answer, one that would seem plausible to the police yet at the same time, lift her above suspicion without diminishing the case against Danny.

'You are right, we *were* getting along well. Right from the beginning we both felt that we were right for each other, but as time went on Danny seemed more and more preoccupied with the case you are looking into. He told me he had worked for Wilson and that both he and the other chap Pete were both bastards, then, when he gave me the very expensive ring, I suspected that he might have been the murderer. He didn't have anything else on him, so I assumed he'd stolen it.'

Daalmans interrupted: 'And that ring is the one in your envelope of possessions held at the desk here?'

'Yes that's correct.' Liliane replied.

'So we can easily check its provenance and place of manufacture. Anyway, carry on with your story.'

'So that started me doubting that we should continue. But then, I got pregnant. When I told him he went mad, saying that he didn't want a kid in tow, but I said that I would soon be too old to have kids, and wanted to keep it. It was starting to tear us apart. So I felt that, given all these circumstances, it might be best to break up, and calling the police seemed to be the best way to do it quickly. I didn't want him murdering me too, so I thought getting him behind bars as quickly as possible would be the safest thing to do.'

'Are you sure the child is his? After all you have only known him for a few weeks.'

Liliane stared at Daalmans in disbelief. I'm not a tart you know. I don't screw around with just anybody.'

'No, of course not, I'm sorry,' Daalmans apologised, 'but you do understand why I had to ask?'

'No actually, I don't,' Liliane replied, her cheeks flushed with anger.

'OK, well let's go back to where we were. Can I ask you…are you still pregnant now?'

'Of course, do you think I've had time to get rid of it?'

'Well, I just want to establish the facts.'

'I wouldn't get rid of it anyway, I'm 34 as I told you, and I want children.'

Daalmans fished through the papers in front of him and pulled out the medical report on Liliane's injuries.

'I understand you had a medical check-up while you were here, following the injuries you received immediately before your arrest?'

'Yes, I did. I was checked for broken bones, as my chest hurt and I had a sprained ankle.'

'Did you have any other tests?

'Yes, I had a blood test and a urine test.'

'Right. But according to the doctor's report, there is no mention of you being pregnant. Yet the tests would have shown you to be so, if you had been.'

Daalmans wasn't sure that this would have been the case, but he thought he'd try it anyway. There was just a chance that Duval would panic and admit the truth.

'Well, I went to the chemist and did the test myself and I'm sure I was pregnant.'

'Well it looks to me, Ma'amselle Duval, as if you are lying, I put it to you that you conjured this whole thing up to put Redmayne off.'

'OK…OK, yes, I'm sorry, you are right, I did, but you surely must understand why I did it, I had to find something that would help drive him away.'

'So you lied to us before, when you insisted you were actually pregnant, didn't you?'

'Well, I suppose so.'

'So why should we believe any other part of your statement?'

'Because I know he did do it, the murders, I'm sure of it. And besides, Why would I lie about anything else, if none of it was true, why would I have phoned you?'

'Because you wanted out?'

'But if I hadn't thought he was the murderer why would I have shopped him?'

'Because you wanted the money?'

'But there isn't any,' Liliane cried in exasperation.

'That remains to be seen,' Daalmans replied, 'but back to the main issue - you don't know that Redmayne actually murdered anyone, do you?'

'Well…No, not as such, though I remember that he said he did, and he also said that he thought it was a good thing Wilson was dead. Why would he say that otherwise?'

'But earlier you said that Redmayne bragged about having killed Radbourne and Wilson. Is that actually true? And, Ma'amselle, please be truthful with your answers.'

'Well, I may have got that bit a little wrong. He told me about it after I had told him about my past. I interpreted what he said as meaning that he had killed them.'

'So can you remember what he *actually* said?'

'No, not exactly, I was so overwhelmed with the situation at the time, maybe I didn't pay enough attention to what he said.'

Daalmans slumped back in his chair and raised his arms in despair. This interview was going backwards.

'But that isn't enough to accuse him, let alone convict him of murder, and unless you can come up with something better than that, then we may have to let him go.' He said forcefully.

'What about me?' Liliane asked urgently.

'Well, we'd probably have to let you go too.'

'But you can't,' Liliane stammered, 'he'll kill me. He knows that I shopped him, and he'll come after me.'

'Not necessarily, but leave that to us,' Daalmans began, 'we'll sort something out. Maybe with the French Police's agreement we can take him back to Amsterdam for further questioning.'

Liliane stared at Daalmans, horror stricken. Her plan seemed to be going terribly wrong. She tried to think of something that might improve the case against Danny, but the only weapon she had was the money and gemstones. She didn't want to give them up. She couldn't afford to lose them.

Liliane was clutching at straws now. 'Could you let me out of custody before him,' she asked, 'So that I can get away from him.'

'That won't be necessary, Mademoiselle, We'll most probably be taking him back to Amsterdam, but if not we can arrange some protection for you. Don't forget that, at the moment, there is no real evidence that he is violent. Meanwhile we have some more questions for Mr Redmayne.'

Daalmans signalled Cuypers to fetch the gendarmes to escort Liliane back to her cell.

She took one last pleading glance at Daalmans. 'Don't worry Mademoiselle,' he said, anticipating her anxiety, 'all will be well.'

The Gendarme took Liliane by the arm and led her to the door.

'Just one more thing before you go, Mademoiselle, Daalmans called, 'Can you confirm whether or not you have paid the rental for your flat?'

'Yes, as I said before, I paid it.'

'Oh yes, so you did.' Daalmans agreed, as he flipped through his notes. 'And how much was that?'

'I paid seven thousand six hundred Euro's.'

'Rather a lot of money, then?'

'Well, it was for the deposit and six months rent.'

'Yet you said you only had a couple of thousand Euro's in your bank accounts. And there's no record on your account statements of your having paid a sum of that magnitude.'

Liliane was trapped. She couldn't say that Danny gave her the money, for that would indicate he had taken it from the heist. She had also admitted not having had much herself. She dug a bigger hole for herself:

'I haven't been entirely truthful, Monsieur,' she conceded, her expression doleful and her eyes moist with tears. 'I am afraid I have a phobia of banks. Although they are useful for day to day transactions, I have never trusted them entirely. So I tend to keep my savings safe in my flat. When I moved from Abbeville I took my hidden savings and it is with that money that I paid the rent. The rest I gave to Danny for safe keeping as we would need some for living expenses and sundry items for the new flat.'

'So the €2,000 you previously said was given to you by Danny Redmayne was actually yours?'

'Yes, I'm sorry, Monsieur.'

So you lied about that as well as everything else?'

'I suppose so, but I was confused and I felt threatened.'

'Miss Duval, you have obstructed this investigation from the start. I suggest that you go back to your cell and straighten out your story. You do nothing to help your case with your lies. Think about that and the consequences that will befall you if you fail to tell the truth. I shall give you only one more chance. Any more lies and you will be charged with obstructing the course of justice and perjury. Do you understand?'

'Yes, I'm sorry Inspecteur.'

Once she had gone, Daalmans turned to Cuypers,

'For two pins I would lock up Duval for quite a while. She has sent us on a wild goose-chase right from the start, by the look of it. We'll probably have to let Redmayne go and eventually, possibly, her. We could charge her, but it probably wouldn't stick. However, I think we should organise some surveillance, on both of them and most importantly on Redmayne. We need to set this up with our French comrades before going back to Amsterdam.'

'I agree,' Cuypers replied, 'It may help in getting some further evidence. Let's see who he contacts and where, but we'll have to make sure he doesn't get to Duval. We'd be a laughing stock if there were a further homicide. We've got their mobiles, so we can set up phone taps before we release their belongings.'

'OK, get that sorted.' agreed Daalmans.

Chapter 39

Jeff and Jenny left the plane and traversed the Air Bridge into the main terminal building at Schiphol. His modified shoes felt little different as far as he could tell and after the success of the last trip, he felt no nervousness. He had successfully passed through the scanners in Johannesburg, but had not been 'patted down' with the hand scanner. Nonetheless he was confident he would safely leave Schiphol airport with his charge intact.

Full of confidence, he approached the small queue of travellers at the EU passport channel. The officer looked carefully at his passport then studied Jeff intently. He passed it over the scanner and handed it back to Jeff without a word.

'So far, so good,' Jeff whispered as he walked over to meet Jenny before moving on to the baggage hall. They had placed only one case in the aircraft hold and Jeff ensured that he was the one to collect it from the belt and take it through the final EU customs section. That way, it would look more normal, and if he was stopped and searched, they would concentrate on the suitcase. Jenny would be passing through the non-EU section as before, and would just have her small pull-along case.

There were a number of passengers with bags open, being searched as Jeff approached the counter and a bottleneck was developing behind them. A customs official by the exit, who had been studying the passing passengers as they walked through, waved the group on towards the exit, Jeff amongst them.

That was it. He had got through without a hitch.

As they settled back in their seats in the taxi, Jeff was tingling with the excitement of it. It had been so easy. He wondered why he had initially worried about his involvement. It was easy money and he was so confident now that he was already working out what method he could engineer for his next drop.

Following Jenny's concern over the accommodations on the last trip, Jeff had booked in at the Hilton Hotel and it was there that he was to meet Alan Redmayne. His meeting had been arranged for 6.30pm in room 211. Redmayne obviously did not want to be seen meeting in public, which suited Jeff fine, as there was always the possibility that Redmayne might be under surveillance and hence he himself would be under scrutiny.

At the reception desk, they signed in and the desk clerk reached for the room key from a hook on the pigeonholes behind him. He also withdrew an envelope and passed it to Jeff.

'You have a letter Mr Blythe,' he said holding it out between his thumb and forefinger, his little finger in the air, in a somewhat effeminate gesture.

The note gave instructions as to how he was to make the exchange:

Later that same evening he was to leave his shoes outside the door of their room for cleaning at precisely 11.30pm, not before, whereupon someone would collect them and exchange them for another similar pair. A 'Do not disturb' notice would be hung on the door handle by the courier to indicate to Jeff that they had been taken by the intended recipient and not by hotel staff.

He wondered why the transfer couldn't have taken place during his meeting with Redmayne, but on further analysis he realised that Redmayne would have no intention of getting caught with the diamonds himself. One of his minions would do the dirty work.

'What's the letter about?' Jenny asked inquisitively.

'Nothing much, just a note from my contact – a sort of reminder really,' Jeff mumbled, stuffing the note in his trouser pocket.

'How long do you think your meeting might last tonight?' Jenny enquired.

'Oh, I don't suppose it will be that long. Probably about an hour, maximum, I would think,' Jeff replied, 'I don't suppose this guy will be inviting me to have dinner with him, he probably knows I'm not on my own and I expect he'll be itching to get home.'

'So we'll be having dinner together then?'

'Yes, of course. You'll just have to while away the next couple of hours with your book while I shower, change and get off to room 211.'

'I think I'll book a massage and have a couple of hours in the spa,' Jenny decided, 'get myself all spruced up for our dinner together,' she added, laughing.

Jeff arrived at room 211 promptly at 6.30 p.m. and knocked lightly on the door. Redmayne must have heard him arrive as the door opened immediately.

'Jeff Blythe, bang on time,' he bellowed jovially, 'come on in.'

He then popped his head out of the doorway, looked up and down the corridor furtively, then closed and locked the door.

'Sorry about all the secrecy and stuff, Jeff, but you never know who's watching you these days, especially in our line of work.'

Jeff noticed he said *our* not *my* line of work, which presumably meant that Redmayne had, at least in part, accepted his enrolment into the 'business'.

'OK. So I guess you are wondering why you are here?'

'No, I fully understand that you would want to personally vet a new man in the business, so it comes as no surprise. It's absolutely no bother either, because I'm due in London tomorrow anyway, so a small diversion just adds a bit of variety to an otherwise stuffy meeting with my company.'

'Right,' Redmayne began, 'that's actually one of the three things I want to discuss with you, the first of which is a somewhat delicate matter, which I imagine might have an emotional effect on you and may even change your mind about your involvement with us.'

Jeff sat forward in the chair, as if galvanising himself for some bombshell of bad news.

Redmayne's expression turned grave and his eyes fell upon the coffee table, his hand brushing imaginary crumbs off its surface onto the floor, while he searched earnestly for the gentlest way to explain the problem. Eventually he spoke.

'When Karl advised me that you were interested, he told me your name. Your surname is the same as a woman I used to know, or I should say…rather…had a connection with. I didn't think much about it at first, but after a while, I decided that I would do a bit of research. It turns out that the Blythe I knew was your mother.

To explain a little more clearly I have to delve a bit more into the background. Many years ago, I met and had an affair with your mother, during a period when we were both working in London. It was very short, largely because your father found out about it fairly soon after it had started.

There was no break-up from my wife or anything, we patched it up, but I never spoke to William again and seldom to your mother. However, after the event, it shortly became apparent that your mother was pregnant, and early the following year, Danny, her son was born – my son too, you see. Your mother didn't want the child, largely because she was separating from your father and would be alone, so my wife and I agreed to bring up the boy as our own. When my wife died about 3 years later, I looked after Danny and brought him up alone.

Until recently he worked in the cartel with a colleague of mine. So you see Jeff, it means that you have a half-brother.'

Redmayne paused and looked into Jeff's face, expecting a reaction.

'Bloody hell!' Jeff whispered, 'I was probably too young at the time to know my mother had been pregnant, but I'm surprised no one said anything to me about it later. I wonder why?'

'As I said, I never saw your mother or father again. We kept quiet so that it looked just as if the kid was our own. Looking back on it now, perhaps we should have been more open, but after your dad died we thought it best to let it lie'

'And my mother was obviously too embarrassed to tell me herself.'

'I expect she wanted the whole episode to be wiped from her life,' Redmayne said, leaning over in his chair and reaching into his briefcase on the bed.

'I've brought a photo – unfortunately it was taken a few years ago, so not quite up to date, but you'll be able to see vague similarities with your mum.'

They were indeed vague, but the eyes and the high cheekbones of Danny's face were inherited from Jeff's mum.

Jeff fell back in the chair and stared up at the ceiling. Both men were quiet for some minutes.

At last Jeff spoke. 'So what's he doing now and where is he?'

'Well it's all a bit complicated – and really this is why I told you about him being your half-brother - but I'll try and explain. I am, as I indicated earlier, or I should say I was, loosely in business with a colleague called George Wilson. I agreed with Wilson that it would be better for Danny to work with him rather than have him in my patch. So Wilson took him on as a courier and sort of soldier. Wilson had another man called Pete Radbourne. The two lads were mates….'

Redmayne recounted the events of the last few weeks and explained how Danny had been sacked and was now somewhere in France with a French girl he had met, whereas Pete Radbourne had gone to do a job in England

and was now missing presumed dead. As he talked, the expression on Jeff's face became increasingly incredulous.

Redmayne continued. 'So that's why we are now looking for new blood, people with a bit more nous and you're one that's been put forward by Karl.'

'I can't believe this,' Jeff stammered, 'it's such an incredible story, and a huge coincidence. To think that I found all this out just by chance, just by doing a run for Karl.'

'The question is, Jeff, will it change the way you view your role, and would you prefer to pull out. I would quite understand, but you would have to remember that you have information that could indict the lot of us, so your silence would be mandatory.'

'I can't see it makes any difference to me personally as far as the business is concerned, but I would like to meet my half-brother. Does he know that my mother is his too?'

'No…He…. We just let him think that we were his parents'

'So, if he doesn't know, and you're not going to tell him, why are you telling me all this? There was no real need.'

'Because firstly, I didn't want to complicate the deception any further and I didn't want you suddenly finding out later. Secondly, you would recognise your mother in Danny and might put two and two together, but I knew Danny wouldn't know you from Adam, so there's no problem as far as Danny's concerned. Thirdly and finally, I didn't want you falling out with him which would be less likely if you knew.'

'Do you think he will ever come back into the business?'

'Well, he's a strange chap is our Danny, he tends to flit about, does his own thing, like now with this bird in France, but I'm sure he'll be back when he's milked her dry and needs the cash.' Redmayne laughed, trying to make light of it all.

'You can think about all this some more over the next few days, but can we now move on to point number two? What are you going to do about your job with The Oil Company?'

'Well, nothing really. Just carry on up the ladder. I'm doing quite well and I need a cover so I plan to keep going with it. There is an added benefit for us, in that I regularly travel back and forth, so that might be useful for us in the future, don't you think? Karl manages to hold down both, so I don't see why I can't.'

'Fair enough, you're not the only one in that company with links to us but you'll have to watch where you put your money. We don't want people thinking the Oil Company pays a fortune, and we certainly don't want the tax people or the law following up fat bank accounts. Best to keep our deals in cash under the mattress as you might say.'

'That's not a problem, I can set something up.' Jeff replied.

'OK! Point number three. Karl tells me that Jenny has moved out, they've separated and she's shacked up with you. Is that true?'

Jeff was taken aback a little. News travels fast.

'It is.' He replied, not without a note of defiance in his tone. 'Jenny was fed up with the way Karl was treating her. He has a terrible temper and can be quite violent at times, especially to her. She too is quite strong willed and that, amongst other things, is why they clashed so often. Karl invited me into his house, as a lodger, when I first moved to Johannesburg and somehow she latched on to me and things developed from there. She will never go back to Karl, in fact I found out that he is due to retire from The Oil Company shortly, as you probably know and intends to move to Belgium. Further, he had previously told me that his plans did not include Jenny and he was going to leave her the house in Johannesburg.'

'So how will your working relationship with Karl end up?'

'Well, it seems that it hasn't affected it. I have talked to Karl over business matters since the bust-up and all was reasonably pleasant and normal. Almost as if nothing had happened. I think most of his ire was directed at Jenny.'

'So you need to keep it that way, at least until he moves from SA. And keep Jenny well away too.'

'Of course. There's no way she'll go near him, not any more.'

'Of course, when Karl does go, then there will be an opening for you to take over the operation in Johannesburg. If you are still based there by then.'

'Even if I'm not I do intend to return regularly if I can. I'm keeping my house on anyway.'

'Good – so that's it Jeff, good to have you on board. You've got your instructions for tonight I gather?'

'Yes, all sorted. One last point…'

'Yes?'

'As we've been talking I've also been thinking about Danny and whether you should tell him or not – I mean about me being his half-brother.'

'Do you want me to?'

Jeff thought for a moment. 'Yes, why not?'

As he walked silently down the carpeted corridor of the hotel, for the second time that day Jeff felt elated. He had made the grade in the diamond smuggling business and gained a half-brother into the bargain. Life was full of surprises.

Chapter 40

Danny was woken at six o'clock by the sudden illumination of the cell-block lighting. He had now been in custody for 36 hours, yet no charges had been brought. Where was his lawyer, he wondered? Surely he should be clamouring to let him out by now?

He lay back on the bunk, awaiting the customary breakfast of baguette and coffee, wondering whether he would be released.

He felt that his interview had gone smoothly enough although there were holes to be found had the police the gumption to follow up his story. He hoped they wouldn't. In fact he was surprised at their failure to drill down deeper during their questioning.

If he was indeed released, what should he do about Liliane? She had done the dirty on him, for reasons he didn't understand. There had been enough money and loot for them both, so why was she being so greedy? He knew that getting back together with her was out of the question and in any case, there would always be the possibility that she might incriminate him again in some way.

She would have to go, he thought, but not immediately. The police would, no doubt, be watching his every move.

Once again he heard the sound of the corridor door and footsteps approaching, but instead of breakfast, it was the two gendarmes again. They marched him back to the interview room where Daalmans and the lawyer were waiting for him. On the table were coffee and baguettes, butter and jam. The two Dutchmen were already tucking in and Daalmans motioned Danny to sit down and join them.

'OK, Danny,' Daalmans began, 'It seems that we have insufficient evidence to hold you in custody any longer, but we have not finished with you yet. We will retain your passport, and we ask that you remain at your current address for the moment until our investigations are completed.

Mademoiselle Duval will be moved to another location in Rouen, under French police protection and you are neither to meet her, nor seek to communicate with her under any circumstances.'

Danny listened intently, sipping his coffee. He was not happy with the proposal at all. For a start he could not continue at the flat. He had told the police that he was virtually destitute. They would wonder how he could afford the rent.

'I don't wanna go back to that flat,' he whined, 'Not without Lil, I wanna see if we can make one last go of it. An' besides, I can't afford the rent on me own.' He desperately needed to stay free in order to keep his options open.

'An' I need to contact her to sort out how we deal with our belongings, the rent for the flat and things like that.' Danny replied, 'I wanna see if we can patch up our relationship. I need to know why she has done this to me. I didn't deserve this.'

Daalmans searched Danny's face for the tell-tale signs of a lie but his eyes reflected anxiety not anger and his mouth, though set firm, was determined rather than mean.

'OK Danny, this is what I'll agree to: I'll allow you one phone call, then, if Duval agrees, you can have one private meeting with her, here at the police station, under supervision…'

Daalmans broke off and turned to Cuypers. 'Give Duval her mobile, but get it back when they've made the call.'

He then continued: 'After that Danny, unless there is reconciliation, you must agree to return to Amsterdam, where you will report to the police station at Elandsgracht at 6pm every evening until we determine otherwise. If you fail to show up, you will be re-arrested. You are not to see

Liliane Duval again, nor are you to seek to communicate with her in any way. Does that seem fair to you?'

The beaming smile on Danny's face belied his true feelings, but it was enough to convince Daalmans that Danny was, in all probability, the innocent party in this liaison.

'I have just two questions for you, Danny,' he said.

'Are you aware that Liliane Duval is pregnant with your child?'

'Yeah! She said that.'

'How did you feel about that?'

'Well I didn't really mind, but I would've preferred to have a kid a bit later after we'd had a bit of fun.'

'But you didn't think it would break up your relationship?'

'Nah! I'd quite like to be a Dad.'

'So you believed it to be true.'

'Yeah, of course.'

Daalmans did not elaborate. 'OK. Second question: Can you explain where you got the ring, which you gave Duval? She tells me that you were virtually penniless when she met you and yet you had such an expensive item on your person, apparently.'

'Yes, she is right there. I didn't have much in the way of cash, other than what I got for me motor bike, but the ring was left to me by me mum when she died. She told me dad to let me have it when I went out into the world to earn me keep. She said I could pawn it, apparently, but I couldn't do it. So I kept it on this chain.' Danny reached into his tee-shirt collar and pulled out a span of the gold chain. When I met Liliane I felt we were an item, so I thought I'd give it to her, not that we was engaged or nothin' but just 'cos I wanted to show her I was serious.'

It all sounded very plausible to Daalmans, it almost brought a tear to his eye as this fictional explanation dribbled from Danny's lips. But he could see no flaw in the story. In fact, by some fluke, after an inspection of the ring, the date inscribed in it roughly matched the likely period when it would have been in Danny's mother's possession, so it quite reasonably supported his testimony.

Daalmans placed Danny's mobile on the table and signalled for everyone but Danny to leave the room.

Danny picked up the phone and selected Liliane's number. He hesitated, determining what he was going to say, before pressing the green circle on the screen.

The phone rang for what seemed an age before she answered. She would know who was calling he thought, the phone would indicate that. It was obvious to Danny that she was deliberating on whether to speak to him or not.

'Hello Danny,' she said weakly, 'I'm sorry....'

'Too bloody right. What did you do that for? I thought we were goin' to have a life together?'

'Yes, well that was my plan too, until I saw all the money. I'm afraid I wanted it all for myself.'

'They're gonna let us have a meeting, here in the interview room, as long as you agree. Will you do it if I promise to act reasonable?'

'Will they be sitting in?'

'No, they'll be outside the door though.'

Liliane was silent for a while before answering. Danny waited impatiently. 'Say somethin' for Gods sake!' he shouted down the phone.

'It'll do no good Danny, I don't want to get back together – never really did. You swallowed a load of bullshit, which helped me get my hands on your stuff, and now its over.'

What are you tellin' me? Are you saying all that crap about livin' the life of luxury was all bullshit? And that when we were in bed it was all fake?'

'At last you understand Danny, bravo, you're not as thick as I thought you were.'

'I'll come after you Lil, you know that.'

'You're too late Danny. The vault's been cleared and I've got police protection now.'

Danny racked his brains trying to think of something that might persuade her to change her mind.

'You know Lil, if we don't have a meeting, they will let me out, and you'll be kept in until they've found a safe address for you. I'll be watchin' and I'll get you in the end if we don't do a deal.'

'What sort of deal did you have in mind?'

'You take the money and I'll take the stones, we could start talking about that.'

'But I've got both, why do I need a deal?'

' You ain't got both, I'll be waitin' for you at the bank.'

'I've told you Danny, I've already cleaned out the vault. The stuff is somewhere where you'll never find it. I showed the deposit box to Daalmans. He saw that all it contained was a tin box containing my dogs' ashes.'

'So that's what was in your drawer at Abbeville! A box of ashes of your fuckin' dogs wrapped up in newspaper? – You're a weirdo!'

'Maybe – but you've obviously been snooping.'

'Anyhow, if you was conning me about your life of luxury, how come you've got a box of dog ash? It's all bollocks and you know it.'

'No – It is ashes, but it's actually my dad. But it got you going didn't it?'

'Look Lil, cut the crap, I need to know it's really over, an' I need that meeting. I wanna look you in the eyes an' hear you say we're through.'

'OK Danny, but it won't be more that a couple of minutes.'

'I don't give a shit. I gotta have it.'

The phone went dead.

Daalmans looked up from the papers he was studying. 'Cuypers, did you get that tap on their phones organised,' he asked.

'It's in progress sir, the permissions have been granted, and the boys are just setting it up.'

'But we've missed the conversation they're having now?'

'Yes it seems so.'

'Bloody gendarmes! Well, make damn sure that we get their conversation if they decide to have the meeting.'

Daalmans was about to resume his study of the papers on his desk when one of the gendarmes came into the room.

'The two suspects have agreed to meet,' he announced, 'but it won't be particularly cordial. They are at each other's throats.'

'So why have they agreed to meet?' Daalmans asked, perplexed.

'We'll listen in and find out in due course I expect,' came the gendarmes reply.

Danny and Liliane were brought to the interview room and made to sit opposite one another. Each had one wrist hand-cuffed to the metal rails either side of the desk, a safety precaution to prevent any physical contact. Once the gendarmes were satisfied that they had taken all possible precautions, they left the room.

Danny looked across at Liliane and put his finger to his lips, gesturing to her to remain silent. He leaned towards her over the desk and motioned for her to do the same until their heads were as close together as their restraints would allow.

'The room may be bugged,' he whispered.

She nodded.

'What have you done with the money? Danny asked'

Liliane sat back and smiled at him but refused to reply.

'How could you do this to me, I mean us? We were getting along fine, and now everything has turned to shit.'

'She leaned forward again and whispered 'It was all part of my plan. I never expected you to have a lot of money and I was just going to take what ever you had, but when I saw it all, I knew I could find a way to take it all. All I had to do was gain your confidence, then I knew I had you all sewn up.'

Outside the room, Daalmans was waiting for them to start talking.

'What the hell is happening in there he bellowed at Cuypers. Are they just staring at each other? Have you got the volume right on the microphones?'

'They are apparently set as always,' Cuypers replied, but I'll ask them to turn the volume up a bit.'

It made no difference however; in fact it just increased the hum of the machine and would have interfered with any conversation had they heard it.

Danny was getting exasperated. It was now clear to him that Liliane meant what she was saying and if it was true that she had moved his loot somewhere else, then he needed to find out where. He no longer cared about Liliane; his sole aim now was to find the loot. Retribution would come much later, when things had cooled down. She would not get away with it.

'So there's no point in me pleading with you?' he whispered.

Again Liliane leaned back in her chair smirking, 'Absolutely not.' She replied.

'OK, meeting over then.' Danny tried to sound nonchalant. 'But you'll spend the rest of your life lookin' over your shoulder, an' I'll get you one day'.

'So be it.' She replied with a shrug of her shoulders.

Danny banged his fist several times on the table and after a short interval Cuypers came into the room.

'Get me outta here.' He shouted.

Chapter 41

'So how did the meeting go Jeff?' Jenny was keen to find out what had taken place.

'It only took about 5 minutes, he retorted, the rest of the time we were chatting about this and that. I couldn't leave too early, as it would have been bad manners. We just had a drink and talked football.'

'But you don't like football'

'I know – it was a bit embarrassing really.'

Jeff couldn't give Jenny any more information without divulging his two secrets, so he changed the subject quickly.

'OK, are you ready to go down to eat?'

The following morning the pair took the shuttle to the airport and boarded their flight to London Heathrow. Before they left Johannesburg, Jeff had e-mailed Sheila's brother Tom, suggesting that as he was in London over Christmas they should get together at some point for a festive drink, but when Tom insisted that Jeff should stay with them over the holiday he had to refuse the offer. It was a bit too soon to introduce his new girlfriend to the brother of his dead wife. 'I'll see if I can fit in a visit between Christmas and New Year,' Jeff had said, 'I'll ring you soon.'

Instead Jeff and Jenny decided upon a hotel in Kensington and spent most of their spare time shopping, taking in a couple of shows, museum visits and entertaining Jenny's auntie Sybil to an outrageously expensive Christmas Lunch at the Connaught in Mayfair.

As the date of Jeff's meeting with David Robinson drew nearer, he began to formulate answers to the most likely questions he believed would be put to him. This was going to be his one big chance and he didn't want to blow it.

To a large extent he was working in the dark. He didn't really know whether the meeting would be good news or bad, but he decided to plan for either event.

Having drawn up a whole series of likely questions, he then composed his answers, honed them into short, but succinct sentences and rehearsed them until he could fluently recall them all. He then put all further thoughts of the meeting aside and enjoyed the last few days with Jenny, knowing that he was as ready as he would ever be for the 3rd of January.

On January 2nd Karl rang Jeff's mobile. 'All sorted I hear. Had a good Christmas? I've got your commission – nice New Year present for you when you get back. Don't tell the slag though, she'll spend it all…'

Jeff didn't wait for him to finish talking. He rang off immediately and put the phone back in his shirt pocket. 'Cheeky bastard,' he swore.

'Who was that?' Jenny enquired from the bathroom.

'Your ex. being rude again I'm afraid.'

'God! I'm so glad I ditched him and moved out, it's really only now that I can see how objectionable he was. I think you slowly get conditioned to things over time and that's exactly what happened to me. I didn't realise quite how bad things were, especially as I didn't have anyone to judge him by until you came along, Jeff.'

He went into the bathroom where she was standing at the mirror, wrapped in a bath towel, applying her make-up. He put his arms around her and kissed the nape of her neck. 'Knight in shining armour eh?'

She turned towards him and let the towel drop, hugging him and pressing her naked body against him.

'Yes,' she replied, with a coy smile, 'and with a pretty fine cod-piece by the feel of it.'

'You're meeting is tomorrow so we'd better have an early night,' she added undoing his belt buckle, unzipping his trousers and searching out the source of his arousal.

January 23rd. The day of the meeting. Jeff woke from his stupor to the shrill beeping of the alarm on his mobile phone. It was 6.30 am. His meeting with David Robinson was scheduled for 9.30a.m. and he didn't have much time.

He quickly washed and shaved then dressed, donning a grey pin-striped suit brought specifically for his meeting. He left Jenny in bed sleeping peacefully and went down to the restaurant in search of a light breakfast.

He walked from the hotel to Hyde Park Corner and took the Piccadilly line to Holborn then continued walking from there to the Company's offices. It was a bright, sunny morning and he made his way briskly, using the time to hone up on his answers to the imaginary questions, which he thought David Robinson might put to him.

He was surprised how quickly he arrived at the building, and he suddenly felt a twinge of apprehension.

He entered the foyer and walked over to the desk to announce himself. The Security man scanned a list in front of him and picked up the phone. He asked Jeff to take a seat and wait for someone to escort him up to the twelfth floor.

A few minutes later the lift doors opened and Daphne Lawrence walked out and across to where Jeff was sitting. She was elegantly dressed as usual, wearing a navy blue pencil skirt, navy high heels and a pale blue long sleeved blouse, unbuttoned just enough to reveal a small triangle of her cleavage, with a discreet necklace of small lapis lazuli. Her hair was neatly tied back and coiled into a bun and Jeff immediately identified her perfume as *Worth - Je Reviens*, he thought.

She smiled sweetly. 'Hello again Mr Blythe, nice to see you, David is expecting you, please follow me.'

They went back into the lift and up to the calm atmosphere of the twelfth floor.

David Robinson's office was furnished with just four items of very substantial and expensive furniture: A large mahogany, leather topped knee-hole desk and chair, a wall of fitted shelving and cupboards in the same wood and two huge, heavily studded, distressed leather armchairs. He waved toward one of the latter inviting Jeff to sit down. He himself moved around the desk and sat down facing him.

'Well my boy, I really didn't think we'd be having this conversation a few weeks ago,' he said, twiddling his gold Parker pen in his fingers, 'of course I hoped we would, but things looked so bleak at the time that I felt that my bet was very safe indeed.'

He looked at Jeff, anticipating a response.

'Well sir, I think to some extent your making the bet galvanised me into doing whatever I could to pull it off, although I was lucky to be right about the minimal duration of the downturn.'

'Absolutely,' Robinson said, 'but you forecast it, and quite correctly. No one else did, not even my board members.'

Jeff decided to push his luck to the limit. 'So when do I move into my new office up here?' he asked, rather tongue in cheek.

'My goodness, you don't mince your words do you, old boy. I don't know what you thought of the meeting we had a couple of months ago, but it was not quite what was 'advertised', as you might say.'

'No – I guessed that at the time.' Jeff replied, trying to look sage.

'Oh really, and what did you think the intent of the meeting was actually?'

'Well, I don't believe that agreement over future policy can be reached in a discussion with 30 diverse people with different agendas, sitting round the table, especially when there is only one board member present. So I immediately started looking for another reason to invite so many delegates. My suspicions were confirmed when I noticed that you were scrutinising a number of people around the table, and forgive me for saying so, but given your age, I did wonder whether you were looking for a suitable successor.'

'My god! You *are* on the button, well, almost. I obviously made the right choice. However, you are a little premature in your presumption that you will be replacing me, nor will you reach the giddy heights of the twelfth floor without some further demonstration of your capability. And don't forget also, that to become a board member, you have to...let's say, 'fit in' and of course, whilst I may feel you are the right man for a job on the board, you would also have to convince another eight members. How do you feel about that?'

'Get me the interviews, I have no problem with that. I think I know enough about the business to make a contribution to its success.'

'Good! I suppose I shouldn't have expected any other answer – how long have you got?'

'Do you mean before I go back to South Africa?'

'Yes, can you fit in a few meetings with some of my compatriots?'

Jeff pretended to be busy. He took out his phone and scanned the screen. 'Well I'm free until about 5.30 today but will be in London until the 5th when I fly back, I do have a number of other engagements, but nothing that can't be rearranged, so yes, whatever you can fit in.'

'Good, then let's start straight away. However, I am not going to introduce you as anything other than our man in Johannesburg, I want the other board members to assess you and decide for themselves whether you are director material. If you get 4 of them on board, with my casting vote you will be in. It's down to you, old boy.'

It was at that point that Jeff felt he should give profound thanks to David Robinson for getting him thus far, but Robinson would have none of it.

'Nonsense, my boy,' he said, picking up the phone, 'you've done this on your own, you know, all I did was to spot the talent. Now lets start by meeting my CEO.'

Chapter 42

Lars Daalmans leaned back in his chair and looked up at Cuypers standing in front of his desk. 'How the Hell did we manage to cock that up? We've got absolutely nothing out of that meeting.'

Cuypers looked sheepish. 'It seems that they must have been whispering. Apparently some words were discernible, just, but the important stuff was missed, probably because they made sure they talked in quieter tones.'

'Well, that was our last chance. We'll just have to let him go,' Daalmans started, 'we've got nothing substantive to charge him with and I doubt we ever will unless we find his colleague Pete Radbourne. No, I think our best approach would be to release him but put a tail on him to see where he goes and what he does. We've got the tap on his mobile, so that will cover any communications he might make. We may even get something we can hang on him to keep him in custody. Let's wait and see.'

Daan Cuypers nodded in agreement. 'What about Liliane Duval?'

'We'll keep her here for a while, there are a few inconsistencies in her statement that need investigation that I would like to get sorted before we release her. Then, once Redmayne is back in Amsterdam, we'll let her go home. If Redmayne fails to report we'll put a watch on Duval.'

'What sort of inconsistencies?' Cuypers asked mystified.

'Well, I tend to accept Redmayne's story rather than Duval's, but I need more detail to be certain. She said that he told her he killed Radbourne and Wilson, but now she agrees that she might have interpreted it wrongly, then she said that her pregnancy had been a major factor causing the aggro. Yet we now know that she wasn't actually pregnant. She's lied about her money, she's been a bloody nuisance with all this. I'm of the opinion that we make her fully aware that we may charge her, for there's no doubt that any future testimony may be deemed unreliable. That will frighten her.'

'So do you want me to get Redmayne up here?' Cuypers asked.

'We might as well get it over with,' Daalmans replied resignedly.

Danny was brought up to the office and given the terms of his release. 'You are free to go,' Daalmans stated, but remember that if you breach our agreement with regard to Duval, you will be immediately sought and re-arrested. Is that clear?'

'No problem,' Danny replied, 'but I need my stuff.

'You can collect that from the front desk, then you are out of here. As you will be reporting to the station in Amsterdam each day, you may have your passport back, you might need it. But they are expecting your first report-in tomorrow evening. Don't miss it.'

Danny couldn't believe his luck. He had come into the police station convinced that he would not see freedom for some time, yet here he was two days later walking back into the sunshine.

In an effort to be polite, he thanked Daalmans and Cuypers. 'When I'm back in Amsterdam, I'll look you up.' He said jovially.

He walked out of the office and over to the main desk to collect his valuables. Then he remembered that he had dropped his keys in the flat. In the turmoil he had forgotten to pick them up. 'I need to get into our flat to get my kit,' he said to the officer, leaning toward the circular hole in the glass of the screen above the counter. I left the keys in the flat. Can I borrow Miss Duval's to get my stuff, then bring 'em back?'

The officer shrugged his shoulders and from the cabinet behind him he produced an identical manila envelope to his own and proceeded to tip out the contents onto the counter in front of him. 'Do you know which they are?' the officer asked in heavily accented English.

It was at that moment that Danny spotted the Left Luggage ticket. He immediately knew what it was. The SNCF logo for the French Railway imprinted on it, with a serial number and one side frayed where it had been torn from its accompanying portion. So that's where she hid the loot, he thought.

Tantalisingly, it was very close to the glass screen, but the slot beneath the glass was not sufficient to get his arm through.

Danny placed his hand under the glass and with one finger pointing at the keys, he strained to cover the ticket with the ball of his thumb. The policeman picked up the keys and slid them toward Danny's pointing finger. The action flipped the ticket a couple of inches nearer. Hooking his finger through the key ring, he withdrew his hand, the ticket sliding with it, stuck to his damp palm. Meanwhile the officer occupied himself by replacing the rest of Liliane's belongings in the manila envelope, oblivious of Danny's sleight of hand.

'Cheers mate,' Danny cooed as he strolled out into the street. He knew he would be followed, and he was aware that the cop in the tan leather jacket, standing outside, smoking a cigarette was his tail, but he pretended not to see him, and marched on up the street. He lit a cigarette and drew upon it, savouring the kick it gave him, accentuated by the taste of freedom. He was sauntering now, in that gait adopted by the teddy boys of an era much previous to his own. It reflected a laid back, 'I'm the main man', attitude, and that's exactly how he felt as he marched on up the street. But he was thinking hard. He had to get to the station to check that he was right about that Left Luggage ticket, but how could he do it with a tail on him?

It was a long walk back to the flat, yet Danny was enjoying every minute of it. He was over Liliane now. She had managed to turn his feeling for her from love to hatred in such a short period, he now found himself questioning his own judgement in getting together with her in the first place. Anyway, he thought, he was now well rid of her and more able to do his own thing – as long as he got his loot back.

He climbed the stairs to the flat, passing the marks of the scuffle with the police, which were still evident on the emulsioned walls, and reached the splendid but now seriously splintered door.

It seemed an age since it had all taken place, so much had happened since. He unlocked the door and after picking up his keys from the floor, went into the bedroom to retrieve his meagre wardrobe. He took Liliane's pull-along suitcase and tipped the few items remaining in it out onto the bed.

Placing his own clothes tidily in the bottom, he gauged whether there would be enough room for his loot. Satisfied, He looked around for the keys to Liliane's 2CV. They were nowhere to be seen. Then he recalled the desk officer's question at the police station: 'Do you know which they are?'

'Shit!' he called out loud. He hadn't realised the significance of the policeman's question; he was so intent on getting the luggage ticket. 'Never mind I'll walk.' He whispered to himself.

On the way back to the police station, he called in at a hardware store and had duplicate keys cut for the flat door. He was hatching a plan to throw Liliane off the scent. He hoped that by returning both *her* set of keys and his own originals, she might believe that he was going away for good, which would encourage her to drop her guard.

He hauled his suitcase back to the police station and handed back the two sets of keys. The policeman at the desk was the same guy Danny saw before and he was surprised to see Danny back so soon, yet he made no comment about the extra keys but just gathered them up and replaced them in the envelope from whence they came.

Danny didn't want to create any more suspicion at such an early stage in his escape so he was happy to let it pass unnoticed.

There was no sign of Liliane in the interview room and he assumed she was still incarcerated in her cell, fuming probably. He wondered if she knew that he had been let out. He hoped so – it would teach her a lesson. He gave a sloppy salute to the officer and bade him *au revoir.*

At the train station he walked over to the train timetables and map in the main concourse. He was looking for a train travelling Northeast. He saw that there was one via a small town called Montville. That was far enough for the moment, he thought. It was due to leave in just under twenty minute's time.

He strolled over to the ticket office and purchased a single, then walked back, through the barrier, to the beginning of the platform. The train was in, but he did not board it and instead, he sat on one of the slatted wooden benches on the concrete walkway. He watched surreptitiously as his tail walked over to the same ticket office and after a brief conversation, walked out again travelling in Danny's direction. The man stopped at the barrier, but did not pass through onto the platform. Instead, he turned his back, leaned on the barrier and lit another cigarette.

Danny wondered how he was going to carry out his little ruse. He had initially planned to get on the train, rush up through the carriages and get off at the top of the platform just at the moment the train departed. He was hoping the tail would board the train looking for him, but now that seemed unlikely. Perhaps the tail had second-guessed his plan?

Could he get off the train on the other side and jump down onto the track, he wondered? He didn't think so as there would be safety locks on all the doors on that side. Maybe I go to Montville after all, he thought.

The tail was pacing back and forth, puffing on his cigarette and glancing at the station clock. He was getting impatient.

As Danny sat there another train rumbled into the station on the adjoining platform behind him. Danny studied the overhead information board. It had come from Le Havre and was due to leave again ten minutes after his train to Montville. Suddenly Danny knew exactly what he was going to do.

He got up and walked quickly over to the carriage door of the Montville train and climbed the metal step into the corridor. Glancing back through the window he could see his tail alternately looking in his direction, then up towards the end of the platform.

Danny raced through the carriages to the front of the train.

The passengers from the Le Havre train had disembarked and were now in a thick mass marching down the platform dragging suitcases, pushing baby buggies and other paraphernalia, offering Danny complete cover from his tail's vision.

He jumped down onto the platform and ran across to the Le Havre train, ducked into a carriage and made his way back down towards the engine. Stopping two carriages short of the barrier, he peered through a window to see if his tail was still there. The policeman was standing right by the barrier, checking every face that went through the now open turnstile. Danny waited patiently until there were no more passengers leaving the train and the platform was clear. His tail was now on his mobile phone, gesticulating wildly, and shouting into the mouthpiece over the noise in the station.

The gong on the Tannoy interrupted Danny's thoughts and a gentle voice announced the imminent departure of the train to Montville. Somebody must have ordered the policeman to get on it because he suddenly ran through the open barrier waving his police badge and disappeared into the first available carriage. About half a minute later, the train slowly departed.

Danny waited a full five minutes before descending the Le Havre train, and after one last furtive look around he picked up his case and walked casually off the platform, looking for the Left Luggage Office.

The desk attendant peered at Danny through his thick pebble glasses, then gathered up the proffered ticket stub.

'C'etait quelle couleur, Monsieur…la valise?'

Danny was stumped. He realised what had been asked, but of course had no idea. He'd never seen it before.

'No speaky French mate.' He replied, with a shrug.

The clerk threw his arms up in resignation. 'Eh bien! Attendez, Monsieur,' he replied and started checking all the tickets on the rows of cases on the rack at the rear of the office. After several minutes he reached up to the top shelf of the rack and pulled out the large brown briefcase, balancing it carefully until it was safely down and transferred to the desk. He checked the two stubs against each other, one final time, then asked Danny for six Euro's.

Danny paid up and while waiting for his change he looked out of the office window across the concourse. He saw nothing to alarm him, so he bent down, opened his pull-along case and put the briefcase inside and zipped it up. After a curt 'Thanks mate' to the attendant he walked back across the concourse taking care to maintain his cover by mingling with a small party of travellers who were leaving the station.

He walked up the street to the taxi rank and took a ride to the main bus terminus. There, he bought a ticket to Amiens on the Flixbus service. While he waited for the bus to come in, he searched out the disabled toilet and went in to check the contents of Liliane's brief case. It was locked, but it was only a pair of combinations, which any self-respecting thief could easily deal with.

Danny made short work of the process and lifted the lid. He was so relieved to see his switch and the Glock pistol sitting upon the pile of money and gemstones. He took the switch and put it in his pocket then closed the lid and placed the briefcase back in the suitcase. 'So Lil, you think you've won eh?' he whispered with a smile, 'well you'll wish you'd never shopped me when you get out. You're gonna pay dear for that, but you can sweat for a while.'

Danny weighed up the chances of Lil moving on. He concluded that she would not leave Rouen for at least six months. She had just paid that much in rent and she would be keen to stay, as she liked the flat so much. Once she had been informed that he had started to report daily to the police in Amsterdam she would feel safe again.

It would be some time during that period that he planned to take his revenge.

Chapter 43

Jeff and Jenny arrived back in Johannesburg at 7.15 am, having slept most of the journey. It was already very warm, the mist over the city that had been visible from the air had all but evaporated in the warm sunshine. They took a taxi back to the house and after dumping their luggage, went straight out to the pool. Jeff was surprised to see Jesse there at the poolside, vacuuming the bottom.

'Hello Sahib Jeff, I knew you were coming back and I clean your pool.'

'That's good of you, Jesse, but does Karl know you are here?'

'Yes Sahib, he asked me to deliver a package to you. He say you know all about it. I wait for you so I saw the pool was a bit green and clean it while I wait.'

'That's very good of you Jesse, but where is the package?'

'In the pump house'

'Good, well, say nothing to Memsahib Jenny about this OK?' Jeff whispered

'I say nothing Sahib.' Jesse whispered back.

Jeff reached into his trouser pocket and took out his money clip. He peeled off two 100 Rand notes and gave them to Jesse. That's for cleaning the pool Jesse, if you want some extra work, you can come and clean it once a week. But do it in your free time, not in Karl's, OK?'

'Yes Sahib, thank you, I come again next week.'

'Good, now be off with you, Karl will be wondering where you've got to.'

Jesse scuttled off and Jeff walked down to the pump house. The 'package' was another manila envelope about an inch thick. He opened it and took out the sheaf of notes, fanning them through his fingers to roughly count them.

He guessed at about eighty thousand Rand, approximately five thousand pounds sterling.

If he had the figures right and his cut was indeed 10%, then the diamonds he had delivered in Amsterdam must have been worth about fifty thousand pounds. He wondered what Karl's take would have been – probably 50 or 60%. Not bad for a day's work and with no risk attached.

He put the money back in the envelope and stuffed it in his trouser pocket. Jenny was already in the pool, naked as usual, savouring the cool water. 'Come on in Jeff, it's gorgeous.'

Jeff waved to her, 'I'll be there in a second or two,' and he trotted into the house to hide his commission, before stripping off and diving into the now crystal clear water.

As he lazily swam back and forth in the pool he reflected on the outcome of his meeting with David Robinson and his board colleagues. He had been able to meet seven of the eight, the last one being absent due to an extended holiday in Australia with his daughter, her husband and - as Robinson referred to them - three unruly grandchildren.

Robinson had suggested that about three weeks would be required before minds would be made up and there was to be no contact during that period. 'Don't ring us, we'll ring you,' Robinson had joked.

Meanwhile, Jeff was requested to continue his role in Jo'burg as if nothing had happened, continuing to report back to Robinson on a weekly basis.

As he swam, he did a quick mental calculation of his earnings. Assuming his current salary at the Company of the equivalent of eighty thousand pounds a year, combined with a diamond run of say ten thousand a month, that makes about two hundred thousand a year and sixty percent of it tax free. He came to the conclusion that he would be stupid to give up the contraband. Unless, of course, he made Director...

Jenny interrupted his thoughts, swimming up behind him and putting her arms around his neck. 'There's something rather special about being naked in the water,' she said, 'It's great to be free of all the constraints of clothing, and the feel of the water on my skin makes me feel quite horny. Shall we…'

Jeff turned towards her and placed his hands on her waist, drawing her to him. 'I know what you're going to say, I seem to remember you asking me that before, I think we'll go into the house,' he replied, nibbling at her ears.

It was now mid afternoon and they had just completed a late poolside lunch. Jeff stood up and announced that he was going to pop over to Karl's house.

'What on earth do you want to see him for?' she asked.

For an instant Jeff had forgotten that Jenny was totally unaware of Karl's shadier profession. 'Well, I'm back at work tomorrow and there are one or two matters I have to discuss – find out what's been happening on the production side while I've been away etc. I won't get time to see him tomorrow as I will be inundated with other stuff and Robinson wants each weeks report on the first day of the following week. So it would help me a lot to get it sorted now.'

'Well I'm certainly not coming with you.'

'No, I didn't really expect you to. To tell you the truth, I also need to sort out him and us – I mean our relationship - you are still married, remember?'

'God! I'd forgotten that.' Jenny retorted sarcastically, 'I'd better get a divorce.'

'No rush,' he countered, ' I'll see you later.' He gathered up his car keys and went out to the Jeep.

Karl seemed surprised to see him so soon after his return. In fact he appeared to be a little wary, almost as if he expected Jeff to start another fight.

'What's the problem?' He asked, 'I didn't expect to see you for a few days. That's why I sent Jesse round with your cut. You're not unhappy with it are you?'

'No, not in the slightest. The reason for my visit is to tell you how I got on with Alan Redmayne.'

'Yeah, I heard. He phoned me straight after your meeting.'

'But did he tell you anything else about me?'

'Like what?'

'Like, I have a half-brother who works in the business?'

'You're kidding me.' Karl was dumbfounded.

'No – really, it's absolutely true. His name's Danny Redmayne.'

'What? Alan Redmayne's son?'

'Yes.'

'Well I'm buggered! It's a bloody small world. But you know he's no longer in the business don't you?'

'Well, Alan Redmayne reckoned he was on some sort of sabbatical, as you might say, in France, and he would probably come crawling back when his money runs out.'

Karl was weighing up in his mind how much he should tell Jeff without embarrassing him and putting him off his new found relation.

'Oh bugger it, I'll tell you the bad news,' he ventured.

'I know all about it,' Jeff replied, there have been one or two problems.'

'You could say that. You are aware that Danny is currently in a cell in a police station in Rouen in France, apparently helping them with their enquiries into a possible four murders?'

'Really? No, Redmayne never told me that. You'd better fill me in on the whole story.'

Karl relayed what he knew to Jeff, based on the information that Alan Redmayne had given him. He also explained the tie up between Redmayne and Wilson and that although Redmayne kept his own business separate from Wilson's the police had interviewed him, only because he was Danny's step father, not because they knew they worked together. 'You'd better remember that, Jeff, there's no tie up between them as far as the law is concerned.'

'Redmayne told me about the Danny situation and that Wilson had been murdered. He also said Danny's mate Pete Radbourne was missing presumed dead, but who are the other two?'

Karl went through the full details, as best he could.

'So you see, the conundrum is: Did Danny do it all, or was it Pete, or could it have been the guy in UK that Pete went to duff up? No one knows.'

'So was Danny in hiding when he went to France?'

'No, apparently not. After he got the sack, he met some backpacking French bird in Holland and went back to her place, so Redmayne told me. Now he's with someone else. Bit of a randy bugger by the sound of it.'

'Anyway, while you're here I might as well tell you, I'm doing one more big run, then packing it in and going to Belgium. I'm leaving The Oil Company and selling the house to help finance an early retirement.'

'But I thought you were leaving the house for Jenny?'

'That was before she started shagging around. I'm not giving her anything now, dirty little tart. I don't blame you, you're a man, it's second nature to take whatever is on offer, and boy did she offer it. She was like that with all men, you know, prick teasing all the time, but luckily none of them came to stay. It's my fault too, I couldn't satisfy her, but she didn't really try to help me either. So she can piss up a rope as far as I'm concerned.'

Jeff sensed that it would be best to leave that particular conversation there. Any further discussion and Karl was likely to become difficult.

'Ok, so where does that leave me – with the business I mean?'

'It's all yours, mate.'

'But I know nothing of your dealings, nor your contacts or anything.'

'Don't worry about that, it'll all come good soon. They won't let me go without sorting out my replacement. But for now, we carry on as we are. I'll get you on board when the time is right.'

Jeff was dubious about the whole thing. He felt that Karl might be spinning him a yarn. Yes, he may be moving on, but maybe he was going to get back at Jeff by shutting him out of the business.

He could do nothing about it now, but he would have to keep the pressure on Karl somehow. Time to hatch a plan, he thought.

Chapter 44

Back at the police station, Daan Cuypers was busy gathering together all the paperwork in preparation for their departure back to Amsterdam. Lars Daalmans was in the middle of a heated conversation on the telephone. Danny's tail, Lacroix, was apparently explaining that somehow he had followed the suspect onto a train to Montville, but between Rouen and Montville, the suspect had disappeared into thin air.

'For Christ's sake, Lacroix, you were given a simple enough task, how could you have messed that up. Are you sure he took the train?'

'Yes I'm certain, Inspecteur, I followed him on, as you specifically commanded, if you remember.'

'And are you sure he didn't leave the train before it departed?'

'Of course sir, I only got on as it was about to leave, and there was no sign of him at that point.'

'Then he must have either got off while the train was moving, or at Montville, where you now are. Are you sure he hasn't evaded you at the station?'

'I'm certain, sir.'

'Then he must still be on the train.'

'I've checked through the carriages twice sir, he's definitely not on it.'

'But why would he get off at Montville? He's supposed to be on his way to Amsterdam. He would do the whole train journey to wherever it ends up.'

'Lille, I think,' said Lacroix..

'Then check again, you idiot!' Daalmans shouted.

'It's too late sir, the train has left now and I'm on the platform here at Montville. I have checked everyone who got off and I am certain that Redmayne was not amongst them.'

‘OK, so you’ve lost him. You’d better get back here, and we’ll have to see if he reports in later at the station at Elandsgracht in Amsterdam. But as far as you are concerned, my report to your superiors won’t make good reading, I can tell you.’

‘Sorry about that sir, but I did my best.’

‘Yes Lacroix, it’s just a shame it wasn’t good enough.’ Daalmans replied dryly.

Daalmans turned to Cuypers, his eyes dark with anger. ‘You’d better get Duval sent up here, ‘he barked. We must get her sorted and out of here as soon as possible, preferably before we leave.’

Cuypers left the room and Daalmans reached for the telephone.

He dialled his office in Elandsgracht. ‘Daalmans here, who’s that?’ he asked curtly as the call was answered.

‘Jesse Hoedemaker, sir’ came the reply.

‘Oh! OK Hoedemaker, Are you the duty officer this week?’

‘Yes sir.’

‘I want you to make sure that you immediately contact me here at the Police headquarter in Rouen or on my mobile, the moment that a Danny Redmayne reports in. It’s likely to be tomorrow around 6 p.m. He has been instructed to report every day at that time until further notice. Is that clear?’

‘Certainly Inspecteur, I shall ensure you are notified.’

‘Good. We shall be returning probably the day after tomorrow, late evening. We’ll see you the following morning.’

Daalmans hung up the phone without waiting for a reply.

He rose from the chair and paced the room a couple of times, deep in thought. There was just the small problem of not knowing quite when it would be safe to release Duval. He was determined that they were to return to Amsterdam very soon, but could he be sure that Redmayne would be back in Amsterdam by that time? Further, could he trust the French police not to release her until the news came through that Danny had actually arrived in Amsterdam?

He dreaded the thought of missing his weekend's fishing trip, he'd been looking forward to it for many weeks now, but he felt it his duty to be still here in Rouen until Duval was safe. He was still contemplating the problem when Cuypers entered the room with Liliane Duval.

'Ah! Mademoiselle Duval, I have just called you up here to fill you in on the current situation. We no longer wish to detain you further, and we shall be shortly arranging your release and leaving ourselves for Amsterdam. You will be free to return to your flat, where you will be…'

'Where's Danny Redmayne?' Liliane interrupted wide-eyed and frightened, 'I'm not leaving here unless he's behind bars. As I said before, he'll kill me.'

'Please calm yourself, Mademoiselle and let me finish. Redmayne has already been released and is returning to Amsterdam as we speak. We are following his every move. We have taken some security measures to ensure your safety, in that he has to report to our police station in Amsterdam each evening at six o'clock. Failure to do this will result in his re-arrest and you will then receive police protection until we apprehend him.

Liliane stared at Daalmans in disbelief. She couldn't understand how her plan had gone so awry. How had Danny managed to convince these people of his innocence? Could she rely on the police solution? To her it seemed a huge risk.

Sensing her disquiet, Daalmans attempted to allay her fears. 'However, Mademoiselle, we don't anticipate your release until we have word that Redmayne has arrived safely in Holland and has made his first visit to the station, so you can rest assured that you will be safe. You must also realise that there is nothing substantial that we can charge Mr. Redmayne with without evidence that he is actually involved and I have to say that your inability to give a truthful account has contributed to this outcome. However, that does not mean that we have given up. We will be investigating further, until we get to the bottom of this mystery.'

Liliane gave out a long sigh, still unhappy about her situation. However, she realised thet there was little she could do. She thought about the loot hidden in the left luggage office. Was it worth giving that up in exchange for her safety? Even if she did declare it to Daalmans, would it be enough to secure Danny's arrest? If not, she might be in even greater danger. On the other hand, her control of the loot might keep Danny from attempting to hurt her.

'Do you know when I might be released?' She asked.

'At a guess, probably the day after tomorrow,' Daalmans replied, and then he had an afterthought: 'unless you would prefer to go immediately with police protection.'

Liliane considered the two options. Somehow she felt she might have overestimated her plight and the thought of being back in her flat appealed to her. Danny was miles away, and even if he wasn't, she could always lock herself in, and she would have the police in attendance. She recalled Pierre Mansard, the estate agent remarking on how impenetrable that particular flat was. It gave her a degree of comfort.

'OK,' she said defiantly, 'I'll go now if you'll escort me home.'

Daalmans smiled serenely. It looked as if his fishing trip was still on. 'Well said, Mademoiselle, you are a brave lady, and we shall not let you down. Now why don't you gather your things together and I'll arrange for a car to take you home.'

Liliane stood up and walked toward the door. Cuypers held out his hand as if to say goodbye, but she ignored it, choosing to leave the room without a word.

Daalmans glanced across to Cuypers and rubbed his hands together. 'Come on,' he said, 'we get to leave early,' a big grin on his face.

Liliane was taken over to the front desk and given her bag and the envelope of her belongings. She took a quick peep inside to check its contents were indeed her own, but then folded the envelope and stuffed it in the handbag, signed the ledger and sat by the entrance door, waiting for the car.

She was pondering over how she might get down to the railway station to collect her briefcase without arousing suspicion. Maybe it would be sensible to just lie low for a while until word came back from Amsterdam, and the police protection was lifted. As she sat there waiting, her earlier anxiety seemed little by little, to fade away. Perhaps things wouldn't be so bad after all, she mused.

One of the gendarmes arrived at the door and asked her to accompany him to the waiting car in the street. As she walked towards it she found herself looking around furtively, as if expecting to see Danny burst out from one of the bushes lining the pathway.

Once inside the car she felt safe again and relaxed a little. She whiled away the journey by sorting her possessions into the compartments of her bag. She noticed the two sets of keys. Danny must have left them for her, she thought. Maybe he had no intention of coming back? No, she thought, that would be ridiculous. He was bound to come looking for her, if only to get his hands on the loot. It didn't make sense.

Then, the penny dropped. Where was the left luggage ticket? She rummaged around in her bag, searching the various pockets within it. She tried to remember where she had put it when she deposited the briefcase. She recalled placing it in one of the inner lining pockets and zipping it up, but it was not there now. Nor had she come across it when she was emptying the envelope. In a panic, she looked around the back of the car – on the seat, under the front seats, on the carpet, everywhere, but to no avail. She re-checked the envelope, then her handbag but there was no sign of the ticket.

'Merde!' she exclaimed, loudly enough to cause the driver to stare at her through the rear view mirror.

'Is there a problem Mademoiselle?' He asked.

'I'm sorry,' she replied, 'but I seem to have lost something, but it is not important, I'm sure it must be in my flat.'

She knew it was unlikely to be there but she didn't want to have to explain what it was she had lost, especially to a policeman.

She felt sick. Had Danny managed to get his hands on the ticket? If so, when? He must have found it before they were arrested.

But if that were true, why did he not believe she had already moved the loot from the bank? No, he must have somehow got hold of it at the police station.

Liliane was furious with herself for not having properly hidden the ticket. Her plans were now in total disarray. However, she realised that there was just a chance that she may never see Danny again. She had both sets of keys and he had the loot. There would be no point in his coming back.

She didn't even have the €2,000 she had collected from the bank. She had stupidly given it to Danny. Yet despite her newfound poverty, she felt - perhaps mistakenly - more at ease.

Back at the flat, she felt drained and tired after her ordeal in police custody and more so by the failure of her little ruse. She had managed to outwit Danny right from the start, yet he'd had the last laugh. She hated him all the more for that.

It was while she was reflecting on how things could have been, that she realised there was a way to make him pay for his deception. She could give the Amsterdam police a full inventory of Danny's booty, after all, she had seen the whole stash. If the police raided his place and found it all, he would be locked away for years and she would be free. Not rich, but free and safe at least.

She quickly phoned the police station and asked for Lars Daalmans. 'I'm sorry, Mamselle, the duty officer replied, 'but both Lars Daalmans and Daan Cuypers have returned to Amsterdam. You should be able to contact them at their station on Monday morning – can I help at all?'

Liliane hesitated, 'No, I think I will wait for Daalmans,' she confirmed, and rang off.

Chapter 45

Jeff was convinced that Karl was going to pull the plug on his involvement. He felt that his view could be reinforced by the fact that there had been no animosity shown him following the fight at his house and that perhaps Karl might be saving up all his ire and spite for a showdown when he left Jo'burg. The best way he could do that was to cut him out of the business.

Had the shoe been on the other foot, Jeff would never have allowed Karl the time of day. But there was another view to consider. Karl was a man's man, who thought he had put up with enough after years of Jenny's un-wifely behaviour. So he blamed Jeff for nothing and her for everything.

Could that be it? Jeff wondered. He would have to bide his time and wait for events to unfold. However he had developed a plan to put pressure on Karl should he threaten Jeff's involvement. He knew that Karl would be relying on him to carry out the next run so all he needed to do was to frustrate him by stalling over the delivery, so putting the pressure on Karl, who was keen to accelerate his move to Belgium. Clearly the next run was to be a big one as it was probably going to fund Karl's retirement.

Jeff's plan, though in it's infancy, involved a firm agreement being made before he undertook the run, but if none was forthcoming, he would agree to carry out the drop in order to get his hands on the merchandise, then hold Karl to ransom. It was somewhat naïve and needed some refinement, but it was a start.

Meanwhile, however, he had a report to prepare for David Robinson. He was motivated to crack on with it because it gave him an excuse to speak with Robinson and, as subtly as possible, find out whether there was any news of his possible move to the 12th floor. It had been two weeks since they had last spoken and he didn't want Robinson to think that he wasn't interested.

He swept up the paperwork on his desk and shuffled it into a neat pile then began carefully extracting the relevant information for his report.

Brent Crude he noticed, was at around $58 a barrel and Karoo was operating well in excess of the original shale gas forecasts. OPEC was in tentative agreement over a cut in production, in the hope of raising the price still further. All these factors, Jeff felt, would increase his chances of a positive outcome with the Company board.

He completed his report, converted it to a .pdf file and emailed it to David Robinson. He decided he would wait a couple of hours before contacting him to check he'd received it.

He was itching to know the result of his interviews with the members of the board and their continuing delay in response increased his impatience and at the same time reduced his optimism.

Maybe he had not gone down that well with them. After all, different people see others in different ways. Robinson may like him, but did the other board members respect his choice? Perhaps in their eyes Jeff was not as sharp as he thought he was.

It was while he was contemplating these points that Mandy, the switchboard operator rang him. 'Jeff? I have a message from Daphne Lawrence in London. Would you ring David Robinson at 8.00 pm London time please.'

Jeff's heart leapt. He looked at his watch. It was 4.15 p.m. South Africa was 2 hours ahead of GMT so the call would have to be made at 10 pm It must be positive, he thought, otherwise Robinson would not bother to phone out of hours. Jeff could think of nothing other than the call, so he cleared the papers on his desk and drove home to tell Jenny the good news. Was he being premature? He wondered.

Chapter 46

Danny arrived back in Amsterdam in the late afternoon on the day after his release. He had spent some of the time on his journey putting together a plan for dealing with Liliane. Despite being many miles from her and having retrieved his loot, he still felt sore over the way she had treated him and his desire for revenge had not diminished.

It was important, he thought, to ensure that from the police viewpoint he was behaving impeccably. He decided that he would be punctual with his reporting to the station, and in order to help his credibility, he would even spend a few minutes with them each day in conversation, trying to be friendly and hopefully demonstrating that he was a reformed character.

He wondered how he could get to Liliane and back in the twenty-four hours time-span between two of his reporting times. It would be a tall order, particularly if there were any unforeseen delay during the execution of his proposed retribution. What form of transport would be anonymous enough? What if someone recognised him on the journey? Or even in Rouen?

He hadn't yet planned how Liliane was to meet her demise, but he was so bitter about her that his only proposal thus far, was to engineer her death. He had no qualms about doing it, not now, not after having killed four others, it had got easier to deal with each time. He now had no conscience. He thought about throwing her off the balcony of her flat, but would she scream? And would he get down the stairs and out of the building in time before someone heard the commotion and spotted him? It was unlikely. He had to find some way to create a delay that gave him enough time to get away unobserved. He reflected on the way he had dealt with the girl, Cheryl. That had been a good one, he thought. Nobody saw him go in or out, nor would they have recognised him in his bike helmet anyway. Could he do it the same way again?

All these thoughts were milling around in his head as he walked back to his flat.

It was several weeks since he'd been there and he expected it would be cold and uninviting. However the first thing he noticed when he opened the door was the stench, which emanated from a curdled bottle of milk he'd left on the kitchen table.

Clearing away the blackened bottle and its contents he then lifted Liliane's pull-along suitcase onto the table. He took one more look at his stash in the briefcase, then took it to the bedroom. He pushed the bed back about a metre and lifted the two loose floorboards. He placed the briefcase next to his suitcase of armaments. Having replaced the boards, he moved the bed back, undressed and took a quick shower, cold because he'd not turned on the heater, and got himself ready for his trip to the police station at Elandsgracht.

At bang on 6pm he walked into the station and up to the desk

'I've come to report in,' Danny began, not really knowing whether the guy behind the desk would understand what it was all about, 'the name's Danny Redmayne.'

'Ah, yes, Mr Redmayne, Inspecteur Daalmans told me to expect you. I am Hoofdagent Jesse Hoedemaker, duty officer this week, you will see quite a bit of me,' he said with a grin, sliding a ledger across to Danny. 'Passport please.'

'Why the passport?'

'Well, I have to check that you are who you say you are, and not some stooge standing in for the real Danny Redmayne.'

Hoedemaker studied the passport then looked at Danny. 'You don't look much like the photo,' he chuckled, 'but I can see that it is you. Had a 70's makeover have you?'

'Yeah! That's women for you.' Danny replied with a wink.

He looked down at the ledger and took the proffered pen and wrote his name, the time and date in the columns of the page, then handed the ledger back to Hoedemaker who also signed the ledger.

'That's it' he said, sliding his passport back across the desk top to Danny, 'you can go now.'

'Thanks,' Danny replied, a note of relief in his voice. 'I didn't think it would be that quick.'

'Well, we're only really interested in you showing up, so if you do, then it's quick. If you don't then your life won't be worth living. See you tomorrow, same time, and for the next week or so, don't forget your passport, it may not always be me on duty.'

Danny smiled, 'OK, see you tomorrow,' he agreed and with a wave he walked out into the dusk.

Hoedemaker picked up the phone and rang Daalmans' mobile.

'Inspecteur Daalmans? Jesse Hoedemaker sir. Just to say that your man Danny Redmayne has reported in. You asked me to let you know sir. He seems a friendly, reasonable kind of guy.'

'Good. Thank you Hoedemaker. You're sure it was him?'

'Yes sir, I checked against his passport. It's him all right.'

'OK, that's great, we can all go home now with a clear conscience.'

Walking back to his flat, Danny took out his mobile. He sent a text to his Father Alan Redmayne, letting him know he was back in Amsterdam.

It was less than five minutes later that his phone pinged and Redmayne's reply came through. 'Call round tonight about eight, for a drink and a chat.'

Danny was grateful for the invitation. He had effectively been alone ever since the bust-up with Liliane, and a bit of family hospitality appealed to him. He had always liked his father. He would do all the things young lads liked, like joining in with them in the football games in the park, taking him down to the pub with his mates or going down the local curry house for a meal on a Saturday night. On the way home, he remembered them whistling at the street walkers, shouting things like 'Hello darlin' fancy a freebie tonight?' All good, bawdy fun, he reflected.

He glanced at his watch. It was just before seven. He hadn't really eaten anything since the day before and he was starving so he went straight round to the local café. The busty, blond waitress recognised him immediately.

'Hi Danny, we haven't seen you in here for a while,' she cooed.

'Nah, I've been away in France for me hols.' He replied.

He ordered a chicken and chips and a glass of ginger beer, then paused and looked up at her.

'I don't suppose you fancy a drink after work, do you Penny?'

'Sorry, Danny, but my girlfriend is back from Denmark today and I'm meeting up with her in town. We're going clubbing.'

'Shame,' he replied, 'maybe another time, eh?'

She smiled but didn't reply and went off to give his order to the kitchen. He lit a cigarette and puffed his way through it, waiting for his food. It was at that point, as his food arrived, that he became aware of a man in a black overcoat on the opposite side of the counter. He seemed to be taking the odd furtive glance in Danny's direction, then turning his attention to his book. There was a single cup of coffee on the table in front of him, which he had made no attempt to drink. Danny immediately recognised the behaviour. The guy was quite obviously watching him, maybe following him wherever he went. Was it the police? Or could it be someone from Wilson's business? Maybe the media? He didn't know. But he knew it would be best to lose him before he got to his father's place.

He ate quickly, washing down each mouthful with a swig from his glass of ginger beer. Having eaten enough, he then rose from the table and walked over to the bar. Catching the eye of the waitress, he quietly paid his bill, then walked over to the toilets through a door at the rear of the room. The corridor split three ways, one each to the ladies and gents, and the third to an office attached to the kitchen. He chose the latter and walked through the office and the steamy wash-up area to the rear door and the yard beyond. Passing round the waste bins at the rear he rejoined the side street and quickly strode down the road in the direction of Alan Redmayne's place. After a few minutes walk, he stopped in the shadow of a doorway, and made certain he wasn't followed, before continuing his journey.

At Alan Redmayne's house he ignored the front door and instead walked through the narrow alley between the houses and jumped over the fence at the rear. He banged on the back door.

He heard the key turn in the lock and Redmayne's face appeared as the door opened a crack, the safety chain still in place.

'Danny boy! You're early, come in, come in,' Redmayne exclaimed, releasing the chain and opening the door wide. 'Didn't expect you to come through the back.'

'Hi Dad, I think I was being followed. I had to get rid of him before comin' over, but thought it best not to advertise me comin' to see you.'

'Good point lad, we'll go in the snug. Fancy a beer?'

Danny gave a thumbs up, and went into the snug. Alan Redmayne followed shortly after with two bottles of *Carlsberg.*

'So how did things go in France,' Alan Redmayne began, 'obviously not too bad 'cos they released you?'

'Yeah, well they had nothin' on me, in fact if it hadn't been for that little tart I was with I wouldn't have been arrested, would I. She saw the news on the TV an' put two an' two together an' made five, silly bitch.'

'So are you back for good, lad?' Redmayne asked.

'I guess so, but I ain't got no job to do.'

'Well, we can soon fix that, Danny, but first I wanna tell you about a new guy we've got with us in Johannesburg. You might wonder why I ain't told you about this before, but I thought it best at the time.'

'What the heck are you on about?'

'Your brother – or should I say half-brother.'

There was a long silence before a frowning Danny spoke again.

'I've got a brother…How come?'

'Well, it's a long story, and not one you might like, but a long time ago, before you were born, I had an affair with the wife of a friend of mine, a chap called William Blythe. It didn't last long, 'cos he found out about it an' put a stop to it. But you were the result. William Blythe already had a son by his wife – so that son was, in effect, your half-brother.

The reason you don't know about any of this is because I broke off all contact with William and his wife, and we brought you up as if you was our own. Of course you never knew your real mum, but you always knew I was your dad, but now you know why.'

Danny gave a low whistle. 'Bloody Hell. After all this time. Where is he?'

'He's in South Africa, Johannesburg as I said. The reason I'm telling you now is because if you come back into the business, you'll be meeting him an' he more or less insisted that he meet you.'

Danny's mind was racing. It shouldn't have been so, but his immediate thought was that he could now see a way of offloading all his gemstones. He hadn't quite worked it out, but the seeds of an idea were forming in his head.

'Great! I'd like to meet him too. How old is he?'

'Pretty similar age, maybe a couple of years older, maybe a little less. I can't exactly remember.'

'Have you got a photo?'

'No, 'fraid not. But you can e-mail him and ask for one.'

Danny took a big swig of his beer and lit a cigarette.

'Yeah! I'll do that. I'd like to meet him too, sometime.'

'You can, and soon. He will be coming over to Amsterdam shortly on a run.'

'So what's been happening here with the investigation and all that? Since I've been away, I haven't seen much news that didn't need translatin'.'

'To be honest Danny, not a lot. The inquiry seems to be dying a bit. They ain't got very far with it and certainly ain't made no arrests, although they say they've got some evidence which most likely points to Pete.'

'What? Pete's the murderer?'

'Not quite, but possibly. They reckon they tested the girl for DNA an' they think she might have been raped and then killed. The swabs they took, or whatever, matched DNA taken from various clothes in the flat belonging to Pete.'

'Yeah, the Inspector told me about that girl – Cheryl somebody, I think.'

'Yeah, well he's not turned up anywhere, but because of the evidence they now think that he's scarpered and there's a Europe–wide search for him. The Press were doin' their usual guesswork an' reporting that there's a likelihood he murdered Wilson too. They said the police were following up that theory. But the heat seems to be off. There's very little in the media about it now. It's all about the elections in England and who's gonna be the next Prime Minister or the war in the middle-east.'

'So what's happening with the business?'

'Well the good news is that the cops don't know that I was tied up with Wilson, so we are carrying on. But the bad news is that they've found a connection between Wilson and the fence in London – the one that was murdered. So they know they was dealing together. We're just hopin' that there's nothing over there in his shop that'll give the game away.'

'Well, that all sounds a bit better than I expected,' Danny said, 'I was a bit worried for you when I was over in France, but maybe things is alright.'

Danny stood up, emptied his beer bottle and made as if to go.

'Not stayin' for a bite to eat, Danny boy?' His Father asked, hoping he'd not leave quite so soon.

'No, sorry Dad, but I've got a few things to sort out an' I haven't had much sleep in jail, so I just wanna get back to me flat and crash. I'll see you tomorrow sometime – give you a bell.'

He walked to the door and Redmayne showed him out.

'Take it easy, Danny, an' don't get too upset about all this. I'll give you a bell when I've got summat for you.'

Danny walked off down the path, and without turning back, gave his father a wave, then disappeared into the night.

Chapter 47

'Now listen, my boy' Robinson began, 'we've had an awful lot of discussion…the board, I mean. The decision wasn't unanimous – in fact I didn't even get a majority verdict, at least, not for you to make Director. But there is some good news.'

He paused, waiting for a reaction from Jeff.

'Are you still there?' He asked, fearing he had rung off.

'Yes I'm here,' came Jeff's delayed reply, 'although I'm a little disappointed.'

'No need to be, my boy. They liked you. It's just that they feel they need to see a little more of your abilities before making any decision – prove yourself, you know.'

'So what's the good news then?'

'You get to move to the Strand, but not the twelfth floor yet. But I can assure you it will happen, eventually. Can you live with that?'

'Oh, I think I can. What do I get to do? What will be my rôle?'

Robinson suddenly sounded very serious. 'We'd like you to head up our Maintenance, Reliability and Turnarounds people. John Brenner, who ran the show previously has had to take early retirement due to illness, so there is a vacancy at senior management level. You would be responsible for co-ordinating procedures, developing global strategy and systems for the future etc. It would be across the whole company. You would be answerable to the board. How would you fancy that?'

'It sounds a very responsible position,' Jeff replied, astounded, 'and one I would be very keen to take on. Although you will understand that I am a little overawed at the magnitude of the rôle.'

'Nonsense my boy, it's just the sort of thing you would be good at, and I can assure you that if you make a good fist of it, it will be the fastest route for you to reach the twelfth floor.'

'When would I start?'

'Soonest. I want you to come over here ASAP and have a thorough grounding of the co-ordinating department - talk to all the key players and that sort of thing. Get fully acquainted with the job. Then we'll make the announcement. Let's say you'll be in position and running the show by the 1st of March. Then in full swing for the new financial year.'

'What do I tell the guys at Jo'burg?'

'Nothing yet. They'll find out when we make the announcement. In the meantime, carry on with what you are doing and a request will come through for you to come over to London for a meeting. I'll get Daphne to set it all up for you. Look forward to having you on board. I've a call on the other line, we'll speak again soon.'

And Robinson rang off.

Jeff fell back against the cushions of the sofa; the adrenaline completely drained from him and replaced with exhaustion. He was suddenly aware that he would have his work cut out if he were to achieve his goal. His previous, somewhat naiive assumption that he would walk into a directorship had been shot away. Could he do it? He wondered.

Chapter 48

As far as he was concerned, Danny Redmayne's plan was coming together nicely. He had decided that the only way he could get down to Rouen and back in time and with sufficient anonymity was to buy himself a cheap second hand car. He would disconnect the speedometer, do the job, re-connect it on his return, then return it to the garage saying that it didn't suit him, and could he swap it for something else? He thought he had worked out a means by which he could dispose of Liliane without raising suspicion of foul play:

Once he was back over the French border, a long way from Rouen, he planned to buy a tin of black paint, some white spirit, a paintbrush and a packet of latex gloves, preferably from a large *'Bricolage'* supermarket, where his purchase would be reasonably anonymous. In case the place had cameras, he would buy himself a pair of cheap reading glasses and a cap to help conceal his identity. He would then set up a scene, where Liliane, intent on re-painting the rusting balustrade around her verandah, would accidentally fall the four storeys to the garden below, preferably onto the stone flowerpots immediately below the balcony to inflict maximum damage. To ensure she would comply with this proposal, he would knock her senseless, place a chair next to the railing, apply some spilt paint to the railings, both her clothes and her painting hand, then toss the brush over the railing after her. The paint tin would be upset all over the edge of the verandah. Hopefully the police would come to the conclusion that while painting the outer side of the railing, Liliane stood or kneeled on the chair, leaned over and lost her balance, falling to the ground.

Danny would set it all up such that, after the final act of pushing her over the balcony railing, he would rush to the door, lock it with his set of spare keys, and quietly go down to his car in the street. Anyone observing the fall would no doubt go to the garden, thus leaving the staircase to the courtyard free and Danny with an uneventful escape. He would then return speedily to Amsterdam, in time for his 6 p.m. report at Elandsgracht.

Danny worked through the plan several times before accepting that there seemed no serious flaw in it. However there were two aspects which needed special consideration: the first, which had haunted him from the beginning, was how he would get back down to his car without being spotted, or worse, recognised? He realised that there had to be an element of drama in whatever plan he devised, so he would just go with the flow and take potluck. If he were reasonably well disguised, there would be a fair chance of not being connected, were he to be seen.

The second was whether he could complete the 1100 kilometre round trip in one 24-hour period. It would not leave him much time to carry out the purchases, the deed itself and the clean up afterwards. If he averaged 70 kilometres an hour, and allowing a couple of hours for possible delays, he would only have about 5 hours. It was going to be tight.

He didn't know whether Liliane would have found herself a job, so he decided that the deed would have to be carried out early on Saturday morning. She would be more likely to be at home then.

Taking an optimistic view, he reckoned it would work, so he decided to sleep on it before touring the garages for a car in the morning. He got a beer from the fridge, sank into his battered leather armchair and turned on the television for the news, just in case there were any further developments regarding his earlier killings.

The local news had a short article concerning two suspects, a man and a women, who had been released without charge in France, following enquiries in connection with the murders of a certain George Wilson and a young woman, Cheryl Carter in Amsterdam.

Danny swung his fist in the air and gave a loud ‘Yeah!’ for he felt that he was now truly free. He’d managed to beat them all. He was the best and no one could touch him now.

He took out his phone and looked up a couple of second hand car dealers he knew in the city. He needed something reliable, cheap and not too conspicuous – perhaps a Ford or a Citroen.

He decided on a Citroen C3, mainly because he was going to travel to France and he felt it would be the most inconspicuous of all. He found one almost immediately. Four years old with 35,000 kilometres on the clock for €2,300. ‘Just the job,’ he said to himself as he noted down the details.

The following morning he made arrangements to call round to the garage for a test drive, get the necessary paperwork sorted and some insurance in place ready for an early departure for Rouen immediately after clocking in at the police station that evening.

At the garage, Anders Jansen, the boss and senior salesman walked Danny around the car, enthusing over the various advantages of that particular model. The petrol consumption was the lowest in its class, the suspension was the smoothest and the accommodation was suitably generous to allow four to travel in comfort, etc., none of which Danny was the least bit interested in.

‘My problem,’ said Danny, ‘is that I have a severe case of spinal compression, so a very high degree of comfort, with as little jarring over bumps and potholes is very important.’ He was enjoying making up his little charade. ‘So, if I buy this model and it proves not to be to my liking, could I change it for another?’

‘Certainly, Sir’, Anders began. He was quite happy to allow Danny two weeks to try out the car, and would exchange it provided there was no damage to the vehicle.

Danny reached into his windcheater and pulled out a wad of notes and peeled off €2,100.

'That's as much as I can afford,' he said 'the rest is for insurance and the tax.'

Anders looked down at the bundle of cash in Danny's hand, a pained expression on his face, 'If you add another €50, we could possibly reach agreement,' he whimpered.

Danny peeled off a single €50 note and held out the money. Anders first took the notes, then shook Danny's outstretched hand vigorously. 'Thank you sir,' he cried, performing an almost imperceptible bow. He rushed over to his desk to write out the receipt.

'We'll get the car serviced and valeted for you and you can pick it up next Monday, sir,' said Anders.

'No, I need it by close of play today,' Danny asserted, otherwise the deal's off,'

'Anders Jansen put on his sheepish, pained expression again, but agreed that he would try to achieve Danny's request. Could he return at 4.30pm to pick the car up?

'That's the latest,' Danny called back at him as he walked out of the showroom.

That evening Danny parked his Citroen some distance from the police station at Elandsgracht. He didn't want the police to make a connection between him and the car. He checked his watch and timed his walk to the station for 6.00 p.m. precisely.

Having checked in, he drove directly for the border, staying within the speed limits in order not to attract attention.

He crossed the border into France near Lille around 10.15 p.m. and it was not for some time before he realised that he would not be able to purchase his props for the planned deed until shops opened again in the morning. Stupidly he had not thought of that.

However, he was making much better time than his original calculations had suggested. Perhaps he could find a Hypermarket still open? No, he thought, it would mean leaving the AutoRoute, and his search might be in vain.

His best bet, he thought was to get nearer to Rouen, then perhaps have a short sleep, buy the paint somewhere and aim to arrive at Liliane's flat at around 9 o'clock. As long as he got away by 10.00 am he'd safely meet his reporting time at Elandsgracht.

At 3.00 am he was 32 km from Rouen and he pulled into a service station car park for some shut-eye, he got out to stretch his legs and enjoy a cigarette before setting the alarm on his phone for 7.30 am

He woke to the shrill warble of his mobile, feeling ragged and bleary eyed. He had not slept enough and instead of being refreshed he felt hung-over. He lit a cigarette to steady his nerves. In the early morning light, he saw - much to his relief - that the service station was in fact part of a much larger industrial site, with a number of outlets. By a stroke of good fortune he would soon be able to buy his paint and materials here. The gods are definitely on my side, he thought.

At eight o'clock he donned his baseball cap and sunglasses before staggering over to the hardware store.

Danny arrived in Rouen at 9.00 am and parked some way short of the flat. The traffic in the town was fairly heavy with commuters, but there were few people about except in the cafés.

Clutching his bag of props, he climbed the stairs to the 4th floor. The damage to the door of the flat had still not been repaired. He peered through the splintered hole, but could see nothing. The interior appeared dark. She must have the shutters closed he thought. She never did that before. Obviously she felt it would give her added protection.

Quietly he inserted his keys and released each of the three locks then, as quietly as he could, he opened the heavy door.

He was right. It was dark inside and he guessed that she would be still asleep. The bedroom door was ajar and he tiptoed across to it and squinted through the narrow gap at the prone figure lying on the bed. The sheet was pulled up to her waist but her upper body was exposed. It was Lil all right, he thought, recognising those dreadful tattoos. She was sleeping soundly.

He crept over to the kitchen, placed his bag on the table and picked up the wooden chopping board, holding it tightly each side with trembling hands then retraced his steps to the bedroom.

Standing over her, he lifted the board above his head aiming to bring it down forcibly on her skull, but he paused.

Could he do this? He realised at that moment that he still loved her. He was weighed down with remorse for what he was about to do.

But she awoke suddenly, her eyes wide with fright and her hands left the sheet and she attempted to raise them in defence, but not soon enough. The heavy chopping board came down straight at her face with a resounding clap. So forceful was the blow that the board split in two and flew from Danny's hands, clattering across the floor.

There was no scream. Liliane was knocked out cold. He took a handful of tissues from the box at the side of the bed and stemmed the bleeding from her flattened and shattered nose.

Then leaving her on the bed he opened the shutters leading out to the balcony and took a chair out to the railing. Carefully, he painted a portion of the exterior of the railing then poured some of the contents of the tin on the chair and the rest on the edge of the balcony together with the upturned tin. He went back into the bedroom, dressed Liliane in her jeans and a T-shirt he found over the back of a chair, slipped on her pumps and wrapping her in a sheet, he carried her over to the balcony. With the brush he daubed some of the spilt paint on her T-shirt and hands then, feeding her gently out of the sheet so as not to get paint on it, he pushed her over the balcony and the brush after her.

He heard the resounding thud as she hit the ground with the simultaneous tinkle of breaking clay-ware on the concrete below as she took out the cluster of flowerpots directly below him.

Without looking down at her, he turned, replaced the sheet roughly on the bed picked up the broken chopping board and let himself out of the flat, taking care to fully lock the door. He listened for any signs of commotion but there was none, so he walked calmly down the stairs and out of the building.

Back at his car, he slipped the broken chopping board beneath the seat and drove away. Shaking severely, he reached into his pocket for a cigarette and lit it with the car's cigar lighter. He took two or three puffs before exhaling, waiting for the nicotine to calm him down. He had achieved his aim, but he was saddened by it. He still could not believe that the woman he thought loved him could have let him down. And equally, he was so ashamed of what he had done to someone he had, even over such a short time, loved dearly.

It haunted him all the way back to Amsterdam.

Danny arrived at the police station at 6.05 p.m.

'You're late!' Hoofdagent Jesse Hoedemaker scolded as Danny approached the desk. 'Not by much, I know, so I won't lock you up,' he jested.

'Yeah, sorry, but the tram was held up. Someone parked a car too near the line and it couldn't get past,' he lied.

'Not to worry, 5 minutes either way is neither here nor there. See you tomorrow.'

Chapter 49

It was Saturday. Jeff called round to Karl having now made a decision in the light of his future move to UK. As he arrived at the estate he rang Karl to open the gate.

'I may be going back to London very soon, Karl,' he ventured as they walked up to the house, 'so you might want to tie it in with the next run.'

'Got a date?' Karl asked curtly as they entered the kitchen.

'No, not yet, but it will be sometime this February. But the reason I'm telling you now is because it will be my last one. I'm not carrying on with it after this last shipment.'

'That's not for you to decide, mate.' Karl responded with a note of venom in his voice. 'You remember what we said at the start? Too many others are reliant on keeping this quiet, so you might come to a sticky end if you spread rumours about like that. They won't believe you can keep your mouth shut.'

'So how am I supposed to get out of it?'

'Never will, mate, you're in for life. Or until you get caught, in which case you're really in trouble.'

'But I've only done two runs and I don't know the people and they don't know me either. It's not as if I could incriminate anyone without incriminating myself as well and I'm hardly likely to do that am I?'

You know me and you've met Redmayne over in Amsterdam. That's enough for a start. These guys won't listen to reason. It's like the Mafia. No one gets their cards, not unless it's condolences.'

'So how come you're able to retire to Belgium and free yourself of it all?

Karl looked sheepish. At first he seemed stuck for a reply, but eventually he spoke in a subdued voice: 'Because I'm the boss here.' He said.

'But you know I wouldn't drop you in it. I'd be daft to even try.'

'Yeah, but I can't trust you any more, not since you started shagging my wife you bastard. How can I ever trust you again? You've brought this upon yourself, so now you've got to live with the consequences.'

Jeff got up from the table and paced around the kitchen desperately trying to think of a way out of this mess.

'But you had no life with Jenny, your marriage was a phoney, you didn't even do things together. You frustrated her into seeking her pleasures elsewhere, so it was hardly my fault that she came on to me. It seems to me that you are intent on punishing me for the misdemeanours of your wife.'

'It takes two to tango, mate, so in my eyes you're both equally guilty. I invited you into my house, I set you up for your job, I confided in you with my problems, yet you repay me by fucking my wife. What kind of a mate does that?'

'So this is really all about getting back at me isn't it. You want to make things hard for me because I took Jenny from you.'

'Yeah, that's about the sum of it,' Karl spat.

'Yet you made a plan to retire and you intended to leave Jenny to her own devices, here in South Africa, while you live like a Lord in Belgium?'

'So what?

'So, in a way, I've helped you achieve that more easily by taking Jenny off your hands, leaving you with no additional responsibilities toward her. You should be grateful.'

Karl laughed.

'You think that would make any difference, mate. Either way I'd not have cared less.'

'You're a hard bastard, Karl,' Jeff whispered, 'I don't know how you can look at yourself.'

'It's a hard life, mate, you do unto others as you have had done to yourself. That's always been my motto.'

Jeff winced at the mis-quote. It was clear that he would get no further with Karl, not without raising the tempo anyway.

'Well, you at least understand my position, Karl, I'm pulling out, and now you can find someone else to do your next run, but it's not going to be me.'

Jeff turned, about to leave.

'Stay where you are, mate,' Karl shouted angrily, simultaneously pulling his pistol from the table drawer and pointing it directly at Jeff's face.

Jeff turned back towards him. 'So now you are going to shoot me? That's very clever. You're sick, do you know that.'

Karl leaned over the table and thrust the gun into Jeff's chest.

'You're a fuckin' dead man if you don't do this run,' he said, 'I mean it.'

Jeff grabbed the barrel and twisted it away from his body, intending solely to prevent injury, but Karl swivelled around the table and grabbed him by the throat with his free hand, at the same time trying to turn the gun back towards him. But Jeff had both hands on the barrel now and had the strength to resist. He turned the gun toward Karl, whose finger was now lodged firmly and inextricably against the trigger. There was a loud bang and suddenly the grip on Jeff's neck fell away.

Karl's eyes were fixed on Jeff's. His face expressionless, his mouth slack as the horror of being shot through the heart was realised. He looked down at the gun in disbelief, Jeff's hands still clutching the barrel. 'You've killed me you bastard' was all he said before collapsing in a heap on the floor.

'Shit…shit, shit, shit!' Jeff wrung his hands in horror. He could not believe what had just happened. He stood there for several minutes, numbed with shock, looking down at Karl's darting eyes and writhing body on the floor at his feet. The soft gurgling sound - as his lungs filled with blood - gently ebbing away. Eventually his eyes were still, staring up at Jeff with his mouth fixed in a toothy grimace.

Although Karl was dead, his eyes were still staring out, as if he could still see what was going on around him. Jeff found it unnerving and quickly knelt beside him to stroke his hand across them to close them. His mind was in turmoil.

How could he deal with this now? He had absolutely no remorse for his actions, but he saw his illustrious future going up in smoke. The syndicate would be after him, Jenny would be alone, while he rotted in a South African jail somewhere. He had to think of something quickly if he was to prevent these thoughts from becoming reality.

He lifted Karl's body and sat him back in the chair, slumped forward over the kitchen table. He checked the floor for blood, but miraculously there was very little. He put the gun in his trouser pocket, wiped up the blood carefully and flushed the soaked paper towel down the toilet. He took one of the two remotes for the gate from the fruit-bowl then he went into the lounge and took the TV and video player from the wall unit out to the Jeep, placing them under the boot load cover. He closed the side door of the house but left it unlocked and drove slowly away, using the remote to open the gate. He hoped no one saw him, but he was surprised that Jessie had not come down when the gun went off. Perhaps he was scared.

As he drove back towards his house he wondered how things would develop. He had never done anything as bad as this before and he was not happy with himself for attempting to pervert the course of events but he knew that he had to try if he and Jenny were to survive this mess he had landed them in.

A couple of miles from home he turned off towards Soweto and finding a quiet spot, he dropped off the TV and the video after quick wipe down with his handkerchief. About a quarter of a mile further down the road he tossed out the gun into some scrub land after first offering it similar treatment, and returned home.

Jenny came out onto the drive to meet him.

'God Jeff, you look terrible. Have you had a bad day? Come and have a drink.'

He gave her a hug but said nothing and walked out onto the patio as Jenny mixed a Pimms.

Jeff sat on the lounger, deep in thought, wondering how this dreadful nightmare he had orchestrated would pan out. He remembered that he had the remote control to the gate in his pocket and got up and walked back into the house, slipping it into Jenny's bag on the hall table. It would not be unusual for her to have it there, after all one of the two was hers anyway.

Jenny came out onto the patio with a glass in each hand. 'I thought we might eat out tonight,' she suggested, hoping it might cheer him up a bit. 'We'll have a quick swim then go eh?'

'That sounds ok,' he replied with little conviction, but seeds were developing in his mind.

It would probably be Jesse who would find Karl's body', he thought, and it would be unlikely that Jesse would phone the police. He would probably phone Jenny or me first, probably ranting down the phone in terror. That might be good, as I would then inform the police, organise the ambulance etc., remotely, at the same time giving the impression that I was unaware of exactly what had happened.

'Let's give the swim a miss, Jenny,' he found himself saying, 'we'll go and eat as soon as I'm changed.'

With any luck, Jesse might leave a message on the phone, which he could then pick up later, giving him an even greater time lag from the event. He just had a feeling it might help.

Chapter 50

Danny's mobile alarm woke him from a deep sleep. It was Alan Redmayne.

'Have you heard the news this morning, Danny?' Redmayne asked earnestly.

'No – what's goin' on?'

' The Amsterdam police have been called down to Rouen to help with an investigation. Apparently they say it involves the death of a girl connected to the Wilson case, which they were involved with earlier. They didn't give a name, but apparently she had only recently been released after questioning and she fell over a balcony railing at her flat. The police haven't ruled out foul play, but it seems that she might have been painting the balcony railings at the time.'

'That sounds like it could be Lil,' Danny exclaimed, with just enough anxiety in his voice to sound genuinely concerned.

'Was that the cheeky tart that shopped you?'

'Yeah! Did the report mention me being investigated too?'

'No, just her, but if it was a hit, who would've done it?'

'Maybe her 'ex', Danny replied. She said he was a bastard. Maybe he found out where she was an' paid her a visit?'

'So it wasn't you then?'

'For fuck's sake Dad, what d'you take me for? Why would it be me? We broke up after she shopped me. I ain't seen her for ages. And in any case, how would I have got down there, done the job and got back before reporting to the cops here in Elandsgracht?'

'No, I s'pose it's quite a long way. Sorry Danny, but I'm just a little bit jumpy with all this at the moment. But I think you'd better prepare yourself for another interview. They'll want to eliminate you from their enquiries.'

'OK Dad, thanks for the warning. I might just mention that I heard the news when I report in tonight – sort of volunteer that I know about it.'

'Good idea son, take care then.' And Redmayne rang off.

Danny sat on the edge of the bed trying to think. Things were moving faster than he had anticipated. He thought he'd better get the speedo fixed on the car and get rid of it straight away.

He quickly donned his jeans and a pullover and went down to the car with his toolbox. He drove round to the lock-ups at the back of his flat and set to work.

At the garage Anders Jansen walked round the car checking for damage before exchanging it. 'I don't think twenty four kilometres is sufficient to determine whether the car is comfortable, sir,' he ventured, 'why not keep it for another week or so?'

'No, I can't do it,' Danny said firmly, 'I must have more lumbar support. What else have you got?'

After a good deal of discussion Danny came away with a nearly new Citroen further up the model range, but he considered that Jansen had conned him and taken a bit of profit from the exchange. However, he didn't have time to argue the point, driving home at the earliest opportunity.

As he arrived outside the flat he saw the police car parked further up the street. It shook him a little and he knew they had come for him. He got out of the car and tried to look nonchalant as he sauntered up to the lobby door. The policeman was inside, working his way along the letterboxes, looking at the names of the various occupants.

'Can I help you?' Danny enquired.

'I'm looking for Mr Danny Redmayne', the policeman replied, 'do you know which is his flat?'

'I'm Danny.' He offered in as natural a voice as he could muster.

‘Can we go up to your flat? I have some rather disturbing news.’

Danny motioned the policeman towards the stairs.

‘Not me dad is it?’ Danny enquired, putting on an anxious expression while trying desperately to sound concerned. ‘Has he had an accident?

‘No, it’s not your father, but apparently your ex girlfriend. You will no doubt remember being interviewed in Rouen by Inspecteur Daalmans? He’s now been asked by the French police to go back as I’m afraid there has been a new development. She has been found dead after a fall from the balcony of her flat. I realise that it might be upsetting for you, but Daalmans asked me to ensure that you were made aware of the situation.’

‘I was hoping it wouldn’t be Liliane when I heard something about it on the news’ Danny replied, ‘but the report didn’t give any name. Not that we are still together or nothing, but I did have a soft spot for her.’

‘Daalmans has suggested that it may not have been an accident,’ the policeman continued, ‘can you think of anyone who might have a reason to harm her?’

Danny could feel the policeman’s eyes piercing the depths of his own, looking for signs that might give him away, but his answer came confidently to his lips: ‘Well, yes I can think of one – her ex-husband. By all accounts he was pretty sick. When she filed for divorce, he killed both her dogs with a shotgun, in revenge. That’s the sort of bastard he was. He was still looking for her, last I heard.’

‘Oh! So she was married before, was she? We didn’t know that.’

‘Well, that’s what she told me anyway.’ Danny replied.

‘And what about you? What were your movements over the last 48 hours?’

‘Not much really, stayed in me flat most of the time, down the café, went to me dad’s place the other night, went down the garage lookin’ at cars…stuff like that.’

‘Which garage?’

'Anders Jansen's place, down the road.'

'So do you have a car now?'

'Yeah! Matter of fact he sold me one. Just picked it up today.'

'From Anders Jansen?'

'Yeah!'

'But you must have had car before, surely?'

'Yeah, but it was a company car and I lost it when I lost me job.'

The policeman made a couple of notes in his diary.

'Thank you Mr Redmayne. Well, commiserations to you. I think that will be all for now, please remain available should we need to talk to you again. I suggest you don't leave Amsterdam for a week or so as I'm sure Inspecteur Daalmans will wish to speak with you again.'

'I'm hardly likely to, seeing as I have to report in every night, am I?' Danny reminded him.

'Of course,' the policeman replied, as he trotted down the stairs back to the lobby. Danny, a big smile on his face, a v-sign in each hand, was gesticulating wildly, once he was sure the copper was out of sight.

'Bollocks to the lot of you!' was all he said, softly, through gritted teeth.

Chapter 51

Jeff woke from a fitful sleep, sweating profusely. He was shocked to find that his nightmare was in fact a reality. For some reason the events of the day before seemed even more horrific with the passing of time. He could not believe that it had happened. He knew he should explain the circumstances to Jenny, but he was unsure how she would react. Further, it would make each other's interrogation by the police that much harder to corroborate. No, he would have to stick to his plan. She must never know that he was involved.

He went downstairs and checked the phone for messages. There were none. Jesse obviously hadn't discovered Karl's body yet, or if he had, he'd not phoned up.

The waiting for something to happen was more than Jeff could endure. He decided that if there were no news in the next couple of days he would make things happen himself by going back to Karl's place to 'discover' the body.

At that moment, Jenny padded down the stairs in her robe and slippers. 'You are up with the birds, darling, are you leaving early this morning?'

'Not particularly,' Jeff replied, 'I just couldn't sleep.'

'I'll make some breakfast,' she replied.

During the course of their meal, Jenny broached the subject of her clothes and other belongings, which had yet to be retrieved from Karl's house.

Jeff's reaction was swift. 'I think you should call round while he's at work and collect it all,' he replied, perhaps in a day or two, when we've made space for it all.'

He saw her visit as an ideal way to set up the discovery of Karl's body, if it was not found beforehand by others.

'Oh I couldn't possibly go round there on my own – not any more. Suppose he was there. I'd probably get slaughtered. Couldn't you come with me Jeff?'

'Well, yes, I could, but I have a busy couple of days at work now. Perhaps we could do it next Friday?'

Jenny sighed with relief. 'Yes, that's a good idea, she said.

Jeff brushed her cheek with a kiss and reached for his car keys. 'See you tonight,' he called as he closed the hall door.

Three days later, there had been no news. It was Thursday morning. Jeff arrived at his office to find a note waiting for him at his desk.

Gordon McKlintock wanted a 'chat'.

Jeff walked round to his office and stuck his head round the door. 'You are looking for me?' He enquired.

McKlintock was in no mood for niceties. His face was like thunder.

'Get in here Blythe and shut the door behind you.'

It was the first time he had referred to Jeff by his surname. It was usually 'laddie' or occasionally 'Jeff' but never Blythe. Something must be seriously wrong. Jeff suddenly felt guilty. He knew what this would be about. He had been reporting to David Robinson behind McKlintock's back. He must have found out.

'We have a serious problem, laddie,' McKlintock started, 'Your ex landlord, our Systems Manager, Karl Jongen has been found dead at his home. You lodged with him for a short while and know his houseboy don't you.'

Jeff nodded.

Well, the motive was robbery, apparently, and his houseboy has fled, leaving most of his stuff behind - except the items he took from Karl's house, that is.

'How was he killed?' Jeff asked.

It seems he was shot in the chest, but there are some anomalies apparently, according to the police.'

'Like what?'

'Don't know yet Laddie, the police wouldn't expand on anything. They are awaiting Forensics.'

'But Jesse wouldn't do a thing like that, he was too timid for one thing, secondly, he was very happy at his job, and a very pleasant lad too.'

'Well, everyone has an unexpected side to them, laddie, so we'll have to wait and see.'

'Anyway, there are two problems now. *Ours*, which is how to we plug his duties, and *yours*, how do you tell his wife.'

'Why me?'

'Because we told the police that she lived with you now, and they asked me to tell you to break the news to her.'

'What, just like that?'

'Yep, that's about the size of it, laddie.'

'Well, I'd better do it straight away. Then get down to the station and offer my help.'

'I think that would be wise, laddie. Now get yourself off quickly.'

The phone rang. McKlintock waved his arms at Jeff in a shooing movement, and then picked up the handset, his eyes following Jeff as he left his office. He didn't answer the call until the door had closed.

'Oh yes, put him through…Alan, thanks for calling back. We've got a hold-up this end. I think we're going to have a problem with the next shipment…'

Chapter 52

Anders Jansen was surprised to see the policeman pacing back and forth across the forecourt of his garage when he arrived at 8 o'clock that morning.

The policeman took a last draw on his cigarette before stubbing it out on the side of a drainpipe by the showroom window, then walked across to Jansen's car as he backed into his usual space.

'Mr Jansen?'

'Anders Jansen, yes, can I help you?'

'I am enquiring about a car you may have sold to an Englishman, a Mr Redmayne, very recently.'

'Oh him,' Jansen replied 'yes, that was a bit of a palaver.'

'How do you mean?'

'Well, he suffered from a lot of back pain and wanted a car with soft suspension, so he tried out a couple before actually committing.'

'What day did he first come to see you?'

'It was last Friday. He initially chose a little C3 and was in a hurry to have it because he insisted that I get it ready for him by that evening. I agreed that I would change it for something else if it did not suit him.'

'So he brought it back?'

'Yes, Yesterday, He said that the seat didn't have enough lumbar support for his bad back.'

'And you exchanged it for another one?'

'Yes…why do you ask? Has something happened to him? Has he had an accident?'

'No, no, nothing like that. We are investigating another matter and just checking alibis and that sort of thing.'

'Well, he didn't strike me as being a criminal.'

The policeman sucked his teeth and sighed. 'Well nonetheless, we need to check his movements. Is the car still here?'

'Yes it is,' Jansen pointed across the forecourt.

'Can you get the keys for me? Oh, and let me know what the kilometrage was when you sold it to him.'

Anders Jansen walked over to the office, the policeman following close behind, and opened up the showroom.

'Searching through the mass of papers on his desk, Jansen found the Spec sheet for the C3 and handed it to the policeman. 'It shows the initial kilometrage there,' he said.

'And what was the kilometrage when Redmayne returned it?

'He only did 24 kilometres, and I remember saying to him that it was not enough of a trial but he insisted.'

Jansen handed the policeman the keys and watched him as he walked out of the showroom and over to the car. He opened all the doors and the boot, and spent some time groping around inside, before taking out a couple of things which Jansen couldn't recognise, then closing up the car again.

Back in the showroom the policeman held out the two pieces of the broken chopping board. 'What are these?' He asked.

Jansen was perplexed. 'I have no idea,' he replied, 'they were not there when I gave Redmayne the car I can assure you.'

The policeman was turning the boards over in his hands and realised that they fitted together to make a whole. Looking closely at the broken edges he could see a thin film of discolouration, maybe grease, near what would have been the middle of the board. 'I'll take these away for further examination,' he said.

It was 10 o'clock. Danny had showered and was standing in the kitchen, making himself a cup of coffee and a couple of slices of toast, still inwardly marvelling at his success in achieving his various goals. He felt he could now relax. He had removed the threat of Liliane, fobbed off the police as to his whereabouts and now could turn his attention to resolving the problem of hawking his stash.

Munching his way through his first slice of toast he reflected on the ease with which he had disposed of Liliane and how he had been so lucky to not be seen in the act. Yet there was something niggling him – some unfulfilled action which he felt he had forgotten – but he couldn't put a finger on it. Obviously it must be trivial, he thought, for it has had no bearing on the out-turn of events. So he carried on with his breakfast and made plans to meet up with his father. He was interested to know when he would be likely to meet his newly acquired half-brother.

The toast was tastier than he expected and he cut himself another slice of bread. His thin and warped bread board, he noticed, was meagre compared with the much more substantial one he had used on Liliane…

'Christ!' It suddenly came to him what had been niggling at the back of his mind. He had forgotten to remove the chopping board from under the seat of the car.

The colour drained from his face and his carefree demeanour turned to one of abject horror.

He knew he had to get that chopping board back, before someone else found it.

He quickly donned a shirt and trousers and grabbing his keys he rushed out to his car.

On the way to the garage he found himself willing Jansen not to have sold the car, not to have valeted it again and not to have discovered the board. But perhaps he was being too neurotic; after all it was only yesterday that he made the exchange. The car would probably not have been touched yet.

Having almost convinced himself that all would be well, he felt a little calmer as he drove, but he knew he would not be fully happy until he had those two pieces of chopping board in his possession.

At the garage, Jansen looked despondent. 'Not back for another exchange, I hope?' He said as he greeted Danny.

'No, but I think I may have left something in the other car – a chopping board I was taking to be repaired?'

'Yes, I know the one,' Jansen replied. 'The police paid me a visit earlier this morning and took it away. What is all this about? They were questioning me, asking about you and your transactions with me.'

'What sort of questions?'

'Oh just which cars you looked at, how many kilometres you have travelled…that sort of thing.'

'Why are they investigating me? Did they say?'

'No,' Jansen replied, 'honestly, they wouldn't tell me. But the copper asked me to open up the car and he gave it a good going over. That's when he found the pieces of board'

'Well, I don't understand that,' Danny said assuredly. 'I'll get round to the station tonight about six o'clock and find out what's going on.'

Jansen looked relieved. It seemed that Danny had convinced him there was nothing to worry about and he dropped his guard.

'The copper said he found a trace of grease on the board, which he was going to get analysed.'

'Well, it's a chopping board. What does he expect, stupid fool.' Danny spat.

He turned and without further acknowledgement, walked back to his car.

Driving back to his flat he was shaking badly. He knew that this could well be his undoing. One sodding little chopping board bringing him a life sentence. It seemed to him to be so unjust.

The cops would undoubtedly come to his flat and maybe search that too. If they found his hoard under the floorboards, that would be the final straw. He had to do something about that, and quickly.

He wondered about the grease on the board. Could they do a test and then compare it with her facial grease, so identifying the board as the instrument used in his attempt to kill her? He hoped not, but he knew he would have to have some plausible answer ready. And what could he do with his haul?

He thought about taking it to his father – maybe in a parcel – with instructions not to open it except in the event of his demise. The sort of thing they did in films. But that might incriminate his father and he didn't really want to do that.

He arrived back at his flat and parked the car some distance from the entrance. He looked around before alighting, checking that there were no police about, but all seemed quite normal.

Once in his flat he locked the door then went over to the bedroom and lifted the floorboard. He lifted out his cache of weapons and the bag containing his haul then gave each a cursory inspection. He wondered whether he could get them out of the flat without being seen, or worse, without the coppers turning up as he was in the act. There was nowhere safe in the flat that he could think of and he was now getting desperate.

Then an idea came to him. He transferred his haul to the leather weapons case and wrapped it up in some old newspapers. After stuffing it into a black bin bag, he took it down to the basement and placed it amongst the pile of similar bags waiting for the Friday waste collection in the corner of the bin room. The concierge would be moving them out to the street on the Thursday night so Danny would have to remember to get his back beforehand. Still, it gave him about 48 hour's respite. The police would never search down there, he thought.

His actions were extremely fortuitous, for the police turned up in force just minutes after Danny had let himself back into his flat. Three of them: Two tall, wiry looking, uniformed young men and a shorter slightly tubby, older man in a grey mackintosh.

'Mr Danny Redmayne?' The tubby detective asked.

'That's me,' replied Danny as casually as he could, 'how can I help?'

It was the best he could come up with and it was not a response that the detective was expecting. He relaxed a little before introducing himself. 'I am Inspecteur Godfried Meijer and I have a warrant to search your flat and while my two colleagues do that, I would like to ask you a few questions.'

'In connection with what?' Danny enquired turning on his inquisitive look.

'Just routine stuff, the continuation of our enquiries into the Liliane Duval affair.'

'OK, no problem, but I don't see how I can help you on that matter, Inspecteur.'

'Nonetheless, perhaps we can try, eh?'

The Inspecteur took out his handkerchief and blew his nose noisily before waving Danny in the direction of the kitchen.

Danny felt confident. This guy seemed a bit of a softy. 'Tell them not to make too much mess Inspecteur, I would like everything back in its place when you're done,' he said before following the Inspecteur into the kitchen.

The two policemen began their search, starting with the furniture.

Meanwhile Meijer took out his notebook and removed a ballpoint from the spine.

'I don't know whether you are yet aware, but a colleague has visited the garage owned by Anders Jansen. Apparently you exchanged cars, but inadvertently left something in it?'

'Yes, that's correct,' Danny replied 'I had a rather nice, fairly expensive chopping board which I wanted to repair, but was unsure which glue would be hygienic and work best, so I was taking it to a hardware store for advice.'

'So how did it break in the first place.'

'I had been stringing up a piece of beef for roasting and I tripped when crossing the kitchen to the oven. The board fell from my hands. I suppose the weight of the meat combined with the angle of the fall made it break on impact.'

'It must have been a big piece of meat?'

'Yes, It was. It was intended to cover a number of meals.'

So what did you do?'

'I picked up the meat, put it in the oven and put the two pieces of board on the worktop. I never gave it another thought until I decided to get it repaired last Sunday.'

'So why conceal it under the seat?'

'I didn't. I didn't want it flying about in the car – it's heavy – so I put it in the rear foot-well. It must have slipped under.'

Again, it was the best Danny could invent and he hoped that the longer the conversation about the board went on, the more trivial the matter might become.

'Look Inspector, I'm answering all your questions, but I am totally perplexed as to why you are homing in on a chopping board. I don't understand the relevance.'

Meijer smoothed his pencil moustache several times with the forefinger of each hand before enlightening Danny. 'The problem, Mr Redmayne, is that the boys down in Rouen believe that Miss Duval had suffered injuries inconsistent with her fall. This might suggest she either met with some accident before falling from the balcony, or even perhaps was murdered by person or persons unknown. Therefore we are looking into the likelihood, and every possible means, by which she might have been injured before falling, being pushed or even thrown off the balcony of her flat. You were obviously considered an immediate suspect because of your previous involvement with her, although we concluded that distance and timing made it barely feasible. This, together with your declared alibi has resulted in your not being taken into custody. However, we have decided to analyse the board, just in case. If nothing untoward is found, then you are in the clear. Simple as that.'

'Yeah, I can see where you're comin' from Inspecteur, but I'm here, in Amsterdam, an' she was in Rouen. If I *was* to have been the one to do it - an' I ain't sayin' I was - do you think I'd be daft enough to take my choppin' board all the way down there to do her in, then bring it all the way back here? That'd be plain nuts. I'd have got shot of it straight away.'

'Nevertheless, Mr Redmayne, we have to ensure no stone is left unturned,' Meijer replied with the flicker of a smile on his chubby face.

There was a knock on the open kitchen door and one of the wiry constables apologised for interrupting, then gave Meijer a sloppily disguised hand signal which Danny interpreted as completion of the search with nothing found.

Meijer sighed, closed his notebook, slid the ballpoint back into the spine and rose to his feet. 'We'll talk again in a couple of days Mr Redmayne. Sorry to disturb you, but please stay available.'

Danny acknowledged and showed the three policemen to the door. He then turned to inspect the damage. The place was a mess, but his relief overcame his anger, his first thoughts being to retrieve his stash from the basement. Well pleased with his performance he walked over to the window and watched as the policemen drove off, then set off down the stairs.

As the police car sped back to the station, Godfried Meijer turned to the Constable seated behind him.

'Do you remember when we were investigating the murder of that Wilson guy?'

The Constable nodded.

'We interviewed a Redmayne then. It was Danny Redmayne's father. I wonder if the murder of Liliane

Duval could possibly be connected in any way? What was his name…the guy who disappeared…'

'You mean Pete Radbourne?'

'Yes, that's the one. Could he have got to France from England without being spotted somehow? Maybe still in touch with Danny. Maybe even murdered the girl, Liliane, for him? Who knows?'

'Seems pretty unlikely to me,' the constable replied, 'If, as is currently believed, he murdered the Cheryl girl and Wilson, then cleaned him out, he would probably be rich and well away by now. Why would he want to do another murder? He'll no doubt be *incognito* sunning himself down in Spain in some grotty resort, shagging some tart or other, I should think'

'Unless he was dead.' Meijer added. 'Don't forget what Redmayne said…he thought maybe the guy in Manchester might have topped him.'

'Yeah, but it's only Redmayne's guess. There's nothing to substantiate it. Suppose Redmayne made it up. Suppose Danny Redmayne *did* go to England with Pete Radbourne and killed him over there. Suppose the guy they were getting money from never existed.'

'In that scenario who killed Wilson and the Girl Cheryl then? Who would have a motive?'

'Maybe Redmayne?' the constable suggested. 'He probably thought that the girl Cheryl knew they were going to Manchester, so Redmayne had to get rid of her too. Wilson had just sacked him, so he wanted to get his revenge. It's another angle on the whole thing.'

'Hmm!' Meijer toyed with his pencil moustache, 'In fact that's a scenario we haven't fully explored' he mused, 'there might be some benefit in working that through, but where would we start? We don't know the UK location, or the guy they went to see – if he exists – we can't trace the car, nobody spotted Danny Redmayne on the ferry, his passport was not recorded and furthermore everyone else who might have any answers is dead.'

'Except Danny Redmayne himself, and we know what he will say.'

'Yeah, but nobody's really pressed him yet, and he might crack under some more aggressive questioning. We've just got to find some small chink in his statement and we can then open up the whole thing...Tell you what...If that leads to an outcome, Constable, I'll recommend your elevation to Detective. Get onto it straight away.'

Chapter 53

Jeff drove back to the house and let himself in. Despite the blustery day, Jenny was taking her usual morning swim, naked as always. He watched her, unseen as she scythed through the water, swimming the whole length without raising her head for breath. She did a rather revealing somersault turn at the end and then swam back towards him, still oblivious of his presence. At his end of the pool she paused and pushed her hair back from her face before opening her eyes to see him standing above her. She jumped.

'Christ, Jeff! You frightened me for a moment,' she said, 'why are you back so soon?'

'Got some bad news I'm afraid,' he retorted, 'you'd better come out and I'll explain.' He went to get the towel off the lounger as she reached for the pool edge and lithely climbed out in one smooth movement and stood, goose-pimpled, before him. He swept the towel around her shoulders and she wrapped the ends across her naked torso.

'It's Karl. He's been found dead at his house. Apparently the police think it was Jesse, he's disappeared without taking any of his belongings.'

'Oh my God!' Jenny began, her hand spontaneously flying up to cover her mouth, her eyes wide in disbelief. Then after a long pause she continued: 'I should be more upset but if I'm honest, I don't really have any feelings about it. I know that sounds awfully callous but after all that has happened, I can't feel anything for him.'

She paused for a moment then her expression changed. 'Jesse wouldn't have done it. He was too gentle and wouldn't have the guts.'

'No, I agree, but until we find Jesse, we won't know for certain.'

'How was he killed?'

'It seems he was shot in the chest but I've only got that information from Gordon McKlintock – he hit me with it first thing this morning when I got to the office and I've come straight back here to tell you.'

'So what next?'

'I'm off to the police station to see if I can be of any assistance.'

'Do you think that's wise?'

'Why on earth not?'

'Well after the way Karl behaved the other night, we might both be considered to have a motive.'

'In which case they'll be round here very soon. So I think it might look better if we went down there instead and asked if we can help with anything.'

'Ok, give me a moment to shower and dress, then we'll go together.' Jenny agreed.

Nothing was said for a while as they drove to the police station in Randberg. Eventually, Jenny broke the silence. 'I wonder what spooked Jesse?' She enquired.

'He probably found Karl first, and was afraid he would be taken in for questioning. Don't forget he's black and liable to be the first suspect – as the police have already indicated.'

'We've got to find him. I can't believe that he would have done this. He was in such good form when he was at our place, It doesn't make sense.'

'I know what you're saying, but we don't know what he went back to when he got home. Karl may have been in a foul mood and started an argument or Jesse may have been distraught at you leaving him, after all he was really fond of you. Maybe Karl took it out on him. Who knows?'

Jeff pulled up outside the police station and parked in one of the visitor bays.

'Well, here goes, let's get it over and done with.' He said with a sigh.

At the desk their explanation of why they were there met with a blank look from the young policeman. 'Karl

Jongen, you say?', a total lack of recognition on his face. 'Who was the officer dealing with the case, do you know?'

'We have no idea,' replied Jeff, 'however, this is Karl's wife, Jenny,' he continued, waving a hand towards her, 'and I am a colleague of his – we both work for the same company and I lodged with him for a while. We thought it might be useful to you if we offered our assistance.'

The policeman raised his eyebrows, 'It's not often we get volunteers to help with our enquiries,' he began, 'but I am not sure who has been allocated to this case. I'm afraid that you will just have to wait until the investigating officer is ready for you. There is no one here to take your statement at the moment. Perhaps if you leave your names, addresses and telephone numbers, you will be called in due course.'

Jeff could detect the note of suspicion in the policeman's voice. Suddenly he wished they had not made the rash decision to go to the police. He found himself wondering why on earth anyone would do that? It would just as likely be read as a means of disguising any indication of guilt, or involvement.

The Policeman slid a form across the desk and Jeff quickly jotted down the requested information and after a short exchange, they departed.

'You were right,' he said as they approached the car, 'maybe it would have been better to leave it.'

'I wouldn't worry,' Jenny replied, 'we've nothing to hide, have we?'

Jeff felt the heat rising under his collar. He hoped it would not show on his face. 'No, of course not.' he said firmly.

'Then let's concentrate on trying to find Jesse, before the police do. If he ends up being arrested we will never see him and he's bound to go to pieces under interrogation. He'll be scared stiff.'

'But where do we start?'

'Well, maybe he's at his mother's place, over in Molapo.'

'Do you know where she lives?'

'No I've no idea, but we might be able to ask around.'

Jenny stared straight ahead through the windscreen, her brow furrowed. 'I'm not sure that would be a good idea either,' she started, then after a short pause she continued: 'I wouldn't want to go down there myself – I don't think it would be entirely safe.'

Jeff turned and stared at her briefly before casting his eyes back to the road. 'I can't believe you just said that. Surely that's not true in this day and age? I know there are some parts that maybe aren't totally safe, but surely not Molapo?'

'Well, It would make me feel as if I was being sized up for a robbery - or worse. Too frightening.'

'Well, I think you're being over sensitive about that but if that's a no-no then how do we find him?'

'Couldn't you ask a few of the black guys at work to find his mother's address for you?'

'I'd rather keep all this as far away as possible from the company. I don't really want to give anyone the impression I'm connected in any way to the suspected murderer. It's bad enough having been involved with Karl.'

'Then perhaps we have to wait and let the police do their work after all. Then, once we know that they have found him, we can give Jesse some support.'

Jeff parked the Jeep in front of the garage and they walked hand in hand up the path to the house entrance. He checked the mailbox and pulled out two white envelopes, then opened the door before slicing open the first envelope with his little finger. It was an electricity bill. The second was half a sheet of A4 paper with a torn edge, upon which was written in a badly spelt, childish scrawl 'I com to clene pool but you out. I com agen tomorow. Jesse.'

'Looks like we've found him,' Jeff called across the hall to Jenny in the kitchen. She immediately came over and snatched the paper from him excitedly. 'Oh thank God!' she cried.

Jesse was true to his word. At ten o'clock the next morning he showed up at the side door.

Jenny rushed over to him and gave him a hug. 'Oh Jesse, we were so worried about you,' she sighed.

Jesse stood there sheepishly, shuffling his feet. He didn't seem to be his usual smiling self.

'I go clean pool,' he said timidly, 'and speak to Sahib Jeff.'

He went out to the pool and started to retrieve the vacuum hose from the pump-house.

'Jesse wants to speak to you Jeff,' Jenny began, 'what do you think that's about?'

' No idea. Probably something to do with the Karl thing. Maybe he wants to explain his recent absence. I'll have a word with him, although I don't suppose there will be much he can tell us.'

Jeff walked out to the pool with a purposeful gate, which seemed to spook Jesse into retreating toward the pool-house, as if he was afraid Jeff was about to assault him.

'Come on Jesse, what's this all about? You know you're safe here, you can tell me why you ran off.'

'I know you kill Sahib Karl,' whispered Jesse, as he shrank back from Jeff, 'I see you fighting in the kitchen. Then the gun goes off. I saw you take TV. Why you do that? Then I run away.'

Jesse waited for a reaction from Jeff, expecting him to lash out.

'But Jesse, if you saw what happened you will realise that it was an accident,' Jeff whispered, 'and that I was only trying to stop Karl from shooting me?'

'Yes but you steal TV. And there was another man.'

'What do you mean, another man?'

'He comes after, asking me who was man who drive away. He had gun too and put it in my mouth. He said he kill me if I not tell him your name.'

Jeff winced. 'Oh God Jesse, did you tell him?'

'Sorry Sahib, I had to tell him. He kill me.'

'What did this man look like?'

'Very big, he talk like you but different. Hairy face.'

'What happened next?'

'He drove away. He told me I was dead if I tell anyone about him. I ran away.'

'Shit!' Jeff exclaimed, under his breath. Suddenly everything had crashed down around him. All his best-laid plans were now in tatters and if that wasn't enough, his life was in danger along with Jesse's and possibly Jenny's too. Who was this guy? Was he part of the ring? Perhaps the Police?

'Jesse, you must not say anything to Memsahib Jenny about this, OK? Don't talk to anybody. You must go straight back to your mother's house and stay there. You will be safe there. Don't come back here again. OK?'

Jeff reached into his pocket and slipped Jesse a bunch of one hundred Rand notes and shoved him toward the gate.

Jesse walked sheepishly away with his head hung low. 'I not say anything,' he called as he passed through the gate.

Chapter 54

Godfried Meijer sat at his desk deep in thought, toying with a pencil and jotting down the odd word as ideas came to him. It seemed that this investigation was thwarted every time a new piece of evidence was uncovered.

The chopping board had come back from the Labs but the forensic examination had proved inconclusive. There were discernible traces of Miss Duval's DNA but it could not be concluded necessarily to be from her face. There was also DNA from a variety of sources, one of which was Danny Redmayne, but it was a chopping board after all and by it's very purpose would have been impregnated with substances from a multitude of sources. Forensics had also looked to see if there were any traces of wood or splinters on the dead woman's face, but none were found.

As a last resort he was trying to find a way to follow up his constable's idea of pursuing Danny Redmayne. However, the more he contemplated the evidence, the less he was convinced that further questioning would advance the investigation.

Eventually, he felt the best course of action would be to build a scenario, implicating Redmayne in the various atrocities and then observe him trying to extricate himself. He might possibly trip himself up on a point, giving the investigators an opportunity to unravel more information.

Finally, he picked up the phone.

'Constable, get a colleague and pick up Redmayne and bring him down to the station for questioning. Treat him politely. Don't arrest him. Just suggest that it would be best if he complies with your request. Say that we just want to ask a few further questions. If he refuses or gets violent, it will be an indication he has something to hide. You can then arrest him.'

Meijer sat back in his chair and started composing his scenario, based on the information he held. After half an hour's jotting, he felt he had enough of a crib-sheet to put together an accusation which he would put before Redmayne once he was in the interview room. With a bit of luck he might just trip himself up.

At 6.30 a call came through to Alan Redmayne's mobile.

'Al…Call me back. Gordon.'

Redmayne went down to his office and took his 'business' mobile from the safe. He dialled a number.

'We've got a problem. The new guy.' McKlintock said.

'Who? Blythe?'

'That's right. He's the one that sorted Karl.'

'You're kidding!'

'No, the houseboy talked after a bit of pressure. He saw the whole thing. What do we do now? If this guy talks we'll all go down.'

'How sure are you about this?'

'Dead sure. We've got to do something serious and quick. The police haven't cottoned on yet but it's just a matter of time.'

'OK leave it with me – I'll sort something and ring you back tomorrow.'

Alan Redmayne was stunned by the news. It was only days since he'd had face to face discussions with Jeff Blythe. He was effectively family. Furthermore he seemed so genuine and capable of raising the image of the business. Was he a stoolie? Why would he kill Karl? Was it business or domestic?

Clearly he had fooled a lot of people and Redmayne was annoyed that he was one.

But he realised he wouldn't have time to find out for sure. He would be forced into taking action before he had investigated the problem properly. The cartel would demand it. Shoot first…

Normally in situations like this he'd send a soldier to sort out the mess, but Danny was the only one left and the police had tied him to Amsterdam. Unless…perhaps he could bring Blythe back to Amsterdam? There was a run due. Perhaps it could be brought forward?

He phoned McKlintock again.

'Can you bring forward the next party to the first available flight?'

'They are ready. I can probably get them on tomorrow.'

'OK. Give them Blythe. Only him.'

He rang off.

Chapter 55

Jeff was still standing frozen to the spot by the pool. He cursed himself for not noticing Jesse at Karl's house or searching for him at the time and also for failing to spot the 'other man'.

Who was he? Big, with hairy face, Jesse had said, spoke like Jeff but not the same. It didn't fit anyone he knew, he thought, so it must be a guy from the cartel. How could he find out?

He thought about phoning Alan Redmayne, but he didn't have a number. With Karl dead he had no idea of any other member in the South African end of the business. But supposing this man had been from another organisation. Jeff felt he should be warning someone in the cartel about it.

He walked back into the house and looked up Alan Redmayne's name in the international phone directories on his computer. There was nothing. He might just have to leave things as they were.

Jenny came down from the bedroom, having changed into something warmer. 'I thought we'd eat on the terrace tonight,' she said, 'where's Jesse?'

'Gone home to his Mum's place,' Jeff replied.

'But he hasn't put the pool hose away.'

'No I told him I would do it and he could go. I don't really want him around here any more.'

Jenny was incredulous. 'Why ever not? He's a poor frightened boy and needs help.'

'Look, he's probably wanted by the police, and the last thing I want is them crawling around here, It wouldn't look good for my chances with David Robinson if he got wind that I might be mixed up in the Karl murder, however much it couldn't be substantiated. He's with his mother, so he's not on his own.'

'Well I think you're being callous.'

'Whatever!' Jeff replied walking back out to the terrace.

He slumped down onto the lounger and shut his eyes, trying to think.

'I'll make a drink,' Jenny said.

The next morning Jeff left the house for work. He idly checked the mailbox for letters as he passed. There was an envelope marked 'Private and Confidential, Addressee Only', with his name upon it.

He tucked it into his jacket pocket, unlocked the Jeep and climbed in before reaching for it again and slitting it open. Inside were an airline ticket and an A4 page of type. He checked the ticket first and to his surprise, saw that it was for him alone on that evening's flight to Amsterdam.

The typed page gave the detailed instructions he was to follow for the pick-up and drop-off of his second 'package'.

It was all too sudden for him, and he swore loudly.

There was no indication of who issued the note, and no means of communicating with the sender.

His first reaction was to throw the whole lot away and ignore it, but he knew that might result in even greater danger not only for himself but for Jesse and for Jenny too.

Jeff was in no doubt now that the 'other man' Jesse had encountered was involved with the cartel. But why was the drop brought forward so suddenly. Could it be that with Karl's death and the police sniffing around, the other members wanted to get one last big haul before everything went down?

Or could it be a stitch-up, a means by which they could deal with him, somewhere where he couldn't be traced?

Jeff rather thought the latter.

He wished there were someone he could look to for advice, Jenny even, but she knew nothing of his involvement and he certainly didn't want to enlighten her.

He racked his brains, but the best he could come up with was Gordon McKlintock. However, that would mean confessing to his involvement in the cartel, and furthermore, he might have to explain away Karl's death. It would also mean giving up any further involvement in the operation, even assisting the police in breaking up the operation.

Eventually, he decided to go to the office, carry on as if nothing had happened, and see what developed. Later, he would follow the instructions in the note. Somebody would have to pass the contraband to him at some point before the flight. He would then decide what action to take.

Jeff got out of the car and walked back to the house. He had to talk to Jenny.

'Something has come up in Amsterdam and I've got to be on the plane this evening, darling,' he began, 'a meeting of some importance, I gather. Not sure what it's about, but I'll be back the day after tomorrow.'

Jenny's brow furrowed. 'Can't I come too?' She queried.

'It's urgent and they've only given me one ticket. Plane's fully booked apparently,' he lied, 'can you manage on your own?'

'Well I'll have to,' she replied with a sigh, 'I'll pack you a case.'

'Great! I'll see you this afternoon.'

Jeff nipped up the stairs to the bedroom and took out his 9mm Magnum Research pistol, checked the magazine then tucked it into his waistband. He felt that he might be glad of it if things got any worse.

He went out to his car and set off for the office.

He mulled over the situation as he drove. Who was the big guy with the hairy face? Was it generally hairy or was it a big beard? He tried to think whether he had seen anyone who might fit that description. Gordon McKlintock might fit, he thought, but he wasn't likely to be involved – not the type.

But wait…Jesse said he talked like me but different. Gordon has a Scottish accent…that's different. Could it be him?

Jeff was dubious, but he decided he would take no chances.

He parked up in his usual space and headed straight for Gordon McKlintock's office.

McKlintock greeted him amiably.

'Well Laddie, what can I do for you?' He asked.

'I need a couple of days off. Some family problems in London. From tomorrow. Is that going to be a problem?' Jeff asked curtly.

For an instant McKlintock's expression changed slightly. His eyes narrowed a little and his mouth turned down at the corners, but it was only for an instant. It was a signal to Jeff of distrust.

McKlintock knew Jeff was lying. Therefore he must know why he really needed the time off.

It was enough for Jeff. He didn't need any further indication. This man was part of the cartel. There was no doubt in his mind. But he needed an answer.

'Sure laddie, we can manage for a couple of days.' McKlintock agreed, 'we'll see you Friday then…God willing!' but his body language did not match his jocular outpourings.

Jeff walked over to his office, unsure of how he was to play out the next two days. The note he had received stated that he was to take a file of data from his in-tray. It would be ready for him when he got to his office. It would be in one of the internal mail transfer envelopes. He was to ensure that he signed and dated the panel on the rear of the envelope, as he would normally do for all other internal mail. The file was apparently titled 'Annual Turnaround Proposals – Rotterdam Terminal'. He was to take the file to an address in Amsterdam for the meeting. No details of the agenda for the meeting were included. These would be distributed at its commencement.

There must be another member of the cartel working in the Oil Company, Jeff surmised. Why else would the drop be arranged on Company premises. He sat at his desk and went through his in-tray. Sure enough, three documents down, there was the transfer envelope containing a file of A4 sheets between light-blue plastic covers all clamped together with a slightly over-large plastic spine.

He looked at it carefully. Peering down the end of the spine, he could see that it had been filled near the end, with some form of glue. He checked the other end. It was the same. He deduced that the goods had been concealed inside the middle portion of the spine.

He took the airline ticket out of his inside jacket pocket and studied it. The outbound flight was booked for the usual 23.15 flight, but there was no inbound return! Did that mean they didn't anticipate him coming back?

Suddenly he felt sick in his stomach. The writing was on the wall. He was going to be liquidated, he felt sure. He tried to think where it might take place. A public place would hardly be likely, so that would narrow down the possible opportunities to perhaps the taxi from the airport in Schiphol, the meeting itself, maybe any post meeting activity that was planned for him, and finally his hotel room.

There was just a faint possibility that they might try something before the flight, but that would defeat the object of making the drop. He also had the safety of his 9mm pistol, at least until he reached the airport.

He reached for the comfort of it at his waistband. He had never fired it, but he was sure he could if provoked.

The likelihood of Jeff completing any real work seemed unlikely, he was too wound up to even think about it, so he made up his mind to go home and spend the last few hours before his flight with Jenny. He was now thinking beyond the so-called meeting.

Suppose he survived the hit, or managed to defeat whoever was due to carry it out – where would he go from there? How would he get his life back together without forever looking over his shoulder? Somehow he had to extricate himself from the grip of the cartel in such a way that he would no longer be a target. How could he do that and yet maintain his meteoric progress through the Company? These were issues that would require his utmost attention over the coming 24 hours.

Chapter 56

Danny was in his flat, making himself a sandwich when the police called. There were two of them, both constables, but armed with holstered pistols.

He tried not to appear nervous. In fact it was not difficult, as he thought he had all but cleared his name in his previous interviews. He put on his best casual air.

'Thought you might want to talk to me some more,' he said resignedly. 'No peace for the wicked!'

The two policemen looked quizzical – their English was poor.

'Come, Inspecteur Meijer wishes to speak again,' said the shorter of the two men, the taller placing a hand on Danny's arm.

Danny looked down at the hand and frowned and the policeman immediately withdrew. You are not under arrest,' he confirmed.

At the station, Meijer commenced his scenario:

'Thank you for coming in Mr Redmayne. As you can imagine, there would have been no need to interview you further had it not been for some new information, which now enables us to piece together the details of the various murders in this case.

It is of great importance to you personally because it quite clearly identifies you as the perpetrator.'

Meijer paused and studied Danny closely, looking for a response. There was none.

'We have now discovered that you did indeed go to England with Pete Radbourne,' he continued, 'this has been confirmed by the Harwich Port Authorities, who presented us with a security videotape showing you both in a silver Mercedes C class automobile, passing through the customs section.

Furthermore, the same car was recorded parked in a McDonalds restaurant on the A14 and again on the M6 North of Birmingham.

You will recall that there was a note at Pete Radbourne's flat, a 'to do' list if you like, which included the statement 'Top Danny'. Clearly the intention was for Radbourne to take you to England and dispose of you. However, Pete Radbourne has not been seen since, neither has the car been found. This lead us to the conclusion that you evaded your demise, in fact you managed to 'turn the tables' so to speak, and do away with Radbourne.

You then disposed of the car and took a ferry back to the continent and took your reprisals firstly against the girl, Cheryl, because she knew of your trip and why, and then Wilson who orchestrated your failed demise. You then stole the contents of his safe and left the country.'

Meijer paused again, looking for a reaction from Danny.

Danny leaned back in his chair, his hands behind his head. 'Go on, don't stop, I'll wait till you've completed this little charade,' he said nonchalantly. He knew exactly what was going on. This was the last ditch attempt to try and obtain a conviction. They were trying to rile him. Meijer's superiors must have put pressure on him due to the length of time this investigation had been going nowhere. But one thing puzzled him. How did they know the car was his old Mercedes? He'd got rid of it. Untraceable. Did it mean there *was* a photograph? Or had they just got a record of the registration and looked up the make from the licensing authority? He decided on the latter.

'No comment.' Danny said emphatically.

Meijer continued:

'You then met the woman Liliane Duval. You realised that she could help you in your quest to hide what you stole from Wilson.

We have discovered that Duval had made two sizeable deposits into her accounts in Rouen. These accounts were virtually empty according to records held at Abbeville, her previous address.

You gave her the money to bank, we believe, because you needed some 'working capital' as you might say. The rest you put into her new deposit box.

Unfortunately for you, she turned against you, probably when she saw how much you had stolen, and being selfish, she wanted it for herself. So she gave you away. But somehow you were able to get your hands on your stolen goods again, later.

Following your return to Amsterdam, you then went back to Rouen and murdered her, before returning in time to appear at your 6 p.m. appointment here at Elandsgracht. The two pieces of chopping board have been confirmed to contain traces of Miss Duval's DNA – *your* chopping board, found in *your* car. You used it to stun her before throwing her off the balcony.'

You will understand that I have abbreviated somewhat the case against you, but I am now going to arrest you for the murders of Peter Radbourne, Cheryl Pieterson, George Wilson and Liliane Duval. Read him his rights, Constable.'

'Hey! Wait a minute. I said I wanted to comment at the end of your spiel.' Danny was now getting carried away. 'You're all gonna look a bit foolish if you arrest me without a shred of evidence. You know I'll walk after 48 hours.

Your case falls flat at the very first hurdle.

Show me the photo of me an' Pete in Harwich. I know you ain't got one. You ain't got photo's of me on the A14 or the M6 neither. Cos I wasn't there.

Danny knew this was all a bit of a gamble, but he felt sure that this information, had it been true, would have been available much earlier on in the investigation, after all, they had consulted with the Port and Highway Authorities as a first step in their enquiries.

'You're just makin' it all up cos you don't know where Pete is, you can't find the car, you think I've nicked stuff from Wilson. You've searched me flat, so you know I haven't got the loot. You know I'm reportin' to the station each day, so how the fuck would I get to kill Lil? Why would I murder anyone? Yeah, I lost me job, yeah, I lost me girl, but I ain't a murderer. As for the bleedin' choppin' board, it was one of the things we bought for our flat in Rouen. I took it, along with a load of other stuff when I left the flat. I bought it, so I took it, simple as that. So I'm gonna walk out of here now, an if you want to arrest me that's your prerogative, but you're gonna look silly when they start askin' you for evidence. You've gotta spend your time lookin' for Pete an' the car, mate.'

He stood up and walked to the door. 'Let me out!' he shouted.

Meijer hesitated for a few seconds, then waived his hand to the constable by the door. 'Let him out,' he said with a weary sigh.

'You brought me here, so are you gonna give me a lift back to my place?' Danny asked mischievously.

'Certainly not,' was all that Meijer replied, a look of disdain on his face.

Danny sauntered out of the station. He couldn't believe his luck. Meijer didn't realise how close he was to the truth, he thought. It was a theory, obviously; otherwise he would have tabled some form of evidence.

Now he knew he was truly safe.

As he strolled back to his flat, he made a short phone call to his father.

'Danny, glad you phoned. We need to talk. Can you come over now? Where are you?'

'Just come out of the police station at Elandsgracht. I'm walking. The bastards wouldn't take me back home.'

'OK, get a taxi and come over here straight away. We can have a bite to eat and a chat. Something's come up, an' I can't discuss it over the phone.'

Danny accepted. He was feeling a bit peckish. He hailed the first cab that was free.

At Redmayne's house, he was handed a plate of ham sandwiches and a couple of beers and the pair sat down in the snug. Redmayne looked worried. Danny didn't touch his sandwich. Instead, he lit a cigarette and inhaled deeply.

'So what's all this cloak an' dagger stuff then, Dad?' He enquired jovially, tilting his head back and casually blowing smoke rings into the air above him.

Redmayne hung his head a little, his eyes darting back and forth across the patterned carpet, as he tried to formulate an easy way to convey his news.

'You're gonna go mad Danny, but Karl, our agent in SA has been killed, and the guy who did it is none other than your half-brother.'

'You're kidding me?'

'No, would I kid about a thing like that? There's more too.'

'Yeah? Like what?'

'Like he was doing some of the runs for us and he knows the ropes so he might squeal if he's caught.'

'He wouldn't do that if he's in the squad would he?'

'Dunno, but they want him out of it. And there's more…'

'Christ! I know what you're gonna say. They want me to do it?'

'Afraid so.'

'But I ain't even met the bloke yet. Am I s'posed to say 'Hi, I'm your brother, then knife him?'

'Something like that.'

'For fuck's sake. What if I won't do it?'

'You know the answer to that, Danny. They'll come after you.'

Danny leaned back in the armchair, took a long drag on his cigarette, and blew the smoke out in a long, whistling sigh.

'This game is getting too much, you know Dad. I was hopin' to get out of it myself soon. Get myself a proper job, get married, settle down, have kids…you know what I mean?'

You can still do all that Danny, but first you've gotta do this job.'

'How do I know they ain't gonna do the same to me after?'

'Look Danny, you've mostly always done what you've been asked to do. You ain't never gone against them, as far as they know. So you've got credit. They'll take that into account.'

'What's the deal?'

'He's on his way over to Schiphol. You meet him at the airport. He won't know who you are, not with that crappy hairstyle and 'tache. You'll have to pick him up at the customs exit – you know – with one of them signs with a name on, like they do. I'll leave it to you to decide whether you tell him who you are, but there's no use in getting him all excited then topping him.'

'Where do I take him?'

'Anywhere you like. Just make sure it's somewhere quiet. Outside the city, definitely. Dump him in a dyke somewhere lonely...I dunno.'

'Jesus! I can't believe this. You're his fuckin' dad. How do you feel about it?'

'Look, Danny. I feel the same way you do, but I hardly know the guy. I've met 'im once and I can't help you on this. The order's come from the top. It's not as if you ain't done one before, by what some guys are saying.'

'Who's sayin'?'

'You were seen in London, doing over the old man. Luckily he was a hood – not one of our guys, but some rival outfit who'd been watchin' and knew about our operation. You beat him to the old man. He admitted that he was gonna get the cash before you got there, then nick the sparklers off of you, after. He couldn't 'cos he was a bit slow off the mark an' he didn't expect you to kill the old man. He thought he might get implicated 'cos he'd been seen casin' the joint, so he cleaned up the place and then tried to get some readies out of us by threatening to go to the old Bill.'

'An' you believed him?'

'Well it all seemed to fit. So I paid him off – twenty grand - and threatened him with his life if he ever came back to me or did anything about it.'

'So you think I stitched up Wilson too? Took his money?'

'Yeah, I thought you might have, but I didn't do nothing about it for two reasons. Firstly we was competing for trade and secondly you were the only real son I had, When you went down to France I thought you were lying low for a while.'

'Bloody Hell! And all the time I was tellin' you I didn't do it!'

'Yeah, but to be honest I was never quite sure.'

Danny was furious. 'Well you'd better keep your mouth shut now, cos if the rest of them think I did the Wilson job, my days are well and truly numbered.'

'Don't worry, Danny lad, I can keep quiet on this, you're my son, and as far as I'm concerned family comes first.'

'Family comes first? That's rich. You just said I had to top Jeff. Family comes first, my arse! I don't wanna do this, Dad, I've had enough killin' an' I'm in the clear with the cops now. But if I do another, they might tie it all in and I'll get done.'

'Looks like you'll get done either way Danny boy, so I think you've gotta do it. Get it over with, then lie low for a while.'

'What flight's the guy on?'

'11.55 tonight – KLM - from Jo'burg. Gets in at 10.15 tomorrow morning.'

'OK. I'll do it, but I want payin'. Tell 'em I want ten grand, how's that?'

'I'll tell them. It won't be a problem.'

'I've gotta go to the station first…tonight at 6.00. I wanna get my curfew cancelled. Now Lil's dead there's no need for me to be reporting in every night. Then I'll do the job and disappear for a few days – you can tell everyone I've gone on holiday.'

'You'll have to use that as an excuse with the police tonight when you check in, Danny boy, otherwise, when they find Blythe, they'll think you've done it and scarpered.'

'Good point, Dad. That could work. I'll sort out a plan on the way home.'

They both rose from their chairs and Danny went over to his father and embraced him, with a pat on the back.

'I'll see you sometime, when the heat's off,' he said, before turning to the door and letting himself out into the street.

Chapter 57

At the airport, Jeff parked up in the short stay car park, reached into his waistband and withdrew the pistol, placing it carefully under his seat. He collected his case from the trunk and – making sure he stayed within the well-lit areas, he walked quickly to the terminal entrance. 'So far, so good,' he thought.

Once inside, he checked in and went immediately to the security barrier, ensuring that he was as close to the other passengers as possible, thereby making it difficult for any possible attacker.

Passing through security without incident, he walked quickly to his gate. He had about twenty minutes to wait before boarding would commence. He found a seat next to a rather large woman with a small child and sat down. To others it might look like husband and wife, he hoped. Trying not to look apprehensive, he glanced around him, looking out for anyone who might fit the description of a hit man, but there were none.

He checked his phone for messages. There was only one – from Jenny, wishing him well for the trip.

On the 'plane he took his aisle seat in row 12, next to a large, rather swarthy looking, but neatly dressed African who was playing some kind of game on his mobile, his thumbs twiddling incessantly on the screen, his elbows constantly invading Jeff's seat space.

For five minutes he put up with it, but then, he felt he had to say something, as otherwise he was afraid that he might be subjected to the frequent nudging all the way to Schiphol.

It served as an introduction, for as it turned out, Thato Khumalo was attending the same meeting too. However, he had apparently forgotten to bring his copy of the Turnaround Proposals document. He said he worked in the maintenance team in Johannesburg as a Supervisor.

'Say, Jeff, can I have a quick scan of yours? Just to get clued up,' he enquired. 'I'll probably get another copy at the meeting anyway.'

Jeff, with some trepidation, was about to reach up for his briefcase in the overhead locker when a passing stewardess restrained him.

'Please remain seated until we have taken off and the seat-belt sign is extinguished, sir,' she whispered firmly.

He slumped back into his seat, relieved for her intervention. With a bit of luck the guy might not ask again.

It was too much of a coincidence. Firstly, finding himself sitting next to this man from the same company, then secondly, discovering that he had mislaid his copy of the document. It all seemed a little contrived. Could this be the switch? If it was happening here on the 'plane he'd be lucky to get out of the airport at Schiphol, except possibly in a coffin.

Jeff re-fastened his seat belt and glanced out of the window. The plane was now gathering speed for take-off. He settled in his seat and closed his eyes. He would feign sleep until the on-board breakfast arrived.

At 7.30 am he was woken with a prod from his fellow passenger, pointing to the trolley being trundled down the isle. Breakfast was being served. Jeff unfolded his seat tray from the armrest.

'Don't forget to give me a shufty at that document,' the big African reminded him, but it was too late now, his tray was in position and his food had arrived.

'I'll get it out for you when we're off the plane,' Jeff suggested, 'we're both going to the same meeting, so we've plenty of opportunity to discuss the document. I'd like to hear your comments too, from the execution side as opposed to my managerial viewpoint.'

So it was agreed that they would discuss it when they arrived at Khumalo's hotel. Jeff assumed that he would be booked into the same one, although he hadn't been advised of it. But it did cross his mind that the lack of a reservation meant that someone somewhere had deemed it unnecessary…

Who if anyone would pick him up? He wondered. Would he meet his demise at the airport? He had no idea.

Chapter 58

At Schiphol Airport, Danny walked across the Arrivals Hall and took up his position at the barrier by the customs exit, holding his clumsily produced card with Jeff's name scrawled across it in black felt tip pen.

He was nervous. He still didn't know what his reaction would be when he met his half-brother for the first time, knowing that it would be the shortest reunion in history. He wondered whether Jeff knew that it would be Danny meeting him. He was dying for a cigarette, but had finished the pack in his pocket on his way over to the Airport. He checked his watch – it was 10.05 a.m. He looked up at the Arrivals screen above his head. The KLM flight from Jo'burg would be landing 10 minutes late. He would have plenty of time to get a coffee and another pack of cigarettes before Jeff Blythe appeared, he thought.

He looked down the long hall, searching for a coffee shop, but of course, he was on the wrong side of the airport. No new arrival would be looking for food and drink on their way out. However he found a soft drinks machine and dispensed a can of coke, and then begged a cigarette off a passing passenger.

Fifteen minutes later, he joined the now enlarged throng of 'people meeters' at the barrier. He studied the names on the various boards being held up. One in particular caught his eye, purely because of the unusual name – Thato Khumalo. He noticed that the board was larger than most, with a company logo in rich colours splashed across the top and the gentleman's name printed meticulously upon it. Not scruffily, like his own. He wondered what a guy with a name like that might do for a living. He was obviously fairly high up in the organisation if the board was anything to go by.

Suddenly, the double doors at the customs exit swung out and a mass of passengers, bags and trolleys poured out through the opening in a continuous stream. Danny held his card up high, as did the other cardholders. He saw a tall burly black guy talking with an equally tall, but slender, fair-haired white guy as they approached the throng. 'I wonder if that's Thato Khumalo,' he muttered under his breath as the big African simultaneously walked over to the fancy card, confirming Danny's guess. The white guy stood beside him, in conversation with the cardholder. There was obviously a problem, as after a good deal of gesticulating, the white guy suddenly turned and started scanning the remaining cards, looking for his own name.

Suddenly his eyes fell upon Danny's card. His face morphed in an instant from apprehension to terror, his eyes darting about over the crowd. Instead of walking over towards Danny, he took off suddenly at a fast trot down the long hallway, dragging his trolley bag behind him, looking about him wildly as he raced across the marble floor. Danny was unsure, but his instinct told him that this was his pick-up. No other had approached him, so he fought his way through the throng of greeters and went after him.

With no luggage to encumber him, Danny found himself quickly gaining upon his quarry. Jeff had almost made it to the revolving exit door by the taxi rank but Danny was now within earshot. He called out to him.

'Hey! Jeff, I'm Danny, your brother!'

Jeff skidded to a halt, his trolley bag slamming into his ankles and he turned to face his executioner.

'They sent you to do it?' he asked, stunned and amazed that this skinny little runt standing before him was his killer, despite being actually related to him. '*You're* my brother? You don't look anything like your photo.'

'Yeah, but don't worry about that, I am your bro' an' I ain't gonna do it yet, I've gotta get to know you a bit first,' he said with a wry smile. 'You never know, if we get on, I might just call off the hit.'

Danny could detect clearly the relief in Jeff's eyes. He had obviously sensed the possible postponement of his demise.

'What was it that scared you into bolting like that?' Danny asked.

'The boards. That big black guy and I – we both work for the same company. When I saw his, then yours, I knew something was wrong.'

'But did you get the goods through?'

'Sure, they're in my briefcase.'

'OK let's go.' Danny motioned toward the exit.

They walked over to the short stay car park, dumped Jeff's stuff in the boot of the Citroen and clambered in.

He didn't start the car immediately, instead, he rummaged around in the glove compartment and was relieved to find a started pack of cigarettes. He wound the window down and lit up.

'Have you got one of those for me?' Jeff asked.

Danny offered him the pack and Jeff nervously plucked one from the crumpled foil with a shaking hand. 'I don't usually smoke,' he started, 'but my nerves are that shot that I'm sure it'll do me good.'

Danny leaned over and held out his bony hand.

'We've not been formally introduced,' he said, 'my name's Danny Redmayne and you must be Jeff Blythe, my half-brother. My dad shagged your mum a long time ago, so now you an' me are related. Funny old world innit?'

'Yes, and now you're going to kill me?'

'Well, I'm getting ten grand for the privilege, an' I don't wanna lose out on that. Maybe you could buy me out? Anyhow, we'll see how things go eh?'

'Can we get something to eat? I'm starving. The food was crap on the plane.'

'Yeah, but we've gotta put a few miles on the clock before we do that. And I've been thinkin' about things and I'm not sure I wanna lose me half-brother too soon. Like me dad said, 'family comes first'. So we need to hatch a plan.'

They drove back to the outskirts of Amsterdam and parked up at a cheap chain restaurant for a late breakfast.

Over ham, eggs and strong coffee, they each divulged their circumstances to the other. Jeff was first off the mark; keen to let Danny know that Karl's death was a complete accident.

Danny listened. He half-believed that the story might be true for he couldn't imagine that this rather refined, well-spoken guy sitting opposite him could be capable of cold-blooded murder.

'So what have you got to go back to in SA?' Danny enquired.

Jeff looked down at his coffee but didn't respond for some seconds. 'I truly don't know,' he eventually blurted. ' I have a job, a house and a girlfriend, but enemies too. If I go back I'll be hunted down by the cartel. If I don't go back, Jenny will probably be abducted and used as a lure. They might even kill her, who knows.

'What's she like this Jenny?'

'Well, I suppose she's the best thing that's happened to me for a while. You know she was Karl's wife I suppose?

'No Shit! No I didn't. You nicked her off him? She must be a cracker. You're bloody lucky to be alive…even if it's not for much longer,' Danny grinned.

Suddenly he was warming to this guy. He wasn't quite the toffee nosed pillock that he first imagined.

'Anyway, What about you?' Jeff queried. 'Do you have a bird?'

'Did have, but she's dead now,' Danny said matter of factly, 'fell off the balcony of our flat in Rouen'.

'Bloody hell! That's unfortunate. Sorry to hear that,' Jeff felt the uncomfortable spasm in his spine as he conjured up the image of the accident in his mind.

'So what are you going to do now, Danny?' he asked.

'Dunno! Me Dad knows I killed the old man, an' he thinks I might have killed Wilson, so if he tells the rest of the Cartel then mebbe my days are over too if I go back to me flat in Amsterdam.'

'You've killed people before? Who was the old man? Who was Wilson?'

Danny realised that Jeff knew little of what had been going on at this end of the organisation. He thought of telling Jeff the whole sordid story, then hesitated. Was it too early? Could he trust him to keep his mouth shut? He was due to be topped anyway, so it probably would make no difference, he concluded. So he lit another cigarette, leaned back in his chair and filled Jeff in on the whole episode, leaving absolutely nothing out.

As he talked, Jeff interjected here and there, either to ask for clarification or to express his view or even simply to issue an expletive.

When Danny had finished they both sat in silence for some time. Jeff, dazed with the seriousness of Danny's misdemeanours, thought more coffee might help and called over the waitress.

'Sounds like we're both in a bit of a hole.' He ventured.

'Fuckin' big hole!' Danny responded, reaching for another cigarette. 'So what do we do about it?'

'That depends on what you want to do with the rest of your life, Danny.'

' I was only just sayin' to me Dad that I was hopin' to get out of the cartel myself soon. Get myself a proper job, get married, settle down, have kids 'n' that.'

'OK, So what was your next move going to be, assuming you'd got rid of me?'

'I was gonna go an' report to the police as usual at 6.00 tonight, tell them I want me curfew stopped, 'cos I'm goin' on holiday.'

'Right, so if your Dad knows that, then the cartel will also know, and if I don't show, they'll assume you finished me off wouldn't they?

'Yeah, that's right'

'OK. So…If I disappear as well, we'd both be good.'

'Yeah – good thinking Batman!'

'How many people in the cartel know who you are?'

'Well, seein' as I've killed most of 'em, only me dad an' you, now.'

'What about Gordon McKlintock over in SA?'

'I've heard of 'im, but never seen 'im.'

'And you're sure there's no-one else?'

'Sure as eggs! But what about you?'

'Well, seeing as I've killed only one, it's Gordon McKlintock and Alan Redmayne, your dad – besides you of course.'

'So we've only got three to deal with?'

'Yes, but no more killing – we've got to plan a way to get them out of our hair without them realising that we did it.'

'I'm not sure I want me dad wrapped up with the rest of 'em.'

'Well that depends on whose side he's on – yours or theirs. What do you think?'

'He'd probably be on my side, but it would cause him a problem with the cartel. Mebbe the best way is to get us both a meet with me dad and thrash it out.'

'But it would show that you hadn't carried out your hit.'

'Yeah, but in a way you're his son too, an' he might just want you to stay alive for his sake or even mine. But I dunno, is it worth the risk?'

'Well, we could try it. I've met your dad before. He seems a reasonable sort of guy. When I explain how Karl came to grief he may just change his mind and help us.'

Danny checked his watch. It was 12.15. 'What time is your meetin' with your company?'

'There is no meeting,' Jeff assured him, 'I'm convinced it was a set-up and besides, the subject was not my field anyway. I'm in Research not Maintenance. It was contrived to give a reason for the drop, and to get me out of the way.'

'But what about that big black guy at the airport – the one you were with – isn't he goin' to it?'

'No, I think he was the pick-up, I think he was hoping to get the goods while I was still on the 'plane and then you could move straight in and do your dirty work. Save on the hotel bills, eh?'

'So if he's not goin' to no meetin' he's in the cartel as well?'

'Christ! Yes – he's another one to put on our list. I forgot about that.'

'So he'll be hangin' around to try and get the goods back and to make sure you're topped?'

'Could be. We'd better keep our eyes open, he may be watching our every move.'

'Shit! That complicates it. We can't go to me Dad's unless we lose him first.'

'Well let's see if he's tailing us first.'

As if it had been orchestrated, both Jeff and Danny turned to stare out of the window of the restaurant. They scanned the car park, looking for a face in one of the vehicles. There was none.

'Well, we'd better go back to me flat,' Danny suggested, 'we'll take a detour and if he's behind us we'll lose him. We can contact me dad from there.'

They rose from the table and Danny tucked a €20 note under the sugar bowl. They left the restaurant, carefully checking there was no-one about.

Danny took an indirect route back to his flat, checking his rear view mirror constantly. After a couple of miles, a taxi caught up with them and followed his route for some time, but eventually it took a left turn and his rear mirror was clear again.

'Can you park somewhere out of sight?' Jeff asked, as they approached the flats, 'just in case they come looking for your car?'

Danny drove around the back, to an enclosed area of parked cars. 'I ain't got a space here, but it's never that full up. It'll be OK for a couple of hours.'

They left the car and cautiously went up to Danny's Flat.

Jeff dropped his bag in Danny's spare bedroom and went back into the living room.

'I've had an idea,' he called to Danny in the kitchen.

Danny re-appeared with two bottles of beer and a bowl of Tortillas. 'What kind'a idea?' He handed a beer to Jeff.

'Well, suppose you say that you never met me at the airport, but you saw me being taken away by the customs officials. The pick-up failed, and the diamonds are in the hands of the authorities?'

'Yeah, but what about the black guy? He came out with you into the Arrivals hall. He knows you didn't get arrested.'

'Well, other than him, we can stitch up everyone else with the story. We might have to sort out the black guy.'

'And how do we do that? We'd have to find him first.'

'That's no problem – I think I know which hotel he's staying at.' Jeff remembered the agreement he had made on the plane.

'So when we get to him, what do we do?'

'I don't know yet. I haven't thought that far ahead yet.'

'I could top him,' Danny offered, after all, I'm getting used to doin' that to folks I don't like.

'No, no more killing Danny, we've got to find a more refined solution.'

'Suppose we get the goods to him an' then tip off the police?'

'Possibly, but he'd probably shop me in the process and they'd come looking.'

'He'll just have to be topped,' Danny insisted, 'I'll sort it out.'

Jeff sat quietly, contemplating that solution. It seemed the only way, but he wasn't happy about it.

'We haven't looked at the goods yet,' Danny reminded him. 'Hadn't we better see what you brought over?'

Jeff stood up, walked over to the bedroom and opened up his case. He took out the blue folder and on the way to his chair he tossed it to Danny.

'What the fuck's this?' Danny exclaimed. 'Where's the goods in this?'

'Look in the spine,' Jeff suggested.

Danny ripped the spine from the folder, loosening the pages, which wafted to the floor. He took out his switchblade and forced apart the plastic spine, carefully levering out the contents. The glue like substance at each end took up about a centimetre of space and the rest of the spines length was filled with diamonds about the size of his little finger nail - twenty in all.

'Jesus!' he swore, 'there's about two hundred grand here. We're made.'

'Haven't you got enough already, Danny? You can't even get rid of your own stuff, never mind worrying about that lot.'

'Yeah, I know, but it would be a shame to lose this. We could take some out, an' just leave a couple in there.'

'But you're forgetting that McKlintock knows how many were there in the first place.'

'Mebbe. But we could pin the difference on the black guy.'

'How?'

'Suppose we put the folder together again with, say, 6 sparklers in there. I'll take it to his hotel tonight and say you were supposed to give it to him, but you're now dead meat. He takes the document, I leave, he thinks you're dead, he phones the cartel to give them the good news, I go on holiday an' you disappear. He won't be opening the file, he'll just hand it over to his contact and by the time the shortage is discovered, we'll be well away and the big black guy will be the suspect.'

'But what about Jenny…and my job with the company? I'm heading for a directorship. I don't want to let that go.'

'Beggars can't be choosers, mate, you're a crook, just like me. You gotta choose. One or the other. You're either in or you're out?'

Jeff fell back into the chair and ran his fingers through his hair several times while he tried to think. How did he allow himself to get into this mess? He wished he'd never met Karl – he was the start of it, but he also blamed himself for showing interest in the first place. He had to find a solution, which took the heat off, ended his involvement yet saved his position in the Company. The key to that would be resolving three issues: His relationship with Danny, converting Alan Redmayne and dealing with McKlintock, none of which were going to prove easy.

'OK, Jeff said eventually, we'll go with your plan to take the folder to Thato Khumalo.'

'Yeah, crazy name. I saw it on his greet card. What kinda name is that? Poor bugger!' Danny laughed.

'Well, he's an African. It's probably quite a common name over there. So…you do that, then we go see your dad and square things with him. Then that only leaves McKlintock. We've got to get your dad to go along with us in convincing him that I'm no longer of this world. Do you think he'd do it?'

'I reckon he might, but how could we persuade him? I could mebbe give him some of me loot, but he might not bite.'

'Well let's give it a try.' Jeff replied. 'We'll see where we go from there.'

Chapter 59

Thato Khumalo fumbled in his pocket for his mobile and dialled a local number.

'Redmayne?'

Alan Redmayne acknowledged.

'The pick-up failed…I don't know where the party is. There was another guy at Arrivals. The party ran off with the other guy chasing him. God knows where they went.'

'So you don't have the goods?'

'No.'

'How the Hell did you lose them? You better find them, and quick.' Redmayne said forcefully. 'There's two fifty k on him.'

'Where do I start? Amsterdam's a big place.'

'That's your problem, mate. But you'd better get out there and find them. Where are you staying?'

'Hotel Zoku on Weesperstraat. Room 204, it's the second floor.'

'OK, that's not far from here, I'll come over tomorrow at 10.00, straight up to your room. Make sure you're there.'

He hung up.

'Shit! Alan Redmayne was furious. He wondered whether Danny had lost his quarry. He cursed himself for not combining the two activities of pick-up and hit on one man. Now he had a pick-up without the goods and a hit man without his target. And he didn't know where either of them was. 'It's a cock-up,' he swore to himself.

He looked at his watch. He might just catch McKlintock in Jo'burg at this time. He went down to his office and took his mobile from the desk drawer and dialled the number.

'McKlintock….'

'Gordon? It's Alan…we've got a problem. Your man didn't make the switch.'

'For fuck's sake! Where is he now?'

'He's in a hotel. He's gonna try to find the party, but there don't seem to be much chance of that unless my lad Danny's kept up with him. I'll let you know when I've got more details. I'm meetin' up with Khumalo at 10 tomorrow. I'd like to beat the shit out of him.'

'You might have a problem there, he's a big guy. Best of luck!'

McKlintock rang off and thumped his desk with his fist in frustration. How had Khumalo failed to collect? How did Danny lose his hit? It was a balls-up. Who's got the goods now? He didn't know. He would have to bring things to a head.

Chapter 60

Alan Redmayne was watching the early evening news when Danny's call came through.

'Where the fuck are you, Danny?' he howled down the phone. What's happened to Blythe? Did you catch him?'

'Don't worry dad, I've got him. Things is all under control.' Danny assured him.

What about the switch? Did you get the stuff to Khumalo?

'Happening as we speak.'

'So you've got it all under control. You can carry out the remaining task in hand?'

'Sure, but I need to see you first. I gotta couple of things to discuss.'

'Well, I'm here, but don't let no-one see you comin' to me. Mebbe I meet you at your flat. Say 8 o'clock tonight?'

'OK dad, we'll be here.'

'Who the fuck's 'we'? Blythe's not with you too, is he?'

''Fraid so dad, that's who I wanna talk about. See ya at eight.'

Danny rang off.

He picked up the modified file, which now looked a little less pristine since fourteen of the diamonds had been removed and the whole thing reassembled by an inexperienced hand. 'OK Jeff, you wait here, I'm off to the Zoku to get this stuff to that Thato fella. Me dad's comin' over at 8 o'clock. I'll be back before then.'

'You'd better be,' said Jeff, I don't want to face him on my own, he'll probably do the job for you.'

Jeff switched on the TV, found a clean patch on Danny's threadbare sofa and sat down. He could do nothing now but wait.

Danny arrived at the Hotel Zoku at 5.30. He walked across the entrance hall to the reception desk and asked for

Thato Khumalo's room number. The desk clerk checked his computer and rang Khumalo's room. 'Who shall I say is calling?' he asked, in perfect English.

'Just tell him that the delivery man is here.' Danny said impatiently.

The clerk repeated Danny's suggestion and nodded into the phone. 'Thank you sir,' was all he said.

'Mr Khumalo says you may go up to his room. Second floor, room number 204.'

Danny turned without any acknowledgement and looked for the lift.

At the second floor he passed through the fire door and followed the signs to rooms 1 – 19 and at number 4 he paused before knocking. He checked the switchblade in his pocket then took a deep breath and tapped on the door.

He heard the peephole cover slide away and he instinctively moved toward the doorjamb as if expecting Khumalo to shoot through, blind.

The door opened a crack and Danny announced himself.

The first thing that struck him was the size of the guy, as he lumbered back into his room with Danny following behind. He was glad he had the forethought to put his switchblade in his pocket.

'How come you're doing the drop?' Khumalo asked.

'Well, the other guy don't exist no more, mate.' Danny replied.

'You've dealt with him?'

'Yeah – he's dead meat.'

'And you've got the file?'

'Yeah, it's all yours, mate.'

Danny handed over the file and apologised for the slightly 'used' look of it. 'Got a bit mangled when I sorted him out,' he said, 'put up a bit of a fight until I got me knife in his ribs.'

Khumalo squirmed slightly as he listened to Danny's story.

'So what did you do with him?'

'Don't worry, he's well hidden, no one will ever find him – at least, not for some time anyway. Then it won't matter – he'll be worm fodder.' Danny assured him. And he got up to leave.

'What's your plan now?' he asked.

Khumalo shrugged his shoulders. 'I'm not sure yet. I've got to contact my boss and he'll tell me. Drop this little lot off then go back home I suppose.'

'Ok. Won't see ya then? Have a good trip.' Danny replied with a smile, as he made for the door.

Alan Redmayne rang Khumalo at his hotel and cancelled his 10 o'clock meeting. Now that Danny had organised the drop there was no point. Instead he just reinforced his feelings about the big black's performance, suggesting that he 'get his arse back home as quickly as possible'.

He then set off for Danny's flat, arriving at bang on 8 o'clock. Danny had only just had time to get back and was in the process of opening a couple of beers. He made it three and went to the door, to let his father in. He handed Alan Redmayne one of the beers and they both walked into the lounge.

Jeff stood up from the sofa, unsure as to what reception he might get. Danny made the introductions.

'Yes, OK, OK, we've already met,' Alan Redmayne said impatiently, totally ignoring Jeff. 'So what's this little plan of yours, Danny?'

Danny took some seconds to reply, trying to compose things in his mind in order to make his solution more plausible. He would have to appeal to his father's softer side and that meant laying it on thick about 'family'.

'Dad, look, I know I had a job to do, and it was easy to say it beforehand, but when I was at the airport an' I saw

Jeff for the first time, I found meself lookin' at me brother, an' I ain't never had one before. It just didn't seem right that I should be toppin' him, he seemed such a nice fella. I wanted to get to know him a bit.

Bedsides, things ain't quite what we thought, an' Jeff is gonna tell you all about what really happened with Karl, aren't you Jeff?' Danny glanced enquiringly across at Jeff, sitting opposite him.

Jeff nodded and turned to Redmayne. He explained about Karl and Jenny's marriage breakdown, how Jenny had latched on to Jeff, how Jeff had tried to extricate himself from his unwanted involvement in the cartel, Karl's mistreatment of Jenny and his threat to kill Jeff, which culminated in the fight resulting in Karl's demise.

At the end of it all, Jeff waited for a reaction from Redmayne but it took some time before he responded. Redmayne was casting his mind back to his own misdemeanours with Jeff's mother. Was he really in a position to judge this situation? He decided it was not quite the same scenario.

'Ok, I hear what you say. And I know that Karl could be a bully at times, but he was entitled to defend his position, especially over Jenny. She was his wife, for God's sake. How would you feel if someone walked into your life and walked out again with your wife, no matter what the relationship was like? You wouldn't tolerate it either.'

'Yes, agreed,' Jeff replied, 'but that wasn't what the argument was about when we had the fight. We had already resolved that issue in a previous fracas during which Jenny was seriously hurt.

The business with the gun was purely as a result of my request to get out of any involvement in the cartel. My position with the Oil Company had changed and I didn't want to lose it. Karl insisted that I continue my involvement, threatening me with statements like 'nobody gets out of the cartel and lives' and suchlike. I wouldn't have it and told him I was not doing another run. That's when he pointed his gun at me and I tried to wrestle it out of his hand. God knows, I would never have dreamt of killing him. It was just a horrible accident.'

'Yeah, and now we are all in the shit,' Redmayne said, 'They want you done away with by Danny and if he don't do it we are all dead meat.'

Danny suddenly sat forward on his chair. 'But dad, you said before, family comes first, an' he's your son too. But we've hatched a plan to put it all right, listen…If Jeff disappears, and I say the job's done and you keep quiet, then we're in the clear. I know it's a bit more complicated than that, but we can work it out. Let's stop all this killin' now – for good.

'But Danny, you're forgetting that McKlintock works for the same company as Jeff. And then there's Khumalo, what does he know?'

'He knows jack shit! I already told him that Jeff's dead meat.'

'So what's his next move?'

'Going home, he thinks.'

'OK, well, I'm not leavin' here tonight until we've got a bullet proof story and it's gotta stand up solid with each of us. We've all gotta say exactly the same thing. OK? It's gonna be a long night so let's get a take-away delivered and some more beers and we'll get our story straight.'

It looked like Redmayne was coming round to the idea.

Chapter 61

There was a knock at the front door, then the bell sounded. Danny jumped up from his chair, grabbed his wallet and went out into the hall.

He reappeared with a pile of slightly damp Pizza boxes. 'I'll get some more beer from the fridge,' he said as he handed a box to Jeff and Alan Redmayne.

Between mouthfuls of limp pepperoni pizza and slugs of cold lager, they concocted their story:

The first step was to safeguard 'kith and kin'. Jeff insisted that this must include Jenny over in Johannesburg. So Redmayne was charged with phoning McKlintock and confirming that the hit on Jeff had been completed. He would probably know already from Khumalo, but Redmayne's call would reinforce the point, and that would prevent any further action by McKlintock.

Jeff would arrange an immediate flight to UK for Jenny, using his purported disappearance as the reason, but the flight would be one-way.

Jenny would call Jim Barber, the estate agent and arrange for the house to be put back on sale. She would have to make all moving arrangements herself. The transactions would be completed from UK, but Jenny would maintain her bank accounts in South Africa at least until the completion of the sale. As she was now the heir to Karl's estate, she would also keep his house for the time being.

Danny would go to the police station at Elandsgracht in the morning and arrange for his curfew to be lifted, using an arranged 2-week touring holiday in his car as a reason. If that didn't wash with the coppers, it would be reinforced with the fact that as Liliane was now dead, there was no need for the reporting to continue. They would no longer be able to justify it.

Danny would then disappear.

Jeff would give notice to his tenants in Chelsea to vacate, as he would be returning to his flat. Pending his move back in, he would lodge with his brother in law. He would then contact his company in the Strand and deliver an ultimatum to David Robinson.

This part of the plan was still in its infancy, but was loosely based on the idea that Jeff would insist that Robinson either took him on board at Head Office with immediate effect, or Jeff would give his notice and seek employment elsewhere with a competitor.

Alan Redmayne would let it be known that he had met with Danny after he had carried out the hit asked him to carry out the switch with Khumalo.

Any attempts by the cartel to accuse Danny of having tampered with the goods prior to the switch would be met with fierce resistance from Redmayne. Instead, he would suggest that either Khumalo or McKlintock were the more likely candidates.

Things were looking good so far. However, there was still the possibility that McKlintock would get wind that the hit on Jeff had not taken place, especially if Jeff remained with the company in any capacity.

How would they get over that particularly crucial issue?

'Somehow we've got to get him sacked.' Jeff suggested.

'Or dealt with by the cartel?' Danny chipped in.

'I don't think that would work,' Jeff replied, 'not unless there was some proof that he had tampered with the package for his own gain.'

'Could we get the diamonds to him, say stashed in his house somewhere for the cartel to find?' Jeff asked.

Redmayne laughed. Although he had now consumed 5 bottles of lager he remained sober enough to recognise the difficulties that Jeff's suggestion might involve.

'That would be the hardest thing to do.' He said, 'You've gotta get through two lots of customs first, then get into his house, then get outta the house without bein' seen, then outta the country again. Too many possible pitfalls, mate'

'Shit! So we're stumped!' Danny rasped, 'If we can't plant the diamonds on 'im, cos we'd have to go there to do it, what else can we do? Get someone to top 'im?'

'You said no more killing, Danny, remember?'

'Yeah, but this is serious an' we ain't gonna resolve it any other way.'

'Hang on a minute,' Jeff said excitedly, maybe we *can* stitch him up some other way. Do we know where any of his relatives live?'

'He's Scottish, so I guess Scotland.' Redmayne replied dryly.

'Yes, but could we find out?'

'Why what's your plan?'

'Well, let's say… that when Danny was supposedly about to kill me, I tried to put him off by offering him the fourteen diamonds. I could say that I'd had instructions to send them to one of McKlintock's relatives at an address - which we've got to find - for safe keeping, till he came back to UK.

Danny then goes to the cartel and returns the diamonds, tells them the story. That gets McKlintock his just desserts, but also makes Danny look really good. McKlintock gets the chop, and if the company hears about it – and I'm sure we can arrange that – he gets the sack too. All we've got to do is find a relative. Job done!'

Danny whooped with delight. 'That's it! That's it,' he shouted, jumping out of his chair, 'no one can prove or disprove it, so they'd have to take action. Jeff, you're a fuckin' mastermind.'

'Thanks Danny, but it does mean we've lost the best part of two hundred grand.'

'Yeah, but you can always have some of mine, Danny replied magnanimously.

Redmayne reached over to his pizza box and peeled the last slice away from the soggy cardboard. It was now cold and congealed. He folded it into three and stuffed it into his mouth. He chewed for a while as he contemplated Jeff's proposal.

He was a senior figure in the organisation, as was McKlintock. Implementation of Jeff's plan would mean that the cartel might break up and that would mean Redmayne might have to pull out too. That wouldn't be so bad. He'd made a fortune already. Which would he prefer? Another son or even more money?

On the other hand, McKlintock was no fool. He would know who had set him up. He would guess that Danny was involved as he knew that Khumalo hadn't achieved the switch on the 'plane. He would assume that Danny had taken the goods off Jeff then killed him, there was therefore every possibility that he was involved in the scam to incriminate him. However, he might not escape the wrath of the rest of the cartel – they might not believe him, especially when they find out he planned to pass on the diamonds to his relatives, whoever they might turn out to be.

On balance however, Redmayne felt the plan might work. There was nothing else on the table. And although he didn't like the idea of stitching up a colleague, he preferred that option rather than dealing with Jeff and upsetting Danny.

'OK, if we can find a suitable relative, we'll go with that.' He murmured, 'but I tell you this…we're all gonna have to play it very carefully with no slip-ups. Danny, you've gotta keep it low key. No shootin' your mouth off. This is just between us three, remember?'

'Yeah, dad, I ain't gonna do that. I don't want to get me balls chewed ya know.'

'OK...Jeff, we'll start with you. Get Jenny's airfare sorted. Speak to her. Explain what's going down and tell her what she's gotta do. When you've spoken to her, let us know how she took it and how soon she can do what she's gotta do. Then I'll sort McKlintock.

We'll start it all in the morning. Khumalo won't be exchanging the goods till then, so we'

re safe for the moment. Let's get some shut-eye now.'

Redmayne rose from the chair and stretched his legs. 'I better be goin'' he said, yawning.

Chapter 62

It was a sunny morning in Jo'burg. Jenny was taking her early morning swim, backstroking down the length of the pool, when she heard the phone ringing. She didn't know how long it had been ringing, for it only became audible as she neared the shallow end by the patio.

She lithely leapt out of the water, donned her towelling robe and rushed into the house. The phone was still ringing. Obviously the caller was not going to give up. She lifted the receiver and purred with delight at the sound of Jeff's voice.

After exchanging a few niceties, Jeff became serious.

'Look, darling, I'm not going to be able to come back to SA. I can't fully explain over the phone, but I need you to organise the sale of the house. We're moving back to UK, immediately, and you're going to have to move quickly…'

'Why what's happened? Why the urgency? Don't get me wrong I'm ecstatic about the idea, but it's all very sudden.'

'As I say, I'll tell you when I see you, but meanwhile get back to Jim Barber and get my house back on the market. We'll deal with yours, or should I call it Karl's, later. Then sort out shipping of our belongings – those that you really want to keep. Leave the rest. Sell the house, as it is, furniture and all. Get the Jeep sold too. Just get the best deal you can. You have to be out of there by tomorrow at the latest. I'm sorting you an air ticket as we speak.

Whatever happens, don't talk to anyone at the Oil Company and put the phone down on them if they call. Keep the house locked up, even when you are there. Don't let anyone in. Check you're not followed if you go out. All I can tell you is that there may be trouble soon so keep your eye out and get cracking. If the worst comes to the worst and people are wondering what you're up to, just tell them that you are doing all this because you are moving back to the UK, the urgency of your return is because I've disappeared and you suspect foul play. I'm very much alive, darling, but it's important that others don't know that. Sorry it all sounds so mysterious, but I promise that you'll understand when I see you. I'll let you know the flight time when it's sorted.'

'Oh, Jeff, I don't like the sound of all this – are you in trouble?' Jenny was in tears now, trying hard not to convey her anxiety to him.

'Sort of, but I can't go into it now. Just do the things I've said, get the balls rolling and get the flight back. Leave your bank accounts open, we'll need those for the transactions when they happen.'

'I don't think I'll get it all done in the time, Jeff, there's a lot to do.'

'Jenny, listen, just do what you can. You can always continue things from the UK. Whatever happens, you must be on that flight. OK?'

'OK, when will you phone me again?'

'As soon as I get the air ticket. Take care now.'

Jeff rang off. He wasn't happy about leaving her exposed like this, but there was no alternative. More than anything else, he hoped that she would be safe.

Thato Khumalo put the folder in the room safe and keyed in the locking code. Picking up his jacket from the bed, he left his room and took the lift down to the hotel bar. He decided to have a few drinks before retiring.

The file was due to be taken to London tomorrow by another courier. All Khumalo had to do was to get it to the guy before his flight. He was due to meet him in the KLM lounge at 11.00 am. No sweat, he'd be on his own flight home by 2.00 pm It hadn't gone entirely smoothly, but fortunately for him, things had worked out in the end.

He approached the bar and found an empty stool. Ordering a Jack Daniel's, he took out his handkerchief and wiped the seat before settling his ample rump upon it. He was always wary of communal seating. One never knew the degree of cleanliness of a previous occupant. The seat was warm and the empty glass upon the bar indicated that it had not been long vacated.

He took a sip of his drink and then glanced casually at his neighbours, left and right. The woman on the left, around fifty, but still reasonably good looking, he thought, stared into her glass, and showed no interest in him. The American guy on the right, younger by perhaps ten years, was itching to talk to somebody and didn't wait for Khumalo to introduce himself.

'Howdy fella! You waitin' fer a flight outta here too?' he asked.

Khumalo looked at him. 'Me? Yes I guess so. I'm meeting somebody first, then going back to South Africa tomorrow.'

'Atlanta. That's me. Via New York. Delta Airlines. I'm in IT. How about you?'

'Diamonds.' Khumalo whispered. 'I'm a trader.'

The woman on his left sat up suddenly on her barstool and turned towards him.

'Did I hear you say diamonds?' she asked huskily.

Suddenly she was interested.

'Can I buy you a drink?' Khumalo asked, his eyes lingering on her slim figure as he appraised her assets.

The woman affirmed and suggested they move to some more comfortable club chairs by the bar windows. The American swallowed the remnants of his whisky and declared that he was going to get some shuteye and he staggered slowly out of the room with a wave.

At 2.15 in the morning, Khumalo decided he'd better get some sleep too. The woman was still very much awake and gushing.

'What's your room number?' she asked.

Khumalo hesitated. Oh! What the hell, he thought. '204,' he replied.

'Mine's on the same floor, 211' she said, but she didn't make any proposal.

They both got up and made for the lift.

At the second floor, they stopped outside Khumalo's room to say goodnight and she reached up and gave him a peck on the cheek.

'See you at breakfast,' she said, 'if not before...'

Khumalo left her invitation hanging in the air, unlocked his room and went in.

By 2.40 Khumalo had undressed. He always slept naked. He was a fitful sleeper, tossing and turning frequently and he didn't like to wear pyjamas for the way they twisted up and constricted his movement.

There was a soft knock at the door.

He checked the peep-hole. It was the woman again. He opened the door a little, hiding his nakedness behind it.

'I've got to see you,' she said with some urgency, 'I can't sleep can I come in?' and without waiting for the reply she pushed the door wide enough to give her passage.

Khumalo woke to find the woman sleeping soundly beside him, her leg entwined with his and her arm over his hairless chest.

He had no idea what time it was, but the room was dark, so it seemed ok to stay with her for a little longer. She felt warm and smelled sweet beside him and he idly stroked her silky body with his free hand. It was not long before he too was asleep again.

A door further down the hotel corridor slammed, waking both of them.

It was still dark. Khumalo fumbled for his watch. 11.15 am. He shot out of bed and drew back a curtain. It was broad daylight. The room was furnished with blackout curtains.

'Shit!' he shouted, 'I've missed the meet.

'What meet?' the woman enquired sleepily.

'I was supposed to be at the airport for 11.00,' he said, struggling into his trousers. 'I've gotta go.' He finished dressing, gathered his things into his bag and went over to the safe.

He didn't feel good and his mind was racing. What was the code he had set? He punched a few numbers but there was no sign of the door opening. Instead, the little red LED lit up and the display read ERROR.

Khumalo was frantic now.

'Phone reception,' the woman suggested, 'they'll be able to override it.'

He walked over to the phone and dialled.

'They're sending someone up,' he sighed, looking at his watch. It was now 11.30.

'What's in the safe?' The woman enquired as she hurriedly dressed. 'Is it really important? Can't you go to the meeting and then get the safe opened later, when you come back?'

'The bloody diamonds are in there,' he blurted, 'I'm supposed to be passing them to a colleague. That was my meeting at 11.00 am.'

There was a knock at the door. It was the bellboy with a master key. Khumalo waved him in and he set to work.

At that moment the phone rang.

Khumalo turned towards the bedside table and picked up the receiver. It was Gordon McKlintock.

'Where the hell are you?' he spat, 'you were supposed to do the swap at 11.00.'

'Yes, I've had a bit of a technical hitch. I'm on my way to the airport now.'

'Well you'd better hurry. Your contact tells me he's missed his plane to London and I've told him to wait there for the next. Get your fat arse over there, and quick.'

Khumalo acknowledged and gave his apologies.

McKlintock rang off.

Khumalo turned to see how the bellboy was doing with the safe, and a lump came up in his throat. There was no sign of him. Even more perturbing, the woman had disappeared too. The safe stood open and empty.

'Fuck! Fuck! Khumalo stood there wringing his hands. He'd been had.

With a sudden burst of foresight, he quickly rang reception.

'There was a woman, room 211, If you see her leaving stop her. She's stolen something from my room.'

'I'm afraid she has already left sir.' The voice replied. 'I saw her getting into a taxi not ten seconds ago. She checked out last night and dropped the keys off on her way out just now. Would you like me to call the police?'

'Er…No, leave it thanks, it was nothing of value.'

Khumalo dropped the phone into its cradle and fell to his knees in despair, his eyes turned to the heavens. 'Oh Lord! Don't do this to me, please…please.' But he knew there was nothing he could do.

He had messed up. His life would now be worthless.

Danny was cooking breakfast – scrambled eggs, toast and coffee – when Jeff phoned Jenny. It was 10.00 am. He'd managed to get her a seat on a British Airways flight for the following evening.

Jenny had obviously taken Jeff at his word and had already spoken to the estate agent, Jim Barber. He had offered her his condolences at her loss, but cheered her up with the news that shortly after their sale had gone through, he'd had another enquiry. He was going to approach the couple again, and he had assured Jenny that a sale would not be far away.

The man from the Jeep garage was coming to inspect the car at the house but had said that his best price might not suit her. She had told him to come anyway.

Meanwhile she had organised a removal firm to come and pack up and ship those items that she wanted to keep. She was currently busy sorting them out and piling them in the hall in readiness.

'Good girl!' Jeff said encouragingly.

'I'm a bit hot and bothered at the moment,' she replied, 'I'm looking forward to my swim later.'

Jeff pictured her lithe, naked body in the pool and wished he were there with her. Still, it would not be long before he saw her now, he thought.

It was 11.30. Alan Redmayne rang McKlintock. 'How's it going?' was all he asked.

'It's a fuckin' lash up,' McKlintock spat down the phone, 'Danny got the goods to Khumalo, but Khumalo didn't make the meeting. Now I've got a guy missing his flight to London and God knows where Khumalo is now. I've contacted him and kicked his arse, but he's still not handed over. I'm giving it another hour, then I'll have to close it.'

'Keep me informed,' Redmayne replied. 'If I hear anything I'll let you know.'

McKlintock rang off.

'That gives us more time,' thought Redmayne and he phoned Danny.

At 12.00 McKlintock's phone rang. 'Gordon?'

'Andrea, is that you?'

'I've got the file. It was easier than I thought, thanks to your perfectly timed phone call. That guy Khumalo is a bit of a wimp and played right into my hands, but he's great in the sack.'

'Dirty girl! Anyway, thanks Andrea. You know where to send it.'

'Sure. Don't forget my cut,' she said.

At 12.30 McKlintock phoned Khumalo.

'How come the hand-over hasn't been made?'

'I've got problems,' Khumalo whimpered down the phone. 'Some woman has taken the file.'

'What woman? What the Hell are you talking about?'

'A woman I had in my room last night.'

'How the Hell did she know about the goods for fuck's sake?'

'She didn't – at least not until the safe wouldn't open. I got the bell boy up with the master-key, then you phoned and when I'd finished the call, they'd both disappeared.'

'You'd better find her, and quick.'

'I can't. I know it sounds stupid, but I don't know her name or anything about her. She just came to my room last night. She checked out and got in a taxi. She could be anywhere.'

'You've got 24 hours. After that you'll be watchin' over your shoulder, laddie, I promise you.'

McKlintock slammed the phone down. He leaned back in his chair and smiled broadly. It looked as if he would be £225k richer, after Andrea's 10% cut. But if Khumalo didn't find her – and he wouldn't – McKlintock would have another hit to set up.

He hoped Khumalo would be sufficiently scared now to do a runner. Any thoughts of chasing after the woman would be farthest from his mind. He would be off. Looking for a way out. He was probably on his way back to SA already. He would never show up at the Oil Company again. He would know that his days were numbered. But it was important that McKlintock played out his little charade to the end if it was to be convincing.

Chapter 63

Redmayne tried to recall Gordon McKlintock's age. About 45 - 50, he thought. So there was a good chances that he might still have a parent alive. Or maybe he had a brother or sister. He just needed to find out where he lived before he became an ex-pat. in South African

He thought about checking through a recent government census, but the latest information allowed into the public domain was 70 odd years old. He would have to trace his family some other way. Maybe the Oil Company had details, although getting them might be difficult without the company seeking McKlintock's permission first.

There had to be another way.

He went over to his laptop and Googled 'Directory Enquiries UK'.

Success! He found a site offering free access to people through the electoral roll. He entered the name McKlintock and in the address box he typed 'Scotland'. A list of three results appeared and a box popped up on the screen suggesting that he subscribe if he wished to get further results.

There probably would be more than three in the whole of Scotland, he thought. But he decided to try those anyway. Using their names and addresses, he obtained the phone numbers. However, there were only two.

He dialled the first one.

A woman answered. Redmayne relayed his pre-prepared spiel.

'Hello, I'm trying to trace an old friend, Gordon McKlintock. I believe he is now in South Africa and I wondered whether you might be a relative and able to help me find his address?'

'Who are you?'

'My name is Angus MacDonald, I'm an old school pal.'

'You don't sound overly-Scottish.'

'No, we come from Edinburgh, and the accent is much softer.'

'Well, I'm not going to give you his phone number or address, but if you give me *your* number, next time I speak with him I'll ask him to phone you. How's that?'

'That sounds good to me. Are you Tracy by any chance?' Redmayne asked, checking that he'd got the right name from the electoral roll.

'Yes I am. I'm his cousin.'

'Well Tracy, I feel like I already know you. Gordon used to mention you often. I'm so glad I've been able to trace him, we were very close at school.'

Redmayne conjured up a phone number in his head and relayed it to the woman.

'Thank you so much Tracy. Goodbye.'

And he rang off.

Redmayne leaned back in his chair and laughed to himself. It had been so easy.

He quickly wrote down the woman's name, her telephone number and her full address from the details on the Internet and shut his laptop.

It was 2.00 pm. Redmayne's mobile rang. It was McKlintock again.

'What the fuck's wrong with that bastard Khumalo,' McKlintock raged. 'The exchange still hasn't been made an' he won't answer his phone. Somethin' tells me he's doing the dirty on us. I've told his pick-up to go home, and we'll do it some other way. Can you send Danny or someone to his hotel and find out what the Hell's going on?'

Redmayne sympathised: 'Yeah, Danny wasn't too impressed with the guy either. He seemed to be a bit dithery, but Danny reckoned he was puttin' it on. He's got somethin' up his sleeve, without a doubt.'

'Well get Danny over there and see if he can knock some sense into him. Duff him up a bit. He's cocked up seriously.'

'Will do.' Redmayne acknowledged.

Redmayne rang Danny.

'Look Danny, we've got loads of time now. Khumalo hasn't handed over the goods yet. McKlintock is fumin'. You better not hand back the fourteen sparklers you've got yet, You need to wait till he's found 'em missin'. I'll call you when I know – he's bound to phone me, but he'll be really pissed off.'

'OK Dad, I'll wait for your call. Who do I pass them to when the time comes?'

'You give 'em to me, and I do the rest. Whatever you do, don't tell McKlintock about them or the whole show will go up in smoke.'

'OK Dad'

'There's summat else Danny…'

'Yeah? What's that?'

'We want ya to get over to Khumalo's hotel and duff him up a bit. Are you up for it?'

'Have you seen the size of that bastard? I'd have to use some equipment.'

'Whatever it takes, son, but don't kill 'im. We've gotta scare him a bit into makin' the switch.'

'Why don't I just nick the folder and make the switch for him?'

''Cos if you do that, it takes the blame for the shortfall off Khumalo and puts it on you, you twat!'

'Oh yeah! Sorry. It's all a bit complicated. OK I'll get over there now.'

Redmayne put the phone down. 'Why am I workin' with turkeys when I could be soarin' with eagles?' he asked himself.

Danny drove to the Hotel Zoku and went over to the reception desk. The same clerk was on duty as on his last visit. He was much more cordial.

'I'm afraid Mr. Khumalo has left the hotel sir, and without paying his bill, I might add. The room maid has confirmed that there are none of his belongings in there.'

'Don't you have his credit card number?' Danny asked scathingly.

'Oh yes, we can charge his account sir, but we prefer to carry out these transactions amicably, face to face during checkout. There was a very large bar bill to agree too.'

'So there's no real problem then?'

'I suppose not sir…are you with the same Company?'

'Yeah! Sort'a', Danny lied, 'but I ain't guaranteeing his bill if that's what you're gonna ask next.'

He took a sweet from the complimentary bowl and walked over to the hotel exit. He wondered what Khumalo was up to. He'd only got six of the diamonds. Perhaps he didn't know that yet. Maybe he hadn't opened the file spine. At least the cartel's losses had been minimised. And it was all thanks to me, he thought.

Back at his flat, Danny phoned Alan Redmayne.

'Khumalo's done a runner. His rooms empty an' he ain't paid his hotel bill. He's nicked the file an' the six diamonds.'

'I had a feelin' he might,' Redmayne replied, 'he's got wind that things are gonna get worse before they get better. I bet he don't turn up at work no more either. So you know what that means for the three of us, don't ya Danny boy?'

'Not exactly, Dad'

'Well, you don't have ta give the diamonds back, lad. The Cartel thinks Khumalo's gottem and we're £200k better off. No one will ever see 'im again.'

The light dawned in Danny's head. 'Fuck me! Yes. Shit! It's over!'

'Yeah! That's about the size of it lad.'

Danny clenched his fist and gave a footballer's salute.

'There's just one last thing to sort out,' Redmayne reminded Danny, 'We've still got to sort McKlintock, We've gotta find some other way to nail 'im.'

Thato Khumalo was well satisfied with himself. After his grilling from McKlintock he'd had a brainwave: Check the taxi rank outside the hotel. Talk to the drivers.

He had laboriously gone down the line of taxi's giving them the woman's description and asking if they had taken her fare. At the ninth taxi, late arriving at the door, he received the news he wanted to hear.

'Where did you take her?' he asked.

'To another hotel. The Blumel Hostel, Kerkstraat'

'Take me there quickly,' he commanded.

'It's a cheapo, mate,' the taxi driver added as he sped through the traffic. 'Not your sort of place at all, I don't think.'

'Never mind, just put your foot down. Its urgent.'

At the hotel, Khumalo dived out of the taxi, dragging his case behind and rushed into the entrance. He addressed the desk clerk breathlessly:

'Has my girlfriend arrived yet? She should have got here and booked a room, probably about an hour or so ago.'

'What name was it sir?' the Clerk enquired.

'Khumalo leaned over the desk and whispered 'I don't think she will have given her real name. She's a married woman. I forgot to ask her what name she might use.'

The clerk tapped the side of his nose with his forefinger. 'I'll say nothing,' he said with a smirk, 'Room 13, first floor.'

Khumalo slapped a €10 note on the desk and went up to the first floor landing, looking for room 13.

At the door, he tapped lightly upon it. A voice called out.

'Who is it?'

'Room service,' Khumalo called back, trying to disguise his voice.

He heard the door unlock so he turned the handle and simultaneously put all his weight against it. The door flew open knocking the woman backward onto the bed. She gasped in disbelief, then horror as she saw the thunder in his expression.

'How did you find me?' she asked, crawling away from him across the bed.

Khumalo grabbed her foot and easily pulled her back towards him. With his right hand he slapped her hard across her face. She fell back on the bed, blood spurting from her split lip.

'Where are the diamonds?' he demanded gruffly, or do I have to hit you again?'

'What diamonds?' she asked, feigning ignorance.

He grabbed her arm and roughly pulled her into a sitting position, then slapped her again, this time with the back of his hand, on the opposite side of her face.

The woman fell back on the bed again, but didn't move or speak. Tears flooded her eyes and rolled down her cheeks to the bed cover below. She raised an arm and pointed to the bag on the desktop at the other side of the bed.

Khumalo walked around the bed and grabbed the bag. The woman suddenly sprang up and attempted to make for the door. But she had no time to unlock it before he reached her and dragged her back. This time he hit her harder, with his fist. Her head rolled first one way and then the other as it recoiled from the blow. He heard something snap and she became limp and flopped backwards to the bed again. This time there was no movement. He ignored her and started rummaging through the bag. In her make-up case he found six uncut diamonds. Where were the rest, he wondered. Six diamonds weren't worth a trip. There must be more. He rummaged around some more, but found nothing. He turned to the woman and prodded her.

'Hey! Where are the rest of them?'

She did not respond. She couldn't. She was dead.

Khumalo rose from the bed, unconcerned, and looked for the waste bin. In it he found the remains of the blue folder.

He reintroduced the diamonds in the spine and put the document back together again.

Satisfied with his work, he put it in his briefcase, gathered his belongings and left the room, locking it carefully and pushing the key back under the door.

As he passed through the lobby he winked at the desk Clerk and gave him a 'thumbs up.'

'Enjoyed that!' he said.

The desk clerk sniggered and tapped his nose with his forefinger again.

Khumalo got out of the taxi at the airport and looked furtively around before entering the departure hall. He went to check in for his flight and then made his way through passport control to the KLM lounge above the Departures concourse.

He ordered a beer, and took a seat in a position where he could observe everyone in the room and watch the door as well. He took out the old copy of the playboy magazine, the signal to his pick-up, and feigned reading, glancing about periodically looking for his man.

He never came.

At 1.30 he heard the announcement of his flight's gate number. He could only afford to stay another five minutes, as he knew he had quite a distance to cover to get to it.

He opened his briefcase and studied the blue folder. What would he do with it now? He wondered. Who could he give it to? Did he actually want to give it to anyone? Why not keep it? The cartel didn't know he'd got the diamonds back. He would need the money where he was going. He couldn't go back to the Company nor could he carry on with the cartel.

Yes, he would need the diamonds to help him financially. They would last him quite a few years in Soweto, he estimated.

Khumalo looked at his watch. It was time to go. He needed to leave enough time to get through gate security. He left the quiet ambience of the lounge and entered the din in the departure concourse, walking swiftly to his gate, where he joined a short queue of passengers awaiting the security check.

Eventually he placed his briefcase and coat in a tray and removed his belt, money, phone and wallet and placed them in another smaller one then watched them disappear through the scanner tunnel. He passed through the body detector and waited for his belongings.

The officer behind the moving belt asked him for his passport. Khumalo handed it to him, wondering why. He had already passed through Passport Control. Another officer came over carrying Khumalo's briefcase and belongings.

'Please come with us, sir,' the officer asked firmly but politely.

Khumalo started sweating heavily. He realised that the scanner had found the diamonds. The two officers accompanied him, one in front and one behind, over to a small room behind the security area.

'Please open your case, sir.'

Khumalo complied, loosening his tie to relieve the heat building up at his neck.

The officer rummaged through the case, taking out all the papers, magazines, files and other paraphernalia, then checked over the lining of the briefcase. He found nothing there. He then went through each file and magazine. He picked up the blue file last, examining it thoroughly before pulling off the plastic spine and peering into the thin gap down its length.

'What's this, sir?' He asked

'I don't know,' stammered Khumalo, 'I was asked to give it to someone.'

'Who and where?'

'He never turned up.'

'Who gave it to you?'

'A guy who flew into Amsterdam with me.'

The officer took a small penknife from his pocket and deftly slid the blade down the length of the spine, then prised it apart. It split evenly all the way along and the six uncut diamonds dropped out onto the table.

'I'm afraid you are going to have to wait here, sir. We will have to summon the Airport Police.'

Khumalo slumped over the table, his head reeling, sweat pouring from his forehead. He felt sick.

He knew his days of freedom were over now, possibly forever.

It was 3.00 pm Redmayne's mobile rang again. McKlintock was still furious.

'Has Danny found that shit Khumalo yet?'

'He's gone, mate,' Redmayne replied, 'probably got the plane home and taken the diamonds with him.'

'Well, in a way I hope he has,' McKlintock said brightly, "cos I gave the customs guys at Schiphol an anonymous tip-off. I told 'em that if they saw a big black guy named Thato Khumalo getting on a plane back to SA today then he's carrying unregistered diamonds.'

'Hope you didn't use your mobile.' Redmayne said anxiously.

'No, course not. Company phone.' McKlintock replied indignantly.

'Whatever happens, we'll have to scrub round that deal' Redmayne replied, 'but there's gonna be an inquisition, you can bet your life on that. And that bastard Khumalo will hopefully rot in a Dutch jail for a while. So we put it to bed an' forget it. Learn ourselves a lesson. Big loss though.'

'Your telling me!' said McKlintock. 'I'm wondering whether we should all pack it in. The cops will be chasing us all the time after this. We've got away clean up to now, but I've got a bad feeling about the future. Talk to you later about that. OK?'

'Yes, OK, Cheers!'

McKlintock smiled and pumped the air with his hairy fist. He was well satisfied with the successful culmination of his little ruse. He had convinced Redmayne that Khumalo had the diamonds. Little did he know…

Redmayne was cock-a-hoop too. He phoned Danny to give him the good news.

'Khumalo's goin' down any time now, Danny boy,' he said, 'McKlintock tipped off the customs people so if he's still got the file, he's finished. Good news eh? One down and one to go. We've still got McKlintock to deal with. Don't know how were gonna do that. We'll sleep on it.'

At the Blumel Hostel in Kerkstraat, the cleaners began their rounds, preparing the rooms for the next intake of guests. Maria - a short middle-aged Spanish lady - was allocated the first floor and she pushed her trolley from one room to another as she sped through the operation.

Clean the bathroom, new towel, vacuum the carpet, wash the coffee cups, make the bed. She had to clean all rooms on that floor, but her pay was fixed, based on two hours work. Some days it worked fine, others not, depending on how many rooms had been let. Today she hoped she would be lucky and get away early. There were only 5 occupied rooms to clean.

At room 11 she inserted the master key and turned the handle. The door opened a fraction but then jammed. She tried shutting it and reopening it again, but to no avail. It seemed that something was trapped under the door. She called the reception from the room opposite and the clerk summoned the handyman.

Maria continued her duties, cleaning the room opposite while she waited for him. Five minutes later, he arrived and she put down her duster and showed him to the room.

The handyman seemed to know the best way to deal with the problem and stepped back a pace then ran at the door, putting his shoulder to it.

There was a noise like a distant gunshot as the wood around the bottom of the jamb split from its hinge, but the door flew open to reveal a woman lying on the bed, apparently sleeping.

But she didn't look right. Her head was at an un-natural angle.

Maria walked over to her and touched her shoulder, shaking it lightly. There was no response. She felt for a pulse but from the state of the woman's face, Maria knew she had not survived the beating she had recently received.

She screamed. Mayhem then ensued.

The desk clerk immediately called for an ambulance and the police. He was agitated for he knew that the woman's demise was probably associated with the big black guy that he had allowed up to her room. He would explain it all to the police, he decided.

McKlintock's mobile rang again. It was the 'Foreman'. So named because he was the leader of the boys at the mines.

'Has the delivery gone ok?' he asked.

'No there's been a cock-up. There will be no deal on this one.'

'But the boy's haven't been paid.'

'So? Nor have I.' McKlintock was prepared for a stand off.

'Well, we've not cocked up, so we should get paid. We got you at least 200k sterling of goods there.'

'I told you before…we get paid, you get paid. Otherwise, we do the next package.'

'Well we're not doin' no more packages, Massa. You don't pay us. You pay us an' then we do another.'

'Look you little shit, your fellow countryman Khumalo fucked up. He never made the switch. So you can go fuck yourselves.'

'OK! So we go fuck ourselves, yeah? Then we fuck you - real good Massa...Real good.'

The phone went dead.

McKlintock was far too worked up to realise the significance of what had been said.

Chapter 64

It had been 24 hours since McKlintock's last phone call. He'd obviously calmed down, Redmayne thought.

He was at home enjoying a barbecue and a few beers with Danny and Jeff, still trying to thrash out a solution to the problem of McKlintock and the failed hit on Jeff.

It was now late in the afternoon and getting cool, so they moved into the house.

Redmayne switched on the television to get the news.

They were idly chatting when Jeff suddenly caught sight of Khumalo being led away in handcuffs into a police van. He turned up the sound on the TV.

'Christ! That's Khumalo,' he shouted, 'look quick!'

Redmayne and Danny stared at the TV.

The newsreader was about to hand over to a local correspondent for details of the story.

Apparently he had been taken into custody for smuggling unregistered diamonds, and further, detained under suspicion of murdering a woman in a hotel room in Kerkstraat in the city. The correspondent was explaining that he had been identified as the killer by the Desk Clerk, who had let him up to her room, after being convinced by him that he was her partner. A Taxi driver had also been interrogated and confirmed that it was the same man that he had transported to the Hotel from another in the city.

Jeff looked across at Danny with a big grin on his face. 'That's him out of the way for good, by the sound of it. Things are getting better for us all the time.'

Redmayne drained his beer, then carefully aimed the can at the waste paper basket. It dropped in with a plop.

'What the Hell was he doin' with a woman in a joint like that?' he queried. 'He was stayin' at the Zoku.'

'Maybe he picked her up and she took him to her place.' Danny suggested. 'Anyway, it don't matter. He's tied up good now, that's all we need to know.'

Redmayne turned to Jeff. 'Have you sent your letter to the Oil Company yet? You know, the 'director or stuff it' letter?'

'Yes, I have, and I gave him my mobile number and asked him to ring me when he'd decided. No news yet though.'

'Do you reckon he'll bite?'

'I guess he might. All the signs were good before. I doubt he's the sort to make a hasty decision though.'

'What happens if he contacts McKlintock for an opinion?'

'Shit! I never thought of that. But I don't think he would 'cos he doesn't trust him. That's why he got me to report back to him direct.'

'OK, so what about your flat?'

'Yep! Notice has been served but I now need to find somewhere to stay for three months until the tenants are out. My brother in law wasn't keen to help. Probably because of Sheila.'

'So when are you going to London?'

'Soon as I get an answer from the Company. Meanwhile I'm hoping Danny can put me up for a few days.'

'You'd be better stayin' here with me, 'specially as you'll have Jenny with you. Danny's place is a shit-hole.'

Danny looked hurt.

'What time are you pickin' her up tomorrow?' Redmayne continued.

'I said I'd be a the airport at 10.30.'

'OK, so you bring her back here then. You can have the back room all to yourselves. It's got an en-suite. It'll also be safer for her, cos Danny's goin' away for a bit and the police is still watching him.'

'Thanks, Alan, that'll do fine. We'll pay our way.'

'Not necessary, boy, now, I think I'd better phone McKlintock and give him the good news about Khumalo. It won't make the South African news channels.'

Redmayne reached for his mobile in his jacket and messaged McKlintock.

Ten minutes later his mobile rang. Redmayne answered, moving the phone some 6 inches back from his ear as McKlintock's thunderous ranting spewed from the earpiece.

"What the fuck's he done, the idiot! He didn't try to take the diamonds through, did he?'

'It seems like it,' Redmayne replied, 'but that's not what'll keep him in jail for long. He also killed some woman in a cheap hotel here, apparently. God knows what he was doin' with her in a place like that.'

'Oh Christ, No! No! No!' was all that McKlintock said before he rang off.

Redmayne was perplexed. He didn't understand why McKlintock was so upset about a scenario that he had engineered in the first place. But then, Redmayne didn't know of McKlintock's own little scam either.

He still wondered how they were going to stitch him up.

Chapter 65

Jeff met Jenny at Schiphol and they got a Taxi back to Redmayne's house. She was beside herself with worry and had not enjoyed the trip one bit.

'Now perhaps you can tell me what all this is about?' she asked. 'I've been so absolutely sick, thinking about you and the trouble you're in.'

'Let's wait 'till we get to the house, Jenny, There's a lot I've got to confess to you…stuff you don't know about, but I want to start at the beginning and get it over with in one hit. As it turns out, things may not get to be as bad as I thought they would, so don't worry unduly.'

They continued the journey in virtual silence.

Redmayne was not there to welcome them when they got to the house. Jeff took the cases up to the bedroom, Jenny following behind.

He turned toward her and put his arms around her, She was quick to fend him off. 'No, we're not getting into any of that until you've come clean,' she said.

At that moment Jeff's mobile rang. It was Daphne Lawrence from the Oil Company. 'Hello Jeffrey,' she cooed, 'David Robinson would like a word. Shall I put you through?'

Jeff was just a little flummoxed. He hadn't yet prepared what he was going to say. He would have to think on the hoof.

'Oh, yes, thank you Daphne,' he replied, happy to continue the conversation on first name terms. It must be a good omen, he thought.

There was a click and then silence for a few seconds before an exuberant sounding David Robinson came on the phone.

'Well my boy, I got your letter, but I'm somewhat perplexed. What has brought on this sudden ultimatum? I thought we had everything cut, dried and sorted last time we spoke?'

'Yes David, they were, but things have changed.'

'In what way?'

'I've been head-hunted by another large organisation in the States. They want me to head up their Fracking Division. They want a very quick response, but I thought I would do you the courtesy of giving you first opportunity, although I doubt you would be able to match the salary package without some dissension in the ranks, as you might say.'

'My goodness! You are a go-getter aren't you.' Robinson replied.

Jeff couldn't determine Robinson's mood on the telephone, he never could.

'Well, I want to make the best of my life, so my ambitions spring from that desire.' Jeff responded. 'I hope you don't think I'm pressuring you.'

'Not in the least, dear boy, in fact I'm glad you had the guts to make the ultimatum. Shows me how you would conduct yourself in the business. I'm impressed.'

'However,' Robinson continued, 'there's been a nasty development over in the Johannesburg office and it gives us a serious problem. I don't know if you've heard?'

'Heard what?'

'Hmm…a really nasty business. The Jo'burg Fracking Team are rudderless at the moment – unfortunately Gordon McKlintock has been shot.'

'What?' Jeff didn't know what to say. He wanted to say how sorry he was to hear the news, but his relief that the last obstacle in his plan might now have been removed overtook his feelings and he was afraid that he would sound insincere.

'Yes, I'm afraid so,' Robinson continued, 'Despite all efforts by the medics, he hasn't survived. Apparently a group of black guys with pistols came over to his car as he was parking in the city, and fired several rounds at him, point blank, through the windscreen. He had no chance I'm afraid. A really messy business. We're now trying to find his next of kin…give them the bad news.'

'That's terrible. Poor guy. But I might be able to help you with his next of kin. I know where his cousin, Tracy lives. Just by chance, Gordon and I were chatting one day and he was telling me about her.' Jeff lied.

'Well my boy, it seems you are a fountain of knowledge. Give the details to Daphne when we've finished our chat. Now, back to the crux of the problem. With no McKlintock, we have a rudderless team, as I said, and if we are to comply with your ultimatum, there will be certain conditions attached. One is that you maintain responsibility for the Jo'burg team, add it to your other responsibilities. Now whether you do that based here in London, flying out as necessary, or perhaps staying over there for a short period until things are sorted, it's up to you. But they will be your bag, do you hear?'

Jeff heard all right. And with McKlintock out of the way he didn't care either way.

'You get me the office in the Strand, David and I'll sort the problem in South Africa. It's no problem. I know all the guys, I know the business and I know the conditions in SA.'

'Good man! But can you manage that as well as the Turnaround Team?'

'I'm sure I can, but it might come more expensive!'

'Hah! You're pushing it a bit today Jeff, aren't you. So, do we have a deal?'

'Not until we agree terms.'

'Well, we are on the ball, aren't we. OK. Why don't you fly over ASAP and we'll settle this here and now. Can you get a flight before Friday? I'm away after that.'

'No problem. I'll get a flight for Thursday and meet you in the afternoon if that suits.'

'I think so, but check with Daphne when you know. Glad to have you aboard, Jeff.' And he transferred the call back to Daphne.

Jeff gave Daphne the details of McKlintock's cousin then rang off and turned to Jenny, his face alight. 'We've got it!' he shouted. 'I'm in on the twelfth floor! Well, at least, almost!'

Jenny hugged him and they both danced a little jig across the bedroom floor. 'Wait till I tell Danny and Alan the news.'

That evening, Redmayne and his son Danny returned to the house and were introduced by Jeff to Jenny. She had bathed and changed her clothes following the flight and chosen something quite alluring for the evening. Danny couldn't take his eyes off her. Even Alan Redmayne was impressed.

Jeff opened a bottle of Champagne – the best he could hurriedly get from the local supermarket – and proposed a toast.

'To us, and our new futures,' he crowed.

'What about Mc…' Danny commenced.

'Gone, no problem.' Jeff replied anticipating Danny's question. 'McKlintock is no more.'

The two of them looked askance. 'How do you mean?' Redmayne asked.

'Although I shouldn't seem so happy about it, McKlintock was shot by some black guys as he parked up some place in Jo'burg. He didn't make it. I'm taking on his position.

Not only that, but…I've as good as got my directorship at the Company.' He looked at the others expectantly, waiting for the congratulations.

They didn't come.

They were contemplating the demise of McKlintock. His death was not what they had envisaged. It was not part of their plan. They just wanted to stitch him up somehow. It left a bad taste in their mouths, especially the manner of his passing. What prompted his murder? Was it unprovoked or was it the failure of the Switch? Redmayne rather thought the latter, although the motive was not clear.

However, wanted or not, the death of McKlintock meant full resolution of all their troubles. But it had also taken away their need for unity. They were no longer dependent upon each other. No need for any further alliance. They could now go their separate ways without feeling exposed. No bonds had been formed - it was too early for that.

Danny was the first to realise it.

'So you'll be leaving us and going back to UK then?' Danny asked Jeff in a subdued whisper.

'Yes, but we'll stay in touch. You can always come over and see us. By the way…aren't you supposed to be going away on holiday for a while, Danny?'

'Yeah! I've got me curfew lifted an' I'm takin' this bird, Penny, that I met in the café, we're goin' to the Spanish coast for while. We've found a villa we can rent cheap for a few months.'

'What about you Alan?' Jeff enquired.

'Well, the cartel's gonna get broken up, so I guess I'll just retire. I might look up Marion and take her for a trip somewhere. She's itchin' for some company.'

'So we're all good then.' Danny suggested, refilling their glasses.

'Let's drink to that eh?'

Epilogue

I first met Danny Redmayne in 1986 when I was five. We lived in the same street in North London. His Dad, Alan, 'bought' and sold stuff in the pub on the corner, like cheap TV's, record players and washing machines. He could get anything you wanted if you were prepared to wait a couple of days.

Danny became my best mate, much to the chagrin of my parents. He came from a poor family of dubious repute and had a thick East London accent, all being factors which led to him being barred from our home and me being told that I couldn't associate with him. I defied these orders as best I could, but at the age of nine I was sent away to boarding school and we lost touch.

Late in 2017, I was on a golfing holiday with some work colleagues in Spain, in a little town overflowing with white sea-front hotels, called Salou, having a drink in a bar.

I got talking to this guy sitting with a busty blonde who was wearing next to nothing. They were drinking Sangria and picking at a pile of olives in a dish on the table in front of them. There was something familiar about him. I don't know whether it was his manner or his looks or what, but I felt I had seen him before somewhere. He introduced himself as Danny Redmayne. Small world, I thought.

'Are you the Danny Redmayne I knew as a kid?' I asked.

He looked at me for a few seconds, and then his face lit up.

'You ain't Tom are you?' He replied, 'This is Penny,' he said, pointing at his partner. 'We ain't married or nothin', she's just me bird. Fancy seein' you here at the same place as us after all this time. Funny Old World, innit?'

That's Danny all right, I thought. He was clearly doing all right too. He had a flashy Rolex and his clothes were pretty expensive looking. And although his 'bird' had little on, she made up for it in heavy make-up and gold jewellery.

We had a few drinks together and I arranged for them to come over to my hotel for dinner the next evening. That's when he began to tell me the story of his life as a black-market courier.

It took four days and cost me the best part of a grand in food and drink!

At the end of it all, I thought his story was so incredible and he had been so lucky to get away with stuff, that it should be immortalised in print, as one might say.

So I wrote this book.

OK, there's a touch of embellishment here and there, to make it flow smoothly, and I've left out all the dross from the earlier part of his life that wasn't particularly exciting, but the essentials are all there. Like…His dad…the family he never knew he had…the birds he picked up on the way…all the really nasty things he did…how he nearly got conned…his money…everything!

As you will now know, the book ends when Danny and his half-brother, Jeff, get out of the mess they are in with the cartel, but Danny did tell me that his dad, Alan, had now retired and he was shacked up with Marion, Danny's old boss Wilson's missus. They were now living in Eton Mews, London. He said that I should look them up, being as I lived so close - I lived in Kensington at the time.

His dad had apparently sold his house in Amsterdam and bought a rather posh house in Northern Italy, on a lake - I forget which one - but he said I could rent it at a discount, if I liked.

Danny had since taken over the remainder of his dad's business, but he had so much money that he was only playing at it really, just to give himself something to do.

He told me that Jeff was a really big nebby in the Oil Company. Danny gave me his address so I could get his side of the tale. But - surprise, surprise - Jenny, Karl's ex, who Jeff took up with, had left him for another bloke almost half her age. I thought she might have been a bit of a flighty piece when he told me the story, but apparently, Danny said it was because Jeff had been seeing that Daphne Lawrence who was now his secretary. Funny how he always went for older women.

Danny and I promised to keep in touch after the holiday. But the trouble was, he lived in Amsterdam. We spoke a couple of times on the phone though, but I never clapped eyes on him again.

Then, shortly after, in the March of 2018, out of the blue, I got a phone call from Penny – she was still with him – she was distraught. She gave me the bad news that Danny had been killed in a motor cycle accident while being chased by the police through Belgium.

He must have been up to his dirty tricks again.

But I suppose everyone gets their just desserts in the end - Karma, I think they call it.

Funny Old World, innit?